Praise for *The Becoming*

"Roberts . . . conjures up an action-packed, magic-infused tale of dragons, danger, and desire that will have readers who got hooked on the first volume fully engaged until the last page, at which point they'll begin anxiously awaiting the upcoming conclusion to Breen and Keegan's story."

—*Booklist*

"As the conflict between good and evil escalates, Roberts's skills with building suspense and crafting stirring relationships truly shine. Readers will eagerly await the final installment." —*Publishers Weekly*

"The world of magick again beckons welcomingly in *The Becoming*. . . . Fantasy lovers will eagerly await this bookend." —*Mountain Times*

Sign of Seven Trilogy
*Blood Brothers* • *The Hollow* • *The Pagan Stone*

Bride Quartet
*Vision in White* • *Bed of Roses* • *Savor the Moment* • *Happy Ever After*

The Inn Boonsboro Trilogy
*The Next Always* • *The Last Boyfriend* • *The Perfect Hope*

The Cousins O'Dwyer Trilogy
*Dark Witch* • *Shadow Spell* • *Blood Magick*

The Guardians Trilogy
*Stars of Fortune* • *Bay of Sighs* • *Island of Glass*

The Chronicles of The One
*Year One* • *Of Blood and Bone* • *The Rise of Magicks*

The Dragon Heart Legacy
*The Awakening* • *The Becoming* • *The Choice*

The Lost Bride Trilogy
*Inheritance*

EBOOKS BY NORA ROBERTS

Cordina's Royal Family
*Affaire Royale* • *Command Performance* • *The Playboy Prince* • *Cordina's Crown Jewel*

The Donovan Legacy
*Captivated* • *Entranced* • *Charmed* • *Enchanted*

The O'Hurleys
*The Last Honest Woman* • *Dance to the Piper* • *Skin Deep* • *Without a Trace*

Night Tales
*Night Shift* • *Night Shadow* • *Nightshade* • *Night Smoke* • *Night Shield*

## ANTHOLOGIES

*From the Heart* • *A Little Magic* • *A Little Fate*

*Moon Shadows*
(with Jill Gregory, Ruth Ryan Langan, and Marianne Willman)

The Once Upon Series
(with Jill Gregory, Ruth Ryan Langan, and Marianne Willman)
*Once Upon a Castle* • *Once Upon a Star* • *Once Upon a
Dream* • *Once Upon a Rose* • *Once Upon a Kiss* • *Once Upon
a Midnight*

*Silent Night*
(with Susan Plunkett, Dee Holmes, and Claire Cross)

*Out of This World*
(with Laurell K. Hamilton, Susan Krinard, and Maggie Shayne)

*Bump in the Night*
(with Mary Blayney, Ruth Ryan Langan, and Mary Kay McComas)

*Dead of Night*
(with Mary Blayney, Ruth Ryan Langan, and Mary Kay McComas)

*Three in Death*

*Suite 606*
(with Mary Blayney, Ruth Ryan Langan, and Mary Kay McComas)

*In Death*

*The Lost*
(with Patricia Gaffney, Ruth Ryan Langan, and Mary Blayney)

*The Other Side*
(with Mary Blayney, Patricia Gaffney, Ruth Ryan Langan,
and Mary Kay McComas)

*Time of Death*

*The Unquiet*
(with Mary Blayney, Patricia Gaffney, Ruth Ryan Langan,
and Mary Kay McComas)

*Mirror, Mirror*
(with Mary Blayney, Elaine Fox, Mary Kay McComas, and
R. C. Ryan)

*Down the Rabbit Hole*
(with Mary Blayney, Elaine Fox, Mary Kay McComas, and
R. C. Ryan)

ALSO AVAILABLE . . .

*The Official Nora Roberts Companion*
(edited by Denise Little and Laura Hayden)

# B THE ecoming

# NORA ROBERTS

St. Martin's Paperbacks

Published in the United States by St. Martin's Paperbacks, an imprint of St. Martin's Publishing Group

THE BECOMING

For information, address St. Martin's Publishing Group, 120 Broadway, New York, NY 10271.

www.stmartins.com

Interior photographs: cottage © PhotoFires/Shutterstock.com; grass © LeManna/Shutterstock.com; flowers © jular seesulai/Shutterstock.com; mountains © Matveev Aleksandr/Shutterstock.com; sky © Valerii_M/Shutterstock.com; birds © boonchob chuaynum/Shutterstock.com

Library of Congress Catalog Card Number: 2021027402

ISBN: 978-1-250-77179-7

Our books may be purchased in bulk for promotional, educational, or business use. Please contact your local bookseller or the Macmillan Corporate and Premium Sales Department at 1-800-221-7945, ext. 5442, or by email at MacmillanSpecialMarkets@macmillan.com.

Printed in the United States of America

St. Martin's Press hardcover edition published 2021
St. Martin's Griffin edition published 2022
St. Martin's Paperbacks edition / December 2023

10  9  8  7  6  5  4  3  2  1

For Laura and JoAnne,
my very own smart girls

# PART I
# THE RETURN

*If by my life or death I can protect you,*
*I will.*

—J.R.R. Tolkien

# PROLOGUE

In the long ago, the worlds of gods and men and Fey co-existed. Through times of peace, through times of war, in times of plenty, in times of loss, the worlds mingled freely.

As the wheel of time turned, there came those who pushed aside the old gods for the gods of greed, for the lust of dominion over the land and the sea, for the glory of what some deemed progress.

In the dunghill of greed and lust and glory, fear and hatred bloomed. Some gods grew angry at the lessening of respect and homage, and some turned anger into a craving to possess and to destroy. More, wiser and more temperate, saw the wheel turn as it must and cast out those who used their great powers to murder and enslave.

As the worlds of man turned the gods into things of myth, those who called themselves holy persecuted any who chose to worship in the old ways. Such acts, once as common as wildflowers in a meadow, brought torture and an ugly death.

Soon, the fear and hatred aimed its brittle fingers toward the Fey. The Wise, once revered for their powers, became twisted into creatures of evil, as were the Sidhe, who no longer dared spread their wings for fear of a hunter's arrow. Weres became cursed monsters who devoured human flesh, and Mers the sirens who lured simple seafarers to their deaths.

With fear and hatred, persecutions raged over the worlds, pitting man against man, Fey against Fey, man against Fey in a bloody, brutal time fueled by those who claimed they stood on holy ground.

So in the world of Talamh, and others, there came a time of choice. The leader of Talamh offered the Fey, all of its tribes, this choice. To turn from the old ways and follow the rules and laws of man, or to preserve their laws, their magicks by closing off from other worlds.

The Fey chose magicks.

In the end, after the windy and righteous debates such matters demanded, the taoiseach and the council found compromise. New laws were written. All were encouraged to travel to other worlds, to learn of them, to sample them. Any who chose to make their home outside Talamh must follow the laws of that world, and but one unbreakable law of Talamh.

Magicks must never be used to harm another but to save a life. And even then, such action demanded a return to Talamh and judgment on the justice of their actions.

So, for generation upon generation, Talamh held peace within its borders. Some left for other worlds; others brought mates from those worlds to settle in Talamh. Crops grew in the green fields, trolls mined the deep caves, game roamed the thick woods, and the two moons shined over the hills and the seas.

But such peaceful worlds, such green and rich land, plants hunger in dark hearts. In time, with vengeful purpose, a castout god slid through the worlds into Talamh. He won the heart of the young taoiseach who saw him as he willed her to see him.

Handsome and good and loving.

They made a child, as it was the child he wanted. A child in whom ran the blood of the taoiseach, of the Wise with more than a dollop of the Sidhe, and with his, blood of a god.

Each night, as the mother slept an enchanted sleep, the dark god drank power from the babe, consuming what it was to add to his own. But the mother woke, saw the god for what he was. She saved her son, and led Talamh in a great battle to cast out the fallen god.

Once this was done, and portals charmed against him and any who followed him, she gave up her staff, threw the sword of the taoiseach back into the Lake of Truth for another to lift, for another to lead.

She raised her son, and when his time came round, as the wheel decreed, he raised the sword from the waters of the lake to take his place as leader of the Fey.

And, a wise leader, he held the peace season by season, year by year. On his travels he met a human woman, and they loved. He brought her to his world, to his people, to the farm that was his and his mother's and her family's before her, and theirs before.

They knew joy, a joy that grew when they made a child. For three years, the child knew nothing but love and wonder and the peace her father held as firmly as he held her hand.

Such a prize was she, this girl child, the only one known who carried the blood of the Wise, the Sidhe, the gods, and the human.

The dark god came for her, using the twisted powers of a turned witch to breach the portal. He caged her in glass, deep in the pale green waters of the river where he plotted to keep her, letting her powers grow a bit longer. No babe this time he would have to sip from, but one he could, when ripe, gulp whole.

Yet she already held more power than he knew. More than she knew. Her cries reached beyond the portal, into Talamh.

Her anger broke through the conjured glass, drove the god back even as the Fey, led by her father, her grandmother, raged into battle.

Even with the child safe, the god's castle destroyed, and the portal protections reinforced, the girl's mother could not, would not rest.

She demanded they return to the world of man, without magick she now viewed as evil, and keep their daughter there without memory of the world of her birth.

Torn between love and duty, the taoiseach lived in both worlds, making a home as best he could for his daughter, returning to Talamh to lead, and, in leading, to keep his world and his child safe.

The marriage could not survive it, and as the wheel turned, neither did the taoiseach survive his next battle, as his father murdered him.

While the girl grew, believing her father had left her, never knowing what she had inside her, raised by a mother whose fear pushed her to demand the daughter think herself less and less, another young boy raised the sword from the lake.

So they grew in their worlds from girl to woman, from boy to man. She, unhappy, did as she was bid. He, determined, guarded the peace. In Talamh, they waited, knowing the god threatened all worlds. He would again seek the blood of his blood, and the wheel would turn so the time would come when the Talamhish could no longer stop him.

She, the bridge between worlds, must return and awaken, must become, and must choose to give all, risk all to help destroy the god.

When she came to Talamh, innocent of all that had come before, she had only begun a journey into herself. Led there by a grandmother's open heart, she learned, she grieved, she embraced.

And awakened.

Like her father, she had love and duty in two worlds. That

love and duty drew her back to the world where she'd been raised, but with a promise to return.

With her heart torn, she prepared to leave what she had known and risk all she was. On the knife's edge, with the taoiseach and Talamh waiting, she shared all with the brother of her heart, a friend like no other.

As she stepped into the portal, he, as true as ever was, leaped with her.

Caught between worlds, between loves, between duties, she began her journey into becoming.

# CHAPTER ONE

With the wind whipping a gale in the portal, Breen felt her grip on Marco's hand start to slip. She couldn't see, as the light had gone bright and blinding. She couldn't hear through the roar of that wind.

As if tossed by the gale, she tumbled, with Keegan's hand a vise grip on hers, and her desperate fingers barely clinging to Marco's.

Then, like a switch flipped, she fell. The air went cool and damp, the light snapped off, and the wind died.

She landed hard enough to rattle bones. On a dirt road, she realized, wet from the soft rain still falling. And in the rain, she smelled Talamh.

Breathless, she rolled to hunker over Marco. He sprawled, limp and still, with eyes wide and shocked.

"Are you okay? Let me see. Marco, you idiot!" Searching, she ran her hands over him. "Nothing's broken."

Now she stroked her hand over Marco's face as she whipped her head around to snarl at Keegan.

"What the hell was that? Even the first time I came through, it wasn't like that."

He shoved his hand through his hair. "I didn't account for the extra passenger. Or all your bloody luggage. And still I got us back, didn't I?"

"What the actual fuck?"

As Marco stirred, she turned back to him. "Don't try to get up yet. You're going to be dizzy and shaky, but you're okay."

He just stared at her, his brown eyes huge and glassy with shock. "Did all this crazy make you a doctor, too?"

"Not exactly. Just catch your breath. What the hell do we do now?" she shot at Keegan.

"Get out of the fecking rain, to start." He pushed to his feet, a tall, irritated man with dark hair curling in the damp. "I aimed to bring us back in the dooryard of the farmhouse." He gestured. "And wasn't far off, considering what came with us."

She could see the stone house now, the silhouette of it a few yards away and across the road.

"Marco isn't a what."

Keegan just strode over, crouched down. "All right now, brother, sit yourself up. Take it slow."

"My laptop!" When Breen spotted it on the road, she scrambled up, sprinted over to grab the case.

"Well now, she will have her priorities."

In the road, in the rain, she clutched it to her. "This is as important to me as your sword is to you."

"If it got banged up, you'll fix it. That's the way," he said to Marco, "slow and easy."

The way he spoke to Marco—slow and easy—reminded Breen that Keegan could be kind. When he wanted to be.

She strapped on the laptop case cross-body, hurried back to them.

"You're going to feel dizzy and weird. The first time I came through I fainted."

"Guys don't faint." But Marco dropped his spinning head

to his updrawn knees. "We can pass out, we can get knocked out, but we don't faint."

"That's the way," Keegan said cheerfully. "Let's get you on your feet. We could use a hand here, Breen."

"Just let me get my suitcase."

"Women, by the gods!" Keegan whipped out a hand, and the suitcase vanished.

"Where did it go?" Marco's voice hitched, this time his eyes rolled. "Where'd it go?"

"Not to worry, it's all fine. Up you come now. Lean on me, and we'll get you there."

"I can't feel my knees. Are they here?"

"Right where they should be."

Breen hurried over to wrap an arm around Marco from the other side. "It's okay. You're okay. It's not far, see? We're going right there."

He managed a few shaky steps. "Men don't faint, but they do puke. I might."

Breen pressed a hand to his stomach, pulled out some of the churning. It made her feel a little queasy, but she told herself she'd handle it. "Better?"

"Yeah, I guess. I think I'm having a really weird dream. Breen has weird dreams," he told Keegan in a voice that sounded a little drunk. "Scary weird sometimes. This one's just weird."

Keegan flicked a hand, and the gate of the dooryard swung open.

"Like that kind of weird. Smells good anyway. Like Ireland. Right, Breen?"

"Yes, but it's not."

"That would be way weird if we're standing in our apartment in Philly one minute and going splat on a road in Ireland the next. 'Beam me up, Scotty' time."

"Those are good stories." Keegan flicked the door open. "Here we are now. You'll have a lie down on the divan here."

"Lying down's good. Hey, Breen, there's your suitcase. It's real homey in here. Old-timey homey. It's nice. Oh, thank Christ," he said when they laid him down on the couch.

"I didn't faint, see. Didn't puke either. Yet."

"I'm going to make you some tea."

He shook his head at Breen. "Rather have a beer."

"And who wouldn't? I'll get that for you. Stay with him," Keegan ordered. "Dry him up, smooth him out."

"He should have the tea, what I had when I came through."

"What goes in the tea can go in the ale."

"Drugs, right?" Marco asked as Keegan strode out. "Because he slipped us lots and lots of drugs so we're in this weird dream together."

"No, Marco. It's real."

She held out a hand to the low, simmering fire in the hearth and had the flames rising and crackling. She lit the candles around the room from where she knelt beside the sofa.

She ran her hands down Marco's sides to dry his clothes, then brushed them over his braids to dry his hair.

"I'm voting for crazy dream."

"You know it's real. Why did you jump with me, Marco? Why did you grab onto me and jump?"

"I wasn't going to let you go without me into some hole of light in our damn living room. And you were all upset. You'd been crying. You—" He looked at the ceiling. "I hear something. Somebody else is in the house."

"Harken—Keegan's brother—lives here. He's a farmer. This is their farm. It was my father's. I was born in his house."

Marco's gaze tracked back to hers. "That's what he told you, but—"

"My grandmother told me, and it's the truth. I'm remembering things I didn't. And I'll explain everything, I promise, but—"

She broke off when Harken and Morena came down the

stairs—in clothes obviously hastily dragged on, as Morena's shirt was inside out.

"Welcome home!" Sunflower hair unbraided and tangled, Morena rushed down to drop beside Breen and grab her in a fierce hug. "We're so happy to see you." She beamed at Marco, blue eyes dancing. "And you brought a friend. Is this Marco then? My nan said you were a handsome one, and she's never wrong."

She grabbed his hand to shake. "That's Finola McGill, my nan. I'm Morena."

"Okay."

"I'm Harken Byrne, and you're welcome here. A rough come through, was it? We'll fix you up."

"I've got it." Keegan came in with a tankard.

Marco darted his gaze back and forth. Brothers, sure, the resemblance was apparent in the strong cheekbones, the shape of the mouth.

"Ale, is it?" Harken considered. "Well then, as long as you remembered—"

"It's a basic potion, Harken. I can handle the basics as well as any."

"Potion?" Marco started to push up, and his rich, dark skin went a little gray at the edges. "I say no to potions."

"It's a kind of medicine," Breen assured him. "You'll feel better for it."

"Breen, maybe they look real good, these three, but they could be sucking you into some cult. Or—"

"Trust me." She reached up to take the tankard from Keegan. "We've always trusted each other. I know it's all hard to believe, or even begin to understand. But of anyone I know, it's going to be easier for you. You already believe in multiverses."

"Maybe you're a pod-person Breen and not my real Breen."

"Would a pod-person Breen know we sang a Gaga duet

while you got a tattoo of an Irish harp inked in Galway? Here now, take a sip. Or would she have packed the pink frog mug you made for me when we were kids?"

"You packed that?" He took a sip when she held the tankard for him. "This messed up my head really good."

"I know the feeling. Drink a little more."

When he had, he scanned the three who stood watching him. "So . . . you're all, like, witches."

"Not me." Smiling, Morena spread her silver-tipped violet wings. "I'm a faerie. Breen has a bit of Sidhe in her as well, but not enough for wings. She wished for them when we were little."

Morena sat on the edge of the couch. "We were friends, you see, good, strong friends—the same as sisters—when we were littles. I know you've been a good, strong friend to her—the same as a brother—for a long time on the other side."

Sitting back on her heels, Breen let Morena take the lead with a cheerful voice and understanding eyes.

"She missed you through the summer, but more, she felt the weight of not telling you, her dear friend, all of this. Now, as her good, strong friend, you'll stand with her, and by her and for her. As we all will."

"That was well done," Harken said quietly, and laid a hand on Morena's shoulder. "You'll feel steadier after the potion, and hungry with it. Such a journey empties you out."

"I'd say that part goes for the lot of us. We didn't come through the Welcoming Tree," Keegan told him. "I had to make a temporary portal, and to add to it, only formed it to bring two."

"Ah well, you'll be starving then. There's enough stew left from supper to fill the holes. I'll warm it up."

"Is everybody really, really pretty here?" Marco wondered.

Morena gave him a light punch on the arm. "Aren't you

the one. Well, I'm no hand in the kitchen, but I'll give Harken what I have with the food. You'll be staying what's left of the night, I take it. There's room enough."

"I wouldn't want Marco to have to go through again so soon, so we couldn't stay in the cottage tonight. And I'd rather not wake Nan and Sedric." Breen looked at Keegan. "I'd appreciate staying for the night."

"You're welcome, of course. Coming around then, are you, Marco?"

"Yeah, actually. I feel good. Better than good. Thanks." Then he frowned at the tankard as he sat fully up. "What's in here?"

"What you needed. Finish that ale, brother, then Breen will bring you in for the meal. Harken's more than a decent cook, so you won't go hungry."

When Keegan left them, Marco looked down at his ale. "You and me, girl, we need to have a real long talk."

"I know it, and we will. And the flash drive I gave you, everything's there. I wrote it as it happened, right back to meeting Morena and her hawk at Dromoland."

"She's the hawk girl?"

"Yes."

"Okay, let me borrow your laptop, and I'll read what you wrote. Then we can talk."

"The laptop won't work here. No tech in Talamh."

For a moment, he—a worshipper of technology—could only stare. "You are shitting me. You can travel the multiverse, light candles across the room, grow wings, but you don't have Wi-Fi?"

"It's a thing. I'll explain everything. I promise. Tomorrow, we'll go back through, and to the cottage—our cottage on the bay. And you can read, and call Sally. You're going to want a couple of nights off. We'll just—we'll say you decided to come back to Ireland with me for a few days, get me settled in again. You can't tell him any of this, Marco."

His eyes filled with dread. "We have to go through one of those portals again?"

"Yes, but it'll be easier. I promise. Come on, you need food, and you need some sleep. Tomorrow . . . we'll deal with everything else tomorrow."

"How much else is there?"

"A lot." She stroked his face, his clever little beard. "A big lot of else."

"You were afraid to come back. I could see that. If it's all magicks and faerie wings, why were you afraid?" He looked toward where Keegan and the others had gone. "Not of any of them. I could see that, too."

"No, not of any of them. It's a long story, Marco. For tonight, let's just say there's a Big Bad."

"How big?"

"Big as they come. I'd be stupid not to be afraid, but I'm stronger than I was. And I'm going to get even stronger."

He took her hand when he got to his feet. "You were always stronger than *you* thought. If this place helped you see that, it gets some points."

"This place, these people, and others I want you to meet before you go home." She gave his hand a squeeze. "Now let's eat, because I can smell that stew, and I'm starving."

He let it go, mostly because he couldn't fit any more in his head at one time. Though after he ate he didn't expect to sleep, he dropped off the moment he rolled into the bed Keegan showed him.

The rooster woke him, which was strange enough. Added to it, he woke in a room not his own with a low fire simmering in a hearth, pale sunlight streaming through the lacy curtains at the windows, and the unsettling realization that none of the night before had been a dream.

He wanted Breen, and coffee, and a long, hot shower, and wasn't sure where to find any of them.

He got up, and the fastidious Marco saw he'd slept in his

clothes. Maybe one of the smoking-hot brothers could lend him something to wear after he got that shower.

He looked at his watch—one that let him keep track of his sleep, his steps, as well as the time—and frowned at the black display.

He crept out of the room—who knew what time it was—and tiptoed his way downstairs.

He heard voices—girl voices—and followed them into the kitchen he'd seen the night before.

At a little worktable that doubled as a small eating space sat Breen and Morena.

Breen popped up. "You're awake. I thought you'd sleep longer."

"There was a rooster. I think."

"Well, it is a farm. Sit, I'll get you some tea."

"Coffee, Breen. My life for coffee."

"Oh. Well."

He could only cover his eyes with his hand. "Don't tell me that."

"The blend of tea's really strong. Next best thing. Hungry?"

"I really need a shower."

She sent him that sorry look again. "Oh. Well."

Now he sat, put his head in his hands. "How does anybody get through a day here without coffee, without showers?"

"We've WCs—water closets," Morena told him. "And nice big tubs."

"Marco's not a tub person."

"You're just sitting there in the dirt you washed off."

"You've a point there, don't you?" Morena decided. "I can do you a shower outside."

"You can?"

"Faeries are connected to the elements. You want a spot of nice warm rain, I can help with that. Outside, of course."

"Sure, of course. Outside." He took the cup Breen held out,

gulped down tea. Blinked. "I think the enamel just melted off my teeth. Any chance of borrowing some fresh clothes?"

"There's less of you than there is of Harken, but I can get you a shirt and trousers. Let's find a spot for your shower." She opened a cupboard, took out a cake of brown soap. "I like your braids," Morena said as she opened the back door. "I wouldn't have the patience to do so many. The far side of the little silo, I think. Private enough."

"I appreciate this."

"The friend of my friend is mine. You'll want the grass under you or you'll end up standing in mud. So." She put her hands on her hips. "How warm for you?"

"Hot. I mean, not burning, but good and hot."

"Hot it is," she said, and handed him the soap.

In her trousers and boots—her shirt right side out now—Morena lifted her hands, palms up. And she curled her fingers in the air as if drawing something to her.

A thin rain, light as feathers, began to fall. As she continued to draw, it came stronger, harder in an area no more than six feet square.

Marco knew his mouth fell open, but he couldn't seem to close it.

"You can test it with your hand if you like, see if it's hot enough for you."

Marco held out his hand, felt the heat, the wet, the wonder. "Yeah, it's good. It's . . . amazing. Jesus, I don't know how to handle all this."

"I think you're doing more than fine." Morena stepped back. "We'll get you some clothes and a towel."

"Thanks. Um. How do I turn it off?"

"I've called it for fifteen minutes. So you'd best get started."

After she strolled away, Marco wasted nearly another minute staring at the magick shower before he stripped down and stepped into its bliss.

Once he'd dressed in what he thought of as farm chic, fortified himself with a fried egg on toast, he felt almost normal.

"I know we need to talk," Breen began, "and go over to the cottage, but I need to see my grandmother first. I need to see her, and I want to get Bollocks."

"I want to meet this dog, and yeah, your granny."

"She doesn't live far. It's a nice walk."

"Okay. I'm trying to roll with this." He stepped outside with her. "It looks like Ireland. They sound Irish. Are you sure it's not—"

"It's not. You tried to use your phone, didn't you?"

Marco rubbed a hand on a pocket of the borrowed trousers. "Yeah. Nothing. And yeah, I took a faerie shower about an hour ago. Best shower of my life. It doesn't feel real."

"I know."

"I mean there's the bay, but it's not the bay in Ireland where we stayed. And I see mountains way over there, but they're not the same ones. Flowers all over, lots of sheep and cows. Horses. Horses on the farm. Did you learn to ride on one of those?"

"Yeah." She decided not to point out the area on the farm where she'd learned to use a sword—poorly—under Keegan's unrelenting training. "You have to know how to ride here. No cars."

"No cars."

"No tech, no machines. They chose magick."

"No toaster," he recalled. "Toast the bread on a rack in the wood stove. Water from a well—or a faerie. You were okay with all that?"

"I had the cottage on the other side for working. But there are ways to write over here—magick ways. And it's pure, Marco. And peaceful, and alive. I guess I fell in love."

"Sense memory—remember? You were actually born here, you said. Are those the hot bros out there in that field?"

"The hot bros? Oh." She laughed, linked her arm with

his. "Yes. Harken's a farmer right down to his toes. Keegan's more a soldier, but he loves the farm, and he works it when he can. He has so much responsibility as taoiseach."

"As what, now?"

"It means leader. He's the leader of Talamh, of the Fey."

"Like King Keegan?"

"No, it's not like that."

So strange, she realized, to explain to him things she'd only learned—or remembered—a few months before.

"No kings here, no rulers. He leads. Chosen and choosing. It's a long tradition with its roots in lore. There's a lake," she began, but Marco grabbed her.

"Holy fuck, Breen. Run. Into those woods there."

"What is— Oh, no, no, it's okay. It's Keegan's dragon."

"His what the fuck?"

"Just breathe. They have dragons—but not like the virgin princess eaters in some stories. I rode that one."

His arm stayed around her in an iron grip. "You did the hell not."

"I the hell did, and it was glorious. They're loyal—they bond with someone, and they're loyal. And they're beautiful. My father had one."

"I might have to sit down. I don't want to wimp out on you, girl, but my knees are going again."

Before he could, right on the road, a joyful bark sounded. Bollocks, topknot and little beard bouncing, bounded toward Breen.

"There you are! There you are." With a laugh, she stumbled back when he leaped on her, every part of him wagging, from that topknot to the skinny whip of his tail. "Oh, you're bigger. You grew on me. I missed you, too. I missed you so much!"

She went down on the road with him for kisses and hugs and rubs. "It's Bollocks."

"I figured. Jeez, he's sort of purple, like you said. Purple

Haze so maybe you should've named him Hendrix. Aren't you something, puppy! Aren't you something else all over again."

Dragon forgotten, Marco crouched down. Bollocks rewarded him with a lapping tongue and wags.

"He likes me!"

"He's the sweetest dog ever. Nan knows I'm here. He knows, so she knows. Come on. Let's go see Nan."

Bollocks ran a few feet ahead, wagged, waited, ran back and forth.

"That's one happy dog. So, your grandmother. She's what now?"

"Of the Wise. A witch, with a little Sidhe. She was taoiseach once."

"So it's got, like, term limits."

"No, she gave it up, so there was another. And then my father led. Now it's Keegan. I'll explain."

"What about your grandfather?"

"He's not here, and we want to keep it that way. He's the Big Bad."

She took Marco's hand, turned on the road that led to Mairghread's cottage. "So much to tell you."

"It's sure piling up."

"She let me go, though it hurt her. After my father died, she sent the money my mother hid from me. And for reasons I'll explain, but one I can tell you now—because she knew I was unhappy—she worked it out so I found out about the money. After that, the choices were mine. To quit teaching, to come to Ireland. And she made me the cottage and sent me Bollocks. He led me here.

"She loves me, in a way I barely remembered my father loving me. The way you and Sally and Derrick love me. For me. And she opened my world."

"Then I guess I'm going to love her, too."

Flowers pooled and spread, spicing the air with autumn.

The cottage stood, sturdy stone under its thatched roof with its bold blue door open.

Mairghread stepped out, wearing one of her long dresses in forest green. Her bright red hair crowned her head. And with her misty blue eyes going damp, she laid a hand on her heart.

"You look a lot like her," Marco murmured. "And she don't look like nobody's granny."

"I know. Nan!"

Marg stretched out her arms as Breen ran into them.

*Mo stór*. Welcome home. Welcome. My sweet girl. You're well." She lifted Breen's face in her hands. "I can feel it, and see it, too. My heart's so full."

She drew Breen to her again, and smiled at Marco over Breen's shoulder. "And it's Marco, isn't it?"

"Yes, ma'am."

"You're welcome here, always." She stretched out a hand for his. "My door is open for you. You've had a strange journey."

She held his hand a moment longer as she studied his face, the deep, dark eyes, the tidy goatee, the anxious smile.

"A good friend to my Breen Siobhan you are, and a good man as well. I can see this, and thank the gods for it. Come in and sit."

She led them through the living room, with its simmering fire and sofa plumped with pretty needlepoint pillows, into the kitchen.

"Kitchens are for family. We'll have some tea, and didn't Sedric bake lemon biscuits just this morning?"

"Where is he?"

"Oh, around and about," Marg told Breen.

"No, I'll get the tea, Nan. You sit with Marco."

"Then I will." Marg sat at the small square table, patted her hand on it so Marco joined her. "And you're a musician."

"I try to be." He saw Breen in her, and Breen's dad—a man he'd loved. "I pay the rent tending bar."

"At Sally's. Breen told me all about Sally and Derrick and their place of business. Sedric says they have good craic."

"He's been there?"

"The silver-haired man you thought I imagined," Breen said as she measured out tea leaves from one of the jars on a shelf.

"Oh. Sorry about that."

"We worried for Breen, you see. In this last year or two, more and more we worried. Dragging herself to the class-room when she didn't feel suited for teaching."

"I wasn't." Breen filled the blue teapot with water from the copper kettle on the stove, then pressed her hands on it to steep the leaves.

"That you weren't, but you were a good teacher just the same, and far better than you gave yourself credit for. This was a worry, you see," Marg said to Marco. "She thought so little of herself, expected so little for herself."

The resemblance had already cracked the ice for him. Her words melted it away. "Speaking to the choir."

That made Marg laugh and lean in as if sharing secrets. "Cover her pretty hair with brown so as not to be noticed, and wearing such dull clothes to hide her fine body."

"Sing it."

Marg laughed again as Breen rolled her eyes. "Would the two of you like to be alone?"

Marco ignored her as Breen set the teapot on the table, went back for white cups and plates. "Her mom pushed her that way. Mrs. Kelly was always good to me, but . . ."

"You won't hear me speak against her. A mother is a mother, and when she and Eian made Breen, they made her with love as true as any."

"I loved him. I want to say how sorry I am he's gone. He gave me music, he taught me. He gave me a guitar on my ninth birthday, and changed my world."

"He spoke of you."

"He did?"

"Oh aye, and often. I knew you as a boy as well through my boy. Such talent, he told me, such a bright light. And as good and true a friend to his girl as he could wish for. He loved you, Marco."

When his eyes filled, Marg reached over to take his hand. "Breen will take you to where he rests while you're here. It's a holy place. I know your visit here wasn't planned, but if I'm honest, I'm so pleased you came. I'm so pleased to meet Breen's dearest friend from the other side."

"I can't get used to it."

"Well now, it's a lot to take in, isn't it?"

"It all happened so fast, and I haven't had time to tell him everything." Breen set the biscuits out, started pouring the tea. "We'll go over to the cottage if that's all right."

"Well, of course. It's yours, isn't it? Finola's having it stocked for you right now. And she's looking forward to seeing the handsome Marco again."

He flushed a little. "She didn't have to do all that. We could go into the village for supplies. Jeez, we have to change money, Breen. I don't know how much I've got on me."

"You don't need any in Talamh." She sat, took a biscuit. "They don't use money here."

"Well, how do you get stuff?"

"Barter and trade," Marg said as she sipped her tea. "And it's our pleasure to make Fey Cottage welcome for you."

"Breen said her dad, then you, sent the money to her."

"That we did. There are ways to come by coin. Trolls mine, and we've craftsmen and so on. We have those on the other side, in other worlds, who buy and sell."

"Ma'am, it changed her life. Not just the money, but the knowing her dad looked out for her. That she could use it to stop doing what she didn't love, and try doing what she did."

He looked down to where Bollocks happily snacked on the

biscuit Breen had given him. "The book she wrote about this guy? It's just great. Did you get to read it?"

"I did. So bright and fun, like its namesake."

"She's got the other going, the one for grown-ups. She won't let me read that one."

"Nor me."

"It's not nearly finished," Breen put in. "I still feel like I should take a walk and leave the two of you alone."

"We've considerable catching up to do, don't we, Marco?"

"Yes, ma'am."

"Oh now, call me Marg, as most do. Or, as you're a brother to my girl, you can call me Nan."

As she spoke, the back door opened, and Marco saw, for the first time, the silver-haired man.

Breen jumped up to embrace him, and Marco recognized pleased surprise. "Welcome home, Breen Siobhan. And welcome to you, Marco Olsen."

"You really are real. Sorry I didn't believe you were."

"Ah well, you wouldn't be the first."

"Sit. No, sit," Breen insisted. "I'll get the desk chair from my room. Is it still there?"

"It will always be there," Marg assured her.

Breen got another cup, another little plate. "When I came back to Philadelphia, and went to confront my mother . . . It was hard."

"I know, honey," Marco said.

"I walked a long way when I left her house, trying to settle myself. She kept all of this from me, all of this, my heritage, my gifts, put me in a box. I know it was fear for me," she added before Marg could speak. "But when I sat down, finally, at the bus stop, Sedric was there. He was there because I needed someone to be. I won't forget that. And I won't forget what Keegan told me. That it's fear of me for her, too. Fear of what I am, what I have. And I think, one day, I'll be able to forgive her because of that.

"I'll get another chair."

When she left, Marg sighed. "Her heart will be easier when she's able to forgive." She picked up the pot, poured Sedric's tea. "Now, Marco, you came through without having a moment to bring what you might need or want during your stay. You've only to make a list for Sedric, and he'll fetch what you like."

"You can do that?"

"I can, and I'd be happy to."

"Because you're . . . a witch? Wizard?"

"Just a touch of that. I'm a Were."

Marco's hand froze as he reached for a lemon biscuit. "You're a werewolf?"

"Not a'tall, though I've the acquaintance of several. Who do not go mad for flesh and blood at the full of the moon, I promise you. A were-cat, I am."

"Like a lion?"

Marg snickered, waved a hand. "Go on then, Sedric, show the lad."

Sedric shrugged, smiled. And became a cat.

Under the table, Bollocks's tail whipped with delight.

"Oh!" Breen carried in the chair as Marco goggled. "I've never seen you transform before. It's so effortless."

The cat became a man, who reached for his tea. "We're one, the man, the spirit animal. For the traveling to worlds, the witch in my bloodline helps. Tell me what you need, and I'll bring it over for you."

Marco held up a finger. "We're going to have really big drinks later."

"We have some lovely wine," Marg began.

"Thanks, but even with this, it's a little early for me. Later, though, really big drinks. And what I'm going to need, I guess, depends. Breen was scared to come back. Damned determined, but scared. Keegan, there was stuff he said—it was all really fast, really confusing—but he said stuff about releasing her from her duty, her promise."

"Did he?" Marg acknowledged.

"Yeah, and Breen told me there's a Big Bad, and she'll explain all that. But I don't know what I'm going to need until I know why he wants to hurt Breen."

"You haven't told him about Odran?"

"Nan, I didn't know he'd jump into the portal that way, and he was—you can imagine—shaken up and sick. I have it all written down, and want Marco to read it all, and I'll tell him all of it."

"This much he should know here and now, and early of day or not, a sip of apple wine hurts no one."

Sedric patted Marg's shoulder. "I'll see to it."

# CHAPTER TWO

W hen I was young," Marg began, "younger than you, I took the sword from the lake, took the staff, and was taoiseach. Odran came to the Capital, and I saw only what he wished I see. Handsome and kind, charming and romantic. And so I fell in love with this illusion, and we married."

She spoke of their return to the family farm in the valley, of the months he deceived her and her family, of the birth of her son, and her joy in him.

And, when she broke from a drugged sleep, her discovery of Odran's purpose. How he drank their son's power from him in the night to increase his own. The war that followed against the dark god and his demons, his slaves, and everything that came after that, up to his abduction of the child Breen had been.

Marco found himself very grateful for the wine.

"But Breen's more than her dad, right? She's got her mom, too. Human, too."

"You're a quick one, Marco. Our Breen is the bridge between the realms of the Fey, humans, and gods. She broke free of the glass cage, this child of three, because of all she is. More than even Odran knew. More than still he knows, I think. So then Eian, as taoiseach, led the battle—the Battle of the Black Castle—and destroyed Odran's fortress, blocked any and all portals from his world again, did all that could be done."

"Mom wanted him to choose, between her, me, and Talamh," Breen added. "How could he? But he gave the farm to the O'Broins—Keegan's family. Their father died in the battle to protect me. They were best friends. He was in Sorcery—the band? From the picture Tom Sweeney gave us in the pub in Doolin."

"We were meant to go there." Marco sipped more wine. "Pretty clear we were meant to meet Tom and hear how your parents met."

"They loved each other. I think they always did. Because he loved, they went to Philadelphia, and he tried to be what she wanted, what his people needed."

"All those out-of-town gigs weren't gigs. He was coming here?"

"Yeah, and she knew, of course, and it just built up resentment. She divorced him, and I think she must have said to him what she said to me when I went back to tell her I knew all this. The aberration—that's what she called my gifts, and really, that's what she called me—wasn't allowed in her home."

Marco reached over to give her hand a squeeze.

"She believed she protected me, she convinced herself of that, but under it, she protected herself. The world as she needed to see it."

"I'm sorry, Breen." Marco kept her hand, gripped it hard.

"Me, too."

"She's wrong. She's been wrong all along, so I'm sorry for her, too. 'Aberration,' well, fuck that. Sorry," he said to Marg immediately.

"No need, as I agree."

"You're a wonder, that's what you are. I always thought so, just didn't figure, you know, witch goddess." He looked back at Marg. "How did Eian die? If you destroyed this Odran's fortress and blocked the portals, how come he's still a threat to Breen?"

"Not just Breen, but she is the key. Odran killed my son. With time, his powers, and the aid of the black magick of a witch who turned to him, he waged his war on Talamh again. This, I think, was a ploy to draw Eian out, to murder him. To kill the son who refused to bend to his father's will."

"Now he wants Breen. Okay, with all the respect I've got, and I'm sorry you have to fight these wars with some crazy god, but it seems to me like the best place for Breen is back home. Where he can't get to her. I'm not agreeing with your mom. You need to be who you are, do what you love, but, girl, you ain't no warrior princess."

"I've been training for it—not the princess part—all summer. With a sword."

He gave her shoulder a push. "Get out."

"I can defend myself. And nowhere's safe, Marco. Not for me. Not for anyone."

"He'll come again," Marg said. "Another battle. More blood, more death. We will stand against him to the last of us. But if he defeats us, if he conquers or destroys Talamh, your world is next. And all the others to follow as he kills and burns. His powers will grow, and so will his thirst for more."

"You mean he'll destroy the Earth, like, everything?"

"Our world, your world, all worlds. Each in turn gives him more. Do I understand Jennifer's drive to lock Breen away? I do. But what she would never believe, never accept, is Breen is the key to the lock. She can't be shut away. He'll find her, in time, or if she has a child of her own? A god has all of time."

"I want children one day. But, Marco, I could never risk that knowing this."

"Jesus, Breen."

"It has to stop with me. These are my people. I know how that sounds, but—"

"It sounds right."

"They'll fight. But they need me."

He nodded, took a long breath. "I watched *Wonder Woman*, I know the drill."

"Four times. You watched it four times."

He held up five fingers. "It takes a god to kill a god, that's how it works, right?"

"The daughter of the son is the bridge between worlds." Breen felt the words, the thoughts, the truth simply flow into and out of her. "The bridge leads to the light or to the dark. Her path is threefold. Awaken, become, choose."

Marco waited a beat. "What was that? Like a prophecy? You do that now, too?"

"Sometimes. I'm still me, Marco."

"Who said you weren't? Okay then, it gives me a better picture on what I'm gonna need. If you're okay with that," he said to Sedric.

"It's my pleasure."

"It's a lot, since there's no telling how long I'm going to be here. I won't be leaving until we kick that asshole god back to hell."

"Marco—"

"I got choices, too, girl, and that's mine."

"You don't have any powers. You have no idea what Odran can do."

"I've been getting a pretty clear picture, and it scares the shit out of me. But I'm staying."

He shot the index finger of each hand in the air. "That's it, that's all. If you start nagging on me about it, I'll ask Nan here if she'll put me up. Look me in the eye, Breen, look me right in the eye and tell me if we switched places, you'd just go on back to Philly and leave me."

"If anything happened to you—"

"Same goes. So that's settled. I guess I need to borrow something to write down this list."

Breen didn't argue with him—she knew better. But she hoped to gradually erode his determination to stay over the next handful of days. Marco, more than anyone she knew, was a creature of urban life and all its conveniences.

The more time he spent in Talamh, without technology, without the basics, the more . . . maneuverable he might be. Especially if she could convince him of something he could do on the other side to help.

At the moment, she couldn't think of a single thing.

On the walk back to the farm, she pointed out a pair of dragons, with riders, gliding through the skies.

"Those are scouts."

"Okay, so, uh, dragons come in all different colors. How about people? Any of my type here?"

"Yes, and of your persuasion. Love is love here."

"That's good to hear. Not looking for romance right now, but it's good to know people around here have open minds."

"And hearts. There are some, like anywhere, that don't. They had a religious cult—the Pious. Didn't start out that way, but they went, well, dark, you could say. And there have been Fey who've turned that way. Marco, I want to point out that if you stay, and you want to get anywhere, you're going to have to learn to ride. A horse."

"You think I can't?" He hooked his thumbs in his waistband and strutted. "I can give cowboying it a try. And if you can learn how to do the sword thing, I can."

"I'm pretty crappy at it."

"Aw, now."

"Just ask Keegan. He trained me, and would be the first to say so."

Marco slid an arm around her shoulders while Bollocks trotted along with them. "You gonna snuggle back up with that fine example?"

"I'm not interested in romance right now either. And I doubt he is. There's something in the air."

"You going all—" He wagged his hands.

"I am all—" She mirrored the gesture. "I can feel something . . . pushing. He wants in. He's not there yet, but he's close."

She shook it off. "But not yet. We'll get my things, go to the cottage. I think it'll be easier if you read what I wrote about everything. Then if you have questions, I'll answer them."

"Okay, so we just walk from here back to Ireland? Through another of those wind tunnels?"

"It won't be like that. Not that dramatic."

Bollocks let out happy barks and raced around. He leaped nimbly over the stone wall and bulleted straight for the two children and the big wolfhound who guarded them.

"Those are Finian and Kavan. And the woman in the vegetable garden? That's Keegan and Harken's sister, Aisling. Their mom."

"So everyone *is* pretty here."

They used the gate. Aisling, her dark hair bundled up, dusted her hands on her trousers, laid one on the mound of her belly, before walking toward them.

"Welcome, Breen Siobhan. Welcome. You came back as you said. I should never have doubted you." She caught Breen in a hug. "I'm sorry for it."

"Don't be. I know how you worried, and why. This is Marco."

"So I hear. You had a tumble into Talamh, I'm told. Are you doing fine now?"

"All good, thanks. It's nice to meet you."

"And you as well. Will you have some tea? Mab will mind the boys while we go in."

"We've just come from Nan's, where we had tea—and wine. I just need to get my things so we can get settled into Fey Cottage."

"Oh, they're sent over already. Morena saw to it, and your very handsome clothes, Marco, had a cleaning."

"Thanks. I borrowed these from your brother. From Harken."

"Not to worry. He has more."

The older boy, Finian, raced over, with his younger brother scrambling in his wake.

"It's almost my birthday," Finian announced. "You'll be here for my birthday."

"On Samhain." Breen crouched down. "I remember. You'll be three."

"Say your hello and welcome to Breen's friend, Fin. This is Marco."

He ducked his head. "Hello, and welcome."

"A bit shy with new people, this one. But," Aisling continued as Kavan reached them and immediately tried to climb Marco's legs, "not a bit with that one."

Marco hauled him up. "And who's this?"

"That's our Kavan," Aisling said as the boy babbled at Marco. "Who's never met a stranger."

Kavan grabbed a handful of Marco's braids, grinned at them. "Like!"

"Me, too."

Then the boy dived to Breen, babbled at her.

"When are you due?" Marco asked.

"Around and about Imbolc. Early in February," she explained at his baffled look. "I'm past the halfway mark as I figure it. Hoping for a girl this time, as you can see I've two heathens already."

"I missed your heathens," Breen said, and gave Kavan a nuzzle before she set him down. "We'll be back tomorrow. I'll work with Nan, as I did before. And if you'd tell Keegan I'll train if he wants."

"No doubt he will. He and Mahon—that's my man," she told Marco, "will be back by moonrise. Come and see me when you can, the both of you are welcome. Come on, lads. Did we or did we not promise Harken we'd see to the kitchen garden? Blessings on you both," she said as she herded her kids away.

"And on you," Breen called. "Come on, Bollocks."

She gestured as they went through the gate again. "The portal's through that tree. Or the portal is the tree, I'm not sure which."

He looked over, beyond the dirt road, another stone fence, a pasture of sheep, and up a hill.

The tree spread more than twenty feet wide as it rose out of a tumble of rock. Its thick branches curved down, some reaching the ground before they arched up again. The leaves Breen remembered as boldly green all summer had a wash of crimson.

"What kind of tree is that?"

"It's the Welcoming Tree, and the portal—or the main one—between Talamh and Ireland."

She led him across. Bollocks bounded ahead, scrambled up the seven stone steps on the hillside. Perched on a branch, he stopped, barked as if to tell them to hurry up.

"Okay. If I pass out, you can go get me the ale again, or whatever was in it."

"I can, but you won't need it. You'll feel the change," she told him as he followed her up the steps. "And there's some wind—but not like the other. A change in light, just a flash. Then we're over. Don't be surprised if it's raining on the other side. You never know."

"I don't think anything's going to surprise me again. Ever."

Standing above him, she reached back. She felt his anxiety, but it couldn't compete with his loyalty.

"Take my hand. Go ahead, Bollocks. We're coming. Step on the branch. It might feel a little like you're falling, but . . ."

The light flashed, the sudden breeze blew through her hair.

"You're not. See?"

"We're through? Gut shook a little, but. Are you sure we're through?"

"Yes. You just need to climb down."

"Little shaky in the knees," he admitted. "But not all whacked like before. And it's not raining."

"Lucky us, we won't get wet. It's about a mile's hike to the cottage."

"It looks pretty much the same."

"It does, but it's not. You didn't get a chance to see last night because it was raining over there, and you were shaken up, but Talamh has two moons."

"Two?"

"One waxes when the other wanes."

"That is so way cool! I want to see that. But you know, Breen, I walked all over these woods when I was here getting my Irish on. I never saw that tree. How could anyone miss that tree? It's huge, and it's growing out of rock. Or there's rock growing out of it."

"You weren't meant to. Look at your watch."

He did, let out a half laugh. "How about that. Working fine." He pulled his phone out of his borrowed pants. "Got a phone, too."

"Sally first," Breen told him. "The best thing to say is you decided to come back with me, and we flew out last night. You're going to stay for a few days, and—"

"I don't know how long I'll stay, and that's what I'll say. Give that one up, Breen, you're stuck with me. We're going to be fine. We're going to get each other right on through this. And I'm going to learn to ride a horse. Giddyup!"

"It's not as easy as you think. My ass had bruises on bruises for days. And I hate myself for being glad you're here."

"You can stop that. Say, in all this you wrote down? Anything in there about sex with Chief Hotness?"

"I— Crap. Listen—"

"Too late. You said I could read all of it. And you two might not be in the mood for snuggling right now, but I saw how he looked at you."

"Like I was one more pain in his ass?"

"No. Like I hope somebody looks at me one day." Marco's romantic heart gave a little sigh. "He didn't even try to punch me back when I hit him, when I thought he'd hurt you. He could've mopped the floor with me, but he didn't. Hell, he could've probably turned me into a kumquat or something. But he didn't."

"He respects loyalty and friendship."

"Sally said he had class."

"I suppose he does."

"I remember this trail now. Son of a bitch! Walk that way, and you end up in the village. The bay's over there. Hey, it was over there, over there. Wrong place. That's— You know what? That's freaking awesome."

He sniffed the air. "Catch that? I can smell the bay, I think. And . . . smoke."

"They lit the fires for us." She gestured as the trees thinned. "See?"

The cottage stood, smoke trailing from the chimneys over its thatched roof. The gardens Seamus had taught her to tend spread as colorfully as ever. And the pots of flowers he'd shown her how to plant thrived still.

"It's your place, Breen. Your grandmother said, and she made it for you. I get that more than ever now. I loved being here, too."

"I know." She looked down at the dog, who danced in place. "Go ahead."

He all but leaped in the air before he raced out, across the green grass, down the slope to the shale beach, and bounded into the water.

"Sea dog," Marco said with a laugh. "He's something."

"Let's go in. I'm used to drinking tea over there—and God, you've got to try Finola's lemonade. It's magickal. But I sure hope they remembered to stock Cokes."

It was like coming home, Breen thought as she grabbed that Coke out of the refrigerator. With the first sips, she scanned her pretty kitchen—the freshly baked bread wrapped in a white cloth on the slate-colored counter, the stoneware bowl of fresh fruit, the fresh flowers on the wide windowsill.

So much as she'd first seen it months before. So much as she'd left it.

"I'm going to make us a pasta dinner," Marco announced as he poked around the kitchen. "Look at these tomatoes. They are prime!" He checked his watch, did the math. "I'll wait about an hour to call Sally. If they're sleeping in any, I'd rather they get some coffee in them before I tell them I flew the coop."

"That works. I'll set up in the bedroom down here for work." She wandered that way and into the room that opened to the garden. "Scratch that. They've done it for me." She brushed a hand over the laptop already on her little desk, noted her yoga mat—which she hadn't thought to grab— neatly rolled and standing in the corner.

"Sedric's already come and gone," she told Marco.

"What? How?"

"You'll sort of get used to it." She walked back to open the door for Bollocks, who pranced his way to the living room fire, and after his habitual three turns, settled down with a contented canine sigh.

"Do you think my stuff's up in the room I used before?"

"Let's go find out. I want to unpack, then I'm going to get some writing in. I should probably do a blog, too, about coming back to the cottage. And you can set up wherever you want to read."

They walked through the living room with its forest-green sofa, its candles, crystals, flowers, its views of the blue water.

The fire sizzled and snapped in the hearth.

Through the foyer, and up the stairs, where the dog scrambled up to follow them, Breen turned at the head toward Marco's room.

His guitar stood on its stand, and the harp, out of its case, gleamed on a table along with his keyboard.

Because he was busy staring, Breen opened a drawer. "Sweaters, shirts."

He opened the closet. "They put everything away."

"It's a kind of welcoming. I'll bet your jackets and rain gear—and mine—are in the closet in the foyer."

"You really think I'm going to get sort of used to it?"

"I hope you do." Her heart squeezed a little. "This is who I am."

"I'm always going to love who you are." He moved over to the table, ran his finger over the harp strings. "I want to learn how to play this. It's the best gift I ever got."

"I remember a little, what my father taught me. I can show you, and I know you can more than take it from there."

"Okay. Okay." He walked around the room he remembered, looked out at the view he remembered. "Maybe we'll have us a musical evening after dinner. Cooking and making music, that might help me with the 'sort of.' I'm going down, start that sauce so it can simmer its way to heaven, then I'll call Sally."

He reached out, ran a hand over her bright red curls. "You do what you do, Breen."

She went down to do what she did, with Bollocks curled on the bed behind her. She'd do the blog first, she decided, just a brief one. And would wait to post it until Marco spoke with Sally.

How to begin? she wondered. She couldn't write, not on the blog, about the taoiseach of Talamh, or Marco jumping through the portal with her.

She simply sat a moment, let it sink in that she was back,

well and truly back. She'd enjoyed her solitude in the cottage over the summer, and finding herself by living on her own for the first time in her life.

But as she sat now, hearing Marco in the kitchen, singing as he did whatever he did to those prime tomatoes, she found his presence like a warm blanket on a chilly morning.

Simple comfort, like the dog napping behind her, or knowing outside the garden doors the flowers bloomed.

So she wrote about returning to Ireland. For the first time on the blog, she wrote about finding her grandmother, learning of the loss of her father. And how the grief of that balanced with the joy of finding family and friends.

How finding them helped her find herself.

Satisfied, she set that aside, and opened herself to the story. She dived in, let it surround her.

# CHAPTER THREE

When she finally surfaced, she found herself a little stunned.

She'd worked well in the apartment in Philadelphia when she'd gone back at the end of the summer. But not like here, she admitted. Maybe it came from the initial burst of energy from being back where she'd really started this part of her journey, but she'd poured out ten pages.

Now, out of the writing haze, she caught the scent of Marco's red sauce, noted the change of light as dusk crept closer.

And saw Bollocks had left his post.

She shut down, stepped out. She saw Marco sitting at the dining room table, his brow furrowed as he read on his laptop. Bollocks rose from his spot in front of the kitchen hearth to lean against her legs.

"Sally?"

"All good. He's glad I came with you." He looked up then, straight into her eyes. "What's in here, Breen, it's not good. It's not good. Holy shitballs, you almost got yourself killed. Twice."

"But I didn't. And he doesn't want me dead, Marco. What

he wants is worse." She walked into the kitchen to fill the dog's food bowl. "I'm stronger than I was, and I'll get stronger yet."

"How are you going to fight him?"

"I don't know the answers right now." She chose a bottle of wine. "But I think it may come down to power against power."

"He's a freaking god. He's Loki, girl, without the fun parts."

"I've got his blood in me, and more. I have more. You're not asking if I'm afraid."

"You're not stupid, you're not crazy, so I know you are. Can't Keegan take him down? Okay." Rising, pacing, Marco waved a hand in the air. "I get he would if he could. I've got a better picture of him, of everybody over there now. I haven't finished it all, but I've got a better picture. Your picture, anyway."

"My father died trying to stop him."

"I know, baby. I know. But that crazy witch lady with the two-headed snakes." He shuddered before he took the wine Breen held out. "I'm with Indiana Jones on snakes."

"Fool me once." She toasted, drank. "She won't catch me off guard again."

He gave her a long look. "You're not as scared as you were last night."

"Maybe I had to come back to lose some of it. Not all because not stupid, not crazy. And I know I'm going to be really scared again. But what I've learned, what I will learn? The more I learn, the more I feel.

"I was afraid to try to write, but you pushed me until I did. And I'm good at it. I'm going to get better, but I'm good at it. And it gives me joy. I'm going to get better at the craft. I've gotten pretty good, and I'll get better. It gives me joy."

He walked into the kitchen, stirred his sauce. "Writing doesn't put you in a death sleep."

"Have you read about my vision—the boy on the altar, what Odran and his demons did to that boy?"

"Made me sick. Made me sick because it wasn't like a movie where it's all pretend. It was real."

"How can I just walk away from that when I might be what stops it from ever happening again?"

"I don't know, but the thing is, lighting some candles? That's wild stuff, girl, but it's not the sort of thing that handles all this."

"Fire is often the first skill learned."

She set down her wine, held out a hand. And brought the red flame over it. "It can burn hot." In her other hand, she brought the blue fire. "Or it can burn cold."

She sent them aloft, then brought them together with a clap like thunder before they sizzled, sparked, died.

"Air can stir." She circled a finger. "A warm breeze." Then held up her other hand, circled it. "Or icy wind."

Both blew through her hair, tossed Marco's braids before she vanished them as she walked to the doors and outside. There she laid a hand on the pot of flowers. "Earth brings life." Buds not yet open bloomed under her hand. "Or takes it."

And the ground trembled.

"Water comes soft for the earth to drink." She lifted her arm, drew down. Held out a palm that cupped the rain she'd taken from the clouds. "Or lashes."

She shot a hand toward the bay, whipped it into a waterspout.

And smoothed it out again.

"These four elements are connected in me with a fifth. The magicks those who came before me gave me. I learned, Marco. My father had what I have, except the human. But he tried, for her, to be human when he was on this side. And I think because he lost so much of his heart, because he was so torn, Odran found a way to exploit that. And killed him.

I have the one thing Dad didn't. I don't know what it means, how to use it, if I'll need to use it, but I have more."

"Okay, okay. I need more wine. I need to fill this glass right up."

He made it back to the kitchen, but his hands shook so hard he couldn't lift the bottle.

Breen went to him, put a hand over his. "Don't be afraid of me. I think it would break me if you were afraid of me."

"Not. Pour that for me, will you? Not afraid. Awed. That's a good word for it. Awed." He gulped down the wine she poured. "You glowed. I mean like you were all lit up inside. I read about some of the stuff you learned to do, but seeing you do it . . ."

He wrapped an arm around her. It still trembled, but he held her against him. "Didn't I always say you were special? It's just going to take me awhile to get to that sort-of-used-to-it part of all this."

"All you need. How about I do something totally normal and make a salad to go with your pasta?"

"That'd be good. I'm going to put the laptop away. I'll read the rest later. I think I'm pretty full up on that for now. I'll put some music on."

Normal, she thought as she peeled and chopped. Would it be normal if she slipped some rosemary and crystals under Marco's pillow to ensure he had a peaceful night's sleep?

Her normal, she decided, so she'd see to that.

They'd have dinner and talk of normal things. And she'd go up for his harp—slide the charm under his pillow—then show him what she remembered. Maybe she'd bring down his guitar, too.

When he came in to boil the water for the noodles, it felt normal—their normal, she thought. With Marco checking her work on the salad, then walking her through some recipe for a dressing before he slid the spaghetti into the pot.

"Like old times," he said, and she laughed.

"Borg mind. I was thinking the same. I'll set the table, and we'll feast."

Bollocks let out a bark—not a warning, but a greeting. When she glanced over, she saw Keegan about to knock on the glass door.

She caught just a glimpse of Cróga's gold-tipped green tail slashing as the dragon rose into the night sky.

She walked, plates in hand, to the door to open it.

"Sorry," he said straight off. "You're about to have your meal. I won't keep you."

"Hey, come on in," Marco called from the stove. "Had dinner yet?"

"Ah, no, I was just—"

"You can have dinner with us. I made plenty. Grab another plate, girl, and let's get the man some wine."

"I don't want to intrude."

"You're not." She stepped back. "Marco's right. He made more than enough."

"It's kind of you. It's smells very good."

"Hope you like spaghetti marinara."

"I do. It's been some time since I've had it."

"You're in for a treat." Not quite sure what it meant for the normality of the evening, Breen went back to pour another glass of wine. "Marco's a terrific cook."

"I wanted to see that you'd settled in, and that I'd meet you, Breen, as usual tomorrow. It seems I've timed myself into a meal."

"You earned it. Take off that really fine coat I lust for," Marco told him. "Go ahead and put the salad out, girl. You can light the candles your way. I'm almost sort of used to that."

Before she did either, she walked to Marco, hugged him hard from behind.

"She worries about me," he said to Keegan.

"Friends will do that. You look steadied up right enough. Morena said you had. And you met Marg and Sedric."

"Sedric's a lucky man. Or cat. Met your sister and her two boys." At home in the kitchen, Marco poured the pasta into a colander. "Saw some dragons. Don't know what to think about that yet, but I read in Breen's journal how she rode on yours."

"You keep a journal?"

"Yes." She concentrated on dishing the salad into bowls.

"We're going to want another bottle of wine," Marco decided. "How about you open one, Keegan? I'm going to mix the pasta and sauce up family style."

Marco fussed, as Marco did, with slices of bread, dipping sauce, with placing basil just so on the pasta. When he sat, he lifted his wine. "It's nice having company for dinner. Back in Philly we didn't have room for many people, so we mostly hung out at Sally's."

"A good place for it."

"The best." Marco dug into his salad, sampled it. "Good job here, Breen. So, Keegan, you're the head guy around here. Or there. Over there."

"I'm taoiseach."

"I read in the journal how that's done. Jumping into the lake and all that. You found the sword, brought it up. And *boom*. Except you could've said, 'Nah, not me,' and doggie-paddled right away."

"It's a choice."

"Not an easy one, I bet. And you were just a kid."

"Old enough." Keegan shrugged that off. "We're taught and trained all but from birth to know the duties of taoiseach."

"And Breen's training and learning now. But not to be the head guy."

"If I fall, she could choose to enter the lake and bring up the sword."

"Don't talk about falling."

Keegan spared her a glance. "He asked. That's the answer."

"She could do that," Marco continued, "even though she's half-human or Earthling or whatever you'd call it."

"She's of Talamh as well, carries the blood of the Wise, of the Sidhe. What comes from her mother, her grandfather, is what makes her unique. Not other, if you understand, but—"

"Special." Marco gave Keegan an approving nod. "I'm always telling her that. Her mom really tried to make her ordinary. Didn't work."

Taking it on himself, Marco dished up a huge portion of spaghetti for Keegan's plate.

"Anyway, I'm glad you came by tonight, because I was going to try to find you tomorrow. Hey, I'm not supposed to call you 'sir' or 'your highness' or something, am I?"

"No," Keegan said, with feeling. "Gods no."

"A third of that, Marco. I mean it. Damn it." Breen only sighed when he served her pasta. "He always gives me too much."

"You're seriously buffed up, girl. Those muscles need some carbs. You helped her get them."

"Ah . . ."

"With training. I was going to be pretty pissed at you, chief dude or not, for knocking my girl down, bruising her up."

"Marco, please." Breen felt the redhead's curse of a flush creeping into her cheeks. "Just eat."

"I'm gonna. But I figured out you were tough on her because you needed her to fight back. To want to. Her mom—and I'm not going to dis her. When I came out, my family didn't support me. My sister did, but my parents, my brother, different story. But Ms. Wilcox did, so I won't slap at her too hard."

"Where did you come out from?"

Marco laughed. "The closet, man. I'm gay."

"Aye, Breen said that means you prefer men for sex and such. We don't have closets for that in Talamh."

While Marco just grinned, Keegan wound spaghetti

around his fork, ate. "Well now, this is brilliant. Better even than I remember eating in Italy."

"You've been to Italy?" Marco pointed at him. "I'm going to ask you all about that, but before I do, I'm going to finish my thoughts here."

"Finish whatever you like. I'm eating this."

"I want to say, it's hard to learn to fight back, to want to fight back, when most of your life, basically all of it, you've been told not to. More, told you'd never win anyway because you'd never be good enough."

Keegan nodded as he continued to eat. "Breen's mother was wrong. Whatever her reasons, it doesn't make her less wrong. You are what you are." He looked at Breen then, straight on with those amber-flecked green eyes. "And you know what you know now. It doesn't mean I won't still knock you down or put bruises on you on the training field."

"Because you want her to live."

"I do, aye, I want her to live."

"That's why I decided not to be pissed at you. Plus, you saved her life. Twice."

"It wasn't her life so much in danger."

"Try the dipping sauce. It's my own blend. You swooped out of the sky on your dragon when some evil faerie dude had her. You—swipe!—cut off his head."

"It's good, your blend here."

"And when the bitch witch's snakes bit her, you got her through it."

"She did much of that herself."

"Not the way she tells it, but I'm going with you on it. Either way, and any way, she's the world to me, so there's nothing you can do—except hurt her—that's going to piss me off very much. I guess I have to stay off the training field."

"You choose your friends well, Breen Siobhan."

"I'll take credit for that. Marco, I don't want you to have to think about any more of this tonight. You've had a day."

"I'm almost done. I'm going to need you, or somebody, to train me. Other than a few lucky punches, I'm crap at fighting."

"He says he's going to stay," Breen began when Keegan looked at her.

"I don't just say it, I mean it. The world to me," Marco repeated. "As long as she's here, I'm here."

"Well then, brother, we'll train you up right enough, though you may not thank me for it. You should learn to fight—to defend yourself and others. But I'll say there are more ways to help than with a sword or a fist."

"Like what? I can't poof up a handful of fire like some of us here can."

"I'm about to ask for a second portion of like what. Not so much as the first, or even Cróga won't be able to carry me home."

"Cooking?"

"Warriors need to eat, and well. I'll see you're trained. Morena'd be a good one to start him with," he said to Breen. "She's steady and firm, but has more patience than I do."

"Who doesn't?"

"Haven't found one yet," Keegan said easily. "You have a gift for cooking, that's more than clear, so it shouldn't be wasted. And I'll say, as one who knows, you throw a solid lucky punch, so I'm thinking—as with Breen—there's more to you than you may know."

Marco rested his chin on his fist. "You're gorgeous and built, and now you say stuff like that to me. It's going to be hard not to fall in love with you."

Keegan laughed, ate more pasta. "If I liked men for that sort of thing, no doubt I'd come courting you, for your cooking alone."

"A boy can dream. So tell me about Italy. Where did you go, what did you see, what did you do?"

They bonded. Breen sat, largely unrequired, and watched

a friendship root, sprout, then bloom as Keegan spoke of art in Florence, fountains in Rome, of twisting roads along the sea and narrow streets in villages.

When they moved to the mountains and plains of Montana, she rose to stack dishes.

"No, sit," she said when both men started to rise. "You cooked. And you can keep Marco entertained."

Which he did, she admitted as she dealt with the dishes, telling tales of other worlds. Worlds of golden sands with mountainous dunes and lush oases, worlds of bustling cities where skyways soared and buildings pierced the clouds.

And the primitive where magicks thrived even as men hunted game with spears and built huts out of mud and straw.

It occurred to her she'd never seen Keegan quite so relaxed, or known him so willing to just sit and talk.

"How many are there?" Marco asked him. "How many worlds out there?"

"Who can say? We know of a score—twenty—but it seems there would be more than we would know."

"Twenty? Have you been to all of them?"

"I haven't, no. My duties don't leave me enough time to travel so freely. Then there are worlds barred to us by law. Some are still evolving, you see, worlds of wild waters and fiery mountains. Volcanoes."

"Whoa. Dinosaurs?"

"I've heard tales of great beasts."

Breen left them to it. She went upstairs, slipped a charm under Marco's pillow.

When she came down with Marco's harp, Keegan rose. "I've kept you long enough," he began, then stepped toward her to study the harp. "Now, that's a true beauty, that is."

"Breen brought it back for me."

"She said you were musical. That's a fine instrument."

"I have to learn to play it. I don't suppose you play."

"A bit."

Marco punched his arm. "Really? Show us."

"I should get back."

"I heard you play the violin."

Keegan frowned at Breen. "When?"

"Right before I left."

"Eian must have taught you to play. The man could make music from a hollow reed."

"He taught me, but I've forgotten so much of it. It'd be nice to hear this played by someone who hasn't forgotten."

When he hesitated, Marco gave him a poke. "Consider it singing for your supper. Your next supper."

"Well, that's a hard thing to turn aside. All right then, one before I go."

He sat in the living room, the harp on his lap, and trailed those long fingers over each string. "It's well tuned."

He paused a moment. Then began to play.

It seemed the notes simply wept from the strings. Beautiful and heart-wrenching so the air sighed with them.

"I know that song," Breen murmured. "I remember that song."

"As you should. It's one of your father's. He called it 'Heart Tears.' It's made you sad," Keegan said, and stopped.

"No, not that way. I can see him playing it. Sitting out in the backyard of the little house we had. Late at night, alone. I watched him out my window, and he seemed so lonely. I sent him butterflies."

Remembering made her smile. "I wished for them, and they came, fluttered all around him. He looked up and saw me, smiled at me, put a finger to his lips. He played in the summer moonlight with butterflies all around him. I fell asleep with my head on the windowsill, and when I woke in my bed in the morning, it was like a dream.

"Play it again, please."

When he had, he switched to something lively and quick to change the mood. Then he held the harp out to Marco. "Have a go."

"We had a pretty good selection of instruments at the music store where I worked, but nothing quite like this."

He plucked at the strings, shifted the harp, plucked a few more. And reached back for something he'd banged out on the piano at Sally's on St. Patrick's Day.

"Well, listen to you." Keegan grinned at him. "You're a rare one, Marco, or you've been pulling one saying you haven't played before."

"It's trying to be 'Black Velvet Band.' It's not quite there. I'm going to YouTube on this."

"Instructions," Breen told Keegan, "demonstrations online, on the computer."

"You could, or you could bring it over with you. Aisling plays the harp, and she'd give you a lesson or two. What I'm hearing, you won't need more than that."

He rose. "Thanks for the meal, and the music. I've got to get back, as Harken will have me up before the sun breaks."

"I live with one of those." Marco wagged a thumb at Breen. "I'm glad you came by. We'll see you tomorrow over there. I guess I'm already sort of used to it," he said to Breen. "Or it's the wine."

"Drink some water, or you'll be sorry tomorrow." She got up. "I'll walk out with you. Bollocks is already dancing by the door. He wants his nighttime swim."

The minute she opened the door, he bolted toward the bay.

Keegan shrugged on his duster. "Good night to you, Marco."

"Check you later."

Breen stepped out in the cool as Bollocks splashed in the lake.

She didn't waste time. "He's determined to stay. You have to understand, he's not built for this. For fighting, for dealing with what's coming. I have to convince him to go back. You're taoiseach."

"And what, I could order him away? I have no sway there, and in any case, he's a man grown, a man who values his friend. You should respect that."

"I do respect that, damn it. But he's powerless, and he's—"

The hem of his duster snapped with his sharp movement—and so did his eyes. "You, of all, should know better than to deem him powerless. He stands for you, so stand for him. Quiet," he ordered before she could object again. "Don't lessen him."

"I wouldn't! I didn't mean—"

"I'll make you this promise. I'll give my life to protect him as I would for you."

"You'd do that for anyone. It's the way you're built. But, Keegan, if anything happens to him, I couldn't bear it. I couldn't."

"I'll see he's protected, and you'll do the same. Don't make him less than he is. You of all people should know what it does to a mind, a heart, a spirit to be made less."

"I don't mean to do that." She pressed her fingers to her eyes. "I am doing that." She dropped her hands. "You're right. Saying he's powerless was stupid and insulting. But he's human, Keegan. He's fully human."

"You have Marg's protection." Keegan tapped the stone she wore around her neck, the dragon's heart stone she'd coupled with her father's wedding ring. "Give him yours. Make him a charm. It's not an impenetrable shield, but it's from you."

"I put rosemary and amethyst under his pillow so he'd sleep."

"I think the wine will add to that. The man has a strong head for wine."

He watched the dog jump from the lake, shake water from his dense curls. "I have something to say to you."

"About training tomorrow."

"Before that. I said it before, but it was rushed, and you were already upset. I'm sorry, truly, for going at you hard as I did when you had to go back, for not believing you, as I should have, that you'd return, even when you swore it."

"It hurt me."

"I know it did, as I meant it to." When Bollocks raced back, Keegan bent to give him a strong rub, and dry him thoroughly. "I'm sorry for that, and it's a fecking burden for me to be sorry over and over again, so I'm getting it done."

"There's more?"

"Before I left the Capital, my mother asked me to be diplomatic and patient with you, even knowing I have little diplomacy or patience. I'm sorry I didn't do as my mother asked. I didn't come at you to hurt you then, but I hurt you nonetheless."

"You didn't, so I'll let you off there. I wasn't hurt, I was terrified and twisted up with worry I'd never see Marco or Sally or Derrick again. That I'd never see my book published, or finish the one I'm writing. That I won't be enough to stop what's coming, and I'll die when I've really just started to live."

"Yet you came, your father's daughter."

She looked up at the moon, the lone moon of this world. And thought of the two in her father's.

Both hers.

"If I don't try to be just that, none of the rest means much of anything. You released me."

"I did, and will again if that's your choice."

"It's not. This is my choice."

"Then come to the training field tomorrow as you did before. If I knock you down, you'll get up."

She looked toward the water and the reflection of the three-quarter moon that swam over it. "There's not much time, is there?"

"Not as much, I think, as we'd like."

"Will we be ready?"

"We will be because we must be. Leave your window open as before. If Odran pushes into your dreams, I'll come."

"He doesn't know I'm back, not yet. He's too busy pushing against the portal."

Keegan gripped her arm. "You see this? Know this?"

"I feel it. Maybe I'm wrong, but—"

"You won't be wrong. Put a charm under your pillow as well. Block him out. It gives us more time."

"All right."

She saw Cróga sail across the moon, then sweep over the water. "When did you bond with him, your dragon?"

"I was eleven." Cróga landed on the grass, shaking the ground. "We were both smaller then."

Keegan strode over, used Cróga's tail to boost him into the saddle. He looked back at her, standing quietly, the moonlight showering silver on her hair.

"*Oíche mhaith*, Breen Siobhan."

Dragon and rider soared up. She felt the wake of wind from the slash of tail before they flew over the woods, through the dark, and into Talamh.

# CHAPTER FOUR

In the morning, with the first cup of coffee in her hand, Breen opened the bay-side door. Bollocks streaked out for his morning swim with his happy barks echoing through the silence.

She followed more leisurely across the patio, over the grass, spongy and damp from a rain that had come and gone while she slept.

She smelled roses and rosemary.

In her bare feet she walked down the slope of the lawn to the edge of the sand and shale beach. There she drank her coffee and watched her dog's curly head bop and bounce through the pale gray of the water and the mists that rose, thin, smoky fingers, toward a sky just awakening.

Philadelphia felt like the dream now, those few weeks she'd spent there between the then and the now all blurred colors and movement.

Standing there in the misty dawn as night gave way to day, with the quiet disturbed only by the call of birds and her dog's cheerful splashes, brought her a peace so complete she wished she could cup that moment in her hands and hold it.

And holding it, make it last to always.

She stood just a bit longer and watched a little red boat slide in and out of the mists, and those mists thin as the sun strengthened.

But there was work to do, and duties to uphold. She went back inside to fill the dog's bowls and left the door open for his return before she started upstairs.

She lit the living room fire with a thought, did the same with the one in her bedroom as she changed for her morning workout.

Marco slept on as she went through her morning routine. Slept still as she settled in at her desk, the dog curled on the bed behind her.

And like the boat, she slipped into the mists of the story.

When she surfaced, craving a Coke, she felt the satisfaction of progress. She thought she might have another hour in her—once she got that hit of cold caffeine—so went out to get it.

Marco sat at the dining room table working on his laptop. He wore his jeans pressed, his red sweater trim, and his gorgeous braids tied back with a matching red band.

How, she often wondered, did he do it?

"Good morning. I didn't even hear you."

"I'm working on being quiet. Plus, the way you were clickety-clacking in there, I figure I could've blasted out some Beyoncé and you wouldn't've heard it."

"I had a groove going." She went in the kitchen for the Coke, sniffed the air. "I smell bacon."

"I got us a good, solid brunch warming in the oven."

To see for herself, Breen opened the oven door to plates of omelets, bacon, breakfast potatoes.

"It looks amazing. I usually grab a piece of toast."

"Not while Marco's here." He rose, went to the fridge. "We've got some mixed berry yogurt parfaits. I'm going to earn my keep, plus I figure you need some good, healthy fuel for all this training business."

"I really didn't want to be glad you're here. You completely screwed that up for me."

"Sit yourself down." He handed her the parfaits. "I'll get the plates. Sweet blog this morning," he added. "Like a bonus since you posted one last night. Did you read the comments?"

"No. I wanted to get right back into the story."

"A lot of people posted condolences about your dad. I'm not ashamed to say I teared up a couple times. Anyway, since we linked your blog to your website, and your website to the blog, got your other social media going, your followers have more than doubled."

"Since you linked," Breen corrected. "I'm so glad I don't have to try to do all that."

"You nagged me into the job." He set the plates on the table. "Did you check your email since we got here?"

She winced. "Well, no."

"Good thing I get copied on the New York stuff. But you need to do that more often, girl. Anyway."

He sat, gestured for her to do the same, then angled his laptop so she could see the screen. "Got this attachment this morning. For your approval."

He brought up an image that had Breen gasping.

Bollocks—or the artist's version—seemed to prance across the screen in all his curly glory. His head turned toward her with his big doggy smile. BOLLOCKS'S MAGIC ADVENTURES arched in bright red over him. And below read: BY BREEN KELLY.

"Oh! Oh! Look at him! Look at you." She turned the screen toward the dog doing his happy body wag beside her. "It looks just like him. It's wonderful. Is it wonderful? Do I just think it's wonderful because my name's on it? It's a book cover, Marco, with my name on it."

"Wrote it, didn't you?"

"Holy shit, I did. I love it. I just love it. Do you love it? Should I love it?"

"Take a breath. Eat some yogurt." He nudged the laptop back so she could see it while she ate. "I think it's fan-fucking-tastic."

"You really do?" She scooped up some yogurt and berries. "I can't trust myself because my eyes are just dazzled."

"I've had some time with it. I've taught music to some kids in the age group you're looking for here. You sure as hell taught plenty of them. First, who's not going to fall for a dog who looks like that? It's got plenty of happy and bright, but then they've got the woods here in the background, right? Like he's happy-go-lucky heading there. What's in them? Maybe something a little bit scary? Maybe something our hero here has to outwit?"

Nodding to himself, Marco picked up his fork, cut into his omelet. "They're going to want to find out, right? And he shines in the story, Breen. The writing shines. And that's going to pull the parents, the teachers right in."

"You make it sound true."

"That's easy, 'cause it is. You eat now."

"A year ago, I wouldn't have believed any of this. But here we are, there that is."

"They're looking for a picture of you with Bollocks for the back cover. I'll take some before we go over to, you know, the other place. But you're going to do something fine with your hair, and get some makeup on."

While he ate, he studied her pale blue sweater, dark brown trousers. "You need boots, and you can use my brown leather vest. Put on some earrings—little studs to keep it cas—and you'll be good to go."

"I need another hour. I focused on the adult book this morning. I need an hour on the next Bollocks adventure."

"That's fine. I've got plenty to do."

She took her hour, then went up to deal with her hair. She considered just doing a glamour for her face, but admitted that was lazy.

When Marco came in with the vest, he nodded approval. "Hair's good. It's fun and easy—they wouldn't want the fancy for a kids' book. You need more on the eyes, girl."

He hung the vest on the hook on the bathroom door, then picked up a brush himself. "Close 'em."

She submitted, let him fuss with shadows and contour and liner.

"Need them to pop some for your first official author photo, right? And there you go."

When he turned her toward the mirror, she let out a breath. "I look good." She put on the vest he held out.

"I gotta hate it looks better on you than me. But I'll put that away, since I think this is just the right look. Let's go do our first photo shoot."

She'd thought he'd take a couple, but it turned into a couple dozen. Standing with Bollocks with the water behind them, sitting on one of the patio chairs with Bollocks sitting beside her, sitting on the grass together.

Then Bollocks planted his forelegs on her thigh, lapped at her face. On a laugh, she hugged him to her.

"There's the money shot! I'm gonna pick out the best five, send them. Don't know why five, it just seems right."

"We really need to go."

"Give me five for the five, and we're off."

When they finally walked into the woods, Bollocks dashed ahead to chase a squirrel, then splashed in the little stream, shook, and raced back.

"There's a dog who makes his own fun," Marco observed. "So . . . what will I be doing over there?"

"I guess that's up to Morena."

"She's not going to want me to do something with that big bird, is she?"

"Amish. I don't know why she'd want you to train with her hawk."

"What'll you be doing?"

"I usually practice with Nan for a while. Magick takes practice."

"Like yoga."

"You could say." Because she sensed his nerves, Breen slid an arm around his waist. "You could come with me today, just give the rest more time."

"Might as well get started. It's stopped feeling real again. Hanging out with Keegan last night—that's like a usual sort of thing. Both of us working this morning. Thinking I'm going to go through a big-ass tree into another world? That's the not-real part right now."

"It's about to get real." She gestured ahead to the Welcoming Tree.

"There it is, all right. Never seen anything like it. So they, ah, put it there?"

"Nan told me a millennium ago—or so—Birget the Wise, then taoiseach of Talamh, brokered a treaty with the other realms. As man turned from magicks, they became suspicious of them, condemned them and all who held powers. Many who didn't."

"Like Salem, and all that crazy shit?"

"Yes, like that, and before that, after that. Talamh chose to preserve what they were, what they had, so the Fey and the world of man used this tree as a boundary, and as a door when Talamh separated from Ireland. Not all respected the treaty, and most on this side of it simply forgot it existed. Most forgot other worlds existed. Talamh remembers, and preserves its peace. Fights for it when it must."

"Like now."

"Like now," she agreed, and took his hand. "Are you ready?"

He sucked in a breath, and his courage with it. "We're going to find out."

He stepped onto one of those thick, curved branches with her.

Then another.

"Go ahead, Bollocks," he heard her say. And with a happy bark, the dog bolted through, and vanished.

The light flashed, but it seemed less shocking. And the wind rose and died. He stood with Breen on a bright, breezy day with the dog deviling the sheep in the field below.

"Okay?"

"Yeah. Weird," Marco admitted. "It's probably always going to be weird. But I don't feel all dizzy and shaky. It's really a sight, Breen, the way it just rolls and rolls. There's Keegan out there doing some farmer thing. No, that's the other one. Harken. And I think that's your friend Morena with those horses. There's a house back there. I don't think I noticed that before."

"Aisling and Mahon's cottage. Keegan's sister—you met her and her boys yesterday. Mahon's her husband, and he's Keegan's good friend. I guess sort of his lieutenant. A soldier. He's of the Sidhe."

"Okay. I'll get it all straight."

He started down the seven steps with her.

After they crossed the field, the wall, the road, Morena hailed them. She had her hair in a long tail with a blue billed cap over it, and the hawk pin Breen had given her on her jacket.

Breen wondered if she spread her wings and flew toward them to give Marco more of a taste of what was.

"I thought to see you about now," she said as she landed. "I've horses saddled and ready for us, Marco."

"Okay." But he was too dazzled by the wings to register horses. "They're beautiful. Can I touch—is that rude or, you know, creepy?"

"Not when you ask. Go ahead."

He reached out, very gently touched his fingers to the silver edges of her lavender wings. "They feel like silk. They just . . . pop out when you want?"

"They do, aye."

"Excellent."

"I'm told Keegan enjoyed a fine meal from your hands, Marco. I'll be looking for some of that."

"Anytime."

"I'm a terrible cook myself."

"I could teach you."

"We'll see about that, but for today, I'll be doing the teaching. You see there is my Blue, and the pretty bay mare is Cindie. You'll ride her today."

"I will?"

"Sure and you will. We'll have you take her around the paddock a few times to get you acquainted."

"How come I didn't get to walk around the paddock a few times when I learned to ride?"

Morena's blue eyes danced. "We'll say Keegan and myself have different styles. Come now and meet our Cindie. You'll see by her eyes what a sweet heart she has. And she's tireless as well. She'll go and go if you ask it of her."

Breen went with her, and didn't need to look into Cindie's dark eyes to feel the sweetness, the loyalty, and the pleasure of having a purpose.

"I'm just going to watch for a few minutes."

And as she stood doing just that at the fence, Breen watched Marco stroke Cindie's cheek before he climbed over and stroked her neck.

"I've never been up on a horse."

"First times are fun times now, aren't they?" Morena claimed. "If you'd like to mount, I'll check the stirrups, see if we've got the length right."

"Here goes."

He didn't, as Breen had, try to mount from the wrong side, or complain about the lack of a pommel. He just boosted himself up, and grinned.

"Yee-haw!"

On a laugh, Morena showed him how to hold the reins, how to use them. "She's a biddable soul," she told Marco, "so you can use a gentle hand with her. Firm enough, of course, but she wants to please."

"I like it up here. Who'da thought?"

"Go ahead, walk her around. Heels down now, knees in. That's the way. Hands down as well."

"I'm riding a horse. I'm rootin'-tootin'! Check me, Breen."

"Can you turn her around now, walk the other way? Look at you. The man's a natural."

Clearly, Breen thought, more than she'd been.

"You can trust me with him," Morena murmured to Breen.

"I can see that. You'll stay close, though? If any of Odran's people get through—"

"I'll have a sword on before we leave the farm. Keegan and Mahon are out with the scouts right now. I'll look after him, my word on it."

"And yourself." Time to trust, Breen thought. "Looking good, Marco. I'll leave you with Morena, and meet you back here later."

"Later. Hey, can we ride around out there?"

Breen left them to it, and with Bollocks racing back to her, started down the road to her grandmother's.

She sent a wave to Harken, checked the sky for any sign of the scouts. She watched a falcon soar, but saw no sign of dragons. And no sign, she realized, of the children she'd seen running the roads or in and out of the woods through the summer.

In school, she thought, like children in other worlds.

Fall added a bite to the air. On the hills some of the hardwoods had donned their autumn reds and golds and oranges as they climbed up among the deep greens of the pines. She saw trolls standing outside of high caves, taking the air before they went back to mine the stones and crystals.

On the turn to her grandmother's cottage, she saw a buck giving her a long, arrogant study before he melted into the woods.

A buck, not a Were, she thought. Keegan was right; she knew. She only had to look into the buck to know.

Marg's cottage stood with its blue door open in welcome, and smoke curling from its chimneys.

She found her grandmother and Finola in the kitchen, adding herbs to jars.

"And welcome home." Finola, her chestnut hair bundled back for the work, stepped over to embrace her. "It's more than pleased I am to see you. And I should tell you, Seamus will be on his way soon to see to your gardens."

"I'm sorry I'll miss him." She leaned over to kiss Marg's cheek. "Do you want some help with this?"

"All but done. Would you be wanting some tea, or a bite to eat?"

"I'm fine, thanks. Marco made us a huge late breakfast."

"Sure I've heard the handsome boy's a brilliant cook."

Breen shook her head at Finola. "Word travels."

"In Talamh it does for certain. I'm looking forward to seeing him again. Is he with Morena now?"

"He's with her, and doing better on a horse in five minutes than I did in five hours."

"I hope I see him on my way back home then. I've got to get along. I just came by to give Marg some of our peach brandy. It has a good kick, it does. You come and see us now, Breen, and bring the handsome Marco."

"I will."

"Take this along." Marg handed her friend a small jar. "Remember, just a pinch when you want to add a kick—like your brandy—to a stew."

"Thanks for that, and thanks from Seamus, who does enjoy that kick. Blessings on you both."

When Finola left, Marg went to the jar of dog treats. Bollocks's ears perked up.

"And what will you do for this?"

"He can dance," Breen told her.

"Is that the truth of it?"

"Dance for Nan, Bollocks. Boogie time!"

He rose up on his hind legs, wagging as he stepped right and left. On a long laugh, Marg tossed the treat so Bollocks snatched it out of the air. "Aren't you the clever pair? Well now, will we go to the workshop?"

"Please. I'd like to make some protection for Marco, since I can't talk him into going back."

"Then we will. Come on, lad, bring your treat. It's a fine, bright day for you to run about outside and splash in the stream. He'll let you know, won't he, when he wants to come in?"

"Yes." They walked out, and since there was no one inside to welcome a visitor, Marg shut the door. "I can just feel him asking. Not words, not really, but a knowing."

"You've bonded well and true."

They walked into the woods, Bollocks prancing with the dog biscuit in his mouth, and to the bridge over the stream.

"You have a gift of connection with living things, and it serves you well." She stopped there, on the arch of the stone bridge with the cottage workshop tucked into the trees ahead of them.

"Do you know the horse they put Marco on today?"

"Morena called her Cindie."

"Aye, a good choice. Sweet-natured, patient, eager to please. Hold her name in your mind, as she knows it well. See her as you did in your mind's eye. Bring her into you."

"Call her?"

"No, no, *mo stór.* Bring her in, as you would with our lad here. Bring her in. Feel what she feels."

She'd seen the mare in Harken's fields before, of course, and had gauged her before Marco mounted, but to connect when she had no idea of distance or . . .

Distance meant nothing, Keegan had told her once.

So she held the name, the image, reached out. For a moment, it felt as if she moved outside herself, then all the deeper in.

"She's content. She likes the human, and the smell of the air. She likes to walk with Blue. She . . . she's mated with him before."

Marg smiled into Breen's eyes. "She has indeed, twice if memory serves. You did very well."

"I didn't know I could do it at all."

"You can, and more. And how is our Marco feeling?"

"I can't—"

"Don't think, just feel. It's not his thoughts, and it takes more, as humans and Fey have filters, you'd say, that horses and dogs and the like don't. But your connection there is already strong. You've already done this without the knowing because you've had this bond with Marco for so long. What does he feel at the moment?"

"Excited." Truly shocked at the clarity of it, Breen laughed. "Proud of himself. A little smug. Oh," she corrected, "more than a little."

"There you are." Marg patted Breen's arm before continuing to the cottage. "So when you worry, you can look. But remember your manners. Don't intrude unless there's cause."

"I won't." Breen followed her grandmother into the cottage, where Marg set the fire to light. "Is it like when I saw the deer—a buck—when I turned to your cottage, and I knew he wasn't a Were, but a buck?"

"It's more. All Fey have this knowing. No one would loose an arrow on the hunt without looking and knowing. But not all have what you have. It's one of Harken's gifts as well. And Aisling in her way, the way of healing a wound or an illness. You have both."

"Do you? I've never asked."

"A bit of both. Your gift is stronger, but needs to be honed as yet."

"I lost all that time. I could've been learning."

"Time's never lost, just spent on other matters. Now." Marg gestured to her many shelves, the jars and baskets, the crystals and tools. "What manner of protection are you wanting for your friend?"

"I'd like to put him inside an impenetrable force field. I don't suppose that's an option."

"With time and practice," Marg said as she lit the little stove with its kettle on the hob.

"Really?"

"Such things can be prisons as well, can't they, taking freedom away as well as giving protection. What I know of him? I'd say something . . ." She circled a finger in the air as if to find the word. "Stylish, that he can wear. Show off a bit."

"You're right about that. A necklace." Breen toyed with her own. "Or a bracelet maybe."

Marg gestured to the shelves. "See what strikes you."

Breen wandered up and down, looking at, picking up, putting down cords and chains, stones, ribbons, strips of leather.

"Do the Trolls mine the crystals?"

"They do, aye."

"And you barter and trade with them for them. I need to expand my stock. You've been more than generous there, but I should start getting my own. Will they barter with me?"

"Sure and they would. Nothing the Trolls favor more than

a good trade. Other than a good meal with a large tankard of ale. It's a good ride to the nearest mines and their trading post. Keegan can take you while he's training you."

"Hmm" was all Breen said to that.

"But you'll choose what you like now for your friend, and mine. And the making of the protection is good practice for you."

"I was thinking the leather. If I could braid some together for a bracelet. These different tones—the black, the browns. And work stones in. Um. Malachite for protection and support—and he'd like the color. Black tourmaline for safety and protection, obsidian for shielding, purifying, and for sending negative energy back to the source. Citrine for positive energy, spiritual cleansing. Amethyst and labradorite for protection against psychic attacks."

She looked back at Marg.

"Good choices, all—you learn, Breen Siobhan. I think add a fire agate, a shield. Choose your stones then—tumbled ones would work best for a bracelet, I'm thinking. I've kept your wand and your athame, so be sure to take them with you when you leave for your training."

Marg went to another shelf, opened a long wooden box. She took out Breen's tools, set them on the worktable.

"Now lay out what you've chosen. The simple task first, to braid the leather with your own hands, with the thought of your friend and your intent in each twist."

She could braid—Marco had seen to that—so she sat and began.

"Each twist, each fold, binding protection for the brother of my heart. Strong leather, dark and light, three into one. And this his pulse beats under."

Marg nodded in approval. "Well done, well said. Lay the stones on the leather as you wish."

Breen arranged them, rearranged them, changed them a third time. "Do you think that's right?"

"It's what you think, what you feel."

"It feels right. He'll like the colors and contrasts. It's a strong combination."

"Aye. Now bring the light, *mo stór*. Charge the stones with its energy, and yours."

It seemed like yesterday, and a year from yesterday all at once since she'd done purposeful magicks. Her heart tripped as she drew her power in and up, as she pulled the light streaming through the window to bathe the stones.

In it, they pulsed.

"Your wand now. Merge them, stone to leather, intent with heart. Give them your power and your words."

"This gift I make for one held dear, to shield him from harms both far and near. With my hands three became one, with my powers I called the sun. And here with these stones selected, I charge he be protected. Body, mind, spirit, three as one."

She passed the wand over the leather and stones, once, twice, three times. "And so by wand and will, my charm is done."

The stones sank into the braided leather, fused with it.

She felt the power tremble inside her another moment, then released it with a breath.

"It's a strong gift." Marg kissed the top of Breen's head. "And a lovely one."

Breen lifted it, turned it over, studied the smooth flat braid, then laid it upside over her wrist to examine the look of the stones. "I've missed this," she murmured, and turned her head to look up at Marg. "And you. Missed all of this and you more than I realized."

"We'll sew a fine pouch for the gift."

Breen took Marg's hand before she could turn back to the shelves. "Odran doesn't see me yet. It's like a curtain, but there's a chink letting in dark instead of light. It's your curtain, your spell holding it."

"For now. You need time yet, as do we all."

"He'll shove it open soon."

"He will, aye, he will. But we have today." Now she cupped Breen's face. "He knows you have more than he thought, but he doesn't understand you have more even than that. Neither do you know it, but you will."

Marg walked back to the shelves. "A red leather pouch, I'm thinking, done with gold cord. Would that suit Marco?"

"To the ground."

And because she sensed Bollocks patiently waiting outside the door, Breen rose to let him in.

"I won't leave again until it's done, Nan. That's my promise, that's my choice. Help me find the more in me to get it done."

"I'll always help you, *mo stór*, but it's you who'll find what you have and what you need."

Soon, Marg hoped, as the tugs and pulls on the curtains grew stronger every day.

# CHAPTER FIVE

After the sublime—an afternoon of conjuring, practicing, and creating with her grandmother—Breen walked to the farm for, if not the ridiculous, the most likely painful.

She felt a spark of hope when she spotted Morena giving Marco pointers in hand-to-hand on the training field. Keegan leaned back against the paddock fence watching. Harken, most usually busy in the fields or with the stock, sat on the fence beside his brother.

The resemblance struck her as Keegan, hands in the pockets of his duster, turned his head to say something that made Harken grin. They shared features with the man in the photo with her father, taken before she was born. The set of the jaw, the shape of the mouth, the plane of the nose.

But whatever the similarities, she'd detected wide differences in their personalities and interests. Keegan wore a sword at his side, and Harken had work gloves sticking out of his trouser pocket. Harken wore an old brown cap on his wave of hair, and Keegan the skinny warrior's braid down one side of his.

The taoiseach and the farmer, she thought. If cameras had

worked in Talamh, she'd have snapped a photo of the moment.

Harken lifted a hand in greeting as she walked along the stone fence to the gate. Keegan just tracked her with his eyes.

On the field, Morena feinted a left jab—slow enough for Marco to block, followed with a right hook she stopped a whisper before his jaw. He tried an uppercut, which Morena deflected with an elbow, and continued up until the back of her fist paused at his nose.

"It's in the eyes as much as the hands, Marco darling, remember that. In the eyes and the stance. And you want your shoulder leading it now. We'll go again."

About the time she spoke, Marco spotted Breen. He grinned.

"Look at me. I'm—"

And ended with an *oof* as Morena swept his legs out from under him.

"On me, Marco." Morena used two fingers to point to her eyes. "Distracted will put you on your arse every time."

She offered a hand to help him up. "You're doing well for a start, so we'll take a few minutes." She grabbed a skin of water, tossed it to him.

"I'm having a hell of a day," he told Breen, and from his tone she interpreted a good hell of a day.

"How'd the riding lesson go?"

"Ask the teacher."

"The man took to horseback like a duck takes to water."

"Really?"

"I've got untapped skills." After guzzling some water, Marco swiped his sweaty face. "Fighting doesn't seem to be one of them."

"That only means you've room to improve. But not today. We have to turn the field over."

"Oh. I can wait," Breen assured her.

"No need. Marco's more than earned the cup of ale I promised him. At dusk then, Keegan?"

"For today, aye."

He swung off his duster, tossed it over the fence.

"I wouldn't mind a late supper," Harken called out. "Dusk would give you time enough to cook it."

Morena shot him a sweet smile. "Dream, my darling. A man should have his dreams. You can ride Blue," she told Marco. "And we'll go get you that ale, and the gingerbread my nan planned to make today."

"I could go for it."

"You'll test those skills by saddling Blue."

On their way to the paddock, Amish swooped down, landed on the gatepost. Marco jumped half a foot.

"Ah now, Marco, I've wings, don't I now, and they don't trouble you."

"It's not the wings so much. It's the beak, and the eyes. The eyes that look right at you and I hear him thinking: I bet your tongue tastes real good."

With a shake of her head, Morena pulled Marco into the paddock. "I'll make you a solemn vow: He won't eat your tongue or any other part of you."

"Does he know that?"

"If I know it, he knows it."

"Wait a minute, Marco. I've got something for you." Breen pulled the pouch out of her pocket as she went into the paddock.

"I get a reward for not falling off a horse? Cool." He opened the pouch, pulled out the bracelet. "Wow. Seriously rocking. Thanks, girl. Where'd you get it? I didn't see any shops around here."

"I made it."

"You did not!" On a half laugh he looked at her, then blinked. "You made it?"

"Oh, and well done, Breen." With her hands behind her

back, Morena leaned closer to examine the work. "It's brilliant."

Harken swung off the fence to get a look for himself. "It's all of that. You chose fine stones as well."

"It's for protection." Breen took it, fastened it onto Marco's wrist. "Mind, body, spirit. I'll sleep better if you wear it. All the time."

"I can do that. You mean it's like magick? You made it with the woo-woo?"

"With the strongest spell I know for it. That doesn't mean you won't break your neck if you jump off a cliff, or Morena can't knock you on your ass. But it's protection."

"And styling." He leaned down to kiss her. "I love it, and you." He blinked again. "Is that a knife? Is that a knife on your belt?"

"It's my athame—it's for rituals. I left it with Nan when I went back to Philadelphia."

"She made that as well, and the wand," Morena told him. "Show him, Breen."

"You got a magic wand? Step off!" His uncertainty about the knife vanished in delight. "Let me see. Do something with it. Where's a rabbit and a hat when you need one?"

"If it's not too much trouble," Keegan said dryly, "I've not all the time in the worlds to stand about while the lot of you admire Breen's crafting skills."

"A hard taskmaster is Keegan. Well then, Marco, show off your skills and let's see you saddle up my big Blue."

"I'll see you in a bit," Breen said as she walked back out of the paddock—and got a supportive squeeze on the shoulder from Harken.

While Morena supervised Marco saddling Blue, Keegan picked up a second sword.

"We'll start with this, and a single wraith." He handed her the sword. "And we'll see how much you've lost and forgotten since you took considerable time off your training."

Marco called out when Breen unsheathed the sword, "You said they won't cut, right, bro? They're all enchanted and like that."

"They won't cut or slash or puncture living flesh. But . . ."

Turning, Keegan circled his hands, drawing them up and down, up and down, stirring the air, swirling the earth through it. And conjuring the dark faerie.

Breen studied the familiar face of one of Odran's followers, one who'd attacked her on her second day in Talamh at her father's grave.

She kept her focus even when she heard Marco's alarmed: "Holy shit. What the fucking fuck!"

"It's a wraith," Morena soothed. "It's not real, not the way you think."

"A training tool," Keegan said without looking around. "All right then, Breen, let's see what you've managed to bring back from your holiday. Defend!"

The faerie leaped, eyes gleaming, sword raised.

Breen blocked the strike, felt the all-too-familiar clash of steel shoot shock up her arm. She shifted, put her weight on her back foot, pumped a side kick into her opponent's belly with her front. Then spun, gripping the hilt in both hands, and using the power of the spin, struck.

As it had on that bright summer day under Keegan's sword, the head thudded on the ground and rolled.

"Shit! Shit! Girl, you go!"

Breen merely tossed her hair back, sent a disdainful stare into Keegan's eyes. "I didn't take time off or go on holiday."

"Feel a little sick."

She turned to see Marco bent over, hands on knees.

"Focus!" Keegan ordered, but she flicked her fingers at him.

"It's not real, Marco. It's like CGI."

He lifted his head, breathing slow. "Like CGI. I can handle that."

"It will be real," Keegan murmured. "Soon enough."

"I'm well aware, and I'm here to train. But he needs time to adjust. You'll give him time, or I'm done for the day."

She thought she heard a snicker from Harken as Keegan angled his head at her.

"Come back altogether full of yourself, haven't you? All right then, take on two."

Rather than conjure another foe, Keegan brought back the first, twinned him. When they rushed her, she shot a stream of fire at the one on the left, impaled the one on the right.

"Three-zip, Breen Kelly!" Marco made wild crowd noises.

"I trained every damn day. You're not the only one who can conjure wraiths." And since she'd anticipated something exactly like this, she'd already done just that, had it—to her way of thinking—on hold.

She released it, a burly, bearded, seven-foot Were. "Now you defend!"

It transformed into a snarling, towering bear as it charged Keegan.

"She made a bear!" she heard Marco shout. "Breen made a bear!"

Keegan drew his sword, pivoted. And didn't quite evade the edge of slicing claws. But he leaped aside, struck out with his blade. As the bear screamed in pain and rage, began the next charge, Keegan opened the ground under him.

And sent fire after it.

Annoyance lost to fascination as Breen studied the mucky mess in the crater. "I don't know that one. Show me."

"Later."

"You'll be filling that hole, brother, or I'll be helping Breen bloody your arse."

Keegan just shrugged at Harken, used two hands and brought the earth back to level ground.

"I want to try that. Let me—"

"Later. Defend."

She managed to block Keegan's strike, but her arm sang all the way to her shoulder. She set her teeth as they eyed each other over the vibrating steel.

"You've improved."

"I trained every damn day."

He hooked a foot around hers, skewed her balance, and before she could regain it, impaled her. "And still you're dead."

Annoyed, she stepped back, set again. She feinted a strike with her sword, used her left hand and her power to shove a blast of air. It knocked him back, and down. She sent fire after it, turning it to water before it struck.

"That makes two of us."

Something lit in those gorgeous eyes of his, she noted, but couldn't tell if it was admiration or the spark of competition.

"Learned some tricks on your own, I see." He got to his feet. "Mind your fire, as I'd sooner not go up in flames."

"It harms no living thing—I bespelled it like the swords. You'll get wet, but you won't burn."

"Well then." He shoved a hand through his dripping hair. "Defend."

They clashed, sword and smoke, fire and fists.

In the paddock, Harken pulled Morena in for a kiss. "I've cows to milk."

As Harken wandered off, Marco pulled himself into the saddle, still craning his neck to watch the action.

He watched fire spew from Breen's fingers, collide with a stream from Keegan's, and burst into a flood of water. Swords sliced through it.

"Okay, I'm saying it right out loud," he decided. "This is getting me hot. Is it like foreplay with them?"

"Sure and that may be a part of it. She's worked hard, and it shows. Still, I can tell you he holds back. Well now, we'll leave them to it and go have ourselves some ale and gingerbread."

Morena spread her wings and rose up, and her hawk with her. "Along with me now, Marco. Blue knows the way home."

Breen heard them leave, ignored them. She already hurt. The swords didn't cut, but they sure as hell packed a sting. And every muscle in her body wanted to weep after ten minutes of sparring with him.

The fire wouldn't burn, but God, her lungs did. And since he'd used her own trick with the fire to water (she'd thought that so very clever), she was soaked to the skin.

She could train with a sword, she knew, for a year—for ten years—and never match him there. But her magicks had grown, sharpened. More to find, more to learn, but if she could ward off his attacks with them, he might not kill her as often.

Still, even with that in her arsenal, she felt herself flagging. He didn't even seem to be winded. Reinforcements, she thought. Why the hell not?

And brought back her were-wraith to charge him from the left flank.

When he shifted to defend, she went for him with fire and blade.

Acknowledging the killing blow, he stepped back. "That was canny."

"You didn't say it was against the rules."

He pushed at his soaked hair. "The only rule in war is to defeat the enemy and live." He lowered his sword, a signal for a break. "Where did you train in your Philadelphia?"

"In the apartment when Marco went out."

"In that little place?"

"It's what I had."

"I mean to say it shows dedication. I reckoned on having to bring you back up to where you were when you left, but you've gained a step or two instead."

"A compliment. Let me mark the day and the hour. Maybe the minute."

Irritation flickered, visibly. "I've given you praise before."

"In this area—pretty scarce."

He dragged a hand through his hair, drying it this time. "Then I'll say this. Your swordplay is weak."

"That's more familiar."

"But," he said, with the faintest edge of annoyance, "it's better than it was, by a small margin. More, as you know it's weak, you've found ways to . . . what is it? Compensate, using where you aren't so weak. That's a good trait and good tactics for any warrior."

"I'm never going to be a warrior."

"Bollocks to that. Apologies," he said to the dog, who stopped chewing on a stick long enough to thump his whip of a tail. "You already are. Odran doesn't know that. You must. You killed me a half dozen times this hour."

She hated the fact his acknowledgment meant so damn much.

"I lost track of how many times you returned that favor."

He shrugged at that. "When we started, you could barely hold the sword, much less use it. And though you're not a clumsy woman, you tripped over your own feet."

He glanced up at the sky, gauged the time by the sun. "Sure it's too late to put you on a horse today. Did you keep up there after you left?"

"No. I didn't have a horse or anywhere to ride."

"Tomorrow then, we'll work there."

"If we're riding, I'd like to go to the mines. I need to increase my crystal supply without always taking from Nan."

He looked back at her, considering. "It's a long ride, and not all of it what you'd think pleasant. Just the thing then, for getting you back in tune there. What do you have to barter?"

"I don't know yet."

"Trolls don't have healers as such. They send a signal if there's a serious hurt or illness, and there hasn't been one.

But they'll have smaller hurts and ills. You can barter basic healing."

"Very basic."

"You've enough for it," he told her. "And if there's a need for more, I've enough to help. And food. Sweets, I think. Biscuits, cakes, pies. Meat pies as well. Anything of the sort. Ask Marco. If he bakes near as well as he cooks, you'll make fine trades."

He looked out, over to the mountains. "A good, long ride," he repeated. "You need the training or we'd take Cróga. We'll have to start an hour earlier than we did today to be back by moonrise."

"All right. If we're done for today, I can get Marco and start baking."

"Does it look like dusk to you?" He lifted his sword, and his smile came more challenging than friendly. "Defend."

When dusk finally came, she felt like she'd been run over by a truck, then dragged behind it for a full mile before being run over by it again.

"You did well enough for the first time back at it."

"Please." Pride ordered her not to just slide to the ground and moan. "Such effusive praise will give me a big head."

He ignored that. "Next for combat, I'm thinking we'll start you with a bow."

"I don't suppose you mean and a fiddle."

"I don't. And here are Morena and Marco now. You pleased him with the bracelet, settled yourself some with the protection of it. When you've gathered your own supplies, you might make more of the sort—for different purposes. For gifts and bartering. You'll want that when we go to the Capital."

"To the Capital? You never said—"

"My mother comes to the valley in a few days more, to visit, to see her grandchildren. To be here for Samhain. And when she goes back in the next month, we'll go with her. The people need to see you, and you them. The valley isn't the whole of the world. For me, perhaps the best of it, but not the whole."

"We don't have until next month."

Because he saw the puzzlement, and some fear, when what she had reached up inside her, he held out a hand to stop Marco and Morena at the gate.

"Let it come, *mo bandia*. It's yours." He took her hand to steady her. "Knowledge is as much a weapon as a sword."

She curled her fingers with his, looked into his eyes. Steadied. "The curtain parts. It cannot hold. And when it clears, he sees. The child, the bridge, the key. The blood of his blood. Daughter of the Fey, of the gods, of man. When he sees, he knows. And they slip and slide through the cracks to bring the dark where the white robes worship, and plot and plan. Blood sacrifice, blood magicks. It begins there."

"When the veil thins," he finished, because he saw it, too. Felt it with her, through her, in himself.

She shuddered. "I don't know what that means, except he's coming."

"No, not he, not yet." Absently, Keegan pressed his lips to her forehead. "But he's picked his time and his place, and the weak-minded among us who'll follow him."

"I couldn't see, not really."

"We'll work on that, won't we?" Keegan said in a tone as absent as the kiss.

"There was water—an ocean, I think—and cliffs, and a stone building on them. Not here, and not Odran's cliffs."

"Not here, no. In the south. South," he said as he gestured Morena and Marco to come ahead.

"You okay, Breen? You're so pale." Instinctively, Marco put an arm around her. "What the hell, Keegan?"

"Sure she's fine. Just not used to the seeing as yet. But she saw well enough, as did I." He looked to Morena. "We know when and where he'll try a strike, and so we'll be ready for it."

"South, you say? The Pious?" She bared her teeth. "Bloody fanatics. They've sworn oaths."

"And some break oaths as easily as a twig underfoot. On Samhain. I need to send a falcon to my mother."

"Amish will take your message. He's faster than most. Should I get Harken?"

"And Mahon as well if you would."

"War's coming. Why are you smiling?" Breen demanded.

"It was coming in any case. But now we know how and when and where. You've given us a weapon, and we'll use it. Ah, pity sakes, woman, he meant—or will mean—to send his demons against us with us unaware, and on a night, a holy night, where we honor those who came before us. When we reach out to them, and them to us. We'd be in ritual, in celebration, in homage. Instead, through your gift, the trap he means to set we spring on him."

"My grandmother. I need to warn her."

"Not to worry, we'll see she knows. And she's nothing to fear tonight, nor do you. Feck it all, woman, you did well. Be pleased with yourself. Now go back over, and help Marco with the baking."

"We're still going? To the mines?"

"And why wouldn't we? Your training doesn't stop, and you need what they mine, don't you? Take her along, Marco. She could use some of the wine she likes."

"Me, too."

"Tomorrow then." Keegan swung on his duster, picked up the sword she'd dropped without realizing it. "An hour earlier. Don't be late."

"He's . . . excited," Breen marveled.

"Okay. Come on, boy, I think we're going back to Ireland. I think I get it," Marco added as the dog scrambled up and raced ahead of them. "Sounds like the bad guys are planning a sneak attack, but now it won't be a sneak because you had one of those vision-type things, so they know the plot. Samhain's Halloween, right?"

"Yeah."

"I'm going to google that, get more juice on it." Marco glanced back when they reached the stone wall across the road. "Wow, man, look up there. Two moons. They really have two moons. I have to think about that later. Let me help you over."

"I'm okay. I've got it. You're right. He's right. Knowing's a weapon. And nothing's going to happen tonight, or until Samhain."

Except Odran would finally push Nan's curtain aside and see her. She wasn't sure how she'd handle that when the time came.

"Hell, I wasn't thinking. We're going to have to walk back through all those woods in the dark."

"It's all right. I can bring light."

"She can bring light," Marco mumbled as they climbed the seven steps. Then laughed when she tossed out all the pretty little balls of it. "You're a wonder, girl. I've got so much to tell you. Just a whole crapload. But I gotta ask . . ."

Distracted, he climbed onto the tree and through without thinking about it. Then stopped, stared. "If I wake up and this is all a dream, I'm going to be pissed. Anyway, I was going to ask before we walked through freaking worlds, what am I baking and why?"

She explained on the walk back to the cottage, and listened to Marco talk about his day. Learning to ride—his favorite part of it—and through to his visit to Morena's grandparents' cottage—his second favorite.

"Is every day over there this wild?" he asked as Bollocks headed straight to the bay.

"At first, I guess so. You just never know what you're going to see or do." She started the fire before heading toward the kitchen.

"Like that. Like watching my best girl start the fire from across the room. Let's have really big glasses of wine."

"Yes, let's."

"Enough leftover pasta for dinner. Good thing," he decided while Breen poured generous glasses. "Since I'm going to be baking for Doc and Sneezy."

"I'll help. I'm completely on cleanup."

"First things first. I'm going to take a long, hot shower, get me some pj's on—you do the same. Then we're going to drink more wine, eat pasta. Then we bake."

"A shower and pj's. Best idea ever. As soon as I fill Bollocks's bowls." But she leaned against the counter first, let the day drain away as much as it could. "How's your ass?"

He turned, wiggled it. "High and tight and proud."

"I meant from the saddle."

"A little sore here and there, but nothing much."

"God, I could barely walk after my first lesson. I could hate you if I didn't love you so much."

She pushed off to fill the dog's bowls. Let Bollocks know his dinner waited.

"You and Keegan went at it hard. And hot."

"The fire-to-water trick was my secret weapon—at first."

"I don't mean that, girl. I mean . . ." Rolling his eyes, Marco waved a hand in front of his face. "Hot."

"Honestly." When Bollocks raced in, she walked over to shut the door and saw the pixies had come to guard. "It's not about sex."

"I know hot when I see hot. And if you don't tap that man again, I feel sorry for you, girl."

"We've got a lot more to think about than sex."

Another eye roll. "That's why you gotta grab the good stuff when you have the chance." He swung an arm around her as they started for the stairs. "And I'd bet my new harp that man brings the good stuff."

"Maybe. Yes. But we're focused on saving worlds here."

"Not much point if you don't grab that good stuff. I'm maybe going to need a cold shower now."

She pushed him toward his room and split off to her own.

# CHAPTER SIX

Always an early riser, Breen started her day before the sun. She watched the pixies flicker and flutter outside the garden door while she squeezed in a predawn workout. She expected Keegan to put her through her paces—in his unrelenting style—so she'd damn well be prepared for it.

By the time the sun streamed through the glass, she'd posted a blog and made some solid progress on Bollocks's next adventure.

Taking what she deemed a well-earned break, she went out to greet Marco.

"You were up early," she said as he guarded a pot of water on the stove. "I heard you puttering around out here on and off, but I was in the groove."

"Me, too." He reached into the pot with a slotted spoon, turned something. "I'm making bagels, baby."

"I think you're supposed to toast bagels, Marco."

"From freaking scratch."

"Come on." She stepped over, saw the circles of dough floating in the boiling water. "You boil them? Did I know that?"

"A minute a side. Then you dip the wet top side into the poppy seeds or sesame seeds—I got both—and bake those suckers."

She looked over to the counter beside him, saw the parchment-lined sheet half full of unbaked bagels.

"We did cookies and the petit fours last night, right, and I got this inspiration. Bagels. How many over there have had the glory of a toasted bagel? We had all the stuff in stock, so I thought why not see if I can do it."

He spooned out three, tapped his watch to set the time, and dropped in another three.

Breen watched as he dipped each into his choice of the seeds in little plates, then put them back on the sheet.

"We're going to split one once they're baked," he told her. "Quality control."

"I'm for it. Do you need help?"

"No, I got this. It's Mr. Science time."

"Let me know when it's testing time."

Since he looked deliriously happy, she grabbed a Coke and left him to it. And made a note at her desk to put a musical bakery in Bollocks's third book.

Bagels and Banjos? Cookies, Cakes, and Concerts? Pies and Piccolos?

With some effort, she pushed it aside and toggled over to her fantasy novel. She surfaced when Marco tapped on the doorjamb.

"You gotta eat, girl. And I got a drumroll going."

"I'm there. Just let me shut down."

She went out to find two places set on the table with the half bagel, some slices of baked apples drizzled with cinnamon, and a scoop of scrambled eggs loaded with chunks of ham.

"I'm going to have to add to my workout time if I keep eating like this."

"Bagel first." He nudged the butter at her while he coated

his with cream cheese. "Never will get how you can turn away from the schmear. But anyway. On three, okay?"

She gave her half a delicate coating of butter. "One, two, three!" And bit in. "God. Good!"

"Good texture." He nodded as he chewed. "Just a touch of sweet from the honey. Chewy, but not tough. These are Troll-worthy bagels. They get a dozen. The other dozen are for Nan and Morena and the rest of them."

"You made two dozen bagels?"

"Two baker's dozens. We keep the extra one for us tomorrow."

"I was thinking you should open a musical bakery, but you should open a musical diner. You'd rock it."

Late in the morning, they carted boxes of baked goods through the woods and over to Talamh.

"This is never going to get old," Marco decided when they stepped from sunlight into a thin, misting rain.

As they approached the road, Breen shifted her boxes and paused. She watched Cróga dive out of the clouds. Shimmering with wet, dragon and rider soared down to land in the center of the road.

The ground trembled, then stilled.

"Jesus, oh Jesus. It's big. It's really big. I think I forgot something back at the cottage."

"Just breathe, Marco."

"What's all this then?" Keegan slid down, running a hand over Cróga's glistening scales.

"The baked goods for bartering."

Keegan scanned the boxes as he walked to them. "And are you after trading for all the stones in Talamh?"

"I wasn't sure how much I'd need. And this little one's for Nan and Sedric. Marco's got separate ones for the farm and for Morena's family."

"Well now, let's have a look." He flipped open one of the boxes himself. "What are these little pastries here?"

"I made mini cream puffs." Marco kept his gaze focused like a laser on Cróga. "Is he just going to stand there looking over here?"

"He won't do you any harm, brother." Keegan took out a tiny cream puff, popped it into his mouth. "Sure and I swear, that's fit for the gods. And you've little tarts as well."

"If you're going to sample everything, maybe we can get out of the rain."

Keegan barely spared Breen a glance as he took out a tart. "'Tisn't for me. Take this, Marco. Cróga's got a taste for sweets. Toss that over to him."

"Oh, you know, you go ahead."

"Ah, sure you've more spine than that. Just toss it out."

Trapped, Marco winged the tart. Cróga just whipped his head, caught it. Then made a sound a pride of lions might after a fine meal of antelope.

"Does that mean he liked it?"

"He did indeed. And it appears he'll make the trip to the mines after all."

"We'll go there on him?"

"We'll ride, but all this he'll take, as we'd need a pack-horse otherwise, and that's too slow for the trip." Standing in the wet, Keegan scanned the sky. "The weather should clear by midday, but it's best if we leave a bit earlier yet. I'll come round to Marg's when it's time."

He snagged two cookies, and as he walked back to his dragon, broke one in two. Tossed half to Bollocks, the other half to Cróga. Ate the other as he swung back into the saddle.

"Sure the gods would weep, Marco."

The dragon glided straight up with his wings sending the air into a whirl. Then they were gone, swallowed by the clouds.

"I fed a dragon a fruit tart."

"Yay. Let's get all this to the farm. I'll take Nan's after we drop them off. I might not see you until it's time to go back."

"I'll be okay. I know the way to Finola's if Morena's not here at the farm. Plus, I fed a fruit tart to a big-ass dragon."

She carried the box to Marg's and spent the rest of the morning learning and practicing a barrier spell.

When the rain cleared as Keegan predicted, Marg led her outside and into the woods.

"Now, tell me what's here."

"Here?" Breen looked around. "Trees, the stream, your workshop."

"You are one with the air, with the earth. You are always connected to the light, to the water. All is connected, all that lives. Open yourself to hearts that beat, to what reaches for the light, what spreads through the earth.

"Hear the beat of my heart."

Understanding the first step was to quiet her mind, Breen closed her eyes, deepened and slowed her breathing. Opening herself to Marg had become as simple as that breathing.

"I hear you, Nan, your strong heart. I feel your light. And Bollocks. The thrill of chasing a squirrel—no, no, a chipmunk. Its heart beats so fast as it races up a tree. A chestnut tree. Old, the tree, it's old, and its bark is deeply furrowed, but its heart is still strong. Its leaves have gone gold for the fall and have begun to drop as the wind stirs them. Year after year, decade by decade, birds sing and shelter and nest in those leaves, green in the spring.

"But the chipmunk's young, and he scolds Bollocks from the safety of the branch. He doesn't understand Bollocks wouldn't hurt him. He only wants to play."

Stunned, as she'd seen it all so clearly, knew it all so surely, she opened her eyes. "Nan—"

"What else is here?"

"The buck, the one I saw only yesterday. He's deeper, so Bollocks hasn't scented him. A doe and their fawn—still spotted—walk behind him. They cross the stream, and the fish scatter away as they pause to drink. Birds, so many.

Nuthatches and jays, magpies and starlings and ravens and woodpeckers.

"A fox." She gestured west. "Streaking from the field to the trees. He has a mouse clamped in his mouth. No heartbeat there. Under an oak, fiery red, a rabbit nurses her young in a burrow, keeps them safe from the hawk. Nearby, mushrooms sprout on a downed tree, finding life where death came."

"There now, that's enough. Too much at once can make you dizzy." Marg reached out to take her hand.

"There's so much, so much life. Beating and growing, sleeping and feeding, hunting and hiding. Can all the Fey do that, feel that?"

"No, no indeed. Elves have their bond with the trees, the stones, the earth, but it's a different knowing than this. As Weres have this bond with their spirit animals. The Sidhe are closer to what you have, and those drops of their blood in yours enhances what you have from the Wise."

"So you can do that?" Breen asked as they walked back toward the cottage.

"Not as quick or far or deep as you."

"It was wonderful, the sensation of it." Filling her, Breen thought. Lifting her. "Affirming."

"It is, aye. And like the barrier spell you've learned, is both defense and offense."

"Because I'll know the heart—or intent—of an enemy?"

"As you didn't before Yseult harmed you, as I hadn't yet taught you the skill."

"I wasn't ready before. I wasn't strong enough before."

"She's powerful, and wily. Her hunger for more, her desires drew her to Odran."

"You knew her, before."

"We were young together. Not friends, never that. I was for the valley, and she lusted for the Capital. A seat of power as she saw it."

When they crossed the bridge, Bollocks leaped out of the

stream to run ahead toward the cottage. Breen didn't need power to know he anticipated a treat in the kitchen.

"She went into the lake that day, as I did. No one could have wanted the sword so much as Yseult. To rule, you see, not to serve, or to protect, or to shoulder the weight of it all. Even then I could feel her envy, the dark of it, when I brought the sword from the lake."

Marg took off her cloak when they stepped into the house, then granted the dog's wish by going straight into the kitchen and his treat jar.

"Such a good, fine boy you are. Ask politely."

Bollocks sat, let out a quiet bark.

"We'll have some soup before your journey. And treat ourselves as well to some of Marco's sweets."

Knowing this routine, Breen sliced bread from the round while Marg warmed the soup.

"Just the two of us today, *mo stór*. Sedric had business elsewhere."

"When did she turn, Nan? Yseult. You've never said."

"She hid it well, from me, from her family, from all. And all the while, from that day, she practiced the darker arts in secret. She went to him, through the portal in the falls, passing in and out without detection. Would I, could I have seen if I had looked deeper? I can't know that, but I know she used her gifts, what she had done to her gifts, to help him come through, to help him blind me to what he was. As I know she helped him rebuild when I thought him defeated. She helped him amass his army, helped him take you on that terrible night.

"This much I've seen in the fire, and in the crystal," Marg added as they began to eat. "These things she did for power, and to strike at me for having what she coveted."

"Does she love him?"

"Ah, no. Such as Yseult don't love. She might lust, but love is a different thing. She worships him, I think. She made him her god. And power—through and of him? That is her true god, her lover, her beloved child. He is the answer for her, you see. She believes in him, of course. Is loyal because she believes."

"They'll destroy each other if it furthers their goals. He was ready to kill her in the vision I had, after she failed to take me to him. He didn't because he cooled off enough to see she was still useful. And she was—like you said—wily in how she played it."

"Remember these things. They're weapons as well. And be wily yourself with the Trolls today. They love a good trade, and a fair one, but won't hesitate to take advantage if you let them. Loga is the chief of the tribe here in the west, and a clever one. His wife, Sul, is more clever yet."

"Give me your opinion." Breen opened the box and set several samples on a plate. "Tell me if these give me an edge on the trade."

Obliging, Marg chose a petit four Marco had frosted a strong green. "This is good. Very good indeed. I've never known a troll without a taste for the sweet. Meat and mead, aye, but the sweet disarms them. You'll do well."

With the door open, Breen heard the sound of horses trotting toward the cottage. "I guess I'm going to find out."

Marg rose with her, walked her out where Keegan waited. "It's a fine day for a ride." She glanced up, watched Cróga circle overhead. "So you take your dragon as well."

"She brought enough sweets for the whole of the Troll clan to have their fill. Cróga carries the trade."

"If it's too much for now, see they give her the proper credit for what she might want in the future. A fine day," Marg repeated. "I believe I'll spend some time in the air myself."

"I'll saddle your horse for you," Breen began, but Marg waved her off.

"No, be off with you. Keegan will want you off the mountain before dark." She kissed Breen's cheek. "Enjoy, and the view from Sliabh Sióg."

Breen bent down to Bollocks. "You can stay here at the cottage or go up to the farm. Go play with the children, or find Marco and Morena. But I'm going too far for you to come today."

He whined when she straightened, took a moment to stroke Boy, the buckskin gelding she'd ride.

"I'll be back with the moons," she promised. "And I'll call out to you."

She mounted, found relief she felt confident in the saddle. "I'll send for him when we're back, and we'll come tomorrow, Nan."

"Trade well, and blessings on you both."

As they trotted down to the road, Breen did a mental review of basic horsemanship. Keegan would, she knew, sneer at any novice mistakes.

When they reached the road, Keegan shot her a glance. "We can make good time for now."

So saying, he kicked his horse into a gallop. The big black stallion ate up the ground.

"Okay, Boy, let's hope we both remember."

She raced after him and found she did remember—and with the memory came the thrill of the speed, the power of the horse under her.

They'd never match the pace of Keegan's Merlin, but it felt as if they flew down the stretch of road. The hair she hadn't thought to tie back streamed behind her, and she found the cool whip of the wind on her face exhilarating.

A wagon drawn by a pair of horses clopped its way toward them. The man drove while the woman held a baby on her lap. The little boy in the back waved and shouted out greetings, first to Keegan—a good ten lengths ahead—then to her.

They neared the turn that led to the round tower, the stone circle, the ruins where the Pious had once prayed. And the graveyard where her father's ashes lay under a garden she and Marg had brought to life.

But ahead of her, Keegan turned away, and rode toward the far curve of the bay.

There, she saw a mermaid sitting on a rock, her luminous jewel of a tail curled around her as she drew a comb through her long golden hair. In the water, blue now like the sky, young ones splashed, rising and diving, glittering tails whipping through the water.

The beauty and wonder had Breen slowing, and listening to the echo of young laughter.

The mermaid turned her head, and after a moment, lifted her hand in an easy wave.

*Blessings on you, Daughter of the Fey.*

Breen's heart tripped as she heard the words in her mind. And her own formed a response.

*And on you, Daughter of the Sea.*

Full of the beauty and the wonder, she rode on to where Keegan had stopped to wait.

"Are they her children?"

"Two are, three are cousins. You can make their acquaintance another day. We've still far to go."

"Boy would run his heart out, and it's as big as Merlin's. But he doesn't have his stamina."

"Right enough." Keegan continued in an easy trot.

"I've only seen one mermaid before. A young girl. Ala. Bollocks likes to play with her."

"If you bring him there, other young will come."

"I'll do that. When Marco feels confident enough riding, I want to take him to my father's grave. He loved him, too. And he'd have a chance to see the Mers."

"I saw him ride yesterday. He doesn't lack for confidence. But when you take him, take a sword as well. The days grow shorter," he said before she could speak. "He strikes for battle on Samhain, and we'll be ready. But between now and then, spies and scouts slip through."

"How will we be ready?" When he hesitated, she shifted. "How can I be so important to stopping Odran if I don't know how we stop an attack I saw coming? Felt," she corrected.

"Mahon and I flew south with some troops last night. He remains there for now with them. We have scouts and spies as well, and those who'll watch and report on what this faction of the Pious plan."

"If you're massing troops, won't they see, and catch on that we know?"

"They'll see what we want them to see. Some fresh novitiates who wish for religious life, others who drink too much ale in the pubs or flirt along the shore, sail on the water, and so on."

He shrugged as if speaking of war was just another conversation.

"My mother travels from the Capital, and some who come with her will veer south. We have barracks there, and this will appear as a troop exchange, but none will leave but to take to the woods or the caves or the fields, where they wait."

"When will you go?"

"Mahon returns for Finian's birthday. We fly south before sunset on Samhain. There's a point," he continued after a moment. "Tactics, you see. Crushing this attack swiftly, completely, taking as many of those who break the treaty or have turned on their own alive, and to the Capital for judgment, shows strength and resolve."

"It won't end it," she murmured.

"It won't end it, no, but it serves to demoralize Odran's faithful, and to lift morale for the Fey."

"You don't want me there."

"You have no place there. I don't insult you. You're not ready for such things, as well you know."

"Will I be?"

"You must be, so you will."

He glanced up, so she followed his gaze. She saw Cróga gliding like a ship over the sea. And with him a dragon of ruby and sapphire, and the rider on it.

"It is— That's Nan! I didn't know she had a dragon, that she rode a dragon. I mean, I did—I saw her in the fire, but what I saw happened years ago."

"Sure she rides. Her dragon is Dilis, and has birthed more than a dozen young. Cróga is from her. A great—no, two greats—grandson."

"She's beautiful. They're beautiful." Then it struck her. "She won't go south, so into this battle? Nan."

"No. There's no need. When there is, if and when there is, she'll fly, and she'll fight. Come, he's rested enough. We have near an hour, then another for the climb to the post."

This time Merlin adjusted his pace to match Boy's, and the way stayed smooth and steady for a time even when the road climbed.

Keegan slowed when they wound through woods, under trees where leaves tumbled down as the air shook them free. Still so much color remained it was like riding within a kaleidoscope with the sun sparkling through.

Testing herself, Breen opened. She felt the heartbeats—deer, a foraging bear. Elves—three on a hunt. Then her own heart slammed as Merlin simply leaped from one bank of a stream to the other.

"I don't know how to do that."

"Boy does. I won't let you fall. Ask him."

"I could just go down, through, and up again."

"Ask him," Keegan repeated. "I said you won't fall."

Since she'd never known him to lie, she held her breath. She had only to think *Jump* and Boy sailed. Maybe the sound she made edged too close to a squeal, but she held her seat.

"Did you help?"

"Only a bit. You're a better rider than you think. And you'll soon need to be."

It didn't take long for her to understand the truth of that. The trail climbed steeper, grew rougher until it was more like the rubble from a small avalanche than a trail at all.

The woods gave way to the open and a kind of skinny, rutted road where the wind kicked higher.

She looked up, farther up, and her mouth went dry. Yes, the green of pines stacked up the hillside, but the way, switchbacks, ledges, seemed more suited to goats than horses.

"You've done this before, right?"

"Sure I have. Boy's surefooted." He turned in the saddle to look back at her. "And I won't let you fall."

She decided the very best way to handle it would be to keep her eyes directly ahead. Not to look down, or up, or sideways. Just trust her horse to put one sure foot in front of the other.

And following her own advice, would have missed it. But Keegan stopped, turned again, and this time turned Merlin as well.

"We call this God's Palm. You rest in it, and from it you see Talamh." He gestured out. "All the way to the south and the Sea of Sorrows."

When she looked, her heart thudded. Not from fear, but from the sheer beauty.

Miles and miles, hills and fields, the patchwork of greens, the brilliance of fall woods, the gray of stone walls and old buildings, of cottages and villages, and under the clear sky to the stunning blue of the water.

"You brought fortune with you to have such a clear day. Often Talamh hides in the mists."

"It's like a painting, but a painting caught in crystal. So sharp and perfect. It doesn't seem like anything so perfect could be real. But I can see movement. Life. Where's the Capital?"

"East, but the mountain blocks it from here, as here is the edge of the west." He put a hand on her shoulder to turn her. "You can see there, where the hills rise and the forest where game runs thick so none ever need know hunger. The high cliffs that slice down to the West Sea, and the sea that rides to the end of the world.

"Your world, as much as mine."

"You needed me to see it, like this, the peace of it." A painting captured in crystal, she thought again—and thought of how she'd wished to hold a moment in a misty morning cupped in her hands.

"The peace you'll fight to hold," she added. "I came back, Keegan."

"No, no. Bloody hell, I don't mean that at all, and I'm damned if I'll apologize yet again. I wanted you to see it like this—which is different from need. I wanted you to see what you protect, as I do."

"I think it's the most beautiful place I've ever seen, or will see. And I feel whatever I've forgotten, whatever I remember I've forgotten, I'm tied to it. And always will be."

She looked at him. "What god holds us here?"

"All of them."

"Not Odran."

"A fallen god is a god in name only." He offered her a skin of water. "He wants you because you're so much more."

Am I? she wondered, and tipped her head back to drink. "There's a goat! A—a ram. Right up there."

He glanced up. "They like the high countries. We're nearly there, and they're expecting us now."

"They are?"

"They've been watching us for some time. Visitors don't climb Sliabh Sióg unnoticed. And if we were unwelcome, they'd have made that clear enough by now."

"Isn't the taoiseach welcome everywhere?"

Keegan took back the skin. "Trolls can be prickly."

He turned away and continued the climb.

She saw more goats, more long-horned sheep, more breathless views.

Then a man with shoulders as wide as a truck, a warrior's braid dangling to his waist, and a face nearly as nut brown as his hair dropped onto the track from above.

He wore a helmet of dull bronze and a breastplate that looked as if it had taken more than a few hits over the years. His eyes, a shockingly bright blue, stayed narrowed as he planted his feet, legs wide, and fisted big, gnarled hands on his hips.

"Greetings to you, Loga, and all your kin. We ask your permission to pass. We bring you trade."

"Do ya?" He sniffed. "And is this the child of Eian O'Ceallaigh?"

"I'm Breen," she said before Keegan could speak again. "And my father's daughter. Blessings on you, Loga, on your wife, Sul, and all your kin."

Loga's eyebrows shot up. "Pretty thing, aren't ya? Got the look of your da, and of Mairghread. I see Odran passed his eyes on to ya."

Turning his head, Loga spat.

"I think of them as from my father, and they don't look kindly on Odran or those who follow him."

"Got some sass. I like sass. Rolled with this one a time or two I hear."

When he jerked a thumb at Keegan, Breen struggled not to blush from embarrassment or insult. "That would be a private matter."

He barked out a laugh. "Sass! You may pass and bring your trade. One pint of ale each you'll have for hospitality."

"She's one for wine," Keegan told him.

"Ah well, a cup of wine for her then."

And like a goat—at least in Breen's imagination—he leaped onto the rocks above. He took a curved horn out of his belt, blew three long notes.

Then seemed to vanish.

"We're welcomed," Keegan told her.

He turned Merlin around the last switchback.

# CHAPTER SEVEN

Stone huts huddled together on the rocky plateau. Others stacked their way up the mountain like deliberately if precariously placed building blocks. The steps and ledges leading up looked as if they'd been hacked out of the rocky rise by axes.

Beyond the huddle, she saw some sort of stable or barn and the mules and husky horses sharing a paddock beside it. A couple of pigs grunted and rooted in a sty beside a narrow track while a handful of fat chickens squawked and pecked away outside a coop.

Small campfires burned inside circles of stones outside each hut. The thin, cool air carried the tang of peat smoke and roasting meat.

Breen was pretty sure she identified an unlucky rabbit rotating on a spit over one of the fires.

Young children played a game involving curved sticks and a small wooden ball that looked somewhat like field hockey. Some women had infants strapped on their backs or in snug slings across their chests. Another took a cup to an old one as he sat on a rough-hewn stone bench in the sunlight.

She saw every shade of skin: black, brown, copper, ruddy, creamy. Most activity stopped when she rode into the camp alongside Keegan.

Loga and two others—one male, one female—leaped down from the rocky point above.

"They have come to trade," Loga announced, "and have permission. Welcome, Taoiseach. Welcome, Daughter of the O'Ceallaigh."

Keegan dismounted. "Greetings to you and your community."

Following his lead, Breen dismounted. "And thank you."

"You'll sit by the fire. Ale," Loga called out, "and wine for the daughter. You, boy, take the horses to water."

Loga led the way to the fire in front of a hut with a high, arched door, then sat on the ground.

"This much is hospitality," he said when Keegan and Breen joined him. "The rest is trade."

"Understood." Keegan gestured up to where Cróga circled. "He carries containers of what the daughter wishes to trade. May he land?"

"He may. And my people will bring the containers."

When Cróga settled on the rocky point above, several scrambled up to untie the boxes hitched to his saddle. A boy stroked a hand over Cróga's scales, his face alive with longing.

"Your grandson. I would gift him a short flight."

The boy looked down, and longing became wild hope.

"Try to soften me up for the trade, will ya?"

"I know the futility of such attempts. And the trade isn't mine."

Loga pointed at the boy. "Short. Once. So," Loga continued as the boy let out a whoop and scrambled up Cróga's side. "First we drink, then we trade."

Breen took the cup a woman handed her, and hoped for the best. "It's very good." And very, very strong, she thought.

Like apple brandy filtered through battery acid.

The door of the hut opened; the woman all but filled it.

Tall, with arms like tree trunks, she stood in rough trousers, rougher boots, and a belted tunic. She had the tawny eyes of a lioness and hair of oak brown braided to her waist. A warrior's braid ran down the side of her wide face.

"Welcome, Taoiseach," she said as Keegan rose. "Welcome, Daughter of the Fey."

As she got to her feet, Breen didn't think about the words; she felt them. Spoke them. "Greetings, Mother of the Trolls."

Sul inclined her head. "Bring wares to trade, do ya?"

"Yes. And also offer in trade my small skills as a healer to any who have the need."

Breen picked up one of the boxes now stacked beside her. "Would you try a sample, to judge?"

Sul stepped forward, peered into the box. "Sweets?"

When Sul took out a cookie, Breen saw the blistered burn on her arm. She started to reach out, froze at Sul's sibilant hiss.

"No one from the world of man touches a troll without consent."

"I'm sorry."

"The fault's mine." Keegan spoke easily as he drank his ale. "She doesn't know the traditions, and I failed to teach her. She is also of Talamh, daughter of a taoiseach, granddaughter of a taoiseach."

"And granddaughter of one who seeks to destroy us."

"Yet she leaves the safety of the world she knew to defend you."

"I apologize for the offense." Breen struggled not to rush the words out through a throat that wanted to snap shut. "I've come to trade for the stones and crystals you mine, so I can use them in magicks to fight Odran."

Sul's eyes narrowed, glittered. "Fear him, don't ya?"

"Yes, I do."

"Yet you wear the word for courage, don't ya? You branded it on your wrist." Sul pointed to Breen's tattoo. "Do you wear it only, or do you have it?"

"I have more than I did, less than I hope to find."

Pursing her lips, Sul nodded slowly. "This is a good answer." She looked down at Loga. "A good answer."

She studied the cookie in her hand, sniffed it. Took a testing bite. Smiled. "You make them?"

"I don't have that talent. A friend. I help a little—and clean up the mess after. But he makes the sweets. There are pastries and tarts, frosted cakes."

Sul took another bite, passed the rest to Loga. Then held out her injured arm. "You have consent."

Breen skimmed her fingertips lightly over the burn. As Aisling had patiently taught her, she opened. Slowly, slowly.

She felt the pain, the heat. Infection.

And something else.

"Your light and your heart are strong."

She could ease the pain. Slowly. Slowly. Diminish the heat. Softly, softly.

It burned, just for an instant, in her own arm. But the blisters soothed away, and the raw redness eased to pink.

"There's a balm," Breen began.

"We have some at the post. I haven't had time to worry with it."

"If you would send for it? And if I could have a moment with you, in private?"

"We'll fetch it when we go to trade." Sul turned, walked to the door. She gestured for Breen to follow.

Inside, Breen saw a rough sort of comfort. Stools by a low fire, a pot simmering on it. A table and chairs, oil lamps and candles. A ladder climbed up to a loft.

"I have an ill?" Sul demanded, her face set, her eyes hard.

"I don't think—"

"I tire too fast and too often. I feel off my feed. Heal me if you can, tell me if you can't. I'm no coward."

"It wasn't an illness I felt. But a . . . a condition."

"What's the difference? You want to speak only to me. Speak."

"I wasn't sure you knew, or would want to let others know yet. I think you're pregnant. I think you're with child."

Sul took a full step back. "Why would you say this?"

"I felt two heartbeats inside you. If I could look again to be sure? With your consent."

Sul nodded, kept her tawny eyes on Breen as Breen laid a hand low on her belly, another on her chest. Breen thought of the lesson with Marg, how to open, feel life.

Closing her eyes, she let it come.

"I feel a heartbeat here." She opened her eyes, pressed lightly on Sul's chest. "And another here." And against her womb. "The second is quiet yet, but strong. I'm not good enough to tell you how far along you are."

Holding up a hand, Sul moved away to the back of the hut. She leaned on a long stone counter, and put her head out the window there to breathe.

"I thought it was the change when my courses stopped. Two courses haven't come, and I'm near enough to the end of the fertile time, so this is what I believed. Then when I felt not good, tired, so often tired, the little pains I should have remembered were from making room for the new life."

She turned back, those lion eyes glistening. "I have grown children, and they have children. Our youngest is fully twelve."

"I'm sorry if this isn't welcome."

"Not welcome? This is a gift." She pressed both hands to her belly. "You've given me the gift of knowing I make life again, and I weep in thanks."

She came back, taking off the triangles dangling from her ears.

"Gold from our mines, hammered by our craftsmen. A gift for a gift."

"They're beautiful, and thank you. But I didn't really have anything to do with it."

On a whoop of laughter, Sul slapped Breen on the shoulder with such cheerful force Breen calculated she'd be sore for a week. "You have sass, don't ya?"

"So Loga told me. I'm honored to wear them," Breen said, and despite her stinging shoulder, put them on.

"Now we trade."

The trading post turned out to be a large, deep cave lit by torchlight and guarded by trolls with thick clubs.

Aladdin's cave, Breen thought, delighted and dazzled by the stones and crystals—some no bigger than a pebble, others bigger than her dog.

Another chamber held gold and silver and copper. Others weapons and armor forged from the metals, and still another held wares. Jewelry, pots, bowls, cups, chalices.

"Think of what you need," Keegan said when she wandered and wandered. "Not of what you want."

"Well, I want and need my own cauldron, so there's that." But she resisted the jewelry and trinkets—this time—and backtracked to select what she'd come for.

"Tell me when I hit the limits of the trade."

Keegan let out a short laugh. "No worries there. Loga will certainly do just that."

She filled a sack with stones, tumbled and rough, copper wire, silver dust. When she started on a second sack, she spared Keegan a look.

"I don't know when I'll be able to get back."

"You've already enough for two life spans."

"I'm almost done, so . . ."

Then she saw the globe, and everything else faded. Labradorite, a perfect circle, large enough she had to cup it in both hands.

When she did, she felt the vibration, in the stone, in her.

It swirled, blues and green, touches of golden brown. Storms and seas, she thought, grass and earth. And she felt she held the worlds in her hands.

In the stone, she saw herself, and then . . .

"Do you see?"

Because he'd already felt the power shimmering, Keegan set a hand on her shoulder. "What do you see?"

"The waterfall, and the river that runs on both sides, the forest, windswept. Two moons, one new, one full, riding the sky.

"Odran."

When she spoke the name, some of the trolls who'd come into the post murmured against the dark and made the sign against evil.

"Do you see? The other side, his side. Yseult. White streaks through her hair. Leaching her power because she pushes and pushes, trembling as she shouts the words against the wind. I can't hear them, not clear. I don't know them. It's a strange tongue to me. As she shouts, as the wind rises, he strikes with his sword. A black goat, a demon dog, a young girl crying for her mother. So the river runs red with their blood, and the red mists rise from it and stain the water from the fall."

Her head spun; her power swelled.

"Rising, rising until the moons are stained with blood. Animal, demon, human in sacrifice. It bubbles and boils, the river, the falls. She drops to her knees, her hair more white than red now. And Odran glides over the boiling river, and with a clap like thunder, with a flash like lightning, his hand passes through the falls and into Talamh."

Shaking now, Breen fought for breath. "Do you see?"

"Not clearly, no, and only through you, not the globe. The globe is yours." With his hand sliding around Breen's waist to keep her upright, Keegan turned to Loga. "I'll trade whatever you need for it, bring it to you this night. My word on it."

"No need. It's hers. We aren't fools here. Is this the now, the before, or the yet to come?"

"Not now. Not before." Breen leaned against Keegan as she clutched the globe. "I don't know when to come. I don't know when, but he can't see me. He still can't see."

"Get the daughter some wine," Sul ordered.

"Water, please. Just water."

"Summer," Keegan said. "Leaves were full, and in Talamh, the foxglove and dog rose stood tall and blooming. The one coming, another after, I can't say, but summer. We'll start back when you feel able."

"I can ride."

"Then we ride."

She tried not to think just how much trickier it could be riding down a mountain than it had been going up. And the fact she could actually see the trickier, the skinny trails or tight turns.

The long, long way down.

"You've learned how to cleanse and charge the crystals?"

"Yes."

"You'll need a proper place to keep them."

"I have one. The table on the second-floor hallway that Seamus made."

"That'll do well enough. It was my fault," he continued. "Not explaining to you about touching a troll. I didn't think of it. And in truth, I didn't expect it from Sul, who's a clever woman, a cagey one, but sensible. Then, as I said, trolls can be prickly."

"Pregnancy can make some even pricklier."

He turned in the saddle so abruptly, her breath caught. "Look where you're going!"

"Merlin knows. You're saying Sul's carrying?"

"If you want my heart to keep beating, watch where you're going. Yes, she's pregnant." She let out a long, relieved breath when Keegan turned back around. "I wasn't sure if she knew, or if she wanted anyone else to know."

"Ah, so you wanted a private word. You came out wearing her earrings, so I take it she didn't know, and was pleased."

"She didn't, and she was very pleased."

"As Loga will be when she tells him. You handled that very well and proper, as you did the rest of it."

"You're talking to me—when you don't usually do a lot of talking—and being nice because you don't want me to panic going down this mountain."

"I talk when I've something to say."

"You can keep talking now because it's working pretty well. You're sure it was summer, what I saw? I was so focused on Odran and Yseult, and what was happening, I didn't notice leaves or flowers."

"I'm sure, aye. We have other seers, and with what I can tell them, they can look."

"You don't want me to look again."

"You will whether I want it or not, won't you? But more eyes are always helpful. It was entertaining, I thought, the way you explained to Loga how to toast and eat a bagel. I'll have to try it myself."

"You haven't had a bagel? Ever?"

"I haven't, no, but expect since Marco made them, they'll be brilliant. So . . . the book you're writing. Is it going well for you?"

He dug for conversation now, she thought, and found that touching. He kept her talking until they'd navigated the rocky trail down into the forest. They were losing the light, so she didn't ask to stop and rest, though every cell in her body longed for ten minutes off the horse.

But when he stopped to let the horses drink from a stream, she stayed mounted. When she got off, she decided, she wasn't entirely sure she could get back on again.

Instead, she ordered herself to relax, to just be.

In the stillness, just the whisper of air through the pines and the hardwoods. Leaves drifting down as their cycle ended, and berries not yet gathered or eaten by birds and bears like little jewels on scraggly bushes. The light going soft, and the shadows deepening and stretching.

The stream rippled as the horses drank, a quiet music that joined the brighter notes of the water tumbling over rocks from higher ground.

The faintest rustle as a fox slunk through the brush, and the barest clicking of talons as an owl woke for the night's hunt.

It struck her that of all the gifts she'd found inside herself, this one, just learned, seemed most precious.

"Amish." Breen gestured up. "Morena must have sent him to scout for us, to be sure we were on our way back."

Looking up, Keegan caught the blur as the hawk swooped down, danced through branches before he chose one. From its perch he gave them a long, cool study.

After returning it, Keegan turned Merlin away from the stream. "You weren't looking at the sky when you said his name. In truth, you looked half-asleep."

"I wasn't sleeping. I felt him. And the owl." She held up a finger as they walked the horses. "Listen." Then let out a laugh at the two-toned hoot. "Nan helped me learn to find the heartbeats and the breath. Can you feel them?"

"Not as you do, no. My power there doesn't go so deep as yours, though there's Sidhe in our bloodline."

"Is there?"

"Aye, Sidhe, and Elfin, Were, a dash of Troll. My father swore a many-times-great-grandmother was of the Mer."

"Basically all the Fey?"

"So it's told."

She barely noticed they'd reached level ground again as she considered it. "That could be important."

"Such a mix isn't unusual given a millennium or so. Others have the same as well."

"But others aren't taoiseach. Others aren't leading the Fey at this time, against Odran. You're all of them, ties to every tribe. It could matter. It feels like it should matter."

"It always just was, so I never thought otherwise."

"I wonder if you should try exploring those other aspects."

"I've a notion if I could sprout wings and fly, I'd have done so by this time of my life."

"You're being too literal. There's more to the Sidhe than wings, or to an elf than speed."

"That's true enough." He kicked Merlin into a trot when the track widened into a path. "Still, I'm damned if I can outrun an elf."

"Maybe, maybe not. Still, you may be faster than you think because you've never pushed at that part of you. Trust me, I know all about accepting limitations, or believing I have them. Lots of them."

"It's interesting. I'll think on it."

"If you were a Were, what would your spirit animal be?"

"It's not a choice, it is."

Literal, she thought. Always so literal.

"If you had a choice. I think I'd be a dog, like Bollocks, making everybody smile. It's a what-if," she pressed. "There's no wrong answer."

"A dragon. Because there aren't any, so I'd be the only."

"Ah, ego intact. No were-dragons in Talamh?"

"Or in any world I know. Still, when you have each other, Fey and dragon, it's all but being as one. Have you got a gallop in you? We're coming to the road, and I'm long past ready for a meal."

She asked Boy, and he stretched into a gallop.

She wanted to ask Keegan how dragon and rider chose each other, how it happened, what it felt like. But the idea of a hot meal and a gallop to clear some of the fatigue won out.

When they reached the road, she felt Boy's anticipation. He knew home was coming, and with it, food and rest. She couldn't agree more.

The moons rose over the bay, and the stars began to wink on. She saw four dragons ride the night sky, riderless, two a quarter the size of the others.

A family, she thought.

She thought of Marg and Sedric in their cottage, and reached out to let her grandmother know she was back.

When they reached the turn, something slid over her, through her, and she slowed her horse.

"What?" Keegan demanded as he rounded back to her. "I'm after a meal and some ale."

"The ruins. There's . . ." She could just see their shadow dark against the night sky. "Not heartbeats, not breath, but something. Awareness?"

"What walks there isn't of the living, and not for a long time."

"Ghosts?"

"Some spirits won't rest, some can't."

"The stones are singing. Not those, not those. The circle. Can you hear them?"

"Aye. I often do, but not from this distance. I expect I hear them through you. They're a holy place, like the graveyard. Sanctified, purified."

"But not the ruins," she said as they walked the road again.

"When some of the Pious turned, they turned sharp and dark. Innocent blood spilled there as offerings to that dark. Rituals, long forbidden even then. And some of it leaves a stain. And some think what they invited in now traps their spirits."

"Do you think it?"

"I've heard them, those damned, and those they tortured and killed who are trapped with them."

She glanced back because fingers of ice scraped down her spine. "Have you gone in?"

"I have, and so have seen them as well, walking along their way, chanting to their false gods." He shot her a look—cool and final. "Best you don't."

He urged Merlin back to a gallop. And, happy to leave the ruins behind, Breen joined him.

Even as she started to reach out for Bollocks, he came running. All the dark and cold that had seeped in vanished with the sheer joy in his eyes as he raced toward the horses, raced around them, leaping, barking, wagging.

"There's one who's had his meal, I'll wager. We'll feed the horses, give them a good rubdown, then have our own."

Lamps glowed in the window; smoke curled from the chimneys. Merlin didn't need a signal to leap over the stone fence. Breen held her breath, put her trust in Boy, and followed.

"And here are our travelers."

Morena came out of the house, with Harken and Marco right behind her. "A long day you've had, and we can hope a successful one."

"I got everything I need and more." Beyond thrilled, Breen eased off the horse. Yoga, she told herself. A lot of yoga in the very near future.

"Go wash up," Harken said, taking the reins. "And go in and have the chicken stew Marco made. Morena and I'll see to the horses, as we've already been to heaven with the stew."

"Thanks, as I'm more than ready for it. They've earned an apple, these two." Keegan gave Merlin a slap on the flank. "Word from Mahon?"

"All's well," Harken told him. "And our mother should be here by midday."

"That's fine then."

Marco put an arm around Breen. "Bet you're ready for some wine and a hot meal."

"Count on it."

"I'm going to have that ready for you. What a day, huh?"

"You can say that again."

She went back to the well with Keegan to wash the dust of it away.

# CHAPTER EIGHT

Despite the stretching, Breen felt the long, challenging ride the next morning. Still, no one could see her hobble when she went down to let the dog out and bring in the stones she'd cleansed and charged the night before.

It took a few trips, but gave her such pleasure to see and hold and arrange all that now belonged to her on the table in the upper hallway.

The globe she took down to her office. She'd keep it there during her workday, and in her bedroom at night.

With the cottage quiet around her, she drank her coffee in the doorway, watching the mists rise off the bay as dawn broke.

She settled down to work, weaving the story with dark magicks, sleep snakes—and a dragon who melted a frozen lake with his fiery breath to drown demons.

She saw the battle as she wrote it, high, high in the mountains, where the wind whirled its ice and snow, where trolls battled to hold the line and demon dogs leaped for throats.

At one point she paused, wondered when she'd gotten so bloodthirsty. Then went right back to it.

By the time she walked with Marco and Bollocks into the woods, she'd worked out the kinks—body and story.

"Ready for more training?"

"Ready and able," he claimed. "I kinda like the sword stuff. It's sort of like cosplay. But I'm seriously digging on the riding. Wherever we end up, girl, we need to get us some horses. I meant to tell you, I've got a Zoom meet with your publicity people tonight. Well, our tonight. I need to be back and ready for it by seven. Trouble is, I've got no way to tell the time over there."

"They do. Don't ask me how. But I know sunset's around five—I always check—so we'll go from there."

"Works. It all kind of works. Don't ask me how."

"I'm hoping to stay off horses myself today. But ask Morena if it's okay if you and I ride to the graveyard tomorrow. I want you to see where Dad's buried."

"I'd like to." He stopped at the tree. "Gets me every time."

But he took her hand, and they passed through.

"Bright today," he commented. "I was hoping." He reached in his pocket, took out sunglasses. "Now I'm styling."

"You're always styling." Before they started down the steps, she shaded her own eyes with the flat of her hand, looked east. "A lot of riders coming."

"I'll say. It's a parade. Flags and everything. Oh man, dragons. Like half a dozen up there."

"It must be Keegan's mother, from the Capital."

Even as she said it, he winged in on Cróga—from the south, she realized. He'd gone to the south. He leaped down as the dragon skimmed the road. Cróga rose up again to join the formation above.

Keegan strode to a woman on a white horse. He took the reins while she swung off, and they embraced standing on the road with two dozen horsemen and women behind and dragons circling the sky.

Her honey-blond hair formed a braided knot at her nape

and left her face unframed. She wore slim pants, almost like leggings, with tall boots over them, a sweater the color of the October sky with a long leather vest.

"If that's Mom," Marco said, tipping down his sunglasses, "Mom's a babe."

After the woman kissed Keegan's cheeks, he stepped over to take the hand of another woman, one with golden skin and ebony hair. He kissed her hand in a surprisingly gallant gesture.

"So's her friend." Hooking his sunglasses on his pocket, Marco started down the steps. "Let's go say hi."

"We ought to let them . . ."

She trailed off when Aisling's two boys raced out of the house. "Nan!" they called, and laughing, the blonde ran to drop down and scoop them into her arms.

Aisling came out next, a hand on her belly as she hurried to the road. With the boys clinging to her legs, the blonde straightened to wrap Aisling tight.

Harken, coming in from the near field, vaulted over the stone wall and moved in for his own hug.

"Let's just wait here," Breen murmured. "It's a family thing."

"It's nice." Marco rested a hand on Breen's shoulder. "It's nice to see."

But Bollocks lacked the willpower and dashed down the steps. For once he ignored the sheep, just sailed over the wall. Breen heard the woman laugh again as she bent down to greet him.

Then she turned her head, looked at Breen.

Breen felt her stomach roll into a single tight knot.

The woman said something to Harken, gestured to Keegan. She started across the road with Keegan at her side.

"Jeez, she walks like a queen. The royal kind," Marco elaborated. "You know what I mean."

Because she did, Breen had to order herself to go down the steps.

"Blessings on you, Breen Siobhan O'Ceallaigh. And to your friend as well. It's Marco, isn't it?"

"Ma'am."

"My mother, Tarryn O'Broin."

"It's pleased and more I am to meet you." Tarryn held out a hand even as Breen wondered if she should bow or attempt a curtsy. "Your grandmother is a treasure to me, and your father, rest him, a good friend, and a father to my children when their own was lost. Keegan, find your manners."

Tarryn swatted a hand at his arm. "Help the girl over the wall."

"Sure she's managed it on her own plenty." He muttered it, but reached out, lifted Breen bodily over.

"I'd say his rudeness is my failure as his ma, but I won't, as he's earned it all on his own. I won't keep you standing on the road, as you must be off to see Marg. Give her my love, will you, and ask if she'd come have a visit with me later today."

"I will."

To Breen's surprise, Tarryn cupped her face, leaned in to kiss her. "You do your father proud," she whispered. "Know that."

Then she stepped back, smiled. "Eian had stories about both of you, and so I know you're both musical. We'll have a ceilidh tonight."

"Ma—"

She waved Keegan away. "Wars and battles come soon enough. We take the good and the bright when we find it. Come back," she told Breen and Marco, "for the good and the bright."

"We don't want to intrude," Breen began as Tarryn crossed the road to lift Kavan onto her hip and take Finian's hand.

"She wants you, she'll have you. But you'll train first. Don't be late," Keegan warned, and walked away to join Harken in the field, where the riders already set up tents.

"That was something," Marco managed after a moment. "It still is something. They're going to camp out here, and they've got all the horses in the field. There are dragons circling overhead. Oh Jesus, they're coming down. Where are they going to put dragons?"

They landed, single file, on the road, shaking the ground as they lined up like planes on a runway.

Jewels, Breen thought. Magnificent jewels with men and women sliding or leaping off their backs.

The riders pulled off saddles, saddlebags, packs. And one by one the dragons lifted up, making Breen's heart shake with wonder, and considerable envy.

The riders hauled their gear, nodding to Breen and Marco as they passed, talking idly among themselves.

One, a saddle over one shoulder, a pack on his back, gave Breen a nodding glance, and Marco a long look.

"A fine head of hair you have there, friend."

"Ah, thanks. You, too."

He stood a moment longer, well over six feet in his boots, a warrior's braid to his shoulder and the rest of his deep blond mane waving down his back.

"And where from the other side are you from now?"

"Um. Philadelphia."

"Phil-a-del-phi-a," he repeated carefully, and smiled. "All right then."

When he walked off, Marco kept watching. "Was he flirting with me?"

"I don't know. I couldn't really tell. Maybe. He sure wasn't flirting with me."

"I think he was flirting with me. It threw me off so I didn't flirt back. He had really blue eyes. I should've flirted back. I didn't even get his name."

"Go train, Marco."

"Right." He put his sunglasses back on. "I'm going this way," he said, but kept looking after the dragon rider. "Don't forget I've got that Zoom, but then we're cleaning up, duding up, and coming back to party."

"I really don't think we—"

"The queen—I know she's not a queen, but she oughta be—the queen commanded it." He gave Breen a light punch. "Catch you later."

She didn't have time for a party, and couldn't think about going to a party where she knew a bare handful of people anyway. So rather than think about it, Breen called the dog and walked down to Marg's cottage.

She found Marg in the back garden harvesting vegetables from her little patch.

And since she didn't see a way out, she told Marg of Tarryn's arrival, the invitation to visit, and the ceilidh.

"A ceilidh's just the thing. I'll walk to the farm with you to spill the tea with Tarryn."

"Spill it?"

"Gossip, it means. And we'll pick a couple of these pumpkins, enough for a pie and soup as well to take to the ceilidh."

"You're going to make a pie and soup out of an actual pumpkin?"

"Well, of course. I can't claim to have the hand with them Sedric does, but no one's yet turned up a nose to either. There's magick in cooking, Breen, as you put your intent into it, and your work, and your love as well."

For the first time in her life Breen carved out a pumpkin. She learned how to separate the seeds, how to toast them while the chunks of pumpkin simmered on the stove to soften.

Instead of a few hours in the workshop, she spent them with Marg in the kitchen with the scents of fall everywhere. She learned how to peel and grate a nut of nutmeg, how to grind cloves and cinnamon into powders with mortar and pestle.

And while she seriously doubted she'd put any of the skills to regular use, she found some pleasure in them.

Whatever they didn't use they stored in jars for ingredients in future cooking or magicks.

In the end, they had a pot of soup, two pies, and two rounds of pumpkin bread.

"You've a fine hand in the kitchen."

"Helping hand," Breen qualified. "Our apartment kitchen's so small I mostly stayed out of Marco's way, but when he wanted a hand, mine did chopping and stirring."

During the washing up—a chore that included hauling in water from the well—she asked about Sedric. She'd realized during the baking time he'd gone south.

"Are you worried for Sedric?"

"Where there's love, there's worry. Worry walks hand in hand with joy on love's path, I think. He's where he's needed. As am I," she added with a brush of her hand on Breen's shoulder.

"Would you be in the south if it wasn't for me?"

"Ah, but there is you, *mo stór*, and if there wasn't, we might not know to be in the south at the ready. So the question's a circle that has countless answers on its ring."

Marg dried her hands, gave a nod to the tidy state of her kitchen. "Now that's done, we'll take our fine work up to the farm, but set by a round of the bread for Sedric on his return."

Breen carried the pot of soup by its handle, and Marg the pie and bread in a basket.

Leaves scuttled across the road, colorful children whisked by the wind. Overhead, dragons glided, with rider and riderless. Breen saw actual children, the group of friends she thought of as the Gang of Six, race across a field toward the bay. Because she felt Bollocks's longing, she glanced down.

"Go on and play awhile."

When he raced off, she laughed. "It's a tough call which he wants more, the kids or a swim."

"And so he'll have both. And how's the new book on our boy there going?"

"Pretty well. I'm going back to it in the morning as a kind of palate cleanser. I've been working on the adult novel, and wrote a really violent battle scene. I'm taking a break from that and switching to the fun."

"Isn't it a gift you have both in you?"

"I'm surprised and grateful for it every day. And for the cottage, Nan, where I can write, and Marco can work. This time last year, I got up every morning to go to a job I never wanted because I thought, I really believed, I had no choice. Now? I get up every morning to do work I love, and it's my choice. I know I have more to make."

"And so you will."

"I will. Just like I'm choosing to let Keegan push, kick, and shove me through another session of training." She sent Marg the side-eye. "Not the favorite part of my day."

"Well now, getting through it makes the good parts that much brighter."

"I'll try to remember that when he kills me half a dozen times. Still, I really enjoyed meeting the Trolls, and the views on the mountain—I'll never forget. I know I couldn't have done it unless he'd taught me to ride, and pushed me hard. I saw you riding your dragon. I won't forget that either. How magnificent you looked."

"Aren't you the one?"

"Can I go up with you sometime?"

"Well and of course you can. Ah, I see Keegan's setting up a target. So it's the bow for you today."

She looked over, saw Keegan in a field putting a target on a stack of hay bales.

"That won't be so bad. I might even be good at archery."

"Then go find out. Here, I'll take the soup in."

"Have a good time, um, spilling the tea with his mother."

"Be sure I will."

Breen split off at the gate. How bad could it be? she asked

herself. She noted he had the sword set aside for her, so there'd be some of that. Which meant getting her ass kicked—not pleasant. But if he'd gone to the trouble of putting up a target, surely they'd spend most of the training there.

One hand resting on the hilt of his sword, he waited for her. She had the muscle for the weight of bow he'd chosen for her. He could hope she showed more talent there than with a sword.

It continued to baffle and frustrate him that a woman with her strength and her grace—for she had more than her share of both—would fumble so much with weapons.

She'd improved, he reminded himself as he dug out some patience. No question she'd improved. Though she'd never be a master or any sort of clever tactician with the blade, she'd hold her own.

Until someone cut off her arm.

And since it was up to him to see that never happened, Keegan felt entitled to some frustration.

To keep his mind focused on the task at hand, he told himself it hardly mattered her hair was brighter than the last fiery show of autumn leaves.

"As with the sword," he said without preamble, "you aim the pointy end at the target."

"I've got that part."

He handed her a bow. "This weight will suit you well enough."

"Weight?"

"The string, you see, the strength you need to draw it back. First watch." He picked up another bow, took his stance.

"We won't nock an arrow yet, but I would use my draw hand to do that, then grip the bowstring with three fingers, the bow I take with the other hand."

He held up his palm. "You know the lifeline on the palm?"

"Yes."

"I hold the bow with thumb inside up to that line before I lift my arm, keep my shoulders level. Level," he repeated. "Then I draw, this way, you see?"

She watched him draw the bowstring smoothly back toward the right side of his face.

"And that eye, that same side—the right for you, for me, the left for others—you train your focus on your target. Now draw the blades in your back together, chest out—for the power, the muscle and strength of your back, you see?"

"All right."

"Then you take your fingers from the string and loose the arrow, and as you do, your hand moves to the rear, under your ear."

"More steps than I realized." And she concentrated on keeping them in order in her head. "I figured you just pulled it back, aimed, let it go."

"No. Try it as I said."

She tried to mimic his stance, reminded herself to keep her shoulders level, gripped the string and the bow as instructed, drew back.

She barely moved the bow an inch, reset, put more muscle into it. When she released, it twanged, and the string slapped against her forearm.

Since she wore a jacket, it was more shock than pain.

"Again. Slow and smooth for now."

She did it again, and again, and again until he deemed her ready for an arrow.

"With your draw hand"—he demonstrated—"you nock the arrow. Your three fingers hold the nocked end and the string."

In what seemed like one fluid move, he nocked the arrow, lifted the bow, drew, and shot. And naturally, hit the center of the target.

Naturally.

She repeated each step in her head, followed them. When

she released the arrow it took a shaky flight before hitting the ground barely four feet from where she stood.

"No," he said simply, and handed her another arrow. "Shoulders level, and pulled back. The draw smooth, steady."

This time the arrow flew a little farther—and a good three feet to the right of the target into a pretty hedgerow of fuchsia.

"No," he said again, and this time moved behind her.

He took her shoulders, turned them. "It goes where you send it. It hasn't a choice in the matter, does it? You do."

He pressed his face close to hers to share her aim, his hands over hers to guide her. "Pull the energy, the power, into your back. Aye, now, release."

The arrow hit the target—not the center, but it hit it.

She smelled of cinnamon, all but hazed his mind with it.

He stepped back.

"What have you been doing?" he demanded.

"I've been trying to shoot a damn arrow."

"Before. What spell have you been working?"

"None today—not really. Why?" She rolled her aching shoulder. "We baked pies and bread, made soup from pumpkins, from the garden. Why?"

"You smell of them."

And the oils from such spices could be used, he knew, in spells to stir lust, even love. Forbidden spells.

He handed her another arrow. "Again."

"Does the smell of pumpkin pie piss you off?"

"No. The scent of the spices is in your hair, on your skin. These can be used for spells and potions as well as cooking."

"I know. I've studied, practiced, used them that way. But today, it was for cooking."

She started to nock the arrow, then it struck her.

Insulted her down to the marrow.

"Love potions? They can be used in love potions. You think I would do that? I know they're forbidden, and I respect the craft. I respect my gift. I respect your choice to feel what you feel. I'm not so damn desperate I'd mix up a love potion so you'd want me again."

"I only asked because . . . bugger it. I'm here to train you, to prepare you for what's coming. There are Fey who will not come back home again after Samhain, and I must send them to fight knowing it. I'm not here to want you, and yet I do."

"And that pisses you off. Your problem, Taoiseach." Furious, she nocked the arrow. It ended up straight down in the grass barely a foot from her boots.

"Shit, shit, shit!"

He laughed, couldn't help himself, and she whirled on him, shoved him.

Still laughing, he caught her close, lifted her to her toes. "Once, gods be damned, just once and we'll be done with it."

He brought his mouth down on hers, took what he needed. And felt the release of it even as the wanting quivered through him like the bowstring.

The scent of her, the taste, the feel, all these weeks without them, demanded that he take what he could, if only for the moment.

She gave him nothing at first, not even a fight. But he felt that wanting in her as in him. And she surrendered to it, taking as he took, wrapping around him in the quieting sunlight in a field that smelled of grass and sheep.

When he let her go, she put her hand on his heart. "Why once?"

"Because some won't come back, and I have to give all I have to them. I have to think of them, not my wants, to think of those who fight knowing they won't come back."

She left her hand on his heart another moment, then let it fall. "All right. We'll both think of them."

She picked up the bow, the arrow, and tried again.

In the house, Marg stood at the window with Tarryn, watching Breen attempt to shoot an arrow.

"She favors you, Marg. Not just the hair—though, gods, it's glorious—but the shape of her face, her build. I know what having her back means to you."

"Such a narrow life Jennifer gave her. Pushing the roundness of the girl into a flat hole, day after day. I think one of the greatest joys of my life has been watching her wake. And the greatest sorrows knowing, now that she has, what she'll face."

"You told me her powers run deep, even deeper than your own."

"Aye. She's yet to tap the whole of them." Marg let out a laugh as Breen's arrow hit the ground. "How long do you figure Keegan's patience will last here?"

"Never long enough. He trains her to fight, and must of course, but it won't be the sword or arrow for her in the end." Another arrow hit the ground, and Tarryn just shook her head.

"And thank the gods for that. Yet she tries, doesn't she now?"

"There, if he'd guided her so in the first of it . . ." Marg smiled to herself as Keegan stood, hands over Breen's hands, face pressed to Breen's face. "They make a picture."

"They do." Enjoying it, Tarryn slipped an arm around Marg's waist. "And there, she's hit the target. I wonder why they seem so careful around each other when I've heard . . . What's all this now? What's the boy angry about?"

Frowning, Tarryn studied the scene in the field. "How could a man with such kindness in his heart have such a stubborn block of a head? She's doing her best, isn't she?"

Tarryn's eyebrows shot up as, after Breen started to nock the arrow again, she turned on Keegan.

"Angry words," she said. "You don't have to hear them to know. Well, I'm pleased to see she'll stand for herself."

"That she does when her temper's stirred."

"Looks to me like she's put him in his place. Good for

her." Then Tarryn winced as the next arrow struck the ground inches from Breen's foot. "Ah, now the eejit's laughing at her. You can't train a body if you're . . . There's the way, give him what for!" She all but cheered as Breen shoved her son.

Then fell silent when Keegan yanked Breen against him.

"Well now," Marg murmured, sipping her tea. "There you have it."

"There you have it," Tarryn agreed. "I'd heard he'd bedded her, but now I see why he no longer glides into the Capital now and again to go to Shana's bed. He thinks I don't know, but I know where my children are."

"Ah, youth." Marg shook her head as in the field Keegan and Breen stepped away from each other, and Breen again picked up the bow. "What a waste of heat."

"He stepped back from Shana some time ago. Not long, not long a'tall after Breen came through. I'm not sorry to tell you I'm glad of it."

Tarryn went back for the pot, and now the two women sat.

"I'll say to you what I've said only to Minga, who's a sister to me. I've great fondness for Shana's parents. Her father is good council, and her mother strong and kind. But when the girl—and a beauty she is, Marg—set her sights on Keegan, I worried. I worried, as it wasn't my boy so much as the taoiseach she aimed for. It was desire and ambition I felt from her, and never love for him. I want love for my children."

"A mother does."

"She's angry now that he told her plainly, and I can hope kindly, he wouldn't pledge to her. Ah, she puts a good face on it, and she's spending her time with Loren Mac Niadh. A more handsome couple you'd be hard finding in the whole of Talamh. I'm hoping the charm of him, for he has it aplenty, will cool that anger I feel from her."

"But you'll worry. Only today I said to Breen that love is worry and joy together."

"That's the truth of it." Tarryn reached out to squeeze Marg's hand. "I've so missed you."

"And I you, the daughter of my heart. I'll say to you now what I couldn't find the way to say before. After Eian and Jennifer ended on the other side, I had hope you'd pledge to each other, you and my boy."

"I'll say to you what I couldn't find the way to say before. We would have, I think, if he'd lived. Near to ten years after we lost Kavan—my husband, my love, Eian's dearest friend, a brother in all but blood to him—it bloomed between us. I'm blessed, Marg, to have loved and been loved by two such men."

"I'm glad of it. I'm glad to know he had that with you before he died."

"And now it may be his daughter, my son." Tangled with hope and worry, Tarryn looked toward the window. "Surely it will be them at the head of the spear against Odran. We can hope they bring each other joy as well."

"She may not stay, Tarryn. When, please the gods, Odran is destroyed and the worlds are safe, she may choose to go back to her other world."

"She may, and must make her choice. Still, it's good she'll come to the Capital soon. She'll see who Keegan is there. See more of Talamh. Politics and war," Tarryn said with a sigh. "There will be much talk of both, but she should see and hear and know what we are and how we govern."

She sat back, drank more tea. "It's a pleasure for me to sit with you awhile and have no talk of politics and war. We can only sit and watch these matters of the heart unfold."

"But we have the pleasure of talking of them."

Tarryn laughed. "Aye. Such as when will Harken finally persuade Morena to pledge so the pair of them can give me more grandchildren?"

"Slow and deliberate is Harken, and a life today and

tomorrow's tomorrow is how Morena sees things. Young Finian might take the leap before those two. How fares her parents, and her brothers and their families?"

"All well. Her da stays at the Capital, as Flynn's on the council. But both Seamus and Phelin flew south, and our light goes with them. Seamus's wife, Maura, you remember, teaches and trains the youngers. Well, she's her hands full with their oldest, who at ten argued hard to join the battle coming in the south. And Noreen's carrying their first."

They whiled away another hour talking of friends and family.

# CHAPTER NINE

When Marg left, Tarryn went outside to gather flowers for fresh displays around the house. Something, she knew, neither of her sons would think of. She noted Keegan had Breen training with a sword, and hand-to-hand, using wraiths.

Though she stayed out of their way, Tarryn watched, and deemed Breen's skill with a sword acceptable for a novice. But her skill with magicks and her strategy with them were well over that mark.

It brought her relief to see it, and gave her more hope. Much depended on Eian's daughter. Too much, she thought, but the fates were so rarely fair.

As she filled her basket, she heard hoofbeats.

She lifted her hand in greeting as Morena and Marco rode toward the paddock.

"You've a fine seat, Marco," she called out, "and a credit you are to your teacher and your mount."

"I got to gallop." The thrill of it still lived in his eyes as he leaned over to rub the mare's neck with both hands. "Man, we flew!"

"I can't take much credit, truth be none a'tall." Morena swung off Blue. "The man was surely a centaur in another life."

He laughed as he dismounted. "You guys don't really have those, right?"

"A smallish tribe in the far north," Morena said easily. "Their home world is known as Greck, but some have migrated here and settled."

He poked her shoulder. "No bull?"

"Not a bit of it. Let's see to the horses now, as you have your meeting—and a cake you promised to bake for tonight. Marco has to talk to people on the other side, in New York City, over the computer."

"Isn't that a wonder? Is this your work then?" Tarryn asked.

"Some of it, yes, ma'am. It's for Breen's book."

"Marg told me she has a story about her dog." Tarryn glanced over to where Bollocks, who'd come around at the end of the archery segment, deviled the cows. "She says it's a fine one."

"It really is."

"And with the apples Grandda gave him, he's going to make an applesauce cake, so he says, to bring to the ceilidh."

"It will be welcome, as its baker is."

As he groomed the horse, Marco glanced toward the tents. "We saw the soldiers training on the ride. Ah . . . do they come to the party?"

"Of course, more than welcome."

"That's good."

"Will you come to the Capital with us, Marco?"

He jolted, blinked at Tarryn. "Me? The Capital?"

"I'm sure Breen would particularly like your company, and so would we all. Sure I'm hoping you'll join us."

"Wow, thanks. Thank you. I'd really like to see it."

"And you, Morena, will you come? I know your mother misses you."

"I'd be pleased to go for a day or two. That's about all the time I can handle the noise and the crowds, even for family, but not this time. This one," she added, wagging a thumb at Marco, "he likes the noise and the crowds."

"I like the quiet, too. But yeah, I'm a city boy." He winced when he saw one of the wraiths, one that looked like something out of a horror movie, swipe at Breen with three-inch claws. When she went down, flat on her back, he started to vault over the paddock fence.

"She's fine, Marco," Morena told him. "Give her a moment."

From flat on her back, she shot out what he thought might be sharp darts of ice. Right from her fingers. The wraith screamed, started to leap on her. Then went poof.

"See what she did? You see that! She is awesome!" Marco did a little victory dance as Breen scrambled up and went after the remaining two wraiths with sword, fists, feet, and—jeez!—lightning.

"Awesome!" he repeated. "The only time I ever saw her fight before? We were, like, ten and I was puny. I mean puny, and this asshole—twenty pounds and two years on me—jumped me on the way home from school. Guess he figured I was too gay to live. He's pounding me into the sidewalk, and my Breen, she comes running. She jumped on his back and started wailing on him. He tried to shake her off, but she latched on, man. He hurt her, bloodied her nose, but she wouldn't stop."

He let out a breath. "I always figured she got in a lucky punch that flattened him, but maybe it wasn't. Maybe it wasn't luck at all. Anyway, her house was closer, so we went there. Breen with her bloody nose, me with the nose, a split lip, a black eye, bruises where he'd punched my guts out. Her mom doctored me up and took me home so she could tell my mom what happened. But she grounded Breen for a week for fighting."

"Grounded?"

Marco looked back at Tarryn. "It's a punishment, pretty popular with parents where I come from. It means you can't go anywhere, well, except for school. Just school and home. No hanging out. That wasn't right. It wasn't right her getting grounded that way."

"Where was Eian?" Tarryn asked him.

"On a gig somewhere. No, I guess he was probably here. We didn't know about here."

It hurt Tarryn's heart to think of it. "He didn't know. If he'd known, he would never have let it pass. He'd never have allowed Breen to be punished for coming to the aid of a friend."

"What happened to the bullying git?" Morena wondered.

"He never bothered me again. He got his ass whupped by a girl, and for his type? Nothing worse."

He shrugged. "I don't know much about gods and all that, but it seems to me this Odran's pretty much what Morena said. A bullying git. My money's on Breen."

"You're a wise one, Marco." Tarryn looked back to where Breen took a break, bent over, hands on knees. "And she'll have the whole of Talamh with her."

"She's got me, too." He lifted his bag of apples. "Hey, Breen! We gotta boogie."

She nodded, straightened. Then she pushed her sword on Keegan and started toward the paddock.

"You're not done." Keegan came after her. "You've an hour more."

"Not today." Her ears still rang from her head slapping the ground; her arm still stung from phantom claws. "Marco has work he has to do from the cottage."

"So he can go do it, sure and he knows the way by now. You have another hour of training."

"I'll make it up."

"We've got to get our party on," Marco reminded him. "Girl's gotta change her duds."

"Why? She's fine. You're fine," Keegan insisted. "It's a ceilidh, not a palace ball."

"Dude," Marco said, with pure pity.

"I'm filthy," Breen snapped. "And I smell like demon dust. So do you. I'm going back, having a really big glass of wine and a really long, hot shower. Deal with it."

She turned, realized she'd completely forgotten Tarryn stood right there. "I'm sorry, Ms. O'Broin."

"No need for that, and Tarryn, if you will. We're not formal in the valley as you've noticed. I'd apologize for my son, but the fact is, he's a man. So there you have it. We look forward to seeing you tonight, and I hope for a song from both of you."

"Thank you. I'll make up the hour," she said to Keegan, and walked away.

"Well now, it's off I go," Morena said brightly, and took Blue's reins. "I'll be back with my dancing shoes on. Tell Harken to be ready for it."

"Be sure I will," Tarryn said, and as Morena walked the horse to the road, turned to Keegan, grinned at him. "I like her."

"She's likable enough, but—"

"She trains hard, Keegan."

"And needs all she can get. Another hour—"

"Makes little difference in the whole of it, as you know. She's not a soldier, *mo chroí*."

"All the more reason she needs to . . . And you're right, as ever. An hour makes no change in it."

"And she was right as well. You smell of demon dust."

Frowning, he sniffed at his arm, then had to shrug in agreement.

"You'll have a scrub. But first, you'll have an ale by the

fire while I fix my flowers, and I'll tell you a story of her that Marco told me."

Breen would not, no matter how Marco wheedled, wear the fancy green dress Sally and Derrick had given her before the first trip to Ireland. Or the fancy shoes that went with it.

Not appropriate, she insisted as she poured her wine and Marco put his apples on the stove to cook.

While he set up for his meeting, she took the wine outside to sit in the fresh air. She put her feet up, sighed with relief as she watched Bollocks splash in the bay.

She sat, even when the dog came back to rest his head on her leg. Sat, even as dusk settled, as it deepened.

She finally stirred, reminded herself Bollocks needed to be fed and she remained filthy and smelly.

When she walked in, Marco stood in the kitchen pouring batter into a Bundt pan.

"Girl, I thought you'd gone upstairs! You've got to get your ass up there, get that shower. We're going to discuss wardrobe after I get this cake in the oven and get my own shower."

"We can discuss, but I'm not wearing the sparkly dress."

She filled the dog's bowls, then accepted the beater Marco offered. Licked batter from it. "God, that's good. Musical bakery or diner, Marco Polo. That's the answer."

Though parties where she didn't know everyone made her anxious, she forbade herself another glass of wine before heading up to shower.

She dealt with bruises under the hot spray, and realized tending to bruises and scrapes equaled another return to the routine of her life here. Add blisters she just noticed.

Archery sucked, she concluded.

By the time she got out of the shower, she'd mired herself in self-pity. And felt entitled. Even as she wished she could just drag on pajamas, pull out a frozen pizza, drink more wine in front of the fire, she did her duty and started on her hair and makeup.

No point in looking tired and out of sorts, she told herself. She'd stay for an hour, be polite and friendly, then slip away. Party-hearty Marco could stay as long as he liked—someone would bring him back to the cottage, or he could just bunk at the farm for the night.

She stepped back, studied herself, and decided she'd pass Marco's critical review. Maybe just, but she'd pass it.

Her good black pants, a sweater, boots, she decided as she cleaned up the hair and makeup debris. She'd put on some earrings, maybe a nice scarf.

And that would have to be good enough.

Then she stepped out and saw the dress on the bed.

It was deep blue, like it had been dipped into the sea under moonlight. Simple, she thought, with its long sleeves and scooped neck. And of velvet, soft to the touch.

She picked up the note beside it, and felt stupid, and more than a little guilty over her self-pity.

> Breen Siobhan, I thought you might enjoy
> wearing this tonight. If it doesn't suit,
> no worries. Nan.

"Of course it suits," she murmured.

Simple, no fuss, soft. How could it not suit?

When she put it on, it fit as though made for her, which she realized it surely had been. It fell in an easy drape to just above her ankles, and made her feel loved.

She chose the earrings Sul had given her, and with her dragon's heart stone and her father's wedding ring on the chain around her neck thought she hit the mark with jewelry.

As she considered her choices of footwear—which didn't amount to much given her hasty packing—Marco knocked on the door.

"Come on in."

"Let's get down to business," he began, then stopped and stared at her. Without a word, he circled his finger in the air so she'd do a turn.

"Where'd you get that dress, girl? It's a killer."

"Nan sent it. It's a killer?"

"The body in it's the killer, and that dress knows how to show it off."

"Oh." Immediately distressed, Breen turned back to the mirror.

"In a classy way, Breen. Jeez. The opposite of a trip to Slut Town—not that there's anything wrong with that. You want the cool boots—the black ones with the stubby heels and the fake laces up the front."

"I do?"

"Yeah, you do." He got them out himself. "Don't want the tall ones or the walking boots with that."

"I'll bow to your far superior fashion sense. Speaking of, you look great."

"I'm rocking it," he agreed, and posed in her mirror.

He wore snug black jeans, black high-top Chucks, a turtle-neck sweater the color of aged bronze with his leather vest over it. He sported a single silver hoop in his left ear, and the protection bracelet she'd made him.

"Put those boots on so we can get a load of our smoking selves."

Obediently, she sat down, put them on, tugged up the zippers on the sides. When she stood beside him, she stuck a hand on her hip and struck a runway pose to make him laugh.

"There we are, and we are lit! It's gonna be hard for us not to get lucky tonight."

"I'm not looking to get lucky tonight."

He heaved a sigh. "Girl, there you go making me sad right before a party. Come on. I'm going to get my guitar."

He detoured to his room, arranged the guitar's colorful

strap cross-body to carry it on his back. As if he knew a party was in his future, Bollocks wagged his way down the steps.

"We just have to figure the best way to carry the cake over there."

"Marco, it's beautiful!" He'd drizzled thin, glossy glaze over the golden-brown dome. It sat on a cooling rack scenting the kitchen. "That's it, decision made. You're going to open your own place."

"Right now, it's getting it there in one piece." Carefully, he transferred it from the rack to a plate. "I guess we put a cloth over it."

"I can do better." She pointed at him. "I've got this." She dashed into the laundry room, came back with a cardboard box.

"Good idea. It won't be pretty, but it'll be safer."

"I've got this," she repeated. She ran her hands over the box, sides, top, bottom, over and over as she visualized what she wanted.

Slowly, the brown turned red, faint at first, then deeper, brighter. For a flourish, she scattered silver stars over it.

"Holy crap! How'd you do that? How'd you do that just touching it?"

"It's more. It's intent and visualization and will. It's just a glamour, so it won't last more than a few hours. Maybe less, since I've never done it on an object before. But long enough to get your cake there in style."

"You're the eighth, ninth, and tenth wonder of the world." He set the plated cake inside, cut some kitchen cord to secure the lid.

"I don't suppose you could do a fancy ribbon."

"Challenge accepted. Silver, I guess, to match the stars."

Now she ran the cord between her fingers until it widened, flattened, began to shine silver. "I've never been really good at tying bows, but maybe this way . . ."

She laughed, ridiculously pleased, when she turned the tiny corded bow into an elaborate one.

Marco picked up the box. "My BFF's an honest-to-God witch. We gonna ride your broomstick to the party?"

"Clichéd much? Let's go, Bollocks. I'm actually in the mood for a party."

She brought light to guide them through the woods, with owls calling and Bollocks racing ahead.

"When I'm ready to go, you don't have to. They can put you up at the farm—or in my room at Nan's—if you want. Or someone will bring you back over."

"We'll see how it goes. No point thinking about leaving before you even get there."

"Give me the cake," she said when they reached the tree. "Go ahead, Bollocks, we're right behind you."

When they passed through, Marco put a hand on her shoulder to balance himself, then left it there as he looked across the road.

Light gleamed in every window of the sprawling farm-house, and campfires dotted the field where the tents stood. Music poured through the air—from the house, from the field.

She could see movement behind the windows. People danced there, and on the grass. Others sat on the stone walls or on bales of hay with plates of food or cups or tankards.

"Now, that looks like a party. Sounds like a party." Marco tugged her down the steps. "Let's go get us some of that."

It didn't matter how many people (so many!) would be there, she told herself. Nan would be there, and Morena, and others she knew. All she had to do was find a safe spot, drink some wine with a friend, listen to the music.

Those seated on the wall shouted greetings as they walked to the door. Marco started to knock.

"They won't hear it anyway," he decided, and opened the door.

Warmth rushed out. The fire crackled, Harken sawed some-thing lively on a fiddle while others played an accordion, a mandolin, a *bodhrán* drum. Kids sat on laps, babies bounced on them. People danced as if their feet could fly.

Through the melee, Finola hurried up to them. "There's my handsome Marco. I'll have a dance with you before the night's over."

"Only one?"

She laughed, patted his cheek. "And how pretty you are, Breen. Ah, Marg will be so pleased the dress suited you."

"It's wonderful. Is she here?"

"She is indeed, in the back now helping Tarryn with the food. Enough for two armies we have, and it's good we do, as we've at least that."

"I'll take the cake back and give them a hand." Having tasks generally put her at ease at a party. "Dance with Finola."

As she walked away, Breen heard Finola ask, "And are you going to play for us, my darling boy?"

Try to stop him, Breen thought.

On her way to the back, Breen spotted a few familiar faces, and that helped, too.

In the kitchen she found Tarryn and Marg setting out yet more food, there and in the dining room, on tables already groaning under pots and plates and bowls and dishes.

Aisling sat, one hand on her growing belly.

"And here's Breen now, bearing gifts. I haven't seen enough of you since you came back."

"I've been selfish with her." Nan walked over, took Breen's shoulders. "I'm so pleased the dress suits you."

"It's beautiful. Thank you."

"You're more than welcome."

"Thank you for inviting us," she said to Tarryn. "Marco baked a cake. I'm not sure where to put it."

"Well then, hand it over." Tarryn, looking resplendent in russet despite the cloth tied around her waist, came over to take the box. "Marco's kitchen skills are already far-famed, so let's see what we have here."

Tarryn made room on a table and opened the box. "Sweet Brigid, the scent alone! And see how lovely." She lifted the cake out to show it off. "If it tastes half so good, it won't last more than a minute."

"From personal experience, I can promise it tastes even better. He's dancing with Finola now, but if we could save a slice for her and Seamus? He used their apples."

"We'll see to that. Marg, why don't you tuck two slices away safe?"

"What can I do to help?"

"You can have some wine to start. No, no, you sit awhile longer," Tarryn told Aisling. "The baby likes the music, it seems, and has been dancing in there all evening."

"This one will be musical, I'm thinking." Aisling smiled as she stroked her belly.

Tarryn handed Breen a cup of wine and a plate of cheeses and bread. "Eat a bit. There's plenty where that came from. The cheeses Harken and Aisling—and Keegan and myself when we're about—make here on the farm."

"It's good," Breen said after she tried a piece. "It's really good."

"Cheeses from the valley are the best in all of Talamh."

Tarryn turned when Morena burst through the back door. "The kids have run me to the ground, so I'll beg for wine. Mab and Bollocks are on them now, and a few of the growns as well.

"Hello to you, Breen," she added as she grabbed for wine.

"You're wearing a dress."

"As are you. I've been known to don one on occasion."

She'd donned one of violet, like her wings, that stopped just below her knees. She'd paired it with tall boots of deep purple, and left her hair long and wavy.

She spotted the cake.

"Is that Marco's? I'm having some." She cut a generous slice, ate the first bite out of her own hand. "Well gods, this is brilliant. Here." She broke off a piece and, to Breen's surprise, fed it to Tarryn from her fingers.

"It's all of that. Ah, Minga," she said as the door opened again. "Come meet Breen, and have a slice of Marco's cake, as you've never had better."

"I will. I've dragooned some of the older children into the washing up, as we'll need more dishes." She walked to Breen, pressed her gold-dust cheek to hers. "The traditional first greeting of my tribe," she explained.

"Minga is my dearest friend. She came from the desert world of Largus to Talamh for love."

"And my love is now out in the field playing dice and telling tall tales. They'll be sending a runner before long for more food, so be warned."

She took the slice of cake from Tarryn, still smiling at Breen. "I've never been to your world, but I know there are places in it not unlike my own of golden sands and heat, and cities rising from it."

"Yes. I've never actually seen. That is, I've never been. I've never really been anywhere until I came to Ireland. And here."

"Not a traveler then? I'm not one myself, or not very much. I'm glad Og was. I met my love when he traveled. I must meet the one who bakes like a god. Introduce me, won't you?"

Smoothly, Minga guided Breen out of the kitchen. And sent Tarryn a quick wink over her shoulder.

"Minga will ease her into things. Now." Tarryn whipped off the cloth. "We've done our duty here, again. So, Morena, pry that fiddle from Harken and get the boy to dance."

"I'll do just that. I'll clear a chair for you, Aisling."

"No need." She hauled herself up. "I've rested enough, and since this one wants to dance, I'll oblige."

The woman from yet another world, in her bold red dress, introduced Breen to a dozen people so their names and faces and words rattled around in her head.

Marco joined the musicians, somehow catching the rhythm and notes of songs she'd never heard. Having the time of his life, she thought, and since everyone was so friendly, she didn't feel awkward.

Then Marco called out to her. "Come on, Breen, let's do one."

"You're doing fine."

But Morena shoved her forward, and people started clapping and stomping. Marco just grinned when she sent him a you'll-pay-later look.

"We don't know any Talamhish songs yet," Marco, the natural MC, announced. "We'll do one from our world. Let's do 'Shallow.'"

She tried to think of something else—something fast and quick and easy—but he'd already found the opening notes on his guitar. The room had already hushed.

When he began to sing, she tuned herself to him as she had hundreds of times before. So when it came to her part, she slid into it, stopped thinking about anyone watching or listening.

She barely noticed when Harken picked up the violin again, filled in some notes, and the mandolin player did as well.

By the time she hit the key change, it was only the music, and the pleasure of making it.

When they finished, voices twined, eyes on each other as the song demanded, the hush held another moment.

Then the applause erupted, and shot her back into herself so a flush rose up into her cheeks. But she saw Marg standing with Tarryn, saw the tears in Marg's eyes.

Her grandmother crossed her hands over heart and, her heart in her eyes, held them out as if giving it to Breen.

"Take a bow, girl," Marco ordered, and took an elaborate one himself. Though she rolled her eyes at him, she dipped into a curtsy that brought more applause.

And calls for more.

"We'll do one more." Marco leaned close to her ear. "Then I've got to get my flirt on."

She glanced where he grinned, and at first saw only Keegan, standing in his leather duster, his hair windswept, his eyes on hers. But the dragon rider Marco had spoken with that morning stood beside him.

They did one more, then yet another by popular demand before Marco managed to pull away. Breen intended to head straight for Marg, but Keegan stepped in front of her, held out a glass of wine.

"Thanks."

"You should sing more." He took her arm, steered her toward the kitchen. "And they'll see you do if you don't move away. Your dog is entertaining those still among the tents."

"I should call him, go back to the cottage."

"Why?"

"I . . ." She decided to just come out with it. "I'm terrible at parties where I don't know people. And I met I don't know how many already, and I'm never going to remember the names."

He nodded, drank some ale. "They're crowded and noisy, and I need breaks from them myself." He sliced a hunk of bread, slapped some cheese and cold meat on it. "Come outside in the air for a bit. I only came back myself as Brian wanted to find Marco."

"Brian? Oh. I didn't know his name."

"Brian Kelly," Keegan said as he nudged her outside. "He's your cousin. His great-grandfather times four or so and yours were brothers, though his traveled to the north, met a north woman named Kate, and settled there. Yours stayed in the valley."

"How do you know all that? How do you remember all that?"

"It's part of my duty, and I suppose some luck with it. He's a good man, is Brian, so you've no worries about Marco."

"All right."

He looked across to the tents, the campfires. "Some will go south tomorrow, some the day after. Not all at once, you see. And some will remain to guard after Samhain, after we break the back of what comes for us that night. And some we'll mourn."

He shook that off, had to. "And some will travel with us to the Capital."

"How long am I supposed to stay there?"

"A few days only. You need to see and be seen. And my mother will have another shagging party."

"A party? At the palace?"

He looked severely pained at the term. "It's not a bleeding palace. A castle is a different thing, which you should know. A castle is for defense, to protect and house and fortify. And don't be packing a case full of things this time. It's a few days, and we'll want to travel straight through, so quickly."

He turned to her, eyes direct and intense. "You look very fine tonight, and you might as well know it's hard for me to keep my hands off you. We'll go back in, as my mother will roast me for keeping you out too long."

"I like your hands on me."

"Gods. Not now." He took her arm, pulled her back inside.

# CHAPTER TEN

While Breen went back into the party, Marco sat on the stone wall out front drinking an ale with Brian Kelly.

"You're telling me you and my best girl are cousins?"

"We are, on our fathers' sides, and well back. My many-times-great-grandfather traveled to the far north for the adventure of it, it's told. There he met my many-times-great-grandmother. They fell in love, pledged. They had eight children, and lived to a ripe age."

"Eight kids?"

Brian smiled and sipped his ale. "Nights are long and cold when winter comes to the north. So I spring from that, and Breen from her many-times-great-grandfather who was mine's brother, who stayed in the valley, worked this very land where we sit, and with his woman had nine children of their own."

"So you live in the north."

"My family's there, or the most of them. I make my place in the Capital for now, or wherever the taoiseach needs me. You're traveling there with Tarryn after Samhain, I'm told."

"Yeah. I'm grateful for the invite because I need to stick close to Breen." Brian's eyes, Marco thought, had a sparkle in them. An actual sparkle. "You're heading back, too, right?"

"I will, aye, once we've settled things in the south."

It struck Marco that *settled things* meant going to war.

"You're going to fight the bad guys?"

"It's what we do when they threaten the peace. We're a world of peace, and laws that hold it for all."

"Are you scared of going south, of, you know, going into battle?"

"Those who don't fear battle seek it. We don't seek it, but we prepare for it, and won't turn from it." Shifting, Brian smiled fully into Marco's face. "Keegan tells me you planted your fist in his face when you believed he threatened your friend."

"Yeah, well, that happened. But I'm not much on fighting."

"Are you for walks? It's a sight to see the moons over the bay on such a night."

Happy butterflies swarmed in Marco's belly. "Sure, I'm big on walks." He rose, and like Brian, left his tankard on the wall. "We walk a lot in the neighborhood where I'm from."

"Philadelphia."

"Lots of shops and restaurants and clubs you can walk to. We don't have a bay, but we've got a river. Only one moon, though."

"I've seen the one moon," Brian said as they walked. "In Ireland and Scotland, and in France when I traveled."

"You've been to France? Like Paris?"

"Aye, I went to Paris."

"Was it wonderful?"

"It was. Full of color and sound, the old and new mixed together. I liked the art, also the old and the new. I like to paint."

The butterfly wings beat even faster. "You're an artist?"

"Ah well, I like to draw and to paint when I can."

"We have art galleries in Philadelphia, one of my favorite things. I can't draw or paint worth crap, but I sure like looking at art."

"When we're in the Capital, I'll show you some I've done, and you can judge if it reaches art. I can judge your music, as I've heard it now, as brilliant. The song—the first I heard when I came in—was passionate, romantic, and your voice mated with Breen's gripped my heart. I'm not musical myself, but admire those who are."

"I could teach you. It's something I do—did, anyway. Taught people to play instruments, did some voice coaching. Oh wow."

Marco paused as he saw the moons, one waxing, one waning, over the bay. "It's awesome."

Still starry-eyed, he pointed. "Look. Mermaids!"

"Merpeople," Brian corrected, taking Marco's hand to draw him toward the beach. "As there are mermen as well."

"They're singing. Hear that?"

"Mers are musical, it seems, by nature, and their voices are part of their powers. They can call other Mers, other creatures of the sea, from far, far distances. And spellbind with a song when threatened. Fierce fighters they are as well. Some of these will go south."

"So, like Aquaman?"

"I don't know this."

"Oh, it's a character, a superhero character, in stories. The guy who played him in the movies is total."

All Marco could think was he stood on a beach watching merpeople swim under two moons while he held hands with a smoking dude who rode a dragon.

Over his head and sinking fast.

"So . . . are you—do you have magickal abilities? Like Breen?"

"None have what she has. I have some Wise from ancestors, but I am of the Sidhe."

As Marco watched, Brian unfurled wings as bold and bright blue as his eyes.

When his heart jumped, Marco reminded himself beaks, not wings but beaks, weirded him.

"Does this trouble you?"

"No. I mean, it's all just fantastic and strange, and fascinating, too. I can't get used to it. I don't want to get used to it," he realized. "Because you can end up taking beautiful things for granted if you get too used to them. And all this, it's beautiful."

You're beautiful, he thought, as those butterflies beat their wings all the way up to his throat. "Look, I have to ask, because I'm real new around here, so I don't know if things work the same. I need to ask if I'm reading the signals right. If there's a thing happening. A spark happening with you and—"

He didn't finish, as Brian simply wrapped arms around him and answered the question with a kiss.

Long and deep, and with a tenderness that melted the muscles in Marco's legs. The Mers' song lifted into the air with the water lapping the shore, and the moons sailed in a sky dazzled with stars.

Sinking fast, sinking fast. Sunk, Marco thought when Brian eased back. Those blue eyes sparkled, the blue wings shimmered.

"You read very well," Brian said, and kissed him again.

"I saw you from above, and something stirred in me." Gently, Brian ran a knuckle down Marco's cheek. "Then on the ground, closer, I saw your eyes, I saw the heart in them— its loyalty and its courage. And you so handsome, such hair. I thought, I'd like a moment or two with that one."

"I was thinking the same thing at the same time."

"But then I heard your song, and knew a moment or two wouldn't be enough. I hope we'll have more."

"I want more." Pressed close, Marco took Brian's lips again. "I want a lot more."

"We'll have what we want when I return."

Going to war, Marco thought. It seemed impossible he was falling for a man with wings who was going to war.

"Come back with me now. We'll go over to the cottage."

"I cannot. None of the Fey can travel outside of Talamh until after we settle things on Samhain. Will you wait for more, Marco, as I need to wait? I want more walks with you, more words, more time. I want to lie with you. But first, I ride for Talamh, for the Fey, for your world and all."

"I'll wait." He held Brian close, felt the brush of wings on the back of his hand.

Breen finally managed to slip away from the ceilidh. She'd done a quick search for Marco, then decided he'd take one of the options they'd discussed. Maybe she'd enjoyed herself more than she'd anticipated, but—no, she admitted, no question she had. Still, she found herself exhausted from talking to so many people, from drinking wine, from dancing (because no one gave her a choice). She really wanted bed.

Then she had Keegan to think about. Or not think about, she corrected, and would think about him if she stayed. She didn't want to think that in two days, her prophecy of the battle in the south could become reality.

She didn't want to think, at least for a few hours, and if she slept, she wouldn't.

It wasn't hiding from that reality, she assured herself. It was more, right now, recharging to prepare for it.

When she started across the road, Bollocks let out a greeting bark. Glancing over, she saw Marco walking with the dragon rider—who was apparently also her cousin.

Holding hands, she noted, and felt her heart melt a little.

"Are you going back?" Marco called out.

"I'm partied out. Go ahead and stay. Your guitar's still in there, and they'll absolutely get you to play it again."

"No, I'll go back with you. I can get the guitar tomorrow. You haven't actually met Brian."

"That's Cousin Brian." He stepped up to Breen, kissed both her cheeks. "I liked your songs, very much."

"Thanks. It's really good to meet you. I didn't know I had family here besides Nan."

"Mairghread the Powerful is family enough for most, but you've quite a number of cousins across Talamh, and on the other side as well. And all are glad you've come, and I'm glad you brought Marco with you."

He glanced toward the Welcoming Tree. "It's sorry I am I can't escort you back over. It's not permitted until after Samhain."

"I didn't realize." Then she did. "You're going to the south."

"Before the day breaks. But I'll see you soon after at the Capital, and we'll have more time to talk." Smiling, he turned to Marco. "And walk. And more. Sleep well."

Breen had to hold back a sigh when they kissed.

"Stay safe." Marco squeezed his hands as Brian drew away.

"To a warrior you say, fight well, stand strong."

"Okay, fight well, stand strong."

"And so I will. Good night to you both."

"And stay safe," Marco whispered when Brian walked away toward the field of tents.

"You've got heart eyes, Marco Polo." Breen grabbed his hands. "And I want to hear all about it on the way back."

"Am I walking?" He went with her across the road. "Because it feels like my feet are way above the ground."

"Your feet are walking. The rest of you's floating. First let me say he's charming, and he's definitely smoking, and

I'm pretty sure I saw stars in his eyes when he looked at you."

"They sparkle." After he climbed the wall, Marco sighed for both of them. "They really do. We sat on the wall out front for a while, just talking."

Breen kept his hand because he still looked dazzled. "About?"

"Oh, about the party, the music, the cousin thing. That's a hell of a thing, right?"

So dazzled, Breen noted, he moved from Talamh to Ireland without the slightest reaction.

"It is. He lives in the north?"

"Not right now. He's in the Capital. Maybe it's like being stationed there. And we walked down to the beach, and there were Mers swimming and singing, and the moons, and he has wings. Blue wings, like his eyes."

"He's of the Sidhe?"

"Yeah, that."

Bollocks pranced along beside them instead of running ahead. He kept his head cocked, and his eyes on Marco as if taking in every word.

"I was feeling all I was feeling, but I wasn't sure if it worked the same in Talamh, you know? So I thought I needed to ask rather than screwing it all up by making a move. And he kissed me."

"You're killing me, Marco. On the beach, with the Mers, the moons?"

"I know, right? And we just kissed and kissed, and he said we needed to wait until after this stupid battle because stuff. And he's an artist, and he's been to Paris. And I think I might be in love. I know I just met him, but I never felt like this. It's more than the lust haze. It's more."

"Then I'm going to love him, too."

"Maybe I'll feel different when we're out of Talamh, back in Ireland."

"Marco, we've been back in Ireland, and we're nearly back to the cottage."

"What?" He tried to look everywhere at once in the light Breen had brought to guide their way. "Wow. Jeez. I don't feel different, so that answers that. He's going to fight those crazies, Breen. What if something happens to him? What if—"

"Don't. Don't think that way. I know it's hard, but we can't think that way."

Fretting now, Marco rubbed a hand over his bracelet. "Can you make him something like this, something like you made me?"

"Yes, and I will. I have everything I need right here in the cottage."

"I know it's too late for tomorrow, but when he gets back . . . Can I help? I know I don't have the woo-woo, but can I help make it?"

"You can pick the leather and the stones."

"Thanks. Can we sit out for a few minutes? I just need to settle a little."

"Sure. Bollocks wants his bedtime swim anyway. We'll sit, and we'll have one more glass of wine. I was too busy talking, singing, and dancing to drink very much. And you were too busy getting kissed in the moonslight. We'll toast those who fight well, stand strong."

He caught her in a hug as they reached the cottage. "No one ever had a better friend than you."

In the morning, Breen got in as much work as possible before she heard Marco in the kitchen. Knowing keeping busy didn't do away with worry, but could cut it back, she shut down.

He stood at the door with his coffee, looking out at the bay. And thinking, no doubt, of the bay on the other side.

She hugged him from behind.

"Did you eat?"

"I think I'm lovesick. Kills the appetite."

"Tell you what. I'll make us a late breakfast." She went into the kitchen, got a box of cold cereal from the cupboard. "My specialty."

It made him laugh. "That'll work."

"And after we eat, we'll make Brian's bracelet."

"It can wait. I know you want to write."

"I'm in a good place to stop, and this is priority."

"Thanks."

"And when we're done?" She glanced up as she poured cereal into bowls. "We'll go over early. We're going to take that ride—our first ride together—to Dad's grave. I told Nan last night we'd stop by on the way back, before I have to go train."

She kept up the chatter as she brought over the bowls, the milk, another bowl with berries. "Let's have pizza tonight, pop some corn, stream a movie. Then tomorrow's Finian's birthday, and I've got an idea for a gift."

"You're trying to keep me busy."

"And me, too. I'm worried, too; afraid, too. And . . . I have powers, Marco, but they're not enough. They don't want me in this because I'm not enough yet."

"I don't want you in it ever. I guess I don't get my way on that."

"I don't know what I need to do yet, or have yet, or be yet. It's hard to know what I don't know. But whatever I have?" She tapped a hand on her heart. "Is going south. Here, tomorrow night—or in Talamh—there'll be ceremonies, rituals. Samhain's a sabbat and important. You can't really be part of that, but you can be there, watch, and send your heart and mind, too."

"Okay. Okay, we're going to do all of that."

"And pack for a few days at the Capital."

"Brian's going to show me his art."

She shook her spoon at him. "Is that a euphemism?"

"Don't need one. I'm going to see his art, then we're going to get each other naked. Or it could be the other way around. What do they wear in the Capital?"

"I haven't the faintest idea."

"I'll ask Nan. And you take that new dress." He smiled at her. "You're making me feel better."

"That's my job. And since I fixed this elaborate breakfast, you get to do the dishes while I get what we need for your gift for your boyfriend."

"Don't be calling him that yet. You could jinx it."

She rose, spoke solemnly. "I saw what I saw, I know what I know."

When she came back, she set out leather strips, selected protective stones.

"He's a big guy." Marco studied his choices. "Can we do a six-strip braid?"

"I have no idea how to braid six together."

"I do. I can show you."

"You do it."

Instantly, Marco snatched his fingers away from the leather. "I don't want to, like, dilute anything."

"You won't—the opposite. You'll add yourself."

"Okay, if you're sure. It's more like weaving, see?" He chose five brown strips of varying hues and a black for the center, and in his practiced way wove them snugly together.

"That's good, already impressive. You choose the stones, place them where you want them."

"Tell me what they are, okay, and what they do?"

As she tutored him, he set stones in a wide zigzag pattern over the leather braid.

"That's not too many, is it?"

"No, and damn it, it's better than the one I made you. It looks like something you'd buy in a high-end arts and crafts shop."

"Don't you insult the bracelet my best girl made me." Satisfied, he sat back. "What's next?"

"Magick." She picked up her wand. "Put your hand over mine on the wand."

He hesitated. "I really can? I won't screw something up?"

"The power's from me, but the heart's from you—so we weave them like you wove the leather."

"That's chill."

"So let your heart and your intent lead. Think of him."

She called the light, said the words, and with Marco's hand on hers trailed the wand over the leather and stones. Once, twice, three times.

"They just . . . They just sort of melted into the leather. I could feel it, Breen." Dazzled, thrilled, he looked over at her. "I could feel the energy just pouring out of you."

"From you, too. Your faith, your heart." She tipped her head to Marco's. "He better appreciate you, or I'll burn the skin off his ass."

"Bet you could. I hope he likes it, and it's not too much, too soon."

"He will, and it isn't. Now you get to sew the pouch. Pick a color. I brought leather because dragon rider."

"I like the blue, like his eyes. Is that completely lame?"

"It's adorable."

Since Marco sewed better than she did, Breen left him to it and put the unused stones and leather away. She pulled on boots, a jacket, added a scarf since the day—at least on this side—held cool and damp.

By the time they left the cottage, the stacked clouds overhead sent down a thin, chilly rain.

In Talamh, they stepped into fresh fall air and sunshine.

Because Aisling's boys played near the kitchen garden, watched over by the patient wolfhound Mab, Breen sent Bollocks ahead.

Finian strutted up to them. "In one more day, it's my birthday."

"I heard that." Marco crouched down so they'd be eye to eye. And Kavan immediately climbed onto his knee. "You're going to be fifteen, right?"

Obviously thrilled, Finian grinned before holding up three fingers. "I get to ride with Harken on his dragon because I don't have wings like Kavan. But one day I'll have my own dragon like Harken and Keegan."

Now Breen hunkered down. "Your gift is of the Wise, like your mother's."

He studied her. "Ma says that, but I can't do anything."

"You will. Good things and great things. I see it. I feel it."

His eyes rounded. "Do you swear it?"

She touched a hand to his heart, and felt that pulse of light, that soft, young power. "I do. I swear it. Your dragon is only this big now." She held out her other hand, measured the distance. "He needs his mother for a while longer. He's green as your fields, with blue like the bay on his wings."

Finian gasped. "You've seen my dragon?"

"I see him in you. You've named him Comrádaí in your heart, for brother, and he'll be, like Kavan, a brother to you."

"I picked his name! I did! But I haven't seen him. I have to tell Ma. Come on, Kavan, I have to tell Ma about my dragon."

Kavan stopped playing with Marco's hair, smiled, and scrambled down to run after Finian.

"Did you really see all that?"

"Yeah. I didn't expect to. I—the longing is so strong in both of them. It was all just there. God, I hope it's all right I told him all that."

"You know what I think?" Marco pushed up, took Breen's

arm to draw her up with him. "I think if you saw and said all that, you were supposed to. And you sure made that kid happy."

Since Mab followed the boys, and Bollocks stood vibrating, watching her with hope, she stroked his topknot. "Go ahead. I'll call for you when we're ready to ride."

"Is it like that with the dragons, you think? Like it is with you and Bollocks?"

"That's what they say. Now, I guess we should find Harken, or check in the house to let them know we're getting the horses."

She led the way to the stables first and found Harken crooning as he ran his hands over a mare. The mare, Breen realized, she'd watched Keegan's stallion impregnate on a rainy summer day.

"Good morning to you both." Harken murmured something to the animal, rubbed his cheek to hers.

"It's Eryn, isn't it? Is she all right?"

"More than fine. Just giving her a once-over before I let her have a run in the field. She and the foal are both well. And how are you faring after the big night?"

"More than fine," Marco answered. "Is it okay if I pet her?"

"Sure she likes the attention. You've just missed Morena, who left to take Amish hunting. And my mother as well, as she and Minga are off for a ride."

"It's still all right if Marco and I ride to the gravesite?"

"It is, of course. I'll get your tack."

"We'll get it. I know where everything is now."

Marco stroked the mare another moment. "I guess some of the soldiers left for the south already."

"Before the sun broke the night, and Keegan with them. He and Mahon will come back for Finian's birthday celebration, then off they'll go again."

Breen laid a hand on his arm. "And you?"

"Not this time. I'm here, as Keegan wants me close to our mother and sister, the boys. They'll not get past them, but we take no chances."

"Will you go to the Capital?"

"No, and thank the gods for that. I'm not one for the crowds and the noise. The farm needs tending, the valley protecting, and that's for me. Well now, you've a fine, fresh day for a ride, so enjoy it. Come on there, Eryn, my beauty."

Without halter or reins, the mare followed him dutifully out of the stables.

"He's a lot like you," Breen said as she watched Harken go.

"Harken? Like me?"

She tapped a hand on her heart. "In here. The kindness, patience, loyalty. I think now that's why I felt comfortable around him so fast."

They gathered the tack and hauled it out to the paddock, where Harken already had Boy and Cindie waiting.

The man himself hooked his muscular plow horse to a plow. As she saddled Boy, Breen watched him walk along behind the horse as the plow turned the earth in a fallow field.

What would he plant there, she wondered, and at this time of year? Or did the plow just aerate the soil? She didn't know the first thing about farming—though her father had been a farmer.

"He doesn't strike me as the, you know, warrior type," Marco commented as the song Harken sung while he worked carried back to them.

"Harken? He's a farmer at his heart, a witch in his gift. He'd rather use a plow than a sword, but you can believe he knows how to use both. His father trained him, then mine continued the training after his died."

She dealt with the gate, then mounted. She called for Bollocks, waited while he ran toward them. Then grinned over at Marco. "What would our friends in the Gayborhood think of us now?"

"They'd think we look sharp, and we look sexy on these horses."

They walked to the road, where Breen tossed her hair back, sent him a challenging look. "Are you up for a gallop?"

"Up for one? Yee-haw!" With the shout, he raced off.

"Urban cowboy," she said to Bollocks. Laughing, Breen clicked to Boy and gave chase.

# PART II
# TRUST

*To believe only possibilities, is not faith,*
*but mere Philosophy.*
                                    —Sir Thomas Browne

# CHAPTER ELEVEN

Marco stopped along the way to call greetings to the woman pegging clothes on a line with a toddler at her feet, to the old man walking with his long-eared dog along the roadside, to a couple harvesting fall vegetables from their garden.

He, like Keegan, knew the names, matched them to faces, so she could follow his lead.

At the turn, she gestured. "We're this way. Did you ride here with Morena?"

"Not this road. We rode down there, and through those woods and all the way to the coastline."

"I haven't seen the coastline. Well, I did from a spot on that mountain. It looked amazing."

"It's not that far, and we've got time if you want to see it. It slays, let me tell you."

"I do want to see it. We can do that before we go back, stop at Nan's." She gestured up at the pair of dragons. "The Magee twins. Ah, Bria and . . ."

"Deaglan. We met them last night. They live near the Capital," Marco remembered. "Came in yesterday."

"Right. They're scouting, or patrolling, I guess."

As they crested the rise, Marco pulled up again. "Just wow. I know we saw stuff like this in Ireland, and that was wow. Here's another. Damn, I wish I could take a picture, you know? The round tower deal, that stone circle up there on the hill, that seriously spooky stone ruin. Big-ass one, too. The graveyard, the woods, the fields. And nobody around right now but the sheep."

From the saddle, he scanned everything. "It's eerie, right? It's like the sky shouldn't be all blue and pretty over that creepy place. It should always be heavy and gray."

"Inside, the air is."

"You've been in there?"

"No." Breen felt the tingle over her skin, like spider legs crawling. "But I can feel it. I didn't before, not like this. It's almost Samhain, so I think that's why.

"The stone dance hums. I can hear it, feel it, too. It's like a balance. Light against dark. Don't go in the ruin, Marco, and don't get too close to it today."

"Trust me, I'm convinced. Is it safe to go to the graveyard?"

"Yes. It's sanctified." She gestured to where Bollocks already sat quietly by the spread of flowers over her father's grave. "See, he knows. He'll stay close today. He's waiting by Dad's grave."

"He's a good dog," Marco managed, though his throat had already started to close with grief. "They're really beautiful, the flowers you planted there. I hate he's gone, Breen. I hate he's really gone."

"I know." When they reached the grave, she dismounted, then took the horses to secure them across the road, where they could snack on the high grass. And to give Marco a few minutes alone.

When she walked back, Marco turned to her, pressed his face to her shoulder for comfort.

"He loved you," she murmured. "You made him laugh. You made him proud whenever you played music."

"He gave me music, and he gave me so much else. He was the first grown-up I came out to."

"I didn't know that."

"It was right before he left that last time. I was afraid to tell him, afraid of what he'd think of me. After he took you back to your mom's that last time, he walked me home. You know it was a couple miles after your mom moved, and I thought we'd take the bus, but he started walking. He said how much he depended on me to help look after you while he was away."

Steadying his breath, swiping at his eyes, Marco eased back to look down at Eian's stone. "How blessed he was to have me in your life and his.

"When he looked at me, I started to cry because I could tell he knew. He put his arm around my shoulders, and kept walking. He said he'd only be disappointed in me if I felt shame for what I was, who I was. I blurted it out, like a big announcement. 'I'm gay!'"

She laughed a little, stroked Marco's cheek. "What did he say?"

"He said he hoped one day, when I was grown and ready, I'd find a man worthy of me, and not to settle for less. 'Be true to yourself, Marco,' he said, 'and anyone who tries to make your truth a lie or shameful isn't worth a single one of your thoughts.'"

Now, in turn, Breen pressed her face to Marco's shoulder as her eyes filled.

"It sounds like him. For so long I nearly forgot what he sounded like, what he was like."

Breathing out, she drew back. "Coming here, coming back, it's helped me remember."

"It meant everything to me, that walk home with him."

Sitting, Marco brushed his hands over the flowers. "It meant everything to me, Eian."

Breen sat with him. "Why didn't you ever tell me?"

"I couldn't really thank him because I got all choked up. I wanted to thank him, talk to him again when he got back. But . . ."

"He died. We didn't know he died, didn't know about Talamh. But he never came back."

"I didn't want to tell you, baby, because you were so sad. You waited and waited, got sadder and sadder. So I get to tell you now, and thank him now. It's beautiful here, and he's home, right? It's beautiful even with that place hulking over there."

"He's home, and it is beautiful. When it was first built," Breen continued, as she shifted to study the ruins, "when they first lived and worked and worshipped there, it was a holy place. A place for good works, for art and prayer and healings. It was some who lived and worked and worshipped there that changed it. Corrupted it, turned it into a place to be feared. A place of intolerance and persecution and torture."

"There's always somebody who just has to screw up the good stuff, and find other somebodies to help them do it."

"I can hear them," she whispered.

"Who?" His eyes widened as he stared at the ruin. "In there?"

"They're stirring. I can't hear clearly, but . . . Wait here."

"No way, no way. You're not going in that place."

"I'm not going in." But she got to her feet. "They'd like me to. They think I'm not ready to stand against them. They're probably right, so I'm not going in."

"Let's just stay away from it." He jumped up, took her arm.

"I can't hear clearly, not from here, and I need to. I swear I won't go a step farther than I know is safe. Stay here. Bollocks, stay with Marco. Stay here."

She broke away, hurried through the graveyard, dodging

the stones, moving closer to the ruins. And to sounds, the thrumming coming from it.

She stopped when she felt the air change—from light and fresh to heavy and dark. And she saw movement through the slits of windows, through the wide opening that had—she knew—once held thick wooden doors carved with holy symbols.

Like thin shadows shifting and sliding.

And like an echo—dim but not distant—she heard voices, the chants, the screams, the calls to dark and damned gods.

On the fresh autumn air, she smelled warm blood and the burning of human flesh.

Bells tolled. Drums beat.

Very slowly, she lifted her hand, pressed the air. And felt the pressure of what pushed back.

She started to reach for her wand, unsure if it would be enough, if she would. Then turned at the sound of a horse coming fast. She watched Tarryn ride straight to her, eyes fierce, hair flying.

"Get back from there. Foolish child, get back!"

"They can't reach me. They can't get out. Yet. Can you hear it? Can you see?"

Tarryn leaped off the horse, gripped Breen's arm. "Not another step. Aye, I can hear them, I can see them. It's too soon, and too much. This is Yseult's doing, by the gods, her and her twisted coven. Do you have anything with you?"

"A few things, just some stones and charms in my saddle-bag. My wand, my athame."

"Get what you have and make it quick. I would wish for five more, or Marg at least to make us three, but we'll make do."

She turned to her horse, opened her saddlebag. "Go now! Be quick about it. Minga, you stay there with Marco."

"What are you doing? What are you guys doing?" Marco demanded when Breen rushed by him to get to her saddle-bag. "What's going on?"

"I don't know exactly. But I'm going to do whatever she tells me. And you stay here."

After slinging her saddlebag over her shoulder, Breen ran back, and up the rise across from the ruin where Tarryn stood. Bollocks charged after her.

"Go back," Breen ordered, but the dog stuck by her side and bared his teeth at the ruin.

"No, let him stay. He's connected to you, so makes us three. We cast the circle—then he must stay in it. Nothing breaks the circle until we're done. Cup your hands."

Tarryn poured salt from a bag into Breen's cupped hands. "We ring with salt. I brought no candles. Draw them in the salt, north and west, south and east, and say the words."

They poured the salt, etched the symbols. Each spoke the words for protection from evil.

Though the sky held blue, Breen heard the rumble of thunder. She felt the wind rise, and the smell of sulfur carried on it.

Bollocks growled low in his throat.

"Protective stones, north and west, south and east, over the symbols in the salt," Tarryn told her. "Say the words."

Breen felt powers rise, felt the storm gathering in the perfect blue sky over the ruin. And as she joined Tarryn in the center of the circle, saw ghostly fingers grip the edge of the stone at what had been the doorway, as if struggling to hold on, pull out.

Screams slashed through the swirl of wind, some hot with rage, others iced with pain and fear.

"Hear us," Tarryn called out. "Know us. Fear us. We hold pity for those imprisoned by the dark, and when at last the key turns in the lock, your spirits rise free to walk into the light. We hold contempt for those who embrace the dark, and you will know the torment you brought to innocents."

A figure, insubstantial as smoke, tried to claw out of one of the slitted windows.

"Yseult and the corrupt god she worships won't free you, not this day, not any day. Hear my name! I am Tarryn of Talamh. I am mother of the taoiseach. I am daughter of the Tuatha Dé Danann, and you will not pass into the world of life and breath."

She gripped Breen's hand. "Draw out what's in you. Release it. Give your name."

Through their joined hands, Breen felt the electric jolt of power.

"I am Breen Siobhan O'Ceallaigh. I am daughter of Eian, granddaughter of Mairghread. I am blood of man and god and Sidhe and Wise. I am daughter of the Fey, and you will not pass into the world of life and breath."

With her hand clasped in Tarryn's, she laid the other on Bollocks's head as he snarled.

"A spell for a spell, a rite for a rite," she called out as the power and the words poured through her.

"From circle cast on holy ground, we lock the dark with light. No matter Yseult's charm or token, by our power her spell is broken."

Lightning flashed across the sky, shooting a bolt to scorch the ground between the rise and the ruin. Smoke, black as ink, blanketed the openings, pulsed there.

"Draw the bolts, shut the locks against whatever spirit knocks." Breen's heart hammered as she heard the *snick* and *thud* as if physical. And with Tarryn spoke the final words of the spell.

"No spell but ours can set you free. As we will, so mote it be."

Though the smoke thinned, the wind whirled still. "Close the circle." Tarryn picked up the bag of salt. "And keep the dog close. Tell him he must not go inside."

"He knows."

"Bring your athame."

With the circle closed, Tarryn walked down the rise toward the opening in the stone.

"She's skilled, and she's powerful, Yseult. And for her spell, innocent blood spilled. One day, the depths of the dark of her own power will consume her. But today, we lay one more defense against it."

She poured a line of salt, then laid her athame over her palm. "You must do this, and also to our third. Blood of power against blood of the damned."

Ignoring the smoke, the stench of it, the cries it couldn't muffle, Breen crouched and took Bollocks's paw. "It's only for a second, and I'll fix it. I'm sorry."

He didn't flinch when she drew his blood, only looked into her eyes. She drew her own, clasped hers to his paw, then rose to clasp it with Tarryn's.

"With salt we bind, with blood we sign, this spell to wind."

On either side of the opening, they drew signs against evil in their joined blood.

The cries died to murmurs, and the smoke to a haze.

"It's done, and well." Tarryn bent down to Bollocks. "What a fine one you are. As fine as ever born."

She waited while Breen healed the cut in Bollocks's paw, smiled as Breen lifted her hand and took that little pain away before healing herself.

"Marg's taught you well. We'll stop by and tell her of this, and get word to Keegan." She walked up the rise again as she spoke to gather what she'd left there. "Odran will be displeased with Yseult when he learns her plans failed."

"They would have come out tomorrow—on Samhain. Not like simply spirits or wraiths, but reanimated. She would have to sacrifice a fawn, a lamb, and a child—human or Fey—to work that spell. And even then . . ."

Tarryn nodded. "A great draw of power needed, and for one night's work."

"So they could attack the valley while the Pious who turned opened the doors to Odran's followers in the south.

Ambushing on two fronts, all while they believed we didn't have a clue."

"Good tactics," Tarryn said simply while they walked back to Marco and Minga and the horses. "But we have a great deal more than a clue." She paused by Eian's grave. "He would be proud of you."

Then she reached out her hands, one to Minga, one to Marco. "Well now, that's more than enough excitement for one pretty afternoon, isn't it then?"

"They were trying to get out," Marco managed. "Minga said you had to break a spell and cast a new one to keep them inside."

"So we did."

"And it's hardly a wonder you were both pulled here on this day, at this time," Minga added. "The work you did spared lives. And you." She leaned over to stroke Bollocks. "What a bright light you are. Do you want to send a falcon to Keegan?"

"I think we don't risk the writing. I'll speak to him directly through the mirror." She mounted and sat a moment studying the ruin. "Thinking this is done, they'll concentrate their attack on the south, but still, best to post guards here.

"Well, I'm after a strong gallop to blow that stench out of my nose," Tarryn continued, "I'll tell you that for certain. And we'll hope for something stronger than tea from Marg."

After his conversation with his mother, Keegan paced the room he currently shared with Mahon. He'd arrived before first light at the southern barracks with only a handful knowing he'd come.

"They dealt with it," Mahon reminded him. "Do you have any reason to doubt otherwise?"

"I haven't, no. If my mother says they have it in hand, they do. But it tells me, plainly, they intended to push for more than a southern attack, and have more followers. They would raise an army of Undead in the valley."

"Where they believe you are, and your mother—the tao-iseach and his strong hand. Where they might hope to find Breen during the sabbat ceremonies."

"Would they risk cutting her down? Corporeal spirits such as this have no restraint, no strategies. They only seek blood."

Frustration poured out of him as he paced and calculated, calculated and paced.

"They must have at least one or two of Odran's closer than we thought. He needs her alive, Mahon. Dead she's of no use to him, and his line through her ends. Someone close enough to lure her away or abduct her during the confusion, I'm thinking."

"There'll be no confusion now. But aye, you've the right of it. And we'll need to root out whoever's been planted close to home."

"And here."

Keegan started to sit, couldn't. The room boasted a single window, but he couldn't make use of it without risking being seen.

"Toric, as we both suspected, is surely the leader of this blood cult here. Ah, he speaks in a quiet voice, keeps his head bowed, wears his simple white robes, but he reeks of ambition."

Mahon poured them both ale. "Sit, by the gods, brother, before you wear me out. I've spoken to him about trading with those who train here and guard the south. Very usual and diplomatic, of course, while letting it be known I leave for my son's birthday tomorrow."

"We've given him his freedom to worship as we must, as is just. And he twists that freedom to take that choice from others, and take lives with it."

From a cautious distance, Keegan stared out the window.

"He won't know the balmy breeze from the sea for much longer."

"What I've yet to tell you, as the news came from the valley before I could, he plans a ritual sacrifice to Odran on Samhain."

Keegan whipped around. "He would dare?"

"He would. They've stolen a child, a little girl, have her under a sleeping spell, locked in the bowels of the round tower. They plan to offer her up to Odran once his soldiers come through. To help keep the portal open. She's to be burned at the stake in the last hour of Samhain."

"And this is what they deem worship." Keegan slammed his tankard down, shoved up again. "How did you come by this?"

"Two of ours, elves, slipped in and, one with the stone walls, heard clearly. I can tell you, with confidence, Toric has no more than a score with him."

"There'll be others across Talamh. Others here in the south as well who don't wear the robes. How many guard the girl?"

"None." Mahon shook his head. "Such is their arrogance— or what they call faith. She sleeps and deep, and is locked away."

"Let's be sure of that. We'll send elves back in to watch over her until tomorrow, when we'll get her to safety. To take her out now reveals too much. Toric and those of Odran's who live through the night will be taken to the Capital for the Judgment."

"They pray. I heard their chanting prayers for peace and bounty when I spoke with Toric. What makes them think burning young girls and slaughtering Fey is the way to peace?"

"Their peace means power over all. They won't have it. I need the air."

"Keegan—"

"And I want to walk through the village, the markets, pay

a visit to the Prayer House." So saying, Keegan covered his face with his hands.

His hair went gray and sparse, his face lined, sagging at the jowls. On his chin grew a small, pointed beard.

Amused, Mahon gestured with his ale. "Your face will work right enough, but there's the rest of you."

"Ah, so there is."

His body thinned to gaunt; his shoulders stooped. He wore roped sandals, a cloth cap, patched trousers, and an aged tunic. His sword became a crooked cane.

"All right, Old Father, we'll get some air. I'll say, should anyone trouble to ask, you're an old friend of my family, newly arrived in the south for the sea air."

Keegan rubbed a hand at his throat so his voice came out in a wispy croak. "Sean, it is. A holy man and hermit who's come to spend his final days by the southern seas."

He had to remember to slow and shorten his gait as Mahon walked with him through the village known for its pretty fruit and fresh fish. Those who bartered had a cheerful air. Many came south, he knew, for holidays.

To take to the water or sail boats over it, to watch their young ones play in the deep gold sand of the beach.

They came, he thought, without knowing a battle would rage in little more than a day.

There could be no warning, or the dark would skulk back to its hole. So he could only protect, defend. And fight to bring those who invited that dark to justice.

He studied the roll of the sea, as lovely as any he'd seen in any world. He heard children laughing, watched lovers stroll along the surf, smelled the sea and the fish and sweets fresh baked.

The world, his world, was a bright and peaceful place, full of joy and plenty. And even now a young girl slept, bespelled so she could be sacrificed to one who wanted dark and blood.

"Do you want to rest, Old Father?"

"I have a thirst, boy, but I would pay respects to the Pious before I slake it. I would add a prayer to theirs for the peace of Talamh and all the worlds."

Keegan hobbled his way from the village proper and its markets, from the balm of the sea air, away from the near woods to where the tower and the Prayer House stood on a rise.

There, they'd pledged to devote themselves to the needs of any who came, to spend their lives in prayer and good works while they rose over the village, the sea, the farms, the boats.

Eian, and the taoiseach before him, and Marg, and the tao-iseach before her, and all for more than six hundred years had honored that pledge. They'd given the Pious who had no part in the persecutions, and those after them who put on the robes, this place in the south to worship in peace.

And he, Keegan thought, would be the one to end that peace.

He climbed, windily, up the steps in the hill even as his eyes—sharp behind the clouds of great age he'd added to them—scanned robed figures who worked gardens or walked with hands clasped under the sleeves of their robes.

He thought of the girl sleeping, and the family who must even now be searching for her. He thought of the tokens and gifts of thanks left on the doorstep of the Prayer House every day.

And the deceit that lived in hearts hiding behind benevolence and piety.

When he stepped inside the nave, he felt the cold, sharp finger of dread scrape down his spine. He'd felt that, and the tightening in his chest, when he'd stepped into the ruins in the valley.

So here, too, he thought, spirits walked among the living. Here, too, blood had been spilled in secret and for dark purpose. The honored dead lay under carved stone slabs on the floor or entombed in chests. Niches held jars of sacred oils, blessed water, holy herbs. Though sunlight streamed through the stained-glass images in the arched windows, candles flickered. Some to bring the light, some for penance or blessings.

Their scent and the thin smoke of incense drifted through the air like the chanting song of the Pious who walked the colonnade in prayer.

He moved slowly, as an old man would, into the altar room where a few robed figures knelt in private, silent prayer.

The carving on the polished stone offered welcome to any in need.

And there, he heard as clearly as he heard the melodious voices chanting for peace, pledging their lives to good works, the cries of the sacrificed.

The goat, the lamb, the fawn, the child.

And through the scent of sweet oils and candles, he caught the stench of black magicks.

Inside, his blood burned as he kept his head bowed as if in reverence. The hand that gripped the cane longed to break the illusion and strike.

"I have waited too long to make this pilgrimage."

"You're here now, Old Father."

Nodding, Keegan turned, started toward an archway. Through it, a passageway opened to a library where three sat at a long table busily writing histories, prayers, songs. Another, as old as Keegan's illusion, dozed by the fire, his soft snores and the scratching of quills the only sounds in the room.

He passed other rooms where men and boys wove baskets and blankets, and others for the carving of wood, the polishing of stone.

The kitchens and eating areas, he recalled, spread on the other side, with some small chambers for those assigned to work in them.

He paused by the stone stairs circling up. Contemplation rooms and chambers, he recalled. He'd like a look at them now, to see how Toric and the other hierarchy lived since he'd visited last.

A full year, he remembered. Aye, he'd waited too long.

A boy of perhaps fourteen hurried down those steps, a basket of dirty linens in his arms. His hair had yet to be shorn close as ordained while taking full vows, and his robe stopped just past his knobby knees.

A novice, and a servant, Keegan thought.

His eyes widened in alarm.

"Blessings on you, pure of heart."

Keegan smiled, returned the traditional Pious greeting. "And on you and yours."

"You may not pass here, good sir. Only the Pious and those who tend their earthly needs may go up."

"Merely resting my old bones a moment. They are many, many years beyond the spry of yours, lad."

"Will I fetch you a chair, or a cup of water?"

"You are kind." Keegan laid a hand on the boy's shoulder. He didn't have what Harken did, but trusted when he felt only innocence.

"You're blessed by a holy man, boy, of great age and wisdom." Mahon kept his tone stern, but not sharp. "Fetch Toric so he can give the pilgrim a proper welcome."

"My thanks, Old Father, for the blessing." The boy raced off without another word.

Satisfied, Keegan continued down the passageway, through a room of small altars and ancient icons, and into the sun-washed colonnade.

In the center stood a dolmen with a ring of stone around it. The grass that spread from there shined green to the stone walls and columns. Pious in their white robes, their hair cropped close to the skull, slowly circled the stone pathway while they sang.

They would do so, he knew, for two hours when the sun broke, two more at midday, and yet two more at eventide.

While archways and doors ringed the area, it spread open to the elements.

Now the sun fell kindly, but when it burned and glared, with the rains and winds swept, they would still walk and sing in prayers for peace and pure hearts.

How many, he wondered, who walked with their hands humbly tucked in their sleeves would take part in the human sacrifice, in the slaughter? How many more who knew or suspected held their silence?

The slap of sandals on stone had Keegan turning slowly.

He recognized Toric, and noted the Pious leader had added a few pounds to his round body. His head, round as well, was topped with the skullcap of his rank.

Over his pale blue eyes his gray eyebrows formed sharp vees. He wore no beard, as such things constituted the vanity the cult eschewed, and his double chins wobbled.

Keegan doubted he observed the weekly day of fasting.

"Mahon. I wasn't informed you'd graced us with another visit. Old Father, you are both welcome. Blessings on you, pure of heart."

"And on you and yours." Keegan laid a hand on his heart and leaned on his cane. "My thanks, brother, for making me welcome."

"Old Father is a friend to my family. A holy man who has made pilgrimage while spreading good works and good words across Talamh."

"Please, please, come and sit." Gesturing, Toric led them through another archway and to stone benches, a quiet fire. There he rang a small bell.

Another boy—females weren't permitted inside the Prayer House, even as servants—scurried in.

"Fruit and wine for our visitors. Do you seek our refuge, Old Father?"

"How kind." Keegan sat, let out a deep and weary breath.

"Ah, the old bones do creak! The young one here"—he patted Mahon's knee—"has offered me a cot for the night."

"I will see you safely housed, Old Father," Mahon promised.

"My needs are few." Keegan held up a hand. "But I fear my days of making my home in a cave in the hills are done."

"How many years have you, Old Father?"

"I count one hundred and sixty, and am coming to the end of this cycle. I journey here for the sea air and the nearness of those of you who live your lives in faith and prayer."

The boy came back with a jug of water and cups, a bowl of fruit.

"Oranges!" Keegan filled his voice with pleasure. "You have Sidhe among your faithful."

"A few. And more who bring offerings from below." Toric studied Keegan closely as the boy poured water in the cups. "One hundred and sixty is a ripe age, but I trust you'll have many more years."

"It is not to be. My thanks." Keegan accepted the cup, drank slowly. "Death is creeping close now, and I have seen my last summer. I do not fear it, as I have lived, always, in faith that what we end here only begins another plane. One of brighter light and deeper faith. I am ready when the gods call me."

"Until that day, you are welcome here, Old Father. I know Mahon returns to his homeplace tomorrow. You would honor us by spending the time left to you on this plane in faith and prayer with us. I will arrange a chamber for you."

Keegan bowed his head. "Your kindness to this pilgrim brings blessings on you."

When they left, Keegan leaned on Mahon, and spoke only of the sea and the hills and the forest.

The minute they were in Mahon's chamber, Keegan shook off the illusion. "Gods, I come to know the old fathers and mothers are the most courageous of us simply for putting their feet on the floor of a morning."

He dropped down in a chair, stretched out his legs. And smiled. "Harken could have gotten every thought, but I found more than enough. They've already sacrificed, and more than once these last months, on the main altar. And Toric plans to slit my throat tomorrow, and offer the blood of a holy man near the end of this cycle of life to Odran, and to his faithful."

"Bloody hell."

"And that's where he'll spend his own cycle, for I've other plans."

# CHAPTER TWELVE

That evening, while Keegan laid out his plans, Breen and Marco spent an hour on Zoom with Sally and Derrick. As expected, she found them both fully geared up for Halloween.

"We're going as Morticia and Gomez," Sally told them.

"Cara Mia!" Derrick ran kisses up his husband's arm to make him laugh.

"We want pictures!" Marco insisted. "And of the club. I'm a hundred percent you've gone wild there."

"Right through with *The Addams Family* theme. Geo's going as Uncle Fester. What about you?"

"I'm getting my cowboy on," Marco decided on the spur of the moment.

"Witch." Easy enough, Breen decided. "A good witch."

"Sexy witch," Sally added. "We want pictures, too. This is the first Halloween we haven't had you here for—has to be close to ten years."

How the hell were they going to get pictures? Breen wondered while Marco chattered on. She'd think of something.

"I know you have to get to the club," she said as the hour

wound up. "We want you to know we're going on a little trip—research—and we'll have spotty internet. Don't worry if you don't hear from us for a few days."

It wasn't exactly lying—and what choice did they have?

But she carried the guilt of it as she carefully sliced butternut squash for Marco's roasted squash dippers.

"Shoulda known they'd want pictures," he said as he prepped chicken breasts for the main. "Where the hell are we going to get costumes?"

"They won't expect anything elaborate." When he just looked at her, she laughed. "Okay, they'll at least expect clever. We'll put something together tonight, do a couple selfies."

"I said 'cowboy.' Can't be a cowboy without a cowboy hat."

She considered while he chopped garlic. "You've got a ball cap."

"No self-respecting cowboy wears a ball cap, girl. Every kind of wrong there."

"I can do an illusion. I can do that. Pretty sure. Like . . ."

She turned to him, put the image in her head, then walked over, ran her hands over him.

He giggled. "No fair tickling. I've got a knife!"

"Pearl-handled six-shooter—toy," she added quickly.

He looked down; his jaw dropped.

"I know you, and you're the 'Rhinestone Cowboy' type."

His shirt glittered with them in a rainbow of colors. She'd changed his belt to a bright red holster, added chaps to his jeans, and turned his high-tops into red cowboy boots with more rhinestones on the pointed toes.

"I gotta get a full load of me!"

"Get the ball cap," she called after him. "And mine, too."

She thought over her own, tried a black dress with a flowing handkerchief hem. Tall, spike-heeled boots.

"I look badass!" He rushed back in, stopped, narrowed his eyes at her. "Vee down that neckline, girl. And try one of those waist-cinchers, laces in the front. A red one. Better, better."

He circled her as she worked. "I want to see red lips, and smoky eyes. Go over-the-top. It's a costume."

He ran his fingers through her hair, fussed until it met his level of witch-wild.

Then he put his ball cap on. "Ten-gallon me, partner."

She gave him a rhinestone band to go with it before putting on her own cap and turning it into a classic witch hat.

"Smaller," he told her, then tipped it off-center for flirty.

Into it now, Breen grabbed a dish towel, laid it over Bollocks, and turned it into a flowing cape.

"Super Bollocks!"

While Marco laughed, Morena walked in the door. "What's all this then?"

"Trick-or-treat!" Marco struck his best cowboy pose. "I'm the Marco Kid."

"I saw cowboys in your west. They didn't shine so bright as you."

"Have you met my friends, Super Bollocks and the Good Witch Breen?"

"I'll tell you, if you wear that dress to the Welcome at the Capital, you won't sit out a dance. Did you bring all that from Philadelphia?"

"It's illusions. Our friends asked for pictures, and we had to think of something."

"I can take them, as I know how to do it, then you'll pour me some wine so I can tell you news."

"Is anything wrong?"

"It's not, and Mahon and Keegan are home. Brian sent his best to you, Marco."

"Aw."

They spent ten minutes posing, mugging, together and separately, before Breen poured wine all around.

"What's the news— Wait."

She broke the illusions and took off her ball cap.

"I really liked that shirt. Anyway, I'm making rosemary chicken in white wine. You in?"

"Who would say no?" Morena wondered. "I'm to remind you to pack, and sensibly. You're to leave from the farm the day after Samhain, an hour after daybreak."

"I wish you'd go," Breen said.

"I'm needed here for now, but I hope you'll take my love to my family and give it to them for me when you meet them. I'll go for a short visit in a week or two."

"So first," she began, "the taoiseach and Mahon bring back news they believe there's someone—perhaps more than one—here in the valley keeping watch for Odran or the Pious, or both."

"Like a spy?" Marco sautéed garlic in a skillet.

"So to speak. Someone we likely know as neighbor knows neighbor here. And more, they both agree it's Toric in the south plotting and planning the attack."

"Who's Toric?" Breen asked.

"He'd be First Brother of the Pious. That's what they call the one in charge—though they say the gods are and so on. They've taken a little girl, and have her spell sleeping, locked away in their round tower. They mean to sacrifice her tomorrow night."

"Do what?" Stunned, Marco stared. "A kid?"

"They didn't leave her there."

"Wait, wait." Morena tossed up her hands. "They know what they're about. No harm will come to her, and they have elves watching over her."

Since the two of them also seemed to know what they were about, Morena boosted herself to sit on the counter and watched them do it.

"Keegan did his own illusion, and walked right into the Prayer House as an old holy man. And as Mahon had already pointed fingers at Toric, Keegan read him, as best he could, while they talked. The Old Father's invited to spend his final days with the Pious. And Toric plans for those days to end tomorrow night, along with the girl, as sacrifice."

"But he's here, so—"

"Oh, he'll be going back, right enough, and as the Old Father, walking right into what Toric thinks is his death. But Toric will be in for what you'd say is a different turn of events."

She boosted herself off the counter. "I'm not much of a one for warring. But I think of what Toric and those like him will do, have done, what those like him did all those years back, before any of us living now were born. How they tortured and killed in the name of their twisted faith. I would lift a sword to right that wrong."

She shook her head, poured herself more wine. "The girl they have, her name is Alanis, Keegan learned, and her family is half-mad searching for her, fearing she's lost or hurt."

"And he couldn't tell them," Breen murmured. "He couldn't because they might not hold back another day and we'd lose the advantage."

"It weighs on him, I'll tell you that. And I'll tell you you'll be seeing more than the shops and craftsmen, the crowds and the dancing at the Welcome. You'll see justice done at the Capital when Keegan sits in the Chair of Justice and brings down his staff on the likes of Toric."

It dragged at her mind, her heart, so Breen's sleep came in patches. When she gave up before sunrise, she found herself unable to escape into the work. Instead, she walked down to the bay, sat, watched Bollocks's joyful splashing while the sun rose.

It bloomed pink in the east, a shimmering line over the hills that spread, spread, spread with hints of gold, streaks of scarlet.

Thin columns of mist twined toward the light from the surface of the water, caught glints, tiny sparks of silver that turned the world into a gauzy curtain. The water shooting up from the dog's happy swim tossed tiny jewels over the curtain.

And the rising sun breathed the night's shadows away.

When he came out of the water, Bollocks sat beside her, and in the quiet, watched with her as the morning came into full bloom.

He tapped his tail when Marco walked down to them, coffee cups steaming in both hands.

But she didn't hear him.

"Saw you down here, so I brought coffee. What a sight." He held out her mug, then saw her eyes. "Hey, girl."

"Before the sun rises again, before the light breaks as day follows night, death comes. Blood flies, and the storm of battle rips the air. As the veil thins on this Samhain, even the dead weep for innocence lost. But the dragon flies, and its fire purges clean. Innocence lost and innocence saved, and the supplicants of the fallen god will meet their fate."

When she drew her knees up, rested her forehead on them, Marco sat beside her, rubbed her back as Bollocks leaned against her updrawn legs.

"I've tried pushing it away, but I know I have to see it. I have to watch it. Tonight."

"You aren't saying you're going down there?"

"No, I don't have to be there to watch. I'd just add more risk if I went. Marco, I feel like there's something I need to find or be or have, that I just can't see yet. Can't reach yet. And I don't know what it's going to mean if I do see it, do reach it."

She lifted her head, leaned it on Marco's shoulder as she put an arm around the dog. "But I do know that in a few more hours people will risk their lives, and some will give them, to protect the rest of us. And I know, in Talamh, a little boy's probably awake right now, so happy, so excited because to-day's his birthday. I know that matters."

"It all matters, Breen." He picked up the coffee he'd set down, pushed the mug into her hand. "That's why there's al-ways some son of a bitch trying to fuck it up."

She let out a half laugh. "Truer words. Let's sit here with this wonderful dog, drink our coffee, and look at all this beauty. It matters."

The wind blew sharp in the valley, flattening the tall grasses this way then that and sending leaves twirling. But the sun pushed through clouds to spread widening spots of blue.

At the farm, in the paddock, Harken walked beside his nephew as Finian rode around and around on a pretty buck-skin with a braided mane. His little brother sat on Keegan's shoulders waving his arms in the air and hooting approval while his parents stood, arms around each other's waists, and watched.

His grandmother perched on the paddock fence like a young girl, her hair blowing free in the wind.

"Look at me! Look at me!" Finian shouted when he saw the newcomers. "Harken gave me my own horse, and I named him Stoirm. Keegan had a saddle made just for me. It even has my name on it. I can ride every day."

"In the paddock, my boy," his mother warned him. "Until I say different."

Kavan leaned down, arms outstretched toward Breen. Taking him, she gave him a little bounce before she set him on her hip so he could play with her hair.

"*Lá breithe shona duit*. And if I mangled that, happy birthday."

"You did well enough," Keegan told her.

"*Míle buíochas!*" Finian called back.

"He thanks you," Keegan translated.

"I actually knew that one, and a little more. My father taught me some of the basics. I'd forgotten. Some's come back to me."

"Ma says the more tongues you speak the more places you'll go." Obviously in love, Finian bent forward to lay his cheek on his horse's neck. "I'm going to learn lots of them like Keegan so I can go many places."

His smile went coy as he spotted the little box Marco carried, the bag in Breen's hand. "Did you bring gifts for me?"

"A gift's best offered, not asked for."

Finian just smiled at his father. "I just wondered."

"I don't think mine can compete with a horse or a saddle with your name on it." Marco held up the box. "But I brought you something of mine I thought you might like."

"Giving something of yours to me makes the gift very portent—important," he corrected.

"Now, that's well said, and as true as true can be. Off the horse now," Aisling told him, "and come accept your important gift."

Harken started to lift him down, but Finian shook his head. "I can do it. I can."

He swung his leg over, shimmied down, and leaped the rest of the way.

"And who will tend this fine horse of yours?" Mahon asked him as Finian climbed through the fence.

"I will, Da. I promise I'll take good care of him always."

"I know you will. Let's see what Marco's got for you."

Finian opened the box to a smaller box inside. The idea made him laugh as he worked out how to open the lid on the gift.

"It shines! It's a— It has a word, but I don't know it."

"Harmonica. It was a gift to me from Breen's dad when I was just a little older than you."

Finian let out a gasp. "A gift from the taoiseach! But you have to keep it."

"I had this strong feeling he wanted me to give it to you. It was the first instrument he taught me to play."

"This is a grand gift indeed, Fin." Tarryn walked over to them. "It has history and heart as well as music."

"A thousand thanks. Will you play it so I can hear?"

Marco took it, played a quick riff.

"It sounds happy."

"It can sound happy, or sad." He played it mournful. "Or scary!" After demonstrating, Marco handed it back. "Try it. Hold it like this."

He coached him through the first notes that had Kavan bouncing and clapping.

Marco grinned up at Aisling. "Apologies in advance for a lot of noise."

"Not a'tall! Music is always welcome."

"Will you teach me to play songs on it?"

"I was hoping you'd ask. We'll work on that. You can keep it in your pocket—that's the handy thing about a harmonica—and play it anytime you want."

Rising, he plucked Kavan off Breen's hip. "Your turn."

"I hope you like it."

After sliding the harmonica into his pocket, Finian opened the bag, peeked in. "A book! I like stories. Ma or Da reads or tells us stories before bed every night."

He pulled it out, puzzled over the hand-drawn (with Morena's help) cover.

"This is my name. I can read my name, and a little more. It says Finian the something and something."

"*Finian the Brave and True*."

"This word is *by*, and the next has the *brr* sound like *brave*."

"It's my name. Breen Kelly."

He looked up at her with stunned eyes. "You wrote a story for me?"

"For you, and about you. An adventure I imagined for you."

"I can't read all the words. Will you read it for me?"

"Absolutely."

"Inside, I'm thinking, out of this wind. We'll have some tea," Tarryn added. "Come, my birthday lad." She hauled him up. "We'll have tea and cake and hear of Finian's tale."

Keegan touched her arm before Breen could follow the others. "That was a very fine gift. He'll never forget it."

"Every child deserves a bright birthday, no matter what else is happening. Morena told us what you learned, and what you plan to do. Are you sure that girl's safe?"

"She is, and will be. It's a blessing she'll sleep through it, and not be frightened." He looked south. "And in a few hours, it's done. But for now, you're right. The boy deserves a bright day. And I'd like to hear his story."

She read the story, then read it again when Marg arrived with her gift and good wishes. Instead of a day of practice and training, she took a ride with Morena and Marco with the hawk circling overhead.

And Marco cringing whenever Amish landed on Morena's arm.

"When we can," Breen began, "I'd love to go hawking again. You're excused," she said to Marco.

"Damn right."

"We'll take Amish on a hunt when you're back from the Capital." Morena looked up, followed the hawk. And the glide of dragons, the sweep of faeries. "Keeping a close eye this day. I'll be more than glad when it's tomorrow. As will Harken. It's hard for him to know his brothers will be in the thick, and he's here in the valley. But he's needed here, to keep watch on Aisling and the boys—and don't ever tell her I said such a thing."

"I won't. He's here to watch over me, too, isn't he?"

"I never said such a thing, but of course."

"And are you watching over me?"

Morena shifted in the saddle. "In my way. But enough of this. I'm saying you'll pay attention to things at the Capital. I'll want all the news—the gossip, as there's always gossip. And I don't mind hearing of the fashions, as I'll have to consider them when I visit myself."

"I'm your man on that." Marco held up a hand. "This is Marco Olsen reporting for Capital Fashion News."

Laughing, Morena reached over and swatted him. "You're a one, you are."

It was all so normal, Breen thought, or as normal as her normal had become. The day passed as days did—a quick shower in the late afternoon that only served to make the green shine. Sheep grazed on the hills, cows in the fields.

She saw children out playing, as Samhain gave them a holiday from school. Farmers worked the fields, bringing in harvest to store away for the winter to come or loaded into wagons for bartering.

They would light bonfires on the beaches that night, and she would join in for her first Samhain.

And she thought of the spirits trapped inside the stone ruin, some hungry to break free and taste blood. Some desperate to find release in the light at last.

She and Marco had the evening meal with Marg before sunset, then gathered what they needed to take to the bay.

"Some," Marg explained as she mounted her mare, "will have their own circle, make their own offerings at their homes, in their hills. All and any are welcome to join ours. Seven are chosen to make the coven, to cast the circle, to complete the ceremony, but all are part of the whole. And there will be seven from each tribe represented."

"How are they chosen?"

"The Sidhe choose theirs, the Weres theirs, and so on. For the Wise who will cast the circle, in most times Keegan would lead—as he is taoiseach, of the Wise, and comes from the valley."

"But he's already gone to the south."

"Aye, and there will be some who wonder why he isn't here. We will say to those who do he's taking part at the Capital. In his place, Tarryn has chosen. She will serve, as will Harken and Aisling, as I will, as will young Declan, who's reached his thirteenth year, and Old Padric, who has reached his century mark, as you will serve."

"Me? But, Nan, I've never—"

"Nor has young Declan. All seven chosen drew their first breath in the valley."

"If I do something wrong—"

"Why do you do that?" Marco demanded. "You're not going to screw up, so stop it. Girl, I've watched you since all this started. And I'm saying you've got more going than you did when I first fell through the rabbit hole. Just that fun shit you did last night with the costumes. Man, you didn't even really think about it. Just, like, abracadabra."

"That was just . . ." Something she'd never done before, Breen realized.

"Marco knows his friend, and I know my granddaughter. He's the right of it, and I've seen the same. Your power grows, and your memories clear. One, I think, connects to the other. This is a solemn night, *mo stór*, but a joyful one as well."

She paused to gesture. "The fires are laid, the altar set, and the Fey gather. As do those from the outside who join us, and are welcome."

And while the balefire burned, Breen thought, the battle would rage in the south. She wouldn't make a mistake, she vowed as they walked the horses toward the beach. And she would open herself and send whatever she had, whatever she could, to those who fought back the dark.

# CHAPTER THIRTEEN

Breen knew some of the faces, some of the names from the ceilidh. Marco, of course, knew more, so she didn't worry about having someone explain the rite to him, walk him through it as she'd planned to do.

In this rite, in this way, her grandmother had told her, any who wished could leave an offering at the altar. A token, an image of an ancestor, food, wine, flowers. All this brought and left before the casting of the circle, before the words were spoken, before the lighting of the fire.

She saw now many had left those offerings, and more laid others. Beside the drawing Marg placed of Eian, Breen laid blooms picked from flowers she'd planted herself. And gave Marco's hand a squeeze as he placed a small boule of bread beside them.

"It's good," he told her. "I didn't know what I'd think of all this, but it's . . . it's personal and respectful. It's good."

He gave her a kiss on the cheek before he moved away.

Personal, Breen thought. Yes, it felt very personal. The images, the tokens, the food, the flowers, they all felt very personal.

She stepped back to wait until she was called, turned when she heard a man ask about the taoiseach.

Before she could answer, the girl beside him rolled her eyes as it seemed girls did in all worlds.

"I told you, Uncle, he's observing Samhain in the Capital."

"He should be here. This is his place."

"All of Talamh is his place," Breen heard herself say. Surprised at herself, she offered a smile to soften the sharpness that had cut through her words.

"What do you know? Who are you to say? You lived your life in the world of man."

"Uncle! Your pardon. My uncle traveled from the north only a few weeks ago to stay with us through Samhain. He hoped to see the taoiseach lead the ritual."

Behind his back, the girl mimed drinking with another eye roll.

Breen struggled not to laugh, tried for sympathetic. "Of course you're disappointed. I hope—"

"You'll know disappointment," he muttered.

Annoyed, she reached out for his arm as he turned. "I'm sure if you—"

She felt it. It poured off him, and for an instant twisted inside her like a snake.

Such hate, such anger. And through it, such dark purpose.

Beside her, Bollocks growled.

"You would lay hands on me, you of tainted blood?"

"Yes."

With his eyes glinting, he started to shove her. She blocked, and swept his legs out from under him in a move that shocked her as much as him.

Bollocks planted his front paws on the man's chest. Snarled.

"Stay down," she ordered as people began to move in. "Harken. I need Harken."

"I'm here. I'm here. What's all this now?" Though he

moved fast, his tone came easy as a stroll. "Has someone had a few too many pints before a solemn rite? Ah well, it happens," he added as he crouched down and patted the dog aside.

"I'm sorry! I'll get my parents." The girl raced off with elf speed.

"I think he's unwell." Breen held the man down with will, murmured into Harken's ear, "A spy. I think—I feel. If I'm wrong—"

Harken merely smiled and laid a hand on the man's shoulder. And because he had his other on Breen's, she felt Harken's quick rage. But his smile never dimmed.

"Sleep," he murmured, and the man went limp. "Passed out, is all. Now, now, have a heart and move back so you don't swallow all his air. We'll just cart him out of the way, let him sleep it off."

"Ah gods, Lordan." The woman who raced back with the girl covered her face. "My father's brother, and a black sheep as ever was. Sure I'm sorry for the trouble. We'll haul him home."

"No need," Harken assured her. "We'll just let him sleep." He signaled to another man to help him carry the unconscious man well away from the altar.

"Out he goes in the morning, kin or no," the woman said. "Your pardon, Breen Siobhan, for his rudeness. My girl said he insulted you."

"No harm done."

She glanced back, saw two men now stood on either side of Lordan from the north.

Harken drew her aside when he came back. "You weren't wrong, and he may not be the only, so we'll keep it as a drunk passed out until it's done. And he'll be taken to the Capital for judgment. Come now, and we're seven."

Before she joined him, she bent down, kissed Bollocks's nose. "What a good dog you are. Go stay with Marco. Right over there with Finola and Seamus and the children. Stay with them."

Her heart tripped a little as she went to stand beside Marg.

She watched others merge. Sidhe, Elfin, Were, Troll, and in the bay, seven Mers formed their ring.

Tarryn lifted her hands, palms up.

"The wheel turns, and the old year gives way. We come to welcome the new. On Samhain, we honor those who have left this world, and welcome them back."

"Blessed be," Breen answered with all the rest.

Each lifted their ritual sword and spoke the words as they walked around the altar three times.

"We cast this circle with sword, with power, with the energy from the Mother who is Earth."

As they called the Quarters, the Guardians of the East, South, West, North, Breen felt it rise in her, and spread, and bloom. The light that was power, the power that was a gift.

As Marg called to the god of the underworld, the candle flames speared high and straight toward the deepening sky.

Inside herself, outside herself, Breen heard her own call to the goddess. "Great Lady, Mistress of the Moons, give us your blessing. Grant us wisdom, grant us courage to face what comes. We are your children, sons and daughters. Help us reach through the thinning veil to those loved and lost. Blessed be."

On the altar fire sparked; smoke rose.

When she lifted her arms like the others drawing down the moons, asking for the light to shine into their spirit, she heard her father, heard him as clearly as if he stood beside her.

*You're my heart, my hope, my abiding love. You are every-thing to me, then, now, always. Be strong, Breen Siobhan, and face what comes, what I failed to spare you from facing.*

With her father's voice inside her, with the others beside

her, Breen lit the Samhain fire. She took a candle, gave it her breath, its flame.

For you, Da, she thought as she placed it in the ground.

"Here is the fire," Tarryn called out. "Here is the light. Here," she said, laying a hand on Aisling, "is the promise of new life."

"Lord and Lady, god and goddess, we bring the bread, we bring the wine to honor you and those who came before." Aisling lifted the chalice, the bread. "Blessed be."

In silence, in reverence, Aisling passed the bread, the wine, took her own, and left the rest for the ancestors.

"We thank the Great Mother for her blessing," Harken said. "Ask her for strength in both darkness and light."

"Blessed be."

"We thank the Lord of the Sun for his blessing," Declan said. "Ask him for strength in both darkness and light."

"Blessed be."

They called to the Quarters to give thanks, then closed the circle.

"Open now this circle, but broken never." Tarryn crossed her hands over her heart. "We stand in hope, in light, in love. We hold the memories of those who have left us in hope, in light, in love. Blessings on you, children of the Fey, and all who stand with you."

Marg laid a hand on Breen's cheek. "You felt him, as I did."

"I heard him, Nan."

"As I did. Such a strong spirit, he is. Such love he has for you." Now she kissed Breen's cheeks, one, then the other. "We were blessed this night. Now, in Fey tradition, we share treats with the children."

"But in the south—it's starting, must be—in the south."

"We have faith."

They needed more than faith, Breen thought. Her father had said strength—to have strength to face what he died fighting.

So she would use her strength and face it. And look.

Even as the children gobbled sugar biscuits and candied fruit, she stepped to the Samhain fire.

Drawing up her power, she looked deep into the flames.

Other fires burned on the beaches in the south as they burned here. And in the hills, as here. In the fields and door-yards.

Circles cast, rings of seven.

Harken stepped beside her.

"I only see the rite, and peace. Maybe the vision was wrong. I was wrong."

He took her hand, and the jolt of new power shot through her.

"We'll watch. And if the vision proves true, send our light."

Marg took her other hand, and more gathered.

"I can't see anything but a big fire," Marco said from behind her.

"Do you want to see?" Harken asked him.

"I . . . Yeah. I've got friends there. I don't have anything to send, but—"

"Oh, there's light in you, brother. As in all living things. A hand on Breen's shoulder, and one on mine. We'll show you what we see."

With hope, with strength, and with faith, those gathered around the fire saw all.

Deep in the round tower, one of the Pious unlocked the door of the small cell where a child slept. As he approached the girl, three elves slid out of the stone walls.

One held a knife, and her hand trembled with the wish to use the blade. Instead, she used the hilt to knock the robed man to the floor.

"Bind him up, lock him in. He'll face his judgment. Then take your places for the battle that comes."

She sheathed the knife, slid her arms under the child to lift her. "I have you, *bláth beag*," she whispered, and cuddling the child close, shot out of the cell in a blur.

On the rise above the beach while the elf whisked the girl to safety, Old Father stood.

"So many Samhains I have known in this life. How bright the ritual fire shines against the dark of the sky and sea." He turned to Toric with a quiet smile. "I understand your faith doesn't observe this night, or ask to reunite so briefly with loved ones lost."

"We do not question the gods who ended those lives, nor wish to disturb the peace or punishment given them in the next. We thank you for honoring our faith while you stay with us."

"All faith that lifts up good works, that harms none and accepts others should be honored." Keegan, as Old Father, leaned heavily on his cane. "I once visited a world where its people professed their world rested on a golden plate lifted from a great sea by a giant fish who held it balanced upon his tail. Not even a starving man would feed upon a fish in this world, as they were sacred. But most there lived good lives, loved their young, had kindness toward neighbor and stranger alike."

"You've traveled many places, Old Father. Will you come inside now, sit, and, over a cup of wine, tell me some of your travels?"

"With pleasure."

Two others stood in the nave, hands inside their sleeves.

What courage, Keegan thought. Three against one old man.

"You have lighted all the candles, I see, though you don't observe Samhain."

"We do not, as it is an unholy night for pagans and heretics. We are the pathway for the true god, the dark god."

Old Father took a stumbling step back. "My son—"

"Not yours, never yours. We are sons of Odran. And you are our sacrifice to him." The hand Toric took out of his sleeve held a knife, and its blade shined keen and black in the candlelight. "We will drink your blood this night, and throw your body on the pyre."

Old Father lifted the cane as if to defend himself. As Toric laughed at the gesture, Keegan lowered what was now his sword, and put the tip against Toric's throat.

"Shall I slit yours as you would an old man's? It would pleasure me to do so."

Instead, he gripped Toric's knife hand, twisted it so that man dropped to his knees. He punched power at one of the two who charged him, short swords gleaming, planted a boot in the belly of the other as elves slid out of the walls.

"Lock these away—take their robes, and lock them tight. Take the house and the hill. Hold this high ground."

He looked up as a bell began to toll.

"Ah, that would be a signal to their god. Shed blood if you must. Only if you must." He looked down at Toric. "There is judgment coming."

He ran out, called to Cróga. He, too, had a signal.

And when the dragon flew, Fey poured out of the woods, over the hills, across the beaches.

Some served to drive villagers to safety, to help gather children. And others waited with unsheathed swords, nocked arrows, clubs, and spears, on land, in air, in sea, for what would come.

And in the west, at the curve of land and sea, on the point of the cliff, Keegan saw the faint glimmer in the dark.

"West!" he shouted, pointing his sword as Cróga flew.

They leaped out of the portal, on horseback, on foot, on wing, on hoof.

"Archers."

Arrows flew, some tipped with flame. And with the fiery flight, the first screams of the dying ripped the night.

He met the sword of a dark faerie, slashed through wing, and sent the snarling female into the sea. As he fought another, Cróga whipped his tail to fling a flying demon after the faerie where the Mers took up the battle.

And still they came, claw and sword, fang and arrow, though Keegan had a coven of the Wise working to close the portal. When he gave the order, Cróga spewed fire to scorch half a dozen who raced toward children huddled behind rocks on the cliffside.

He felt the burn of power sear his side, spun toward it.

He spotted the wizard robes, black and flowing, and the fallen Fey around him. He flung out power in sheets of ice to strike against the vicious heat.

The air sizzled; steam spewed. Keegan flew down through it. He slapped back, power against power, until the circle of mist spread thick.

And with it, protection against the dark within to those outside its ring.

He leaped from Cróga, met his foe on the scorched sand.

"I know you." Aye, Keegan thought, he knew that face, the wild dark eyes, the sharp cheeks, the flow of black hair and beard. "Nori the Mad."

"And I you, Keegan the Weak. What a prize you are." He flung out a bolt of lightning. Keegan batted it away so it dissolved in the mist.

The mad eyes laughed. "The taoiseach before you sought to banish me, and where is he now? Dead by Odran's hand, and lost in the underworld, where he cries for mercy. As you will when you die by mine, and Odran sips your blood, when his demon dogs feast on your—"

Keegan pierced Nori's heart with his sword and lopped the head from the body as it fell. "Too much talking."

With a wave of his hand, he dissolved the mists.

He called out for healers to help the fallen and rushed back into battle.

At the verge of the sea, he saw Sedric battling three, his silver hair flying as he whirled. Before Keegan could lash out power to even the odds, Sedric impaled the leaping demon dog. He used its body as both shield and battering ram. He cleaved one enemy's arm at the elbow, and in the fountain of blood, slashed the sword upward to disembowel the third.

"It's closing," Keegan heard someone shout over the clash of steel, the screams and cries of war. "The portal's closing."

Once again he called for Cróga and took to the air to help cut off escape, to cut down the enemy, combat dark magicks with light.

Even when the portal shut, when the coven worked to seal it, the battle raged. Rolls of smoke spread from burning shops and cottages, stinging the air, muffling the pleas for help.

Sweat ran down his body, blood stained his clothes, his face as he fought those trapped in Talamh, as he shouted orders to pursue any who tried to escape over the hills, over the sea, into the woods, through the fields.

He turned a gargoyle to stone as it leaped on the back of a soldier, crushed it underfoot when it fell. Slashing, hacking his way through the enemy, he called for Cróga to pluck three he saw climbing the cliffs. Cursed when he stepped in the ooze of what had been a demon, and fought on, until he found himself back-to-back with Mahon, taking on the dwindling foe.

And at last, when there was only the weeping and the moans, the stench and smoke, he lowered his sword.

He said, "It's done. We'll send scouts to root out any that got through. There won't be many."

He turned, cursed again. "That's your own blood." He lifted a hand toward the gash in Mahon's arm.

"Heal yourself," Mahon told him, and pointed to the blood seeping from Keegan's side and through his shirt.

"Fuck me, three of the dogs at once, and one got through for a bite. You first, as I have to face my sister."

But the pain was seeping through now as well, after the numbing blur of war. Still, he closed Mahon's gash, hissed when he closed the punctures on his side.

"We'll have someone with more skill than mine do the rest of it." He swiped at his face with the back of his hand as he looked around the beach, the hills, the pretty village and saw the burning, the blood, the ruin. The death.

"We'll heal our own, and theirs after. Bind any of theirs who live for the Judgment. We'll burn their dead and salt the ash. We'll carry our dead home. Gods, I want a vat of ale and a bed."

"I'll take the ale, a scrub, and what I wouldn't give for my lady's arms around me. I'll have to settle for yours."

Mahon laid his hands on Keegan's shoulders, and when Keegan laughed, rested his forehead on his friend's. "Well fought, brother."

"Well fought. And fuck me again, and you along with me, this was nothing. A scratch, a prick of a needle to what's coming still."

"And so we'll fight on, heal our wounds, honor our dead. And fight on again. For Talamh, and all the worlds."

"For Talamh, and all the worlds." Keegan sheathed his sword. "Gods, but the taste of the kill is foul. I will dance, I swear it, on the day I never have to drink it again. But for now."

He looked up the hill to the Prayer House. "I will see Toric and his lot are bound and taken in for judgment."

"Taoiseach!" One of the elves he'd positioned inside the Prayer House raced to him.

"You hold the house and all in it?"

"Aye, aye, but . . ." His eyes filled. "We found one in a chamber below the bell tower. And three boys, just boys. Two already dead with their throats slit. His knife with their blood dripping. And he had the third sliced open before we could stop him. They were children. Just boys."

"Does he live?"

"I killed him. I didn't have to, I didn't obey. I—"

"Do you think I would find blame in you for this? It's, ah, Colm, isn't it?"

"Aye, sir."

And you barely more than a boy yourself, Keegan thought.

"Know there is no blame for this, and know we will seek out the family of the murdered boys. If they have none, we will take them in honor with our dead."

He looked up the hill again, and it burned through him. Rage and grief, grief and rage building a fire that scorched his soul.

"And know this, as I am taoiseach. This house falls. Every stone of it. There will be nothing left of it, and the evil that grew inside. We will build a monument in its place, on ground so sanctified. A monument to the fallen, to the innocent, to the brave, and all who walk in the light will be welcome."

He let out a breath. "So I have spoken."

He put a hand on the elf's shoulder before he walked toward the steps leading up. "Well fought," he said, and carried his rage and grief with him.

The first stars began to gutter out when Keegan flew toward the valley. He'd ordered Mahon and Sedric to bring the valley's dead home, assigned others to do the same across Talamh.

And he'd stayed in the south until the pyre of enemy dead went to ash under dragon fire.

The warriors he'd left there would help rebuild what was destroyed. And would raze the Prayer House to the ground.

He wanted home, and for a few hours he'd take it.

As Cróga glided down, Keegan stretched across his neck. Words were never needed between them, but he spoke them.

"Rest well, *mo dheartháir*. A thousand thanks for your courage and skill this night."

Weary to the bone, Keegan slid to the ground, then trudged toward the farmhouse, where a light beamed welcome from the window.

He might have gone straight upstairs, might have simply fallen into his bed in the clothes stained with blood and sweat and smoke, but he saw light glowed in the kitchen as well.

There he found his mother and his brother drinking tea. And from the scent of it, tea with a good dose of whiskey.

Tarryn rose, and though he would have held her off, embraced him.

"I'm filthy."

"You're whole and safe, as are Mahon and Sedric. We kept watch." She drew back far enough to kiss his cheek, look into his eyes. "Well fought," she told him.

"The portal's closed and sealed," he began.

"We kept watch," Tarryn repeated. "Throughout. Breen opened the Samhain fire, and all kept watch. Sit. You'll have a whiskey. We'll save the tea for this round."

He sat. "You haven't slept."

"Nor have you," Harken said. "I spoke with Mahon and Sedric not two hours ago. Our dead are home. Tomorrow at sunset we'll send them on, as you will send the dead on from the Capital. As all of Talamh will. This I'll see to."

Painfully grateful, Keegan nodded before he lifted the cup his mother poured. "We'll drink to those we lost, and the light that takes them in."

When they had, Tarryn pressed a kiss to the top of his head. "Now you'll eat."

When she got a skillet, Harken started to rise. "I'll fix a meal, Ma."

She sent him a cool stare. "Are you thinking I can't manage some eggs and bacon for my boys?"

"I'm thinking you don't do much cooking in the Capital."

"Sit your arse back down. You'll eat what I give you, and like it."

Then she set the skillet on the stove, turned to put an arm around each of them. "My boys," she said again, and this time kissed both of them. "And after you've eaten, Keegan, you'll scrub and well. You reek."

"As I've been living with myself, I'm more than aware." As he leaned into her, he closed a hand over Harken's. "I'm having the Prayer House razed, the ground sanctified, and a memorial to the dead built in its place. They've betrayed us twice," he went on when Harken simply watched him and his mother said nothing. "I won't give them the chance to betray us a third time."

Tarryn turned, put slabs of bacon in the skillet to sizzle. "Some on the council will object, as will others, on the grounds of freedom and of choice."

"Will you?"

She shook her head as she selected eggs. "The child they stole and would have sacrificed would be enough. The plotting with Odran would be enough. But Mahon told us they killed three boys who'd come to serve and study."

"And others who'd had no part in the plot, no knowledge of the blood sacrifices done under Toric's orders."

"Empaths can confirm all of this," Harken said. "If you sent three, to walk and feel and look, no argument would hold."

"I saw the young boys myself," Keegan began, then held up a hand. "You've the right of it, and I'll have that done. And there will be no more shelter and serving and secrecy for those who would spill our blood to honor Odran, or any god."

"I, time and again, urge you to temper your anger with diplomacy," Tarryn commented as she cooked. "But in this, let your anger lead. Will the child they stole and her family come to the Capital for the Judgment?"

"Aye, it's arranged."

"Good. Let them see and be seen. Let them know and be known."

She piled food on plates, set them on the table. "Now eat. Then we'll rest—well, you'll scrub off the battle stink, then rest. There's more work to be done."

# CHAPTER FOURTEEN

With what she'd seen in the fire haunting her, Breen slept poorly. She'd already packed what she hoped would see her through this trip east—kept it light as ordered. But she'd included the paper and pen her grandmother had conjured for her so she could continue to write.

Should the opportunity arise.

She went down before sunrise for coffee, to let Bollocks out. And worried about the dog, afraid if she tried to leave him behind with Marg, he'd somehow follow her—scent and mind.

The alternative, as she saw it, was for him to ride with her, at least for stretches of the journey. He'd gotten so big, she thought as she watched him swim in the bay. But she'd manage.

Marco came down for coffee of his own. "You're sure about Brian, right? He's okay."

"He's fine, and already back at the Capital." Because he'd led the transport of the dead, Breen thought, but didn't say. "You'll see for yourself in a few hours."

"I'll feel better when I do. I'm going to make us a hot breakfast. It's a long ride."

Five to six hours on horseback, Marg had told her, depending on the pace. A fraction of that, of course, on dragon or faerie wing.

She ate, she dressed, she added food and treats for Bollocks to her packing when she admitted to herself she wanted him with her as much as he wanted to go with her.

"Is it okay if I take my harp? I know it's extra, but—"

"I'm taking a dog. I think you can take your harp."

"He's going?" Immediately, Marco brightened. "All right! I feel better about that, too, after seeing how he went for that guy who came at you last night. I know it's still early, but—"

"Better early than late."

She brought light to guide their way, and they crossed into Talamh, into the cool and thinning mists of dawn.

She heard voices, and the jingle of bits as travelers saddled horses, and saw the movement of those already gathering.

As they crossed the road, she saw her grandmother in her hooded cloak standing with Sedric.

She went to them, embraced them. "I saw you in the fire. I saw you fight," she told Sedric. "I'm glad you're on our side." She gripped his hand an extra moment. "I'm glad you're safe and well. Are you going to the Capital?"

"I'm needed here. But we'll see you on your way. Stand tall, Breen Siobhan. You're your father's daughter."

She looked over as Harken led Boy to her. "Safe journey," he said.

"Thanks. Will Boy have a problem if Bollocks rides with me when he gets tired?"

"Not a bit of it, but it'll crowd you considerable. Keegan rides Merlin, but Cróga travels as well. He'd carry our lad here."

"Oh, I'm not sure that's . . ." Even possible, she thought.

She let it go as others rode or led horses to the road, as dragons glided and circled through the wakening sky.

She watched Keegan ride out of the mists. "We're all of us here and ready, so we'll go."

He leaned over to tap Harken's shoulder, murmured something to him. Mahon embraced Aisling and his boys before he took to the air.

Sedric took Breen's tote bag and hooked it with the saddlebags on the horse.

"I packed the scrying mirror," she told Marg.

"I'm here when you need me." Marg kissed her cheek. "Find the pleasure in the journey."

"I will." Or try, she thought. She mounted, and with Marco, fell in line, and into a brisk trot. Bollocks, already finding the pleasure, trotted along between them.

They rode toward the east, where the sun painted the sky with light and color, where the hills rolled and rose, where lakes glimmered and rivers snaked.

She saw children trudging or riding toward a building perched in a field and realized it was the school for that end of the valley.

Here and there cottages huddled closer together, then spread apart again. Stone fences ran between fields where sheep, horses, or cows grazed. Gardens burgeoned with cool weather crops; flowers splashed color wherever they willed.

When she sensed Bollocks tiring, she veered to the grass between road and wall. Before she could dismount to help him onto the horse, Cróga glided down—scattering sheep like tossed cotton balls. He folded his wings as he landed in the field.

"Come on back over here, girl." Marco turned his horse to the other side of the road. "Maybe Mr. Big-Ass Dragon wants to take a nap. Let's just keep going awhile."

"As soon as I get Bollocks up with me."

Again, she started to dismount, but Keegan circled back.

"Tell him to get on Cróga. He won't leave you otherwise."

"I'm not sure he should—"

"He'll be fine, as you'll see for yourself. It's not the first dog he's carried. We'll stop to rest and water the horses in another hour, but the dog's flagging. Show her what you're made of," he told Bollocks.

To Breen's surprise and worry, Bollocks leaped over the wall, and when Cróga dipped a wing, scrambled right up it onto the dragon's back.

"You don't baby a warrior, and he proved himself one only last night I'm told." He signaled to Cróga, and with the dog perched on his back, the dragon glided into the air.

"Now he's a dragon rider." Satisfied, Keegan galloped away.

"That dog's getting a piggyback ride from a dragon." Shaking his head, Marco rode over to watch with her. "That's something you don't see in Philadelphia."

"He's loving it." Breen felt the dog's delight in the flight, in the wind, the speed.

They rode on through the green.

The land gentled in wide, deep patchworks of that green and gold and brown. Forests rose with trees so wide it would take three with arms outstretched, hands joined, to circle their trunks.

And when she opened herself, she felt the life beating in them. The fox and the bear, sparrow and hawk, deer and rabbit, elf and Were.

They came to a river, brown as tea, and the bridge spanning it. To the north, high mountains speared through clouds so their peaks seemed to float over them.

"The Giant's Steps," one of the outriders told her. "And the highest there to the west is Dragon's Nest. The peaks will go white soon, and remain covered in the snow until Lammas."

Breen knew his face—young, ruddy, handsome—from the ceilidh, but struggled to find the name.

Marco had no problem. "Do you ever get snow down here, Hugh?"

"A sweep perhaps, frost for certain in the higher lands. But the sort a man sinks into past his boots? Only once I know of in my life span in the foothills of the Giant's Steps. I was born there."

"You know Brian Kelly?"

"Sure and I know Brian. We came up together, we did, as my mother and his are cousins. Northmen of Talamh we are."

"You miss it." Breen could feel it, that yearning. "The north."

"I do, aye. And when peace covers all of Talamh again, home I'll go. I've a wife waiting, and a son not yet two. After we honor those we lost in the south, I'm for home until called again."

On the other side of the bridge, they walked the horses toward the trees and the lively stream that weaved through them.

Breen dismounted, then handed the reins to Marco before she rushed to where Cróga landed. Bollocks scrambled down as happily as he had scrambled up.

"Look at you, dragon-rider dog. We'll write about that in the next one." She gave him long strokes before letting him race to the stream for a quick splash and a drink.

As she started back, Keegan walked toward her.

Hours on horseback, and that following a night of brutal combat, didn't appear to wear him down. He looked as ridiculously romantic now as he had when he'd ridden the black stallion out of the morning mists.

Smarter, she reminded herself, not to think about how he looked, but about what needed to be done.

"You were right. About Bollocks. I've lost any track of time, so I don't know how much longer we have to ride."

He pointed up. "Do you see the sun?"

"Yes, I see the sun." That came in and out of the clouds that washed over it, streamed by it.

"It's traveled three hours since we left the valley, so we've traveled three hours. Two and a bit more left, as we've made good time. We take time here for the horses, for the riders to eat. You have food in your saddlebag—my mother saw to it."

"Oh. That was nice of her."

"The dog . . ." Frowning, he trailed off. "Why do you do that? Is something wrong with your leg?"

"What?" She'd brought her left leg behind her, pulling her heel to her butt to stretch her quadriceps. "No. I'm just stretching." She tapped a hand on her thigh as she did the same with the right. "These muscles."

"Hm. Well then, the dog should ride with Cróga until we near the Capital. Then he should go with you. And you should ride in the front with my mother and me."

"Why would I ride up front?"

"You are granddaughter to Mairghread, daughter of Eian. Both were taoiseach. You are . . . who you are. They'll know you by your hair, by your eyes. They will expect it. Ride where you like until then. I'll send someone for you when it's time."

"What do I do? Give me a break, will you? I've never done any of this before."

Keegan shoved his fingers through his hair. "People will be out, or come out. They'll know about the battle, and our victory. That brings pride. They'll know about our dead, and those brought back to families who'll grieve for them. This brings sorrow. Keep your back straight, and your head up. Meet eyes that need yours to see them. And it would be best if you came to the ceremony for the fallen."

He gestured for her to follow him, then pointed at her saddlebag. "Eat."

"What did you do with the Pious you captured? And the man—the spy—from the valley?"

"They're secured and guarded. Those with powers, those

powers have been bound, and will remain bound until the Judgment."

She found bread and cheese wrapped in her saddlebags, along with an apple. "When is the Judgment?"

"Tomorrow. Two days if two days are needed."

"Am I allowed to be there?"

"Aye, and it would be best if you came." He held up a hand before she could ask another question. "Eat, stretch, or what suits you. Ten minutes more, then we ride. Someone will instruct you where you need it, answer what you need. Let the dog go with Cróga until I send for you."

When he walked away, Breen bit into the bread.

"Weight of the world on his shoulders," Marco commented. "I was going to say something to cheer him up, but it seemed wrong."

"He talked about us riding into pride and sorrow. I only saw the sorrow." She took the apple around to feed to Boy. "Before, I thought how he looked . . ." She searched for a safe word. "Fresh, fresh and strong, considering the last twenty-four hours. But you're right, Marco. Over and under and through all that? The weight of the world. Or more, the worlds."

"You're carting some of that, my Breen."

"Not like he does."

When they mounted again, she watched Bollocks fly overhead on Cróga. The road rose and fell with the land, and the gentle patchworks of the midlands gave way to the rolling east.

She saw a stone circle ringed in a field with a stone column in its center. She heard its hum as they passed. A graveyard where sheep wandered through the stones near a small building that looked like a little chapel of some sort.

She felt no dark from it, only quiet and soft light.

Near her, Marco chatted with other riders. She let the

voices lull her, along with the steady rhythm of the horse under her, the cool air that brought the scent of peat smoke and grass, the occasional rider or wagon that went by with a salute or a greeting.

The long night with only snatches of sleep had her half dozing.

She found herself near the waterfall, in the green light where moss grew in thick carpets on the trees, and the river reflected it.

Pixies danced there, over and through the tumble of water, white against green. All the hearts beating—so many—filled her own. Dragons, tiny zips of color, winged and dipped. Enchanted, she walked closer to the bank of the river.

In this river years before, she knew, she'd been closed in glass, held under the surface. In this place not so long ago, Yseult had bespelled her—but that was done.

She was safe here, with the pixies, the baby dragons, and the music they made.

In the river, its green clear as glass, she saw the gleam of the red pendant as she had in a dream once before. The dragon's heart stone just beyond her reach.

She started to kneel down, to stretch her arm out and down. And a shadow passed over the river, over her.

She looked up, her own heart beating fast now. Above, circling above, the dragon. Red as the stone, gold tips as bright as the chain.

She wanted to reach up. She wanted to reach down.

The dragon circled, gold eyes watching. The pendant shimmering, waiting for her hand to bring it to the surface.

*Choose and become.* She heard Marg's voice in her head. *Choose to become. Take your place, and both are yours.*

*I can't reach either. I can't quite reach.*

She held one hand toward the sky, the other toward the water. And feeling herself slip, pulled back.

And stood on the other side of the falls. Like a ghost she

stood behind Odran. His voice boomed, made her want to press her hands to her ears.

Yseult, her hair liberally streaked with white, chanted with him.

As did the demons and the damned who gathered.

She didn't know the language, but still she knew the words.

*Run with blood, feed on death. And with the feast break this lock. Unseal the door, by my command. I will take what is mine, what was denied me. Be this blood, be this death only the next in what will come.*

She saw the child now, a young faerie whose pale pink wings frantically beat, as she screamed for her mother, as she tried to escape the chains that held her in the river shallows.

When he lifted the knife, Breen didn't think. Only acted.

She threw power out so the knife spun from his hands, threw it so he cried out in shock and pain. Threw it out so the chains broke and sank under the water.

And the young faerie flew into the trees.

On the wrong side, the wrong side, Breen thought as Odran whirled.

For an instant their eyes—gray and gray—met.

She felt dark close in around her.

And someone said her name.

She jerked back, found Keegan gripping her arm. "Back straight," he snapped, then saw her face.

"Where were you?"

"I—Odran. He had a child, a faerie child. The waterfall, a sacrifice. I stopped him. I don't know how. I don't know when. Now, before, yet. I don't know. But she flew away, and he saw me. He saw me, and she's on the other side."

"Not before, or I'd know. If now, she'll hide, and we'll find her. We'll find if any child from Talamh is missing. If yet, we'll see she's protected. Stop," he ordered. "There isn't time now. I'll see to it. You ride in the front. Cróga will bring the dog to you. Ride behind my mother."

The hand on her arm gripped tighter. "We'll find her. We'll look, and we'll find."

"Dilly—her name, the name she calls herself. She has brown hair, gold eyes, brown skin, pink wings. She was . . . about six, I think. No more than seven."

"We'll find her."

He gave Boy a slap on the flank to send him forward before signaling to one of the faeries overhead.

He gave orders, and as he rode to the front, three veered off in different directions.

"I was talking to Hugh and Cait." Marco edged his horse closer to Keegan. "I wasn't watching her. I—"

"She'll be fine. Ride up to the front with me now, and fall in beside her."

Keegan rode ahead, took point with his mother. Other riders made way so Marco could move in beside Breen.

"I'm okay," she said before he could ask. "She was such a little girl, and so scared. I'm going to believe they'll find her, and I have to think about the rest. But not now. The castle or fortress or whatever it's called—you can see it up on that hill. And there are already so many more cottages, and people."

"It's like the burbs." He shot her a smile, hoping to help settle her as Bollocks now pranced between them. "Talamh's version, with some urban sprawl. And holy shit, Breen, it is a castle. Good thing I'm all used to that, since we stayed in one in Ireland."

"I wouldn't count on Wi-Fi and in-room movies in this one."

"It's a downside."

She'd live without them, Breen thought, and she'd think about the dream or vision or experience when she had some quiet and alone. But now she studied the cottages and outlying farms spreading over hill and field, and the people who stopped their work or spilled out of doors.

Babies on hips or shoulders, kids gawking and grinning. Young Sidhe spreading wings to fly alongside the riders and shower them with flickers of light.

She saw what she thought must be workshops, as those who stepped out wore leather or cloth aprons and some still held tools in their hands.

She watched a woman run out of a cottage, take wing, and one of the faeries fly toward her. They met in an embrace, circled in midair with the kiss.

"They pledged before we left for the valley," Minga told her. "Keegan will pretend not to see Dalla broke ranks to greet her love. You'll see some with a black band on their right arm. These are the mothers, fathers, brothers, sisters, sons, daughters, wives, or husbands of a fallen."

"How many fell? Do you know?"

Minga shook her head. "Keegan knows."

She could feel her dog's delight.

*Children! People! Sheep! Cows!*

She glanced down as he looked up at her. No one could mistake his expression for anything other than a grin.

"No running off to explore," she told him. "Not until we have the lay of the land."

Oh, he wanted to—she sensed that as well. But he kept pace with the horses and contented himself by looking everywhere.

They rode over a bridge spanning a narrow ribbon of river where gates stood wide and people lined the road. Others stood on the thatched roofs of cottages and what she saw were shops, pubs, workshops. She thought the clothes somehow more urban as she spotted some waistcoats worn by both sexes, dresses that skimmed above the ankles, or snug pants in bold patterns worn by some of the women.

Shawls—bright colors—or long coats protected against

the autumn chill. She heard music streaming out of pubs, voices raised in welcome. She smelled the spice of stews on the simmer, meat in the skillet, a whiff of the flowers spilling from baskets, and another whiff of livestock.

It made her think of the visit to the folk park at Bunratty, how charmed by it she'd been, how oddly connected to it she'd felt. But then she'd been to the Capital before. She hadn't re-membered, didn't remember still, but knew she'd come with her parents for the Judgment of those who'd helped Odran abduct her.

"There are five wells in the Capital." Minga gestured to one where people gathered with buckets and jugs. "Schools, of course, and the fields for crops and livestock here, and on the castle grounds. Most of the wheat has been harvested, taken to the mills. We have three. Those who live on the castle grounds contribute to the whole."

"Like a commune," Marco said.

"If this is community, yes. We barter and trade what we grow, what we make, our skills, our service. Some will come to the taoiseach if there's a conflict or question, and he will judge. Or the council in his place. We value peace, and train to hold it."

"Do you sit on the council?" Breen asked.

"I do. Though I was not born in Talamh, I was given this honor, this duty. We are seven, and with the taoiseach and Tarryn as his hand, nine."

Breen saw roads splitting off from the main as the main climbed the rise toward the castle with its many shades of gray stone, its battlements and towers and turrets.

On the topmost, the banner snapped in the wind so the red dragon seemed to fly against the white field. He carried a sword in one claw, a staff in the other.

She saw Cróga glide over the castle, and a boy—a winged boy—rode on his back. The boy's joyful laugh spilled down like sunlight.

They came to another stone bridge, another gate. A fountain shot water clear as crystal toward the sky. It fell in rainbows. Gardens spread and speared in islands of texture, in rivers of color. More flowers flowed over walls of terraces and balconies that graced the castle. Beyond them and the roll of green stood a forest, thick and deep.

She heard the cry of a hawk, saw a stunning sweep of butterflies rise like a wave. They swirled around her, once, twice, a third time, before flying as one toward an island of blooms.

"They welcome you," Minga said with a smile.

"That was wild." Marco's own smile dimmed as he studied Breen's face. "Did they scare you, girl?"

"No, no, just surprised."

And scratched the surface of some memory. Riding in front of her father, gulping in all the sights like water with the castle rising and spreading, the banner snapping, the fountain spewing and spilling. Those first sounds of waves slapping rock on the cliffs.

And butterflies swirling. How she'd laughed and lifted her arms so they'd land on them. Her father's laugh as he'd kissed the top of her head.

*Dragon Hearts, like your hair.*

She knew Minga spoke about the falcon mews, the cliffs, the gardens as Keegan led them around to the side and back of the great stone building. She barely listened as she tried to hang on to the memory.

But it faded away as riders began to dismount around her.

Mahon walked up to take her reins. "They'll see to the horses and have your things taken up. Minga will show you to your chambers—and anywhere else you want to go or see, as Keegan and Tarryn will be busy for a while yet. You've time before the Leaving to rest or wander, have some food. One of us will come fetch you, or find you if you go out and about, when it's time."

"I expect you'd like to walk a bit after the long ride." Minga gestured. "We'll go this way, and in through the doors to the entrance hall."

"It's big," Marco commented as he craned his neck up. "And tall."

"It's all of that, but home nonetheless. I think you'll be comfortable in the rooms Tarryn chose for you. Right next to each other, they are."

"The gardens are beautiful. You said there was a falcon mews?"

"Aye." Minga nodded at Breen, gestured again. "Down this path, a school for training as well—both hawks and students. Other training areas for horses and horsemanship, for archery, for combat. If you walk or ride down to the village, there are shops for trading. Fabrics and jewelry, leather goods, ironworks, tools for magicks, cobblers and tailors. Pubs for food and drink and music."

She led the way around, winding through the garden, along stone paths, over wide terraces, and to the steps leading to massive double doors.

"The gates are only closed during times of defense. These doors are only barred at such times."

Minga pressed her hand on the dragon image carved in the stone by the doors, and they opened.

They walked into a towering hall with stone floors polished smooth, with tapestries and bronze works gracing the walls. Archways opened up in all directions, and the sun spilled through the glass dome in the soaring ceiling.

Fabric-covered benches and high-backed chairs offered seating, flowers more beauty, and a fire, snapping in a hearth she could have stood in, warmth.

"It's beautiful. I thought it would be more . . . fortified."

"When necessary, it is. Those stairs?" She nodded toward the staircase—stone, but wide and straight rather than the curving pie shape Breen had seen in ruins and restorations in

Ireland. "When the gates and doors must be locked, they . . . I have to find the word."

Minga paused, closed her eyes. "Ah, they go . . ." She smoothed her hand in the air.

"The treads go into the stone, make a platform. A steep one."

"This. But now, the grand stairs are convenient."

"And pretty freaking grand," Marco added.

As he spoke, a young woman in snug pants and a green sweater raced down. Her dark hair coiled to her shoulder blades; her dark eyes sparkled against gold-dust skin.

"Mama!"

Though she didn't use full speed, Breen recognized elfin blood.

"You're home! You're home." She threw her arms around Minga. "I was minding Gwain's children when I heard you were riding through the village. And here you are!"

"Here we all are." Minga hugged hard before drawing her daughter back. "My daughter, Kiara. Make your welcome to Breen Siobhan and Marco."

"You're most welcome! How exciting to meet you. Oh, your hair is wonderful! Both!"

"Our Kiara has a talent for hair," Minga told them. "They've traveled long today, my precious. Come, help me show them their chambers."

"They're so pretty! I peeked when Brigid and Lo were do-ing the linens and flowers."

As she chattered, they started for the stairs. And the vision glided down them.

Her silvery blond hair fell in long, loose waves to her tiny waist. Her eyes were tawny like a cat's and sparkled with the faintest of glitter on the lids. Her lips, pink and perfectly carved, curved in a smile in a face narrow and delicate and impossibly lovely.

She wore a tawny tunic to match her eyes, belted with gold

at that tiny waist, over pants that followed every curve down to tall boots.

She smelled, Breen thought, seductively of wild things that grew in the forest.

"Minga, welcome home. You've been missed." She sent Marco a flirtatious flutter of long, dark lashes before turning that smile on Breen. "And is it Breen Siobhan? Your arrival has been much anticipated."

"This is Shana," Minga began. "Daughter of Uwin, who serves on the council as I do, and Gwen. Breen, daughter of Eian, granddaughter of Mairghread, brings her friend, Marco, from the other side."

"I haven't yet traveled to your world. But now I see I must." She offered Marco a hand in a way that invited a kiss.

He shook it instead. "If you make it to Philly, I'll show you around."

"Sure and now I will for certain. Have you just arrived then, and I'm keeping you standing? Minga, if you wish to rest or see the rest of your family, Kiara and I can show the guests to their chambers."

"That's kind of you, but the taoiseach requested it of me."

She led the way up and up, explaining various rooms as they went. A vast library, a contemplation room, a kind of nursery area for young children, a room for magicks, another for crafting.

They took, single file, the pie-shaped winding stairs to the next level. Rooms for music, for dance instruction, for art.

Another set of stairs, and Minga led the way down a corridor.

"Your room, Marco." Minga opened the door.

The tall bed had four soaring posts, and the drape of a blanket in midnight blue. The two moons floated over a quiet sea on the chest at its feet. A tray of fruit, cheeses, bread, decanters sat on it. A wide wardrobe that gleamed from a recent polish, a winged chair and footstool, a table where flowers graced a deep blue vase all offered a strange sort of sophistication.

His harp stood on the table with the flowers.

Doors opened to a terrace with views of a pretty courtyard and, to the east, the rolling sea.

"This is a view and a half."

"I hope you'll play for us." Shana walked over to the harp, trailed her finger over the strings. "I've heard you're very musical."

"I'm still learning to play the harp. Breen bought it for me."

Shana turned. "What a fine friend."

"And your fine friend is in the next room." Minga took her daughter's hand, moved back into the corridor and down. "As with Marco, if anything doesn't suit your needs, you've only to say."

She had the big bed, but this with a gauze canopy that sparkled like stars. The fire simmered; the flowers scented the air.

She had a desk as well as the wardrobe and chest—hers painted with a meadow in full flower. On the desk that faced the side of the room toward the sea, sat her paper, her pen.

Unable to resist, she opened the doors to let the sea air flood in, and saw the terrace wrapped around the corner.

"It's beautiful, inside and out. Thank you, Minga."

"I'm pleased, as will Tarryn be, that you like it. Now, we'll let you refresh after the long journey. If you have a need or a wish or a question, you've only to ask. Come now, come, let's leave them in peace."

Minga pointed the others out, closed the door behind them.

"This rocks it out, back again, then out one more time."

So saying, Marco flopped on Breen's bed. "How about we have ourselves a snack and some wine? Then I want to clean myself up, because I'm hoping to find Brian."

Breen poured wine for both of them. And wondered why the gorgeous elf—she'd caught that—with the perfect face despised her.

She'd caught that, too.

# CHAPTER FIFTEEN

Keegan spoke with the families of the fallen, the most miserable duty he held. When he'd finished, he went out to check on the arrangements for the Leaving. As taoiseach, he would send the fire himself and provide the families of the lost with the urns for the return of the ashes.

Once satisfied, he went down to the dungeons to be certain the bindings on those who would be judged held fast.

They slept, each and all, under the same spell they'd used on the child they'd meant to kill. The sleep would hold, he determined, until they faced him, their magicks bound, the next day.

He went up again, wishing for nothing more than an ale, a fire, and a soft bed for an hour.

Shana waited for him near the grand stairs.

"Taoiseach. If I could speak with you."

"I've little time now," he began.

"For my apology." She looked up at him, looked deeply.

"There's no need."

"For me, there is need. Please, a few moments only, as

I know you have important matters. In the air, Taoiseach. Grant me this."

"A few moments," he agreed, and thought longingly of the ale, the fire, the bed. And the quiet.

She wound her way through to the courtyard near the seawall, which to his mind ate up unnecessary time when he had so little. But they'd ended things badly, he reminded himself. And some of the fault had been his own.

She stepped out, breathed deep. "First I want to say I know you fought well and bravely, and I know you grieve for the fallen, as we all do."

She laid a hand on his heart, the other on her own.

"My own friend Cullin O'Donahue is one who goes to the gods."

"I'm sorry. He was a strong warrior, and true."

"He was." Tears sparkled in her eyes as she took Keegan's hand. "And now I will say I'm sorry, and shamed, for what I said to you when we last met."

"We misunderstood each other, and part of that blame is mine."

"No, it's mine alone. You made no promises." She brought his hand to her cheek. "I wanted what I knew you didn't, and I struck out at you. I was angry because I built a dream, and you never shared it. And never pretended to. Will you forgive me?"

"There's nothing to forgive, Shana."

She lowered her eyes because those words flashed fire into them. "I would be friends again, if you'd have it."

"Friends we were, are, and will be."

She took a moment more before she looked up, put the flirt back in her eyes. "Sharing a bed with you is a very fond memory, for you're skilled. I would invite you back into mine, but—" she said quickly, because she read refusal, rejection on his face, "I'm with Loren Mac Niadh now."

"I'm glad of it," he said simply, and enraged her. "He cares for you, and always has."

"He does." She toyed with one of the baubles at her ears, which Loren had given her. "And though I haven't pledged to him, I will, I think. In time."

"When the time comes, he'll be fortunate. I wish you happy, Shana, in all choices. In all ways."

"I know you do, and always have, so I'm only the more sorry for my angry words. I wish you the same, Keegan. Are you happy?"

"I'll know true happiness when peace holds in Talamh."

"So speaks the taoiseach." She used a smile with those words, though they lay bitter on her tongue. "But is Keegan happy? I'm told you've a taste now for red hair."

When he looked blank, she felt a rise of hope. "The O'Ceallaigh's daughter. The one you brought with you from the valley. She's a quiet one, and some say the quiet ones hold the most fire."

"She's not always quiet, but she holds fire enough for any. She needs more time and more training, and neither of us can waste that time on . . . flirtations."

"Ah well. From what I know"—she tapped a finger to his cheek—"she doesn't suit you. But I wish you happy, Keegan, whatever and whoever brings it to you.

"A kiss to seal it," she added before laying her lips softly on his. Sighed. "And an admission that I'll miss finding you with me in the dark. Blessed be, Keegan."

As she glided back inside, she flicked a quick glance upward and congratulated herself on her timing when she saw Breen standing on the terrace of her room.

She wouldn't need to trick Kiara into gossiping about a tryst between herself and Keegan now. The woman she fully believed stood in the way of all she wanted had seen for herself.

Keegan didn't get the ale or the fire. As a falcon arrived with reports from the south, he called a council meeting.

"Time's short before the final preparation for the Leaving," Tarryn told him as a few helpers scrambled to set cups and pitchers of water on the council table.

No spirits were consumed during council meetings, though by the gods, Keegan thought, that's when he wanted them most.

"Everything is at the ready, Ma, and this won't take long."

"You've yet to wash off the travel dust and change."

"I was detained. No more fussing now." He gave her an absent pat on the arm before he walked to the window he'd opened so he could breathe.

"Until the council convenes, I'm just your ma, and my boy is tired."

"So's my ma, isn't she? So let's make this quick and done."

Minga entered first, along with the representative from the Trolls. Bok wore a black band in honor of his granddaughter, who'd fallen on the beach in the south.

The others came quickly enough, talking and muttering among themselves as they entered the room with its murals and map of Talamh, its tapestries depicting all the tribes of the Fey.

Each stood behind the tall chair of their place at the long table. Keegan escorted his mother to hers at one end, then strode to his at the head.

"Greetings and blessings, and my thanks to all for their counsel."

When he took his seat, the others followed suit. "We ask, as always, for wisdom in all choices made here, and that all choices strengthen the peace of Talamh and all who dwell within it."

"So ask we all," the council answered.

With that formality done, Keegan held up a hand. "I know there's much to discuss, but the time is short before the Leaving. Tomorrow is for the Judgment, and the Welcome. Between those duties, we will meet again. But I've asked you to come now for only this. The battle in the south is won, but at great cost. Every life leaving us is a cost to all. More, a great many more, would have been lost through the treachery hiding behind robes and folded hands, for those who took our tolerance and forgiveness for weakness."

"They will be judged for it," Bok said.

"Aye, they will be judged. The Pious, as before in the dark past, used their Prayer House to hide their true purpose in false piety, and within walls deemed sacred and holy, tortured Fey, made blood sacrifice to Odran."

He saw the flash and heat in Flynn's eyes, and knew an ally in the friend of his father's, and the representative of the Sidhe.

"Taoiseach." Uwin, Shana's elfin father, spoke up. "You cannot be certain of this."

"I am certain of it. As the child they stole and bespelled and planned to offer to Odran will testify tomorrow. As I myself, in the guise of an old holy man, was to be offered."

"For the stolen child, they must be judged." Rowan of the Wise spoke up. "For bespelling her, they must be judged. But can there be judgment on what was not done, even through intervention?"

"This is for tomorrow. I say now and here, she would not have been the first. I tell you, in walking through that unholy place, I felt the deaths that came before, I heard the echoes of chants to Odran. This will not pass. This will not stand. And neither will stand the unholy place. It will be razed."

"Taoiseach!" Uwin held up both hands. "This strikes as vengeance, and justice rarely follows vengeance. Not all, surely not all, of the Pious took part in this."

"Not all."

"Then we must allow them their choices, their place of contemplation and good works."

"If I may speak." Tarryn did so, softly, as arguments erupted around the table. "We did not destroy the Prayer

House in the valley where the Pious once lived, prayed, did those good works, then turned to persecution, blood magicks, torture. This was long ago, long before any here took first breath, but the Fey remember. The Fey forgave, and gave the Pious their place in the south. And in repayment for forgiveness, they used what remains of it, near the God's Dance, near the graveyard where Eian O'Ceallaigh's ashes lay, and the ashes of many loved and lost, to stir the spirits trapped within. The sacrificed, and those who sacrificed them. To stir them to walk free on Samhain, through the thinning veil."

Neo, of the Mer, with legs given when called, fisted both hands on the table. "You're sure of this?"

"The fates decreed I go there, see, hear, feel, as did Breen Siobhan, daughter of the O'Ceallaigh. I tell you without her, I would have needed a coven to break the spell—Yseult's spell, strong with the help of the Pious. And I tell you that on Samhain, the Undead would have swept over the valley and beyond."

She nodded at Minga. "Minga is witness to this."

"I am. And though I am not Fey, though I haven't the gift, even I felt the battle of power, dark and light. Even I saw the shadows taking form, clawing to get out."

Rowan of the Wise spoke again. "The ruins must be cleansed."

"More," Tarryn said. "The spirits must be sent to the dark and the light. This will take time and power, but must be done. And the cleansing, and the sanctification, all of it."

"We can do the same with the south," Uwin began.

"They have twice turned on us." Flynn's voice whipped out. "Betrayed us, sacrificed innocents. Would we give them leave to do so again?"

"We will not. The walls come down, every stone. Vengeance, you say?" As his mother advised, Keegan let his anger free. "So be it, as it is justice as well. See!"

He rose, lifted his hands, spread his fingers, and threw his memory, the images of it, onto the wall. And there the young boys lay, throats slit, blood spilling, pooling.

"Children, children sent to serve and learn and begin a life of good works, murdered by the hand of the Pious. Murdered in hopes their blood would strengthen the attack against us. More!"

He threw another image, one of men sprawled in their own blood. "Those who wore the robes and knew nothing, or pretended to know nothing of the evil inside those walls, the true purpose inside those walls. Murdered. Not by our hands, but their brothers so they could not speak against them."

He looked at every face around the table. "It will not stand, and every stone torn down will be a sign of strength, of justice, of our purpose. I sent three empaths to walk inside that evil, and the falcon has brought their report. You are free to read it, as I did. And I'll tell you all three were sickened by what they saw, heard, felt.

"It will not stand," he repeated. "The ground will be cleansed and sanctified. And in its place on the rise, we will build a memorial to those who gave their lives for us yesterday, and for those whose lives were taken by those who vowed to heal and help and honor. I am taoiseach, and this is my word. I will not be swayed on this, whatever your counsel. I swear by all I am, I will tear it down with my own hands if need be."

With both pride and rage on his face, Flynn rose. "I stand with you, for this is justice. This is right, and honorable."

Rowan got to her feet. "I stand with you. Let the light rise from the dark. Let honor grow from the blood of the innocent and the brave."

"I stand with you." Neo rose. "Let this tribute rise high to be seen from the sea, from the land."

One by one, they stood.

Uwin got to his feet. "I'm one for caution, for tolerance,

for forgiveness, in hopes that all of this will hold peace. But there are times, I know, all of this gives a path to the evil in some hearts to walk. Children, the most precious of all gifts, murdered. I stand with the taoiseach."

"Then we are one. My thanks for your counsel. I will ask for more of it tomorrow on other matters. Blessed be."

It was dismissal, and though some might have lingered, Tarryn nudged them along in her easy, inarguable way.

"Well fought," she told Keegan from the doorway. "Rest a bit now. There'll be more battles to come."

Breen gave the scene in the courtyard the consideration she thought it deserved.

Very little.

Instead, she took a long soak in the copper tub, let herself drift awhile. Then, because packing light had meant—to her—the bare minimum of makeup, she used what she had.

Then boosted it a little with a glamour.

Maybe she'd given that scene in the courtyard a medium amount of consideration.

She'd yet to develop a real talent for hair, but since they'd be outside, the wind would make hay of any attempt anyway.

She should've bartered for a shawl somewhere, she thought, but she'd make do with her jacket. With the blue dress—that seemed right for a kind of funeral—and her boots, she'd be warm enough.

Maybe.

"All I've got anyway," she said to Bollocks, then opened her wardrobe to find a hooded cape, the same shade as the dress, and another note from Marg.

Coastal winds blow brisk. This and the blue dress are suitable for a Leaving in the Capital. Be safe and warm, mo stór. Nan.

She smiled down at Bollocks. "Aren't we lucky to have her?"

Though it was early, she dressed, not only to see how it all looked, but maybe—now appropriately dressed—to see if Marco wanted to wander around.

She gave the cape a couple of swirls, laughed at herself. "I don't know why, exactly, but wearing this makes me feel like the heroine in a novel. And I like it! Let's go see what Marco thinks."

She started to turn to the door; Bollocks went on alert.

And someone knocked.

"Probably Marco thinking what I'm thinking."

She opened the door to Shana.

"Ah! I thought to come help you get ready for the Leaving, but I see you are."

"Yeah."

As you are, Breen thought, in a forest-green dress cut square at the bodice, and cut just low enough so the fat citrine pendant she wore nestled between the rounded tops of her breasts.

"What a . . ." Just the slightest hesitation as Shana let her gaze travel down, then up. "Sweet dress. Did you bring it from the other side?"

"No. My grandmother gave it to me."

"Ah." Smiling, Shana strolled in without invitation. "Grandmothers will be old-fashioned, won't they? Are you comfortable in your room then? And happy with the view?"

"Yes, to both. Thanks." And since her visitor made no move to leave but wandered over to the desk, Breen laid the cloak on the bed. "Can I offer you something?"

"So kind! I would love a cup of wine. You're a scribe, I'm told. Myself, I could never sit still long enough to write words on paper. And sitting can . . ." She spread her hands to indicate wide hips.

She took the wine Breen offered, then dropped into a chair, very much at home. "It must be so strange for you to be here."

Oh, I know your type, Breen thought, and sat on the chest. I've dealt with you before.

Not well then, she admitted. But this was now.

"Why?"

"Ah well, a strange land, strange people."

"I find the land beautiful, and the people wonderful. I was born here."

"Were you? I think I heard that somewhere. And, of course, that's part of the problem altogether, isn't it? You being what you are, your father breeding with a human, it's what has Odran waging war. Not that it's your fault, not at all. And still we'll have a Leaving tonight for those who died because he wants you. It must weigh on you."

Very deliberately Breen poured herself a cup of wine. "It does. It weighs that he wants to use what I am to lay waste to Talamh, and other worlds. That he wants to make slaves of someone like you." Breen sipped her wine, and thought of all the times she'd stepped back, lowered her head, taken the nasty little flicks.

No more of that.

"Because it weighs, I'm learning how to fight back. With magicks." She circled a finger and set the candles alight on the mantel. "And with fists, with sword, with whatever it takes."

"Mmm." Shana leaned back in the chair, held the cup in both hands as she studied Breen over the rim. "It's said that Keegan trains you, and you often end with your face in the dirt. Not a patient one, is Keegan."

"How are you with a sword?"

Shana laughed. "Not all are trained for combat—not in the Capital. Elves, as you may know, have other skills. Speed, concealment. And I'm considered a fine archer."

She twirled a finger through the curl at her ear. The rest of her hair she'd braided back into a coil at the base of her neck.

"I'm told you shared a bed with Keegan a time or two." Her smile just before she sipped more wine edged toward a smirk. "I hope you haven't set your sights so high."

"My sights?"

"I say this to you, woman to woman, and in friendship. He is not for one such as you."

Breen tried the most innocent of smiles. "Such as me?"

"Much is expected of the mate of the taoiseach, and the duties are many. Too many, I'm sure you agree, for one not raised to know them, perform them."

For the hell of it, Breen smiled again, and not so innocently. "I'm a fast learner."

The mask slipped just a little as Shana leaned forward. "Then learn this. The taoiseach and I have what you would call an understanding."

"Would I call it that?"

"Sure we both enjoy a dalliance here and there, and why not, as his duties often separate us. Now of course, he flies back to my bed as often as he can, but when he can't, we've both agreed to take our pleasures, such as they are, where we find them. And when this business around you is finished, and you're back in your own world, we'll pledge and wed, make our life together here in the Capital."

She smiled her pretty smile. "I'm more than happy, of course, to make you acquainted with others who would dally with you during your—I imagine—brief stay in the Capital."

Rather than return the smile, Breen angled her head and studied that unquestionably stunning face. "I find it so interesting, and flattering, that someone like you feels threatened by someone like me."

"What a foolish thing to say. You're no threat to me."

"You're here because you think I am. And oddly, that makes me feel . . ." She rolled her shoulders, gave them a little shake. "Competitive. I'm not usually a competitive sort, and Keegan isn't a trophy or prize, but there you go.

"More wine?"

Shana set down the cup, got to her feet. "I warn you, I can be friend, or I can be foe."

Surprised at herself, Breen got to hers, as did Bollocks beside her. Breen laid a hand on his head to keep him still.

"You've already chosen, so take a warning yourself. You don't scare me. You don't even intimidate me, because all I'm seeing is a desperate and poorly disguised attempt to make me feel less, feel unwanted and unworthy. And I've got more important things to fight over than a man."

For a humming moment, they faced off.

The knock came, and Marco poked his head. "Hey, Breen, get a load— Oh, hey. Ah, Sharla, right?"

"Shana," she said, and instantly switched to the friendly flirt. "And how handsome you look."

"Thanks. You look nice."

"Charming and handsome. I'll take my leave. So pleased to have had time to know you better, Breen Siobhan."

"Likewise."

"You mustn't be late for the Leaving," she said as she sailed out. "It's considered rude."

When Marco closed the door behind her, Breen grinned. "You never forget a name, and when Marco Olsen tells someone they look 'nice' in that tone, it's a roast."

"She looked awesome, but I don't like her. Strikes me as a bad kitty. She's got Mean Girl all over her."

Breen walked right up to him, grabbed his face, kissed him loudly on the mouth. "That's one of the many reasons I love you. She is totally Mean Girl."

"What did she want?"

"I'll tell you, but first! That is some excellent coat."

"Right?" He did a turn in the rich brown, just-past-knee-length leather. "Nan sent it. Top nan in the history of nans."

"She really is." To prove it, Breen picked up her cape, swirled it on with plenty of drama.

"Look at you! Look at us!" He grabbed her, lowered her into a dip. "We're like the cover of a romance novel."

"I feel like a heroine, especially after that little scene with Shana."

"Dish it."

"Let's walk and talk—head down and outside. I could use some cool air after all that blowhard hot."

"And listen to you." Delighted, Marco added a little elbow jab. "Breen the ass-kicker."

"I was ready to kick her perfect elfin ass, let me tell you. And, more? It gave me a nice big thrill to anticipate it. What's happened to me?"

"Whatever it is, I like it. Now tell me a story."

She told him in snippets on the way down, careful to break off if they passed someone, or saw someone close enough to hear.

Because she really did want the air, and she'd worked out the direction from her terrace, she led the way to the courtyard they could see from their rooms.

"She got dumped." Marco said it firmly. "I'm telling you, Keegan kicked her to the curb, and she's pissed. And she figures you're why."

"Since I've been dumped, I recognize the signs. I'd say the reason was more he recognized naked ambition and that core of mean than anything to do with me."

"Don't underestimate the power of Breen."

"I'm not, I'm really not. But I believe her about them not being monogamous. So I'm saying it's not about me. It's about her. I saw them out here earlier, and—"

She broke off because stars popped into Marco's eyes. Bollocks's tail wagged as she turned and saw Brian striding across the courtyard.

"To be continued," she murmured.

She stood back as they walked to each other.

"Breen said you were okay. Everyone said—and I saw—but I needed to see you."

"I only have a few moments, as I've duties at the Leaving. But I needed to see you, and here you are."

Breen felt her heart just roll over and sigh as they embraced, as they kissed.

Then she patted a hand on her dog. "Come on, Bollocks, let's go somewhere else, and give them that few minutes."

# CHAPTER SIXTEEN

Of all the memories she'd banked during her time in Talamh, Breen knew, almost from the beginning of the ceremony, the Leaving would be the most heartrending.

She stood, as did so many others, in the whip of wind between the castle and the seawall. Below, waves crashed against the rocks like drumbeats. Overhead, dragons and their riders flew in formation across a sky going moody with twilight.

Others who had fought with the fallen stood at the wall, swords or spears or bows raised.

Across from them stood the families of those lost in the battle in the south. And while a piper played mournfully, one from each family stepped forward and said the name of their fallen.

The rest gathered repeated the name. One by one.

While the raft carrying the dead crested the first wave, the second, and began its journey on the sea, Keegan strode out to stand between the warriors and the families.

He wore black, unrelieved, the sword at his side, the staff in his left hand.

"We send to the gods the brave and the true. Even as we're

lessened by their loss, we are strengthened by their valor. Heroes of Talamh, father, mother, son, daughter, brother, sister, friend, never to be forgot, always to be honored, we give you to the light."

He turned toward the sea, unsheathing his sword, lifting it up.

When the shine of silver turned to flame, he sent the fire out like an arching arrow. Then lifted his voice, clear and strong, in song.

Other voices joined, all joined, and though the words were in Talamhish, the old tongue, Breen heard the grieving in them, and the faith, the pride. Beside her, Marco reached for her hand, gripped it tight.

His tears fell, as hers did. When Bollocks lifted his head, let loose a long howl, Breen knew he wept, too.

And in the deepening sky with only the dying shimmer of sunlight, the dragons sent out a roar and blew flame.

Drummers joined the piper now, with beats like the waves that rose and rose and rose.

And in those dying shimmers of the light, in the flashing dragon fire, streams lifted from the raft. The one who'd spoken the name of their fallen held an urn, held it high. So one by one, those streams, soaring over the sea, came home.

Keegan extinguished his sword, sheathed it. Turning back, he lifted the staff. "From the earth, on the water, by the fire, through the air. Into the light, into the arms of the gods, go the brave and true."

The mourners and witnesses echoed the words. At their end, Keegan brought his staff down. He turned to the families, fisted his sword hand over his heart.

"So it is done."

Some remained, murmuring among themselves as Keegan walked to the families. Others, Breen noted, slipped away. She saw Shana, a green cloak trimmed in gold, with a man in black and silver, deep brown hair a sweep around a narrow, handsome face.

He lifted her hand and kissed it, and she leaned into him to whisper something in his ear that made him smile. Together they wound through the crowd and away.

Breen wondered if the man noticed Shana looked back once, fixed her gaze on Keegan.

"Man, that was beautiful. Tore me up." Marco knuckled a tear away. "You told me how they did all this, but seeing it . . . wrecked me."

She leaned her head on his shoulder. "Right there with you." She took his hand again as they started back in. "Where are you meeting Brian?"

"Oh, right about here. He just needs to, you know, land, then he's, like, off duty. We talked about maybe getting dinner or something. You should come with us."

"Oh yeah, that's just what I'll do." She drilled a finger in his side. "Idiot."

"I'm not leaving you on your own."

"Truth? I'm actually ready for some on my own—with my dog. Maybe write a little, then turn in early."

"You gotta eat something, girl, and Brian said something about a pub. The Cackling Chicken or Ugly Duck or like that."

"Honest to God, besides refusing to be a third wheel on your romantic reunion, I don't have a pub meal in me tonight. I want some quiet time, Marco."

"Let me see your face." He gripped it, turned it, studied it. "Okay, that's the truth, so I'll let you off. But you need to eat something."

"Minga said just to ask, so when I'm hungry, I'll ask. Stop worrying about me. Especially since I see your hot new boyfriend coming this way."

When Marco turned, and the stars popped back into his eyes, Breen signaled to the dog and escaped.

Marco just stood, heart tripping, then extended a hand as Brian reached for it.

"I need to say that was the most moving ceremony or ritual or whatever it's called I've ever seen."

"You wept," Brian said, and traced a finger under one of Marco's damp eyes.

"I was just telling Breen—" He broke off when he realized she'd gone inside.

"Is she coming back then? Isn't she going with us?"

"She said she wanted some quiet, and since I could see she meant it, I let her off." Then he looked back at Brian, and couldn't think of anything else. "Do you want to go to the pub right now?"

"I don't, no. I was thinking later for that. Later."

"Later's good." Stepping in, Marco put a hand on Brian's cheek. "So for now, your place or mine?"

With a grin, Brian gave him a light kiss that promised more. "Yours is closer."

Kiara caught Breen just before she reached her room.

"I was after finding you!" She wore red—not bright but deep and dark with her hair tied back with a black ribbon. "My mother wanted me— Oh, first, I have to say I love your cloak."

She reached out to touch it. "So soft! Simple beauty and it looks so well on you, and with the dress. Simple often looks dull on me, but it shines on you."

A genuine compliment, Breen judged. "Thanks. I didn't see you outside. There were so many people. It was all so beautiful."

"A Leaving is sad and lovely all at once."

"Did you know any of the fallen?"

"Aye. All." Her voice wavered. "I knew all."

"I'm so sorry, Kiara." Instinctively, Breen took her hands. "I'm so sorry."

"As I am. But it's a comfort to know they walk in the light now. It helps thinking of them in the light. My mother would like to say you're welcome to sup with her and my father, as Tarryn and the taoiseach have duties. Or if you and Marco and this sweet dog want the more lively, some of us are going to the village, and you're welcome to join us."

"I appreciate that, but—"

"She said as well you might be weary after such a long day, and want a meal in your room. And not to pester you if you did. I pester," she admitted without shame. "I like talking, and I've so many questions, as I've never been to your part of the other side."

Breen had to laugh. "I'm going with my room for tonight, but I'd love to talk another time, and try to answer your questions."

"Well, that's perfect then. I could do your hair in the morning. I can't do it for you before the Welcome, as I'm already promised, but I would love to do your hair. It's glorious."

"That would . . . yes. Great. Thank you."

"Oh, it's my pleasure, and that's the truth of it. So I'll find you in the morning, before the Judgment. And I'll see a meal's brought for you. And Marco?"

"He's going out with a friend."

"Ah." Her eyes danced. "Well, a meal for you, and your fine boy here." She bent down to rub an enchanted Bollocks. "In the morning then, and if you change your mind, we'll be at the Spotted Duck."

She dashed away, leaving Breen smiling as she went into her room.

The fire still simmered, but she gave it a boost, lit the candles and lamps. She wanted to change into pajamas, but since she'd have to walk Bollocks outside before bed, she decided to stay in the dress.

With Bollocks already curled up in front of the fire, she sat at the desk. She would, at another point in her story, incorporate a Leaving, but for now, her characters needed a little quiet, too. And some happy, maybe a hint of romance.

Because the dark there would creep in before much longer.

After she'd written a little, and while she and Bollocks sat down to the meal a couple of cheerful teenagers brought them, Marco and Brian lay tangled together in the bed in the next room.

With his eyes closed, Brian stroked Marco's back. "I've thought of this almost since the moment I first saw you, standing on the road, your eyes full of wonder. Now I find my thoughts were small and thin compared to the having of you."

"Maybe we could just stay here, like this, for—I don't know—ever."

With a laugh, Brian shifted a bit so they lay nose to nose. "We could wander our way to the village for food and music, then find our way back. Right here again. I would stay with you tonight if you'll have me."

"I'll have you tonight, tomorrow, any night you want. I know that's moving fast, but—"

"No. Not for me, no, not with you."

"It's all just racing through me, you know? Everything." He pressed his lips to Brian's, then drew the warrior's braid through his fingers. "I was so scared, watching what was happening in the fire. Breen made it so I could see, because I needed to see. You. All the smoke, the blood—"

"Don't think of it now, *mo chroí*."

"No, I want to say, I saw you. I saw you fighting. Flying and fighting, tearing through the smoke. And I saw why, and I always . . . War sucks, Brian. It just sucks, but I saw why you had to. Most of this, for me, it's been like a fairy tale, right? Some weird parts, sure. Some jump scares, but mostly the seriously cool. I knew I'd stick with Breen no matter what, for the duration, but—"

"Because loyalty is who you are." Brian trailed a finger

down Marco's cheek, down his throat, then up again. "It's your great gift. I love this gift."

"She's my girl. Thick and thin. But I saw you, and the others. What you were fighting and why. And tonight, I saw all this, and what it meant. A hell of a long way from the Gayborhood."

Brian smiled. "This is your place on the other side?"

"Yeah, and I really want to show it to you sometime. Show you off to Sally and Derrick and the gang. But right now? I'm here, and I'm in all the way. For Breen, for you, for, ah, the light. I'm crap at fighting, but—"

Brian touched a finger to Marco's lips. "You have other skills and strengths and gifts." He ran a hand down Marco's flank—smooth skin, slim build, toned muscle. "You're beautiful. Body, heart, spirit."

"So are you." Levering up, Marco ran his lips over those broad shoulders. "I want you again. God, I want you again."

"I'm yours for the taking."

Breen woke early, and throwing the cloak over her pajamas, shoving on her boots, took Bollocks outside. She dreamed of coffee, or at least some strong tea, as she let him race and wander and sniff, and do what he had to do.

She wasn't the only early riser, as she'd heard activity and movement inside before she'd taken Bollocks out the door closest to the stables.

And she heard laughter behind the high walls of the falcon mews. When they walked on, she saw people already working in gardens, others drawing water from a wide stone well. Another carrying pails—milk?—away from what she took for a barn.

She saw a couple of cats slink out of it—and so did Bollocks.

"Oh no, not today. No chasing cats or squirrels or anything until we know our way around."

To make up for it, she walked him down to the bridge so he could jump in the river for a swim.

From there she watched what she took as young recruits—or whatever they were called here—drilling in a field. Swords, spears, archery, hand-to-hand.

Overhead, a handful of faeries sparred in midair.

She recognized Keegan, his leather duster flapping as he gave the woman beside him a friendly punch on the shoulder. When he turned her way, she called to the dog.

"Okay, let's go now. That water has to be cold. Let's dry off, go inside."

He came out, but reluctantly, and stalling. Then he spotted Keegan, and with a happy bark, raced to him instead of her.

"Great. Perfect," she muttered. No caffeine, pajamas, and bed head.

And, of course, he looked exactly that. Great and perfect as the dog leaped around him, as he laughed and gave Bollocks a good rub.

Stuck, she waited as Keegan walked to her, and the dog trotted beside him as if bringing her a present.

"Good morning. I trust you slept well."

"I did, thanks." She gathered the cloak close as the wind snapped at it. "He needed to go out, and he wanted a swim."

"We've dogs around if he wants their company. A pair of wolfhounds, some spaniels and mutts as well."

"Oh. I haven't seen any."

"You will. Are you walking on?"

"No, I was going back."

"As am I."

"The Leaving was beautiful," she said as they started back. "Heartbreakingly beautiful. I didn't know you sang."

He shrugged. "I enjoy it more with a pint or two in me."

"Who doesn't? I don't know when or where I'm supposed to go later."

"In two hours, we'll have the Judgment. Someone will fetch you."

"Is there a dress code—what I should wear? It may sound silly to you, but I don't want to be disrespectful."

He gave her a glance. "I'm thinking you might change what you're wearing presently."

"Funny. I packed light, as instructed, so I don't have a lot of choices."

"It's not a fancy matter, so what you usually wear, what I've seen of it, will do very well. I'm sorry I haven't had time to show you and Marco around—and I've kept my mother busy as well. Or haven't yet introduced you to those who live and work here."

"I've met a few. Brigid and Lo—they brought me up dinner last night."

He stopped, hissed. "You ate in your rooms? So again, I'm sorry."

"You're off the hook. I wanted the quiet, and Marco was with Brian. Kiara, who I already like a lot, brought me invitations—to eat with her parents, or go with her and some friends into the village. I really just wanted to write some and have the quiet."

"All right then. Kiara's a likable sort. She'll talk both your ears off your head, but she's entertaining and good-natured about it."

"She's determined to do my hair this morning."

He took a longer look and reached out, twisted one of her curls around his finger. "I like your hair as it is, but she's a skill for it."

"I also met Shana."

"Hmm. Not surprising, as she and Kiara are tight as ticks."

"Are they? I'd say that surprises me, because they strike me as opposite types. One being friendly and charming, and the other being . . . what's the term. Oh yeah. A stone-cold bitch."

He stopped again, spoke carefully—and she assumed as taoiseach. "Sure it's a pity you found her so, but it should be a simple matter to avoid her company while you're here."

"You think?" She couldn't help herself—in fact, she enjoyed herself by shooting him a big smile. "Harder to do that when she waltzes into my room uninvited."

His face went blank, but she saw annoyance clearly under the shield. "I'll speak to her about that, as we prize good manners here."

"I spoke to her myself, thanks all the same. She made a point of coming to my room shortly after you were with her in the courtyard—the one my room looks over."

"Plead the gods! If this is some female drama, I haven't the time or—"

She punched him, solid, in the gut.

Rather than flinch, he nodded. "You've improved there."

"Consider yourself lucky I aimed above the belt. The drama was all hers. She flounced her way in to subtly insult my looks, my clothes—that I'm used to. And she topped it by warning me off you."

"Sure that's nonsense, and I—"

"Shut up. She made it clear you and she were together, not that either of you minded a little dalliance—such as me. And whoever she dallies with when you're not around. But poor, unworthy me shouldn't get my hopes up where you're concerned. Added to it, people are dead because of me. If I hadn't been born—"

Now he gripped Breen's arm. "Stop. Stop now. She had no right to say such a thing to you. A lie, and a cruel one. I'm ashamed of her and for her. I will speak with her."

She'd been angrier than she'd realized, Breen admitted, and had bottled it up.

Well, she'd uncorked it now.

"I don't care if you speak to her or not. I know I'm not to

blame for any of this. And I don't care—why should I?—that you slept with her."

"Sleeping wasn't much of it. I don't have time for this, but I'll take this time, as it's wrong what she said, what she did. And that business in the courtyard was nothing."

"It was something," she corrected, and felt considerably calmer now that she'd popped the cork. "Since she staged it hoping I'd see—or someone would and it would get back to me."

"You can't—"

"I've spent most of my life watching people, Keegan," she interrupted, "because I had such a hard time interacting with them. I'd sit on the bus and watch them, and from their faces, their gestures, and so on, I'd decide who they were, what they were feeling.

"I saw your body language out there with her."

"My body speaks now, does it?"

"The way you stood, the way you made certain not to touch her when she insisted on touching you. Polite and cool, that's what you were. You dumped her—I know the signs there, too, as I've been dumped. And she didn't want to be. Broke things off with her," she explained when he frowned at her.

"As I was trying to say before you went off on your speech there. I ended it, as I began to see she wanted what I couldn't and wouldn't give. I never went to her bed after I went to yours."

And that mattered, Breen thought, for the simple respect.

"I don't want to make this about you and me."

"Well, we're in it, aren't we?" he countered. "I never wanted her the way I wanted you, and that was unfair to her. I don't have time to want you now, and still I do."

And that, though she might wish otherwise, mattered, too.

"I didn't tell you all this because I wanted you to be angry with her, or make me feel wanted. Or only partly there, because I can be as petty and needy as anyone. But I felt such rage in her, and desperation and . . . ambition."

"I'm aware it's more the taoiseach she's wanted than myself. I've always been, but what did it matter? Now it does. I'll speak with her."

"I'd be careful there if I were you."

"Well, you're not me, are you?" he said simply. "Now I have work, and you need to change out of your nightclothes."

When he walked away, she looked down at Bollocks. "Did that go well? I'm not sure it did. But I got it out of my system, so there's that. Let's go make ourselves presentable and find some breakfast."

When she walked back into her room, she found Marco waiting, Bollocks's bowls filled, the table ready for breakfast for two, and her bed tidily made.

"Well, hi, and . . ." She looked around as Bollocks made a beeline for his breakfast. "Who did all this?"

"Brigid and Lo. They're assigned to look after us. Somebody spotted you out walking, and they came in like—what's that thing?—dervishes. I don't know what that is except it moves fast. I said how maybe you and me could have breakfast together, and *bam*."

She went straight for the pot of tea. "Where's Brian?"

"Back on duty."

"Sit," she ordered, and did so herself. "Tell all." Then she lifted the lid off a pot. "I think this is porridge. We'll give it a shot. All," she repeated.

"We spent a lot of time next door."

"No! Let me find my shocked face."

Laughing, Marco spooned up some porridge of his own. "We talked a lot, too. And we did finally walk down to the village—cool place—had a pub meal, listened to music. Kiara was there with some other people, so we hung out for a little while. But we wanted to come back, and he stayed until he had to report in this morning."

"You look so happy, Marco."

"Girl, I'm stupid with the happy. I think I love him. I think he loves me."

Those big brown eyes of his looked into hers, implored. "Can you just fall in love—the real deal—just like that? Because I've fallen in the lusties, and the guy is hot or fun or interesting—all that real fast. But nothing like this, not for me."

"I don't think love has a time clock. Fast or slow or anywhere in between, it just is. And you look happy."

"When we're together, everything else goes away. I gave him the bracelet. He said it would be like carrying me with him wherever he went."

"I may fall for him myself." She slathered a slice of brown bread with butter and jam, passed it to him. "Eat, Happy Boy."

"So. What did you do last night?"

"Well, I wasn't busy falling in love, taking romantic walks, or having a lot of sex, but I did exactly what I wanted. I wrote, had the quiet, and got a good night's sleep. Oh, I also ran into Kiara again, and she wants to do my hair this morning."

"I really like her."

"Me, too! And I can't figure out why she's best pals with the Mean Girl. I ran into Keegan this morning, and that was interesting."

Marco grinned. "Tell all."

She told him all so they dished the dirt over breakfast. Then she kicked him out so she could dress.

"Wear the leather pants with the white shirt and the heathery V-neck black sweater," Marco suggested. "Leave the shirt out so the bottom shows under the sweater."

"I didn't bring the leather pants—which I wouldn't have bought in the first place if you hadn't worn me down."

"Which is why I put them in your bag when you weren't looking. Wear the leather. You look fine in them. Kick-ass. Tuck the legs into the boots. Brian says the Judgment's serious business."

He shot a finger at her, then hurried out.

Mostly because it meant she didn't have to think or second-guess, she put on what he told her to put on, then did what she hoped was serious-business makeup.

She'd barely finished when Brigid and Lo scurried in to take away breakfast, and Kiara came in with them.

"Ah!" Kiara pressed her palms together. "You look lovely and strong. It would be a mannish look, but you have such a fine form it isn't."

"Thanks. It's hard to know what's appropriate."

"You've done very well indeed. Now, I'll give you hair, for certain, that complements the rest."

"I love what you've done with yours."

Kiara flipped at her high, curly ponytail. "Very simple, as I'll be helping to mind the littles."

"You're not going to the Judgment?"

"For some of it, aye." She gestured for Breen to sit, then opened a case full of brushes and combs, pins and jars, bands and ribbons. "Some will bring their children, of course—it's good for children to see justice done. But the littles go fussy, after all."

She ran her hands through Breen's hair as she spoke. "Ah, sure and there's so much of it! And healthy. What a fine color. I saw your father when he came to the Capital. He was very handsome."

"He was."

"Oh, and I met with Marco and Brian, speaking of handsome. We had some good craic at the pub."

She chattered away as she worked, about the music, the man she'd decided to fall in love with, about people Breen didn't know and who flirted with whom, who was angry about what.

"Have you been to your mother's home world?"

"I have, aye. It's beautiful, all gold and blue—sand and sea—and the cities have great colorful towers. And the sun bakes so you forget what cold and rain are. But Talamh is home, and we protect it, and so protect all."

She stepped back, gave Breen a critical study. "I'm after simple for this again, and I think it's working very well indeed. If I can find even a tiny bit of time before the Welcome, I'd love to fancy it up for you."

Kiara took two mirrors out of her case, held the first up to Breen's face, the other behind.

"If you don't like it, I'll change it."

Breen saw her face framed by a few wispy curls, and the rest worked back into a long, loose fishtail braid.

"I don't like it, I love it. You made it seem so easy. I could've struggled for an hour and not managed this. I wore it straight for so long, and Marco's been trying to teach me how to style it, but I barely fumble through."

"He's the gods' own hair, doesn't he now? And such a voice, and . . . But wait."

Kiara stopped, frowned. "You said— You're meaning you took out the curls? Now why would you do such a thing when they're so beautiful, and look so well on you?"

"Long story."

"Sure that's one I'd like to hear when we've time for it. I love stories."

"Thank you for this, Kiara," Breen said as Kiara packed away her tools. "Is there something I can trade?"

"Another time, but this is a welcome gift."

"Prettiest one I've ever had," she said, and made Kiara beam. "Can I ask—about Bollocks. Am I allowed to take him to the Judgment?"

Kiara glanced down at him where he sat—as he had throughout the hairstyling. "Of course, and why not, as he's so well-behaved. Look at that sweet face." She made kissy noises as she rubbed it, and Bollocks thumped his tail. "But I'm thinking he's a young one as well, and like the young ones might rather be playing than sitting and behaving. Would he come with me?"

Breen looked at the way Bollocks looked at Kiara. Adoringly.

"Clearly."

"Why don't I take him along with me when I leave the Judgment? Then he can come play with the littles, and some of the other dogs, romp about outside."

She smiled at Breen. "You have the gift for living things, as I do. I'll know when he knows you call him back to you. Until then I'd enjoy him. And so would the littles."

"You're making all this very easy for me."

"And sure why wouldn't I?" Kiara's hair gave a cheerful bounce as she turned. "I'll let you know when I need to leave, and Bollocks and I will go have a fine time. And if I don't see you before, I'll see you at the Welcome."

When she left, Bollocks laid his head on Breen's knee. "I think we've made a friend at the Capital."

# CHAPTER SEVENTEEN

Kiara hurried back to her own room. She needed to put her case away, then make full certain she looked her best. Aiden O'Brian would be at the Judgment, and she wanted to add a bit of scent before she went down to take her seat—beside him.

Still, she called out greetings to any she saw on her way, and even stopped to gossip a bit with a friend over a mutual friend's recent public row with a lover.

She laughed to herself as she stepped into her room.

Shana rose from Kiara's reading chair.

"Well, so there you are. I haven't seen a sign of you since yesterday—when I saw you and Loren slip away together. So were you—"

"How could you?" Fury snapped and sizzled in the words. "How dare you?"

"What—what! What is it?" Horrified, Kiara dropped her case to rush to the closest friend of her lifetime. But as she tried to embrace her, Shana shoved her away.

"You did her hair? Did you think I wouldn't find out?

Doing her hair, inviting her to the pub, chattering with that one from away she brought with her."

"I—well, why shouldn't I do her hair, or give her an invitation?"

"She was rude to me! She was cruel."

"No!" Sincerely shocked, Kiara pressed her hand to her throat. "Oh, Shana, I'm so sorry. I'm more than sorry. I . . . She seems so pleasant, does Breen, I can't imagine— What did she say to you? What did she do?"

This time when Kiara reached out, Shana let herself be hugged. "She thinks to steal Keegan from me, to put herself above me."

Slowly, stroking Shana's lovely waves in comfort, Kiara drew back. "But, Shana, you told me you'd put Keegan off, that you preferred Loren, as Keegan thought more of his duties than of you. That when he wished to pledge to you the last he was here, you realized he wasn't for you."

If the lies she'd told her friend bit back at her, Shana shrugged them off and viewed them as truth. "I've changed my mind, and why shouldn't I? She's no right to him, and no right to speak to me as she did. And you, doing up her hair? How can you say you're my friend?"

"I didn't know, did I? And . . . But, Shana, what of Loren? You've been with him and no other since . . . before," she said carefully. "You told me he's said he loves only you, and has asked for your pledge twice now."

"Loren isn't taoiseach, is he?"

"No." Sorrow filled Kiara's heart. "No, he isn't. Here now, let's sit."

"I don't want to sit!"

"I do." Because she needed a moment. She knew how to soothe or joke Shana out of a temper or mood, but this felt different.

"You know how long I've wanted Keegan, and how I gave

myself to him anytime he flicked a finger. That he would brush me aside for such as her? I will not have it."

"But you refused him." Even as she said it, Kiara found the lie, and the sorrow grew. "I'm so sorry."

"I don't want your sorry." Hands fisted tight at her sides, Shana whipped around.

And Kiara knew the signs. Her friend was caught in one of her rages, and little could be done until it burned itself out.

"What you'll do is whisper in ears, you're good at it and have many ears eager to listen. You'll say how ugly she is inside her smiles and quiet manner. How she looks down her nose at the Fey and uses her powers to hide it."

"Shana, I could not. These are terrible lies."

"They are truth! They are my truth! You will say how she insulted me, and the taoiseach." Pacing now, skirt swirling, Shana built the lies. "She wants to rule over the Fey, and will bewitch Keegan to get her way. And having her way, will offer Talamh to Odran. He is her blood."

"Stop!" Appalled, and fearful with it, Kiara leaped up. "This is your anger talking, and you must stop. To say such things against another? Shana, this is wicked."

Shana strode away to the window, stared out. Then her shoulders slumped, and she began to weep. "Not anger, hurt. Oh, I hurt so, Kiara. When I saw Keegan again, I understood I'd made such a terrible mistake. I only want to right it. And she said such hard things to me."

"There now, there." Moving to her, Shana held her, stroked her. "We'll make it better, we will. I know it. A misunderstanding, that's all it is. Keegan declared his love for you, and that won't have changed, not a bit. His pride may be stung a bit, but you'll fix that right enough. And you'll be gentle with Loren when you tell him."

"She's in the way, don't you see?" Shana lifted her

tear-streaked face to Kiara's. "Keegan thinks he needs her, for Talamh."

"She is needed. And if you had hard words with her, we'll fix that as well, won't we? I'll help you fix it. There's a kindness in her, Shana."

Shana jerked away. "I've seen the truth. If you are my friend, you will shun her, and tell others to do the same."

Yes, she thought, she knew how to soothe Shana when her moods whipped so fast and hard, but this was different.

"I am your friend. You are a sister to me. But my parents have asked me to make both Breen and Marco welcome, to be a friend to them while they're in the Capital. You can't ask me to go against my parents' wishes."

"Do as you like then," Shana said in a tone so cold it might have frosted the glass.

"Shana—"

"You've shown me who you are." Shana stormed to the door. "I won't forget it." And slammed it behind her.

Minga came to escort Breen and Marco to the Judgment. Though she smiled, Breen felt hints of worry.

"Kiara's needed with the children," she began. "But Brigid would be happy to take our fine boy here to her if that's all right."

"Oh, sure. Thank you, Brigid. You go on with Brigid now, and you can play with the kids. I'll call you when we're all done."

He went off happily as Minga led them in the other direction.

"It will be crowded, as this Judgment is very important, but there are seats for you. If at any time you wish to leave, this is permitted. Any may witness the Judgment, any may choose not to." They walked to the main floor, where people crowded the entrance hall and voices buzzed. She continued on until they reached a wide archway with its doors opened.

More people crowded there, and inside a windowless room lit by torches and candles.

A huge room, Breen noted, with rows of benches almost like church pews. Portraits lined the walls, and with some shock she saw her father, her grandmother. Keegan.

"The taoisigh, all who have sat in the Chair of Justice, who have delivered the Judgment."

Minga worked her way through the crowd of people to the second set of benches on the left. "The council and their families sit there," she explained, and gestured to the right. "These first seats are for witnesses. You may be called to bear witness, as you watched the battle, and it was your vision that warned us of what was to come."

"Oh." Anxiety had her reaching over to grip Marco's hand. "I didn't realize."

"Only speak truth if the taoiseach asks of you. You may refuse to speak. You may leave." Minga set a hand on Breen's shoulder. "I hope you won't."

She walked over to sit with the council.

"Don't be nervous," Marco whispered.

"Easy for you to say."

"Hey, I saw it, too. He could ask me."

Not much comfort there, Breen thought, so focused on the chair. The Chair of Justice.

She wouldn't have called it a throne, though there were faint hints of one, as its back speared high in front of the dragon banner.

Deeply carved, its wood dark and gleaming, it looked ancient and impressive. But, she admitted, not royal.

More . . . sober.

She imagined her grandmother sitting there, her father.

Her father, she thought again, bringing justice to and judgment on the men who'd helped Odran abduct her.

She looked back at the portraits and felt a new shock as she saw her grandmother—young, vibrant in white. And the pendant, the dragon's heart stone, the gold chain. The pendant she'd seen in dreams and visions glowed around Marg's neck in the portrait.

"The pendant," she began, only to break off when Keegan strode in.

All in black again, with a vest—or maybe it was a doublet—over his shirt. He, too, wore a dragon's heart stone, on a black cord around his neck.

It gleamed there as the room fell silent, and he walked to, sat in the Chair of Justice.

Catching movement out of the corner of her eye, Breen shot a glance over and saw Shana, dressed in ruby red, take a seat beside a man with silvery hair who patted her hand, then nodded—though his brows drew together when the brown-haired man in black sat on Shana's other side.

Others came now, down the aisle between the benches.

Breen recognized the little girl—she'd seen her sleeping on a pallet in a dark, locked cell when she'd looked into the balefire on Samhain.

Her hair, walnut brown, fell down her back. She gripped the hands of the man and woman who walked with her.

Her parents, Breen decided. And the elf who'd carried her out of that cell walked behind them.

They took their seats on the first bench. Others followed to fill in the witness area.

Still no one spoke.

Brian came through a door in the front, and Marco squeezed Breen's hand. Behind him came other men—prisoners, she thought, as their hands were bound, their eyes downcast.

Eleven, she counted—with the spy from the valley among them—led to benches on the side of the room where Brian flanked one side, a woman the other, and Mahon with two more stood behind.

She jolted when Keegan brought down the staff.

"This is the Judgment. I am taoiseach, and I sit in the

Chair of Justice. These eleven are accused of crimes against the Fey, against Talamh, against the rules of law so written. I ask the hand of the taoiseach to speak these crimes."

Tarryn rose, walked out to stand and face the prisoners. She, too, wore black, slim pants, tall boots, a long open coat.

"You who await judgment are accused of the abduction of children. You are accused of blood sacrifice of children and of other Fey. You are accused of the murder of innocents. You are accused of treachery against Talamh in the name of Odran, the damned god."

Murmurs spread through the benches. Tarryn merely held up a hand to silence them.

"You will, one and all, have the choice to speak to these accusations, to explain, to deny, to rebuke. You will hear the account of witnesses to the accusations brought against you. Before the taoiseach renders his judgment, you will be given the right to speak to your innocence or to plead for mercy."

She stepped back, turned to her son. "This is the law of Talamh. This is the law of the Fey."

"This is the law," he said, and waited until his mother took her seat again.

"Alanis Doyle." He looked at the little girl, smiled at her. "You are safe here. Will you stand? Your ma and da can stand with you."

They stood together, hands clutched tight.

"I only ask you to tell your story, and speak it true."

When she pressed her lips together, her mother leaned down, murmured to her, kissed her cheek.

"Taoiseach, I was gathering the last of the autumn berries, for my ma and sister would bake a pie. And the man came."

"Is the man here?"

The girl pointed to the second prisoner on the left. "He's there, and he came and he said there was a puppy, and the puppy was hurt, and would I help. I heard the puppy—I heard it crying, so I went with the man to help. I'm not supposed to go beyond the berry bushes, but . . ."

"You only wanted to help," Keegan finished.

"Aye, aye, to help. And then . . . I don't know. I was somewhere else, and I had bad dreams. I couldn't wake."

"Can you tell about the dreams?"

"The men in the robes would come, and it was dark and cold. The man there with the puppy, and this one there."

She gestured to Toric.

"They made chants, and I felt sick when they did. And they said, or the one there—not the one with the puppy, the other—said—he said—" She pressed her face to her father's leg.

"Taoiseach, may I speak for her?" Her father crouched down to stroke her hair. "May I speak the truth she spoke to us? Please."

Before Keegan could agree, the girl shook her head. Tears spilled, but she turned back to Keegan. "He said on Samhain, we will wake her after she is bound to the stake on the pyre. And then her . . . her screams will rise as she burns. And the crackle of young flesh and bones will honor Odran."

She swiped her face with her hands. "I was so afraid. Taoiseach, I wanted my ma to come. I wanted my da. But I couldn't call out."

"Anyone would have been afraid, little sister."

"You wouldn't. You're taoiseach."

"I would've been afraid. And can only hope as brave as you are now to speak these words. How did you get back to your family?"

"She came." Alanis turned, pointed at, smiled at the elf sitting on the bench. "I could see a little, like a dream, and she came and picked me up, and carried me. She ran fast, fast. She's an elf, you see, is Nila, and talked to me all the while, saying I was safe, and all was well, and saying my name."

She knuckled more tears away, but continued her story.

"And I wasn't so afraid, and started to wake. Truly wake. And then I was home, and everyone was crying and hugging me, and hugging Nila, who said she couldn't stay for ale, thank you, because she was needed, but she'd come back when she could."

"You've done well, Alanis. You may stay, of course, through to judgment, but if you like, there are other children you may wish to meet, and as your parents have agreed . . ."

Brigid came through another door, a wriggling spotted puppy in her arms.

"This bit of a girl here needs someone to look after her and give her a home."

Tears vanished in joy as the girl reached for the puppy. "I can keep her as my own?"

"Sure she's been waiting for you. Show them where they can run around a bit, won't you, Brigid?"

"A thousand thanks." As Alanis left with giggles, her father's hand on her shoulder, her mother turned to Keegan, laid a hand on her heart.

"Bright blessings on you, Taoiseach."

"And on you."

He waited until the door closed behind them.

"Nila, will you speak?"

"I will, and gladly."

She was tall, slender, young, but her voice carried strong.

When the elf finished her story, she sat, and Keegan called on another.

The man rose, twisting his cap in his hands as the woman beside him wept silently.

"They killed our boy, sir, our youngest boy. Toric himself came to us and said he'd heard our boy had a calling. In truth he'd spoken about joining the order, living a life of prayer, doing good works. And Toric said he would take the boy as an initiate, and he would begin service, continue his education.

We thought it an honor, and he would be close, you see. He could come home once every week. He said—he said—they worked hard, the initiates, and slept rough, but it was good for the soul. And they ate well, and learned much."

The man choked back a sob. "The last time or two he came home, he was so quiet, and seemed troubled. But he said he needed to pray on it, and was sad, as two of the other boys had run off."

The man gathered himself. "And on Samhain, after the attack, and we couldn't get through to try to get to our youngest, but thought him safe in those walls, you came yourself, to tell us he was dead."

Keegan called on the Fey who'd seen the boys murdered, on the parents of the other boys. On others.

Then he looked at Breen, and even as dread at having to stand and speak filled her, he turned to the accused.

"What do you say to these words, these crimes of abduction and murder and sacrifice?"

All of them kept silent, refused to speak, until one of them fell forward, prostrated himself, bound hands outstretched. "I was misled. I ask for mercy. I was only a boy when I entered the order, and I believed all they taught. All Toric preached. I was misled, and never did I shed blood myself."

"Only watched it shed?" Keegan said.

"Had I spoken out, my life would be forfeit."

"Coward," Toric sneered from his seat.

"Let him speak," Keegan ordered as Brian turned to him.

"A coward and a liar, and a traitor to the true faith. He shed blood, drank it, offered it as is demanded by Odran, and now he whimpers like a child."

"You do not deny the accusations, the words spoken here?"

"I deny nothing, and I defy the weak laws, the thin faith of the Fey to stop the rise of the god. And with his rise, we crush your bones to dust. With his rise."

He stood now, aimed his gaze at Breen. "He will drink

you dry, abomination, and give us your husk to burn in his name.

"In his name!" Toric shouted, and as his bindings fell, as Lordan, the spy from the valley, collapsed, he shot power at Breen.

Even as Keegan surged from the chair, she pushed her hand out, met power with power. As the furnace of power in her ignited, she lifted her other hand high, rose.

She heard herself speak, but the words, the knowledge, the light burning in her came from so deep.

"You would test me here, in this place, at this time? You, murderer of children, slayer of the innocents, defiler of true faith, traitor to the Fey, to Talamh and all the worlds?"

As the air stirred around her, she stepped forward, pushing, pushing against what he threw at her, watching, watching the fear grow in his eyes.

"I am granddaughter of Mairghread, daughter of Eian. I am child of the Fey. I am of the Wise, of the Sidhe, of man, and of the gods. Hear my words and know truth. See me. See me and tremble at what will come for you and your dark god."

Her power whirled. It spun around him, locked him inside a cage of light.

Moving toward him, moving closer, she angled her head, left, right, as he cowered inside the bars.

"I see your death, your blood on the stones, your eyes staring without life in the dark. Be glad, Toric, murderer of children, you don't face my judgment this day, but that of the taoiseach, that of the rule of law. But know, the time may come when you will."

She brought down her lifted arm, and he fell to the ground.

It emptied out of her as quickly as it had filled. The room spun, and she waited to just slide down like water from a jar.

An arm came around her, took her weight. Tarryn's voice murmured in her ear.

"You'll not faint and be spoiling such a moment as this."

"Okay."

"I want you to walk back on your own now, look straight in front of you, head high. And sit."

She did as she was told, though the murmurs and confusion in the room got through finally. She sat, and even with his hand shaking, Marco took hers.

"Put the accused back where they belong, would you, Mahon, Brian."

Mahon started to lift the one who'd collapsed, then knelt. "This one's dead, Taoiseach, and cold with it."

Keegan held up a hand as the room threatened to fall into chaos.

"That's how you broke your bindings," he said to Toric. "You found the weakest, drained him, left him only enough to walk in here. Strengthened yourself, and took the rest of his light and life to attack. And now, we are all of us witnesses. We have all of us heard your own words damning you. You have each of you been accused, had testimony given against you. You have each of you broken sacred trusts, sacred laws. And you will each of you pay for this. You are, one and all, banished to the Dark World. You will, one and all, be taken there immediately, and sealed there for all time."

"He will free us!" Toric shouted, but fear cracked through the words. "He will free his faithful."

"I think he will not," Keegan said easily. "I think he will see what you are, cowards and weaklings. But should I be wrong, you should hope that I meet you on the field, and not Breen Siobhan O'Ceallaigh.

"Banishment, for all time," he repeated, and brought down the staff. "This is the Judgment. Take them out, and to the dolmen in the woods. I will open and seal the portal myself."

He brought down the staff again, then rose. "So it is done."

"I really want some air," Breen managed.

"Okay, honey, let's just sit here until the place clears out a little."

"Best leave now." Tarryn walked up, took one of Breen's hands. "Others will want to speak to you. So come with me now, and I'll take you out this way."

She led them out a side door, down a corridor, around a turn, and into the library.

"You'll have quiet here, and some wine. Open the doors there, Marco darling, so she can have some air as well."

"I don't know how that happened."

"If you don't, you will." Speaking easily, Tarryn poured from a decanter. "I'd take you up to my rooms and mix a potion for you, but this will do. You're stronger than you think, and showed that well and fine this day. Marg will be so proud."

"I was so angry, and so twisted up listening to those parents—those boys—and then it was so fast."

"Your gift, your power comes from your heart and your belly as much as your mind. Your belly holds the anger, your heart the compassion. Your mind the will."

She patted Breen into a chair before pouring wine for Marco. "Drink some wine now, Marco. What a good friend you are. He stood beside you, Breen, did you know? The whole time. He stood with you, for you."

"No, I didn't know. But of course he would."

"You'd do the same for me."

"I have to leave you now, as Keegan needs me for the rest. But you stay here as long as you wish. No one will disturb you."

"Tarryn, thank you. Thanks for giving me a hand when I might've—probably would've—passed out and spoiled the moment."

"Can't have that now, can we? It was such a bloody thrilling one."

When she left by the open doors, Marco dropped down with Breen.

"All but shit my pants, girl. It was a damn close thing. You were— It was more than the other night. More than anything. You were practically on fire. You were that bright, that fierce. And the air's spinning around, and the light's pulsing, and . . . Whew. I'm gonna need more wine."

"I don't know where the words came from, Marco, but I knew them. I meant them. And what was in me? It was so strong, but it didn't scare me. Because it was mine. Right after, I felt shaky, sort of like I did the first time I came through the portal. But that's going now."

"What do you feel like now?"

"Steady," she realized, and held out a hand, nodded when it didn't tremble. "Steady."

"That's my girl. Told you to wear that outfit, didn't I? Kick-ass. And that's what you did."

She laughed, gulped some wine. "Yeah, the pants did the job."

Deep in the woods, Keegan stood. Only his mother and Mahon remained now. He'd looked at the dark, listened to the howling wind through the portal he'd opened. As only the taoiseach had the power and the words to unlock it and seal it again. He'd seen that maw swallow the judged and the banished, and knew this was justice.

They could live in that dark world, but without magicks, without joy, without the peace and freedom Talamh offered all.

That, he thought, was the keen, cruel edge of justice.

They could live.

He held the staff, pulsing still from the energy called, but it had already begun to quiet. His mind, Keegan knew, would take longer to quiet.

He turned to Mahon. "Go home to your wife and children."

"I go when the taoiseach goes."

Keegan shook his head. "There's no need for you to stay. What needed to be done is done. The rest, gods spare me, is bloody politics and formalities. The Welcome tonight, a full council meeting, and the open Judgment tomorrow. Take this time, brother, as I'll want you with me when I go south to see to the razing."

"Fly home." Tarryn cupped Mahon's face. "My daughter is strong, but a woman creating life welcomes a steadying hand. Take this time, as Keegan says, for we can't know how much we have before Odran strikes again."

"All right then. I can do some scouting on the way home. I can detour to the south and see how it's holding."

"We left Mallo and Rory overseeing the cleanup and re-building. That's enough for the now. But you could take a swing to the north so we're certain all's well."

"And so I will, and I'll round back again if there's anything you need to know. Well then, you'll feast well tonight, that's certain, but I've the better bargain by far, as I'll be at my own table without having to put on the fancy."

"Push my face into that, I'll have you stay in my stead while I go home."

"Too late for that. I follow the orders of the taoiseach. Blessed be." He kissed Tarryn, gripped Keegan's shoulder. Then, spreading his wings, he rose up and flew north.

"You asked him to scout north so he'd go willingly and without argument. This," Tarryn said, tapping a finger on her son's chest, "is politics and diplomacy."

"I spared myself the headache, as I've one coming soon enough."

"And what is this?"

"Let's leave this place, walk in brighter air."

As they did, he told her of his conversation with Breen that morning.

"Ah gods, the girl's sly and selfish and has always been so."

Keegan's eyebrows shot up as he stopped short. "So, is it politics and diplomacy that had you holding that opinion back before this?"

"You visited her bed often enough in the last year or more, and as you're a man grown, I held my tongue. And I'm fond, very fond, of her parents. It's a pity, I think, they weren't blessed with more children so they wouldn't have had all this time and inclination to thoroughly spoil their only young."

"I mean to speak with her about this."

"Aye, you must. Have a care with this one, Keegan. Beautiful girls who grow into beautiful women who grow too used to having their own way can be vicious when denied. And as I'm done holding my tongue, that one has the vicious in her."

"She's no threat to me. And as all there saw clearly, by the gods, Breen Siobhan O'Ceallaigh can hold her own and more."

"Have a care," Tarryn repeated. "Revenge doesn't always come at the end of a blade, it doesn't always come hot. Sly and selfish finds ways to wound." Then she sighed. "Ah, Uwin and Gwen would be humiliated by her behavior to Breen."

"There's no need for them to know of this. I'll speak to her as, aye, that must be done. Then it's done."

Men, Tarryn thought, were so often naive when it came to women. But he was a man grown, and must learn such things for himself.

# CHAPTER EIGHTEEN

Because she had a plan, one she'd toyed with in the past then shut away, Shana went with Loren to his cottage after the Judgment.

They went on horseback, over the fields, and into the south edge of the woods near the village. And along the way, it seemed to her, Loren could speak of nothing else but Breen, and the sudden, unexpected power she'd displayed at the Judgment.

And why, she wondered, by all the gods why was she hampered by men who looked upon the redheaded slag as some sort of goddess?

"Perhaps you'd rather be riding with her," Shana said, voice dripping sugar. "Sure I can turn around and go back, see if I can find her for you."

Because he knew that tone, far too well, Loren turned to her. He let his heart come into his eyes. "There's no one but you for me, Shana. No one my heart, my mind, my body and spirit crave but you. For the power I saw in Breen Siobhan, I'm grateful knowing she'll be helping keep Talamh safe. And you. Most of all, you."

And because he knew her, because he loved her, he said nothing more about Breen—or anyone but Shana.

"What will you wear tonight to enchant me and everyone who sees you?"

"If I told you, you might not be as enchanted."

"You enchant me every day, every hour, every moment. No one in all the worlds is as fortunate as I, as you'll sit with me tonight, and dance with me tonight, and be with me tonight."

She smiled at him now, and meant it, as she knew he meant those words. He loved her, and that love was his weakness.

If only he'd been taoiseach, all would be perfect.

But he wasn't, and as he had no ambitions to lead, never would be. How could she settle for the weakness of love without the power and standing she craved?

In some ways, he was more handsome than Keegan. Smoother, for certain, in looks and in manner. His clothes were fine and fashionable always.

She knew whether they walked, rode, or danced together, they made a striking pair.

And Loren enjoyed giving her pretty gifts, creating glittering jewels and rich fabrics for her with his alchemy. And he never tired, it seemed, of paying her pretty little compliments, giving her the whole of his attention.

But.

He lived in a quiet cottage in the woods, and didn't possess the tower rooms of the taoiseach. He would never sit at the head of the council or have the people cheer for him.

Never would he sit in the Chair of Justice and punish her enemies.

And with him, she would never become the hand of the taoiseach, never have that power and sway.

Have it she would. One way or the other.

When they reached his cottage, she let him lift her from the horse, then linked her arms around his neck.

She knew genuine want when his mouth took hers. A skilled lover, he knew how to meet all her needs and stir more. When she and Keegan pledged, when they wed, she would keep Loren Mac Niadh with his soft, skilled hands as her lover. He'd fill her nights when the taoiseach had duties away from the Capital.

Though she intended to make certain Keegan spent most of his time with her and not in the west. His mother would go back there, as she would not be needed here.

Oh aye, Shana thought, she would see Tarryn sent back to the valley. She wouldn't tolerate vying for attention with Keegan's hawkeyed mother.

"I have a thirst for you." She murmured it as she pressed against him. "And wine." She laughed when she said it. "A cup of wine, then you. And you can enchant me, Loren of the Wise."

He waved his arm, turned his hand—right, then left.

The door—always locked by his spell, as was all the cottage—opened.

"Pour the wine, *mo chroí*, and I'll settle the horses. I want nothing more in my life than to enchant you."

She walked inside, then moved elf fast to pour the wine, to add two drops—only two—of the sleeping potion she had in her pocket to his.

He would sleep minutes only, but she only needed minutes.

She glanced up at the loft that was his workshop, imagined it in her head from the memories of times he'd spun spells for her, or made her a pretty bauble.

Harmless things, of course, small things. Though he had considerable powers. And for the larger things, the less harmless, he kept a cupboard locked with another spell.

Only his hand could open it—and since she'd professed to

love him, had pouted prettily that he didn't love her enough to allow her to open the cupboard, her hand could do so now as well.

Taking love, to her mind, forged the keenest of weapons.

When he came in, she sent a beckoning look over her shoulder and strolled, with the wine, to his bedchamber.

She gave a little shiver. "Would you light the fire, *mo leannán*?"

He flicked his fingers, set the fire blazing. As he continued toward her, she shook her head. "Oh no, my golden god, I would have you disrobe." She sipped from the cup in her right hand. "I would see what's mine."

When he simply snapped his fingers to send his clothes to the floor, she laughed. "I like what I see. Into the bed with you, as I will have you do my bidding."

He stretched on the bed, one with posts tipped in gold, one she knew was thick and soft, as he liked fine things as she did.

"I'm your slave, now and always," he told her.

She sipped more wine as she walked to the side of the bed. She set down her wine, handed him his. "Would you battle all my foes?" she asked as she took down her hair.

"Battle and defeat them, first to last."

"And drape me in silks and satins and jewels?"

"All you want, and more."

"Drink your wine, my slave, so I can soon taste it on your lips, your tongue."

As he did, she unhooked her dress, let it fall so he could see she wore nothing but herself under it.

"Shana. You are a vision, a dream. And so wicked."

She laughed, tossed back her hair. "You will lie still now, so I can have my way, so I can take my pleasure first while you wait."

She crawled onto the bed, slid up him very slowly. With

her eyes on him she used her tongue, her teeth, felt him ripple, pulse, strain for control.

"Wait and see." She trailed her fingers up his sides. "See there is so much more we can do in a bed than . . ." She paused, her lips a breath from his. "Sleep."

And with that word, and the two drops of potion, he slept.

She lifted the chain with the key from around his neck, raced from the room, up to the loft in a blur. Heart hammering, she laid her hand on the first of a trio of stars carved into the cupboard. Then to the first of the two moons, and last to smallest of a group of seven planets.

And when she fit the key in the lock, the doors opened for her.

She knew what she needed—she'd wheedled the spell out of him once when he'd been pliable from sex.

She gathered everything quickly—quickly, quickly. Such small amounts, she held certain he wouldn't notice the difference.

She closed and locked the cupboard again, sped down to put everything in the bag waiting in the pocket of her discarded skirt.

Thrilled, excited now at the thought of what she would do, what she would gain, she lay over him again.

"Wake," she whispered, and as he did, crushed her mouth to his.

His head spun, his mind clouded. His limbs felt oddly weak.

Then she rose up, straddled him, took him into her.

And nothing else existed for him.


More than an hour later, pleased, utterly relaxed, Shana rode back to the castle. Oh aye, she would absolutely keep Loren for her lover once she had her rightful place in Talamh.

And at the Welcoming, she'd give him all her attention

so Keegan would suffer—surely suffer—believing he meant nothing to her any longer.

And when all was done, the taoiseach would kneel at her feet and beg her to belong to him. He would give her everything she wanted; she would take everything she deserved.

She gazed at the busy village, at the gardens, the castle, and her heart swelled with the knowledge all would soon belong to her.

In the happiest of moods, she rode to the stables, and though she'd been taught to tend to her own horse, she passed him off to one of the boys there. After all, she needed all the time she had left to ready herself for the evening.

She tossed her hood back as she went inside and, fingering the bag in her pocket, crossed the grand entryway.

"Good lady!" One of the men who did—whatever they did—around the castle called out to her. "The taoiseach sent for you. Wishes to speak to you on your return."

"Does he then? And where is he?"

"He's in the Map Room, but—"

She just waved a hand, walked on. Beyond the Justice Hall, beyond the library, near the council room—where she would one day sit—the Map Room stood two stories high, with its maps of every known world, even the cities in them, or the jungles, the villages, and the seas, rolled on tall cases.

In the center of the room stood a large round table where those maps could be studied. Smaller tables lined walls where scholars and travelers could sit to update maps as needed.

Worlds, she thought, still riding on her happy mood, surely possessed of pretty things. When she was in charge, travelers would, by law, bring her some pretty thing for the privilege of using a portal.

Keegan stood at the large table now with several others. Shana recognized the elf who'd spoken at the Judgment, she knew Brian—Sidhe, dragon rider—the twins who were scouts, one of Morena's brothers, and Tarryn, of course, who in Shana's opinion held far too much power for a mere mother.

Keegan rolled up a map as she came to the archway.

"Thanks to you all," he said. "I'll see you all at the Welcome."

As they left, he walked over, poured himself a half tankard of ale. "If you'd close the door, Shana."

"Of course." Her pulse jumped. Maybe he'd come to his senses, and she wouldn't have to use what she held in her pocket.

"I speak to you now, first as taoiseach, and must tell you of my great disappointment in your behavior."

"Mine?" Her chin snapped up.

"And I speak to you second as one who thought of you as a friend, and must tell you of my anger you would use that friendship against another."

She looked him straight in the eye, and the distress in her own was genuine. It masked a rage rising into her throat, but was genuine. "I don't know what you mean, what you think I've done, but you hurt me." That rage, barely suppressed, made her voice quiver. "You hurt me, Keegan, and insult me by scolding me like a schoolmaster."

He took a slow drink, and because she knew him, she saw he held in his own temper. And that added the first licks of fear.

"Tell me this, did you seek out Breen yesterday?"

"Breen? Well, of course, as Minga asked me, and Kiara as well, to show her and her friend warmth and welcome. Why would you slap at me so for it?"

"You sought her out to tell her you and I continue to share a bed, and when I shared one with her it was of no matter. I don't take kindly to being used in a lie to hurt another."

"This is nonsense. Nonsense! Oh, sure and I should've known better than to offer her a bit of kindness." She swirled around the room as Keegan stood, quiet and still. "I should've known better than to hold my tongue when she raged at me and called me foul names."

"Did she now?" Keegan responded before setting the tankard aside.

"I told her plain that what had been between us was in the past, and that I loved another, but she wouldn't relent, so jealous, so furious she was. Now she's twisted it all around, hasn't she? Running to you to speak these lies."

"So these are lies?"

"Of course!" Eyes wide, she put a little tremble in her bottom lip. "How could you think . . . Didn't I apologize to you only yesterday? Though you'd hurt me, I gave you my regret for how I behaved. And though, even upon our first meeting, she gave me a look that chilled me, I went to offer her friendship and whatever help or companionship she might want or need while she's in the Capital."

Again, Shana pressed a hand to her heart. "And she flew at me, with such fury I thought she might strike me."

"And did she fly at you before or after you told her she held responsibility for the fallen?"

She dropped her hand to her side. It burned, Shana discovered, the anger. But more scalding, the realization she'd misjudged her quarry. "Why would I say such a horrible thing?"

"Why indeed, Shana?"

"I tell you I did not, would not. But I see, oh aye, I see you take her word over mine, this woman from the outside, this woman you've known only months. You take her word over that of one of your own."

She snatched up his tankard, drank to wash the bitter taste from her mouth. "She's bespelled you, that has to be the truth of this. All saw the anger of her power this day."

She heaved the tankard at the wall. "You are bewitched, and how can any trust you as taoiseach when one from outside, one with the blood of Odran, grips your will in her hand?"

When he let the silence hold a moment, another, she felt

another lick of fear. When Keegan took time to hold his temper, when he chose his words deliberately, they could bite.

"Have a care, Shana, with what you say to me here. Have a care before you make accusations unfounded and untrue. As if you say them to others, make them to others outside this room, you won't like the consequences."

His words shocked her, but no more than the cold look on his face, the hard ice in his eyes. "You—you threaten me?"

"I warn you. I am taoiseach, and your taoiseach tells you now to guard your words. I tell you to keep good space between yourself and Breen Siobhan O'Ceallaigh. I release you from the courtesy of offering her welcome."

At her sides, Shana's hands fisted until her nails dug into her palms. "You would bar me from the Welcome tonight?"

"I won't, no, as it would bring shame on your parents. But I warn you, for their sakes and your own, keep clear of her. She'll only be in the Capital for a short time. I trust—must trust—that whenever she returns, you'll have settled yourself."

"I am settled, Taoiseach." She spoke coldly now, her face like stone. "I am well settled. And I tell you in turn, you'll regret your alliance with such as her."

When she turned away, he let her storm out.

Twice now, he thought, Shana had clearly shown him what she was. So he regretted, very much, his alliance with such as her.

But considered the matter closed.

He walked over to pick up the dented tankard, and holding it, studied the map of Talamh on the wall.

And there were so many things, so many far more important things to worry about than a former lover's ire.

With Brian on duty, Marco insisted on taking Breen down to the village. The long walk pleased Bollocks—and gave him another chance to jump in the river.

And it gave Breen a chance to see life in the Capital outside the castle.

She decided people gathering around the well equaled Talamh's version of the office watercooler. Men and women chatted away while they filled jugs and buckets. Others leaned on the well, taking their ease while they talked.

Clothes flapped on lines behind cottages; sheep and cows grazed in pastures.

She watched a man and woman unloading bricks of peat from a wagon, and a woman—ripely pregnant—carrying a basket of fall vegetables into a pub where the music of a flute piped out like laughter.

Though the air blew brisk, the sun beamed, and that combined to create an ideal autumn day. Shopkeepers brought wares out into stalls to tempt passersby with more vegetables as colorful as a carnival, baked goods and leather goods, wooden toys and bowls and spoons, trinkets and jewelry, ribbons and buttons.

Shawls and scarves, caps and sweaters hung from pegs while in the next stall a cobbler hummed as he hammered the sole of a boot into place.

"Brian says it stays pretty busy," Marco told her. "People come in to trade or set up a stall, maybe visit the castle grounds or some of the local sights."

"It's all bigger than I imagined."

And full of life, she thought. Energy, movement.

"If we have a chance to come down again, we should bring something to trade. I made a few bracelets, but I didn't think to bring them today. I've got a charm bag in my pocket, and a little bag of crystals. I'll put something more together for next time. I'd like to find something to give Nan."

As she thought of it, she saw a woman sitting in a rocking chair. Raven-black hair piled in a loose knot on top of her head, and a pumpkin-colored shawl wrapped around her shoulders.

As she rocked, she worked snow-white wool with knitting needles and tapped one booted foot to some internal rhythm.

The sign over her head read OF THE WISE.

She paused her knitting only to crook a finger at Breen.

As Breen stepped closer, she saw the red dragon flying over the field of white wool.

"It's beautiful."

"It's for my great-grandchild who'll come into the world by Yule. My twelfth she'll be, and for each I make such a blanket so wherever they go through their life they know the dragon flies over Talamh."

"A wonderful gift."

"I know you," she added, and set the knitting in the basket beside her chair. "You've the look of those who came before you. I, carrying in me my last child of seven, stood on the road right there when first Mairghread rode to the Capital as taoiseach. And so I stood when your father made that ride."

She rose. "Come inside, Breen Siobhan. You and your friend and your fine dog there are welcome."

"I don't have anything to trade today," Breen began as they followed the woman inside. Then she stopped, simply looked.

"You like what you see?"

"It's wonderful. It's a wonderful shop." Though smaller by far, it made Breen think of the Troll cave.

"Wow." Marco turned a circle. "It smells amazing in here."

As he spoke, a black cat—who'd sat so still on a table Breen had taken it for a statue—leaped down. Instead of giving chase, Bollocks sat while the cat circled him.

"My Sira won't harm your boy there. She's only showing him who's in charge." With a laugh in her voice, the woman spoke to the cat in the old tongue.

The cat made one more circle before jumping back on the table. And sitting, began to wash.

"Here now." The woman went to a shelf holding a variety of

crystals in wedges and squares and rounds. She lifted down a perfect square of deep purple amethyst.

"It's beautiful," Breen began when the woman held it out to her. "But I . . . Oh, for a candle." Intrigued, she took it, studied the round hole in the center.

And heard the voice of the stone.

"For peace and calm of mind in these turbulent times. You're after taking a gift back to your nan, aren't you now?"

"Yes, and this is perfect. But I didn't bring anything to trade."

"No, no, you've come to Talamh, and in trade for that, I give you this to give to Mairghread. My man, the father of my seven, he fell at the Battle of the Black Castle."

"I'm so sorry."

"He stood for the light. For you, for me, our children, and all who come after. A good man, he was a good man, and I see him in our children, and theirs, and theirs. As I see your father, his mother in you. So, as they stood for the light, you will stand, and the child I'll wrap in the blanket I made will know peace.

"Will you tell her Ninia Colconnan from the Capital sends blessings? She may remember me."

"I will. And I'll remember you, Mother."

When Breen offered her hand, Ninia took it, then gripped it. Her eyes went from soft blue to deep. "Have a care, child. Look behind and beneath. Someone wishes you harm."

"Odran and his followers."

"Him and them, always, but on this side, and close. Have a care, for you're precious to us. Have a care," she said a third time. "This will fail, this time, this way, but it won't be the end of it."

She closed her other hand over Breen's. "I can't see more, but I hear the hard thoughts sent toward you, and thoughts so hard and sharp can cut as true as a blade."

"I'll be careful."

With a nod, she stepped back. "You wear protection, I see," she said to Marco. "So take this." She walked over, chose a small white candle. "The scent comes from the blossom of the jasmine flower that blooms at night. As the pleasures of love often do. You love and are loved, and when you take those pleasures, this scent and light will . . . enhance. And you, do you think I'd be forgetting you?"

She gave Bollocks a pat as the cat looked on from her superior height. She chose a trio of tiny stones from little jars, then placed them on Bollocks's collar.

"This true heart this charm protect, as this is my wish and my intent. Shield him on land and air and sea. As I will, so mote it be."

With a faint shimmer of light, the stones fixed into the collar.

"You've been so kind," Breen began.

"You've had trials and face more to come. This is thanks. Kindness? This costs nothing."

Marco leaned down to kiss her cheek. "I'm awfully glad we met you, um, Mother."

"Ah, what woman doesn't like a kiss from a handsome young man." She kissed his in turn. "We'll see each other again. Now you need to be off, to make yourselves lovely for the Welcome."

She took Breen's hand one last time. "And have a care, Daughter."

"She was great," Marco said as they walked back. "A little spooky with the someone wants to hurt you bit, but great."

"I think I know who she sensed, and it's nothing. Hard thoughts don't worry me."

"Who? So I can give them the hard eye."

"Shana. She embarrassed herself—and women everywhere—trying to get me into a fight over Keegan."

"Oh, that." Since she'd already told him the story, he shrugged it off as she did. "But I'm giving her the Marco Olsen Terrifying Hard Eye anyway. Nobody snipes at my girl."

"That'll teach her." She gave him a body bump. "But on to more important things. Is it dumb if I changed the color on the blue dress—it's all I've got—just for tonight?"

"You can do that?"

"I can. Maybe to purple or something bronzy."

"Not dumb, but totally on. How about after we get all done up, I come over and you can try out different colors on me? And what else you should do? Hunt up Kiara, see if she's got any sparkly pins or whatever for your hair. Just fancy it up a little."

"She said she'd promised to do someone else's, so wouldn't have time. But . . . maybe I could hit her up for a loan, and you could help me fancy it."

"Something sparkly," he said again. "Or, you know, if you can't find her, we could maybe work some flowers into the braid."

Now she hooked an arm through his. "I'm almost, sort of, nearly looking forward to this thing tonight."

"Almost, sort of, nearly? Come on, girl. Party in the castle! Can't nothing be more lit than that. We had the sad and solemn last night, and man, I'm never going to forget that. We had the drama and your I'm-a-kick-ass-witch turn this morning. Now it's party time. Welcome to the Capital, Breen Siobhan Kelly."

"Yeah, it's— Wait, what? You think this is about me tonight?"

"Don't think, know. Girl, what'd you think? Besides, Brian told me for sure. Welcoming you—and I get a piece of that as the BFF of the star."

She lost three shades of color on the spot. "Oh God, Marco, I don't want to be the star."

"It's not like you have to get up and sing. Though you

could. And no speeches required or anything, Brian said. I asked because I know you. You just talk to people, and there's a big-ass feast, lots of drinking, and there's dancing. A party, Breen."

He laughed when Bollocks leaped off the bridge into the river. "That dog can't pass up a puddle, much less a stream. Oh, and he gets to come, too. Toss away the nervous face, girlfriend. Everybody said tonight's nothing but fun."

# CHAPTER NINETEEN

In her room, blood boiling, mind burning, Shana set out the crystals and herbs, the oils and essences she'd taken from Loren's cottage. From a box hidden in her wardrobe, she retrieved the strands of hair she'd taken and secreted away months before when she'd playfully insisted on brushing Keegan's hair.

In her heart she knew she'd always planned to do this, just this, even when she'd believed Keegan would pledge to her. Because to attain all she wanted, she needed him to look at her and no other. To want her and no other.

Love her, and no other. Even his mother. How could she take Tarryn's place as the hand of the taoiseach if he took love that should be hers and gave even drops of it to his mother?

She used a bowl of rose quartz Keegan had given her and, with that anger and ambition fueling her intention, lit a red candle.

"Red for passion and for the heart, light his love for me alone." Her own pounded as she poured the oils into the bowl. "Oils of cinnamon and poppy cloud his mind to all save me, and to this I add the stone. A weight on his heart when we must part."

Carefully, she tapped in powdered herbs. "Rosemary, valerian, remember and sigh till nothing I ask of him will he deny." One by one, she added three strands of hair.

"This part of him, three, two, one, and so the spell is nearly done." She picked up a small knife, ran a shallow slice across the heart line of her left palm. "Now add my heart blood and my tears . . ."

She let the blood drip into the bowl and, as she'd had the talent since childhood, willed tears to her eyes. Leaning over, she let them fall into the mix. "So when he drinks, he drinks of me, and his love is mine for all my years.

"Stir and seal and bubble and blend." Circling the candle over the bowl, she watched three drops of red wax slide in, and with it, the mix simmered and smoked. "And so his love will never end. When this potion he drinks, his heart with mine links. It will forever belong to me. As I will, so mote it be."

With a little shiver, Shana blew the candle out.

She'd done a few spells before—coaxing Loren to show her. But she'd never done anything this complex, or anything on her own.

Now she smiled at the clear, quiet liquid in the bowl. She would learn more, she decided. She had a few drops of Wise in her, after all, from her mother's mother's mother.

She poured the potion from the bowl into a small vial, closed it with a stopper.

She would dress, aye, she would be sure to look her very best, then go up to Keegan's chambers before the Welcome.

She knew just what to do, what to say.

And before the moons rose, she would have all she'd ever wanted.

Breen Kelly would be sent back to her own world, Tarryn back to the valley.

And she would take her place at the council table. She'd share Keegan's handsome chambers in the tower—and make a few changes there, of course. And she'd plan a lavish wedding, one suited for a queen.

Imagining it, she opened her wardrobe to select which gown she should wear when Keegan pronounced his love.

Even as she reached for one, someone tap-tapped on her door. Before she could call out, it opened.

With a hesitant smile, her styling case in hand, Kiara poked her head in. "I've come to do your hair. Are you still angry with me? Oh, Shana, I don't want you to be angry with me. I can't bear it!"

As she hadn't given Kiara a thought all day, it took Shana a moment. Remembering, she put on a pout. She wanted her hair styled, of course, but wanted a bit of groveling first.

"Ah, so you've done your new friend's hair already, have you then? And now have a bit of time for me?"

"Oh, Shana, no!" Hurrying in, Kiara closed the door behind her. "I've come straight to you after minding some of the littles. Never would I want to hurt your feelings so, and I've been half-sick on it all day. I won't do her hair again, I promise you. So come and sit, won't you? I've a style in mind for you that will turn heads."

Kiara started for the dressing table, and stopped when she saw the red candle, the bowl, the remainder of the ingredients used in the spell.

"What are you doing here, Shana?"

Cursing herself, Shana waved a hand as she strolled over to gather up herbs and oils. "I thought to try making a scent for myself, but I couldn't get it right."

Kiara laid a hand on Shana's arm. "No, that's not what you were about, no, it isn't. You mustn't do this, Shana, you mustn't do such a bad thing as this."

"I don't know what you could be talking about." Furious

all over again, Shana yanked open a drawer, intending to shove everything inside to deal with later.

"You've already done it, I can see it on your face." Heart-sick, fearful with it, Kiara tightened her grip. "I can see the candle's already been lit and put out again. Oh, Shana, why would you do such a thing? It's against our laws, and you know full well. A love spell takes choice away, and can cause the one bespelled to do things he'd never do, do them out of jealousy or despair."

"Now you lecture me? Go, just go. I'll do my own hair."

Truly shocked, Kiara took a step back. "Oh, gods help us, Shana, you mean to bespell Keegan. The taoiseach! Shana, you would be banned from the Capital, and your family disgraced! Worse, you could be banished altogether, for you'd break one of the First Laws."

"I'll not be banned or banished or anything of the sort, as he'll be devoted to me, as I'll take my place as his wife and his hand. And I've earned that, right enough.

"And you'll be quiet about this," Shana added, giving Kiara a shove. "You'll say nothing, do you hear me, or you'll be the one sent from the Capital."

"You're angry now, and hurt more than I knew, and I'm so sorry for it. You're just not thinking clear, that's what this is." Even as her eyes pleaded, Kiara kept her tone gentle. "Give me the potion, and I'll destroy it. We'll never speak of it. I'll tell no one of it."

"You'd best be telling no one, or you'll pay for it, I promise you that." Snarling it, she shoved Kiara back another full step. "Now take your bloody case and go. You're a false friend, I see that clear enough."

"I'm as true a friend as you've ever had, and so I'll save you from yourself." She didn't pick up the case, but turned to the door. "You won't give me the potion, but you'll give it to my mother right enough."

"You'd betray me?"

Eyes full of tears, Kiara looked back. "I would save you."

She'd nearly reached the door when Shana grabbed the vase, rushed after her. Brought it down on her.

When Kiara fell, when Shana saw the blood, she thought she'd struck harder than perhaps she'd meant.

"Can't be helped," she mumbled. "You turned on me, and would have ruined everything. The fault's your own."

No time now to put on her dress, to style her hair. When Kiara woke—if she woke—she'd go running to her ma.

But when Keegan drank the potion, when she had his heart, he'd deal with them.

With all of them.

She stepped around Kiara, closed and locked the door, and began to make her way to the tower rooms of the taoiseach.

In her room, Breen put away the gift for Marg. She filled Bollocks's water bowl, brought the fire up to a satisfying snap, then poured herself a glass of wine.

"The Capital's interesting," she told the dog. "But I'll be ready to get back to the valley. And to our cottage. But right now, I have to work myself up to a party mood."

She opened the wardrobe to lay out the blue dress, and instead pulled out the one hanging beside it, and read the note from her grandmother.

A Welcome is a bit fancier than a ceilidh, less so than a ball. Remember all the years I couldn't give you pretty things, and enjoy this, as I enjoy the giving of it. Bright blessings, mo stór.

"Nan." Breen sighed it as she took out a dress the color of moonlight mists.

It felt just as soft, she thought as she held it up, turned

to the mirror. The thin layers of the skirt floated down to just above her ankles with the faintest of sparkles, like faerie lights through that mist. The long sleeves came to points, and the square bodice dipped considerably lower than the more modest neckline of the blue.

"Well, it's gorgeous, and it deserves some sparkly pins in the hair, like Marco said. Let's go find Kiara, Bollocks, and see about a loan."

The dog went out with her, and she realized she had no idea where Kiara's room might be. She started to tap on Marco's door to see if he did, and saw Brigid.

"Is there something you're needing?"

"I was hoping to ask Kiara for something, but I don't know where her room is."

"Well now, I'm happy to show you. It's down in the other wing."

"I appreciate it."

"And so did you enjoy your afternoon in the village?" Brigid asked as she led the way.

"I did. So much to see."

"Yes, and a fine day to see it. And tonight should be fine as well. Here's Kiara's room. Will she be doing your hair? She's brilliant with hair."

"I just wanted to see if she had some pins I could use tonight." Breen knocked. "She told me she already promised to do someone else's."

Brigid slid her gaze to the door one down from Kiara's. "Likely that one. Shana, that is. She's likely in Shana's room now, fixing it up for her."

"Oh. Well, I won't bother her."

"I'll wager I can find what you want. What sort of pins are you after?"

"That's all right. It's not important. I was just . . ."

She trailed off because Bollocks had gone to the other door, and now began to whine.

"Come on, Bollocks, come away from there. Let's go back and—"

But because he felt distress, she did. Because he scented blood, she did.

"Something's wrong." Stepping over, Breen didn't bother to knock, but tried to turn the handle. "It's locked, but something's wrong," she repeated as Bollocks let out a howl.

"Are you sure?" Brigid clasped her hands tight. "I can fetch a key from Tarryn if you're sure. It's just—"

"No time." Using power, Breen turned the lock, then opened the door.

Kiara sprawled just inside, and Breen dropped down beside her.

"She's hurt!" Brigid spun on her heel. "I'll get help."

"Wait."

Slow, Breen reminded herself. Easy. She pulled back everything Aisling had taught her, then laid her hands on the wound seeping blood at the back of Kiara's head.

"I can see it. I can feel it."

Slow, easy, she brought the light.

"It's not deep," she murmured. "But there'll be pain. So gently." She breathed in, breathed out, closing the wound that ran long but shallow. Soothing, shrinking the ugly knot, and the bruising.

When Kiara moaned, stirred, Breen spoke softly. "Lie still a minute. I know it pounds, I feel it. You feel sick, but lie still, let me finish."

"I can fetch a potion from one of the healers," Brigid began.

Kiara moaned again, stirred again. "Shana."

"It's all right. Another minute."

But eyes wheeling now, Kiara shoved up to her hands and knees. "Shana. The taoiseach!"

"What happened? Was it Odran or—"

"Oh gods." Kiara grabbed Brigid's arm, dragged on it so she could stand. "Where is the taoiseach?"

"In his chamber. I—"

"Get help. His mother, mine, send them to him. Hurry, hurry."

As Brigid raced off, Kiara swayed.

"You're dizzy, come sit. Let me finish."

"There's no time. We have to stop her. Help me. I can't run."

"All right. Lean on me. What happened?"

"She struck me."

"Shana? She hit you?"

"She's so angry, and I think she's lost her mind. Oh gods. She's brewed a love potion and means him to drink it. I have to stop her. Oh, she's damned herself, my dearest friend, and I must be the one to accuse her."

While Kiara had lain unconscious, Shana climbed the tower steps. She put on her most contrite expression and knocked on Keegan's door.

"Come."

She kept her expression in place even when irritation rose on seeing he wasn't alone. And clearly didn't look pleased to see her.

"I'm interrupting," she said, and smiled at Flynn.

"A pretty woman is always a welcome interruption, and we were just finished. Aye, Keegan?"

"Aye. I'll see you at the Welcome, and we'll speak again tomorrow."

"Save a dance for me, won't you?" Flynn said to Shana.

She gave him a smile, a flutter of lashes. "I will, of course."

When he went out, Shana put the sorrowful look in her eyes, folded her hands at her waist. "And again I must apologize. I don't like making it a habit, I can tell you, so hope this is the last I must."

"It's not to me you owe one."

She nodded, moved to the fire in the generous sitting room—one she intended to make her own. "I know you believe that, and so I will, as when I cooled my temper, I realized how what I said to Breen could be misunderstood. I never meant to insult her, Keegan, but I see now I did, and I was only joking, as women often do, about you—and us. She was so upset by it, and said hard things, so I said hard things."

Shaking her head, she turned back to him and saw—on that face she knew so well—he'd had more than enough of the entire matter.

"Women can be foolish about men, and I confess I felt a bit of jealousy myself, as a woman does when she meets the lover of one she's bedded herself. Silly and foolish, and I'll apologize to her. When I leave, I'll go straight to her chamber and do so. But I owe you one for how I spoke to you. I was embarrassed."

She smiled again, lifted her hands. "As you know well, my pride runs wide and runs deep. Will you, again, forgive me?"

"I will, of course."

But she heard, clearly, the stiffness in his voice. Saw, clearly, the coolness in his eyes.

"Will you have a cup of wine with me—a bit of courage for me before I face Breen—and so we put the matter behind us?"

"I've other matters to see to before—"

"One cup of wine," she said as she walked to the table holding the decanter. "And behind us it goes for well and good."

With her back to him, she poured the potion from vial to cup.

She handed him a cup, tapped hers to it. When she sipped and he didn't, she tried again.

"And you can drink to me on my pledging with Loren, and wish me happy."

He looked into her eyes. "I would drink to such news as that, and wish you happy."

As he lifted the cup, Kiara stumbled in the door. "No, Taoiseach, no. Don't drink it."

When her knees buckled, Breen lowered her into a chair.

"She made a love potion," Breen told him.

"What terrible lie is this! What have you done to Kiara, my friend? Why, there's blood! Keegan, she's—"

"Silence!" He set the cup down and, waving his hand over it, sealed the potion inside. "Did you think I wouldn't sense it, couldn't smell it? What do you take me for?"

He grabbed Shana's arm before she could move, and, thrusting his hand into the pocket of her skirt, pulled out the vial.

"That you would do such a thing to another. Someone with all you have would do this to take more. You would break a sacred law, betray my trust, harm a friend, all for your pride."

Her fury snapped so strong she couldn't call the tears.

"I gave you what you asked for, what you wanted, and you spurned me."

"We gave each other what we wanted, for a time, then it wasn't enough, it seems, for either of us."

"You would take her over me?"

He looked into her eyes, spoke the cruel truth. "I would never have taken you."

"Bloody bastard, you'll pay." She jerked her arm free. "I swear you'll pay. Your mongrel whore will know my wrath, as will you."

With Kiara weeping, Shana blurred from the room.

"She won't get far." After pressing his fingers to his eyes, he walked over to crouch in front of Kiara. "There now, darling, where are you hurt?"

"She hit me. I think she hit me."

As Kiara started to lift her hand to the back of her head, Breen took it, laid her other on Kiara's head. "I know it hurts. Let me finish."

"I saw—I saw on her dressing table, and I said no, she couldn't. I said she had to give the potion to me, and I'd destroy it. I wouldn't tell anyone. I'm sorry, I'm sorry. She's my friend, and I wouldn't have told anyone even though it's law."

"It's all right now." He shot a glance up at Breen, saw the flickers of pain, the concentrated focus as she worked. "Who wouldn't do the same for a friend?"

Weeping, Kiara clung to Keegan's hand. "But I think . . . After all, I think she was never my friend."

"No, darling, but you were hers."

Minga flew into the room with Tarryn right behind her. "Oh, my baby!"

"Let Breen finish, let her finish, Minga. Kiara's doing fine now, just fine. Aren't you, darling?"

Tears continued to fall in a flood, but she nodded as Minga dropped down beside Keegan and took Kiara's hand.

"She hit me. I think. I said if she wouldn't listen to me, she would listen to my mother. I was going to get you, Ma, bring you, but she hit me, I think, because my head—a terrible pain, and then Breen was there, and Brigid with her. It doesn't hurt so much now, truly it doesn't."

"Feel a bit unsettled in your belly, don't you?" Tarryn got another cup, poured some of what she carried in a bottle into it.

"I do, aye, but not as much now. What will happen to Shana? She wasn't thinking right, she couldn't have been. It was more than one of her tempers. If she—"

"Ah now, that's not for you to worry about." Soothing, gentle, Tarryn stroked Kiara's face. "You drink this now, my good girl. That's the way, every drop."

When Breen stepped back, Tarryn ran her hands over Kiara's head, her neck, her shoulders. Then, with a smile, nodded at Breen.

"Now, you'll go with your ma, have a bit of a lie down, and you'll be fine." She stepped over to lay a hand on Minga's shoulder. "She'll be fine, I promise you."

"Aye, she will, with a head as hard as my girl's. Come, my love, you can rest in my bed as you did when you were a little."

"Tell me this if you can, Kiara." Keegan helped her stand. "Do you know where she would've gotten what she needed? Where she would have learned the words?"

"Not for certain, and if I'd known she was even thinking of such a thing, I'd have found a way to stop her, for her own sake. I swear it."

"The fault's not yours." He kissed her forehead. "You did all that was right. Go and rest."

Minga put an arm around her waist to lead her out, and as she did, she reached out to grip Breen's hand. "I'll never forget."

Rubbing the back of his neck as they went out, Keegan turned to Breen. "Sit."

"I'd really just like to go get some air."

He swiped a free hand to his window so it flew up. "Now you have it. Sit. You're pale as the moons."

"And of course the way to fix that is barking at her. Get her some wine, boy, and three drops—three's enough—of a restorative," Tarryn said.

"I have to . . . She needs to be found. I have to send a few, quiet as I can, to do that."

"Gods. Aye, go on then. I'll see to Breen."

"Stay," Keegan ordered Breen before he strode out.

"He's angry." Tarryn walked to a cabinet, and opening it chose a small bottle. "My boy's patience runs thin at the best of times, but it vanishes like mist in the sun when he's angry."

"Yeah, I've noticed that." Because she didn't want to sit, and did want the air, Breen stepped over to the window. It looked out, she saw, on the gardens, the fountain, the river, the village, and the hills and fields beyond.

"Drink this, just a few drops of restorative in some lovely wine from our own vineyards. He'll be less angry when you've color back in your cheeks. I'm after some wine myself with all this."

She poured her own. "How bad was she hurt, our Kiara?"

"I'm not really sure. I'm still learning, and I've never healed a head wound like that. I had to try. She was on the floor, in Shana's room. Bollocks sensed it first."

His tail thumped as he sat by the fire.

"And I sensed it through him. A lot of blood—head wounds bleed so much. I'm guessing a concussion because her vision was blurry when she started to come out of it, and she felt queasy, dizzy. There was a vase—crystal, I think—on the floor, and the water from it, and the flowers strewn. The door was locked. She'd locked the door and left Kiara bleeding."

"It would have been worse for her if you hadn't found her. I blame myself for some of this."

Now Breen turned. "How? Why?"

"Because I knew some of what she was, the ambition so raw, so deep. The slyness in her. But I'm fond of her mother, and her father, and they love her so. Indulge her far too much, but from love."

"She had a choice; she made it. That's not on you, or Kiara, or her parents or anyone but her."

Tarryn studied her as she drank some wine. "So Keegan would say, and just as firm—even as he holds some of the blame inside himself."

"Then he's stupid."

Tarryn threw back her head and laughed. "Oh, I like you. I do like you."

"What happens when they find Shana?"

"Judgment," Tarryn said simply. "And there I worry about my boy, as whatever he does will weigh heavy on him." She walked over to pour a third cup of wine as Keegan came back.

"I've three elves combing the castle itself, as it's dead easy for an elf to hide—though she couldn't for long. A couple of faeries will take the grounds, the woods, the village. I've had to send for Loren—and they'll look in his cottage and the woods there as well. She might go to him for help. She might have gotten the spell from him, and I need to know."

He drank, looked at Breen. "Tell me what you know."

Precious little, she thought, but told him.

"You weren't going to drink it," she added. "When we came in to warn you, you already knew."

"I did. What did you call it once? Body language. The way she turned to pour wine, insisting we had to have it to seal her apology to me. And I thought, why, she's putting something in the wine, and wondered if she meant to sicken me before the Welcome, as her apology rang as false as a cracked bell."

He picked up the cup he'd sealed. "But then she used a bit too much oil of cinnamon, and I caught that scent, and the rest as well, as she's no hand with mixing potions."

He sat, looked as weary as Breen had ever seen him. "I'd have sent her away. Her father has family in the north, and I'd have sent her there for a year, I think. If it had been just between her and me, I would have felt that enough. But I didn't know about Kiara. So now there'll be a Judgment, and her parents shamed."

"Let me speak to them. Let me tell them."

"Ma, I'll grant you that, and gladly. And please the gods, we find her quickly."

"It was never about you." Tarryn went over, sat on the arm of his chair. "Or only a little—the little that's her vanity and pride sore because a man didn't want her. But it was always about the staff and sword."

"I know it, and fortunate for me neither my vanity nor pride is harmed by it."

"I'd be disappointed in you if they were. I'll be going now to tell her parents, and after, I'll check on Kiara. Her heart's broken by this. You did more than well in this, Breen. Kiara's all but one of my own. And now I must tell friends what their only child has done." She rose. "I'll see you then at the Welcome."

"I—I thought you'd call that off," Breen said to Keegan when his mother left them.

"No, best to go forward than to have everyone and their brother besides nattering about why we didn't."

"Wow, won't this be fun?"

He met her sour look with one of his own. "It's duty, yours as well as mine, though I wish it all to the devil myself. But it matters that people welcome you and meet you."

He closed his eyes, just for a moment. "It matters we don't let this, all of this, take from that."

"Okay. All right. Keegan, all of this? It was more than temper or hurt feelings. She's not . . . I don't think she's stable."

"I know it. I saw it. We'll find her."

The man she'd seen with Shana came to the open door. This would be Loren, she thought, and set her cup aside. "Then I should go get ready."

"Taoiseach." Loren nodded to Keegan, then beamed at Breen. "Breen Siobhan O'Ceallaigh, it's a great pleasure to meet you at last."

"Loren Mac Niadh," Keegan said as Loren took Breen's hand, lifted it to his lips.

"It's nice to meet you. I'm just leaving."

"I'll see you again at your Welcome. I hope I can claim a dance."

Because she couldn't think what to say, she just smiled and got out. Since it seemed right, she closed the door behind her.

Loren took a seat. "I'm told you wanted to see me, and urgently. Is there trouble? Odran and his demons?"

"Trouble there is, but not, at the moment, from him." Rising, Keegan retrieved the sealed cup, and unsealing it, offered it to Loren. "Don't drink. Do you know what this is?"

Obviously puzzled, Loren frowned into the cup. "Well, it's wine, isn't it? A bit of a cloud in it, and . . ." He lifted it to sniff, then his gaze shot up to Keegan's.

"Why would you brew this? Why does the taoiseach break one of the First Laws with a love potion?"

"I didn't. It was meant for me to drink, but like you, I knew it for what it was."

"You're not telling me the O'Ceallaigh's daughter would—"

"Not Breen, no." Keegan took back the cup, sealed it again before setting it aside. "Shana."

"That's wild talk, and I don't know who would have told you such a lie, but—"

"It's not a lie." Now he picked up the vial. "She brought it with her in this, slipped it into wine she poured. And before she came to me, Kiara went to her room, saw what Shana was about. When Kiara tried to stop her, to save her friend from harsh judgment, Shana struck her down. She left Kiara stunned and bleeding on the floor, locked her in, and came here."

"There's a mistake, surely." He pushed up. "Some misunderstanding, confusion. Kiara, is she badly hurt?"

"Breen found her, and we'll thank the gods for it. She healed her wound enough that Kiara could come to me, afraid I'd drink. And I'll tell you, she had blood on her face, in her hair, on her clothes. Blood spilled by a friend. I'm asking you, did you give her what she needed for the spell?"

"Gods, no, and I'm not convinced of any of this. I'll say I know we're not fast friends, you and I, but never would I use my magicks for such a purpose, or help another to do so. A rape of the heart and mind? And the danger that may . . ."

Loren fell silent; his eyes went dull.

"You've remembered."

"No, nothing, no. A game, a lover's lark. Where is she? Where is Shana?"

"We're looking for her. What game?"

"It was just a pretending, and well back in the summer. A pretending to mix the potion, but only pretending. But, gods, I gave her the words, I told her how it's done, so she could pretend to enslave my heart to hers.

"I knew she didn't love me full, but I thought she was coming to it. Let me take her away."

"There must be a Judgment."

"I'll take her away." Desperate, Loren gripped Keegan's arm. "Wherever you say, out of Talamh if that's your wish. I beg you not to banish her to that place. Ban her, a lifetime, and I'll take her away."

"Knowing all this, you'd want her?"

"I love her."

"Then you'll speak at the Judgment, make your offer. If she'll go with you, and you're willing, I would grant that. In truth, it would relieve me to grant that. But first we have to find her."

# CHAPTER TWENTY

Marco sat on the chest at the foot of his bed while Breen paced and told him everything.

"Holy freaking shit monkeys!"

He'd said that or equivalents throughout her monologue, then just stared at her when she dropped down in a chair.

"She was going to vamp him with a love potion. Who the hell wants somebody you have to drug into thinking they want you?"

"Apparently, she does, or the upshot I got was she wanted the status—Keegan just came with it."

"That's way over the Mean Girl line. You're sure Kiara's okay?"

"Yeah, but I don't know how she gets over it, Marco. It would be like me doing that to you, or you to me. At least from Kiara's side."

The sad filled his eyes. "Shana broke her heart as much as her head."

"She did. I guess I don't believe now that Shana's capable of real friendship, or love, or loyalty, but Kiara is. Anyway, I had to vent it out. I can't believe we're going to a damn party after all this."

"It's going to be just what you need. And if Kiara's feeling up to coming, we're going to make sure she has some fun, take her mind off all this."

"We can try."

He knew his girl, and switched tacks to lighten it all up. "We're gonna do it, and we're gonna look extreme doing it. Nan sent me a 'fit, and I'm betting she sent one for you."

"She did."

He jumped up to open his wardrobe. "Gander this."

She walked over to see pants—and damned if they weren't leather—in a bronzy shade, a cream-colored tunic, and a long velvet vest in deep green to go over it.

"You'll look great, and I'd better go get started on putting myself together. Let's go put our party on, Bollocks."

When she'd dressed, indulged herself with a couple of turns in front of the mirror, someone knocked on the door. Assuming Marco, she called out.

"Come on and gander this!"

And flushed a little when Minga came in.

"Sorry, I thought it was Marco. How's Kiara?"

"Much better, thanks to you, and the boy—man, I have to remind myself she's a woman grown—the man she's busy falling in love with came with flowers and has coaxed her into going tonight. It's good for her to go, and not sit and mope over Shana.

"And I've brought you these." She held out jeweled hairpins. "Brigid tells me this is what you were after, and if you hadn't been, my baby would have lain there for who knows how long. I think they go well with your dress, which I had a peek at when Marg gave it to me to bring to surprise you."

"They're perfect, thank you. I just have to figure out where to put them in."

"I'm happy to do that for you. Kiara may have gotten

her elfin gifts from her father, but her skill with hair ran through me."

"Yours is . . ." Half swept up, half floating down in coils. "Fabulous."

"Thank you. Here now, turn around. Oh, aye, here's how it should be.

"They've not yet found Shana," she said as she placed pins in and along the braid. "Her parents are crushed, Tarryn tells me."

"I'm so sorry."

"As am I. I'm told as well that when she's found, when there's a Judgment, Loren will offer to take her away, to make a life with her, if she's willing. This would be best for all. She's never had to fend for herself, you see, and though being sent from the Capital, and perhaps from Talamh altogether, will be hard for her, she's earned that right enough. And she can make a good life with Loren."

"He must really love her."

"I think he does. Aye, he does, though I think he mistakes he can, with love and indulgence, temper the edges of her. There, they set your hair off, they do, and go very well indeed with the dress."

"Thanks. I'd never have figured out how to do it myself. I lean on Marco for this sort of thing."

"Do you think he's ready? I'll take you both down to the banquet hall."

"We'll find out. And it's really okay if Bollocks comes?"

"He's an honored guest, and another love in my life." In her dress of shimmering copper, Minga bent down to him. "You knew my Kiara needed help, and saw she got it. You are a hero to me." Minga smiled as they started out. "I would so like to read the book you wrote about him."

"Sure. It's not going to be published until next summer, but I'll send you a copy."

Marco opened the door before the knock. "I was just

coming over to see if you were ready. And, girl, are you ever! That dress is snatched. Minga, you look fierce!"

"That's a compliment," Breen explained.

"And so I took it. You are fierce as well, Marco."

"Look here, Bollocks, we got ourselves two gorgeous women. I got two arms, ladies."

He cocked them both out.

Music piped and poured from the balcony above the banquet hall. Candles blazed in tall iron stands and from iron wheels hung by chains from the soaring ceiling. Their light added a sheen to the long tables and benches arranged on either side of the room to face another at its head. Behind it, the dragon banner flew over a huge roaring fire.

Voices echoed, bouncing off the wide-planked floors, off the walls where colorful tapestries hung between arched windows of leaded glass.

People milled about or gathered in groups. Some already sat, drinking wine or ale while they talked.

"Ah, I see some I know are waiting to see you again."

Minga led the way to a table where three men and three women talked, nearly all at once and with elaborate gestures.

One of the men, older than the other two, glanced over. And his eyes fixed on Breen's face.

She thought she'd seen him sitting with the council at the Judgment, but there'd been so many people.

He rose, a tall man with hair the color of roasted chestnuts, a warrior's braid tucked behind his ear, a trim beard.

A fist squeezed Breen's heart as he looked at her. He hadn't had the beard before, but she knew him. She recognized him as one of the three with her father in the photograph taken when they'd played in a pub in Doolin. On the other side.

As he watched her come, he laid a hand on the shoulder of the woman who sat beside him and waved his hand in the air as she talked to the others.

Still talking, she glanced up, then over. Breen saw her eyes fill as she scrambled to her feet. And not stopping there, rushed over to fold Breen into a hug.

"Ah, sweet Mother of all, here she is. There's the girl." She drew back, tears sliding out of eyes of soft, dreamy green. "Would you look at her, Flynn, a woman grown, and so lovely! Have you forgotten me, darling? Well, that's no matter, no matter at all, for I've not forgotten you."

"You're . . . Morena's mother. You're . . ." It was all swimming up to the surface of her memory. "You're Sinead, and you used to make us sugar biscuits shaped like flowers."

"That's right, that's right, so I did. And you liked the cornflowers best of all."

"I— Morena said to tell you she'd come visit soon."

"I hope she will, as we miss her, but we know she's no liking for the Capital." She brushed a tear from Breen's cheek. "Would you look at the two of us. Why, we'll have splotchy faces if we don't stop. Isn't she a sight to see, Flynn?"

"She is, aye, she's all of that. And how are you then, little red rabbit?"

With a half laugh, half sob, she went into his arms. "You called me that because I was always running, and you'd sneak us all gumdrops when our mothers weren't looking."

"And here, after all these years, she's telling on me."

"I have a picture of you with my father and Keegan's and another—Brian—taken in a pub in Doolin."

"So my mother's told me. Those were days, fine days indeed." He cupped her face in his big hands to kiss her. "Your da was my brother in all but blood, and as dear a friend as ever I've had."

"I know. I'm sorry, this is Marco, as dear a friend as I've ever had."

"And sure we've heard all about Marco." Sinead pulled him into a hug. "And I see Finola had the right of it as usual. Handsome as they come. Come, come, meet the family. You may not remember my boys, Breen, and you've never met their wives. Here's our Seamus, named for Flynn's da, and our Phelin, named for my own, and—"

"I set the frogs on you," Breen said to Phelin. "You— Morena and I were having a tea party in the garden, and you made it rain on us, and we were so mad. I called the frogs and toads, and they chased you away."

"Wouldn't she remember that of all things?" A near carbon copy of his father from the photo, he laughed as he hugged Breen. "And here's my wife, Noreen."

"Don't get up," Breen said to the pretty and very pregnant woman with a crown of sunny braids. "It's nice to meet you."

"And you, and I hope for more stories on my man's disreputable youth."

"It's coming back to me. I remember you," she said to Seamus. "You had a cat named Maeve, and she had a litter of kittens. You promised me one when they were weaned. But . . . we left before they were."

"We kept one, and named her for you, and a fierce mouser she was. A thousand welcomes."

He had his mother's eyes, his father's build, and bent to kiss her. "And here's my Maura."

"We named our youngest for your father," she told Breen. "He was a great man, and a good one. My parents both fought beside him. I train others to fight beside our taoiseach."

Bold green eyes gleamed against her dark skin. A warrior's braid fell beyond Maura's shoulder while she wore the rest of her hair short and sleek.

"He'd thank you for the honor, and wish bright blessings on your son."

"I know you have much to say to each other," Minga said. "But I see the taoiseach has come, and I need to take Breen and Marco to the table, or we'll all starve."

"I'll come back," Breen promised, and took Sinead's hands. "I didn't know how much I missed you until now."

"My sweet girl." Sinead moved in for another hug, mur- mured in Breen's ear, "I loved you like my own, and do still."

"I know. I'll come back."

"And well done," Minga said as she led Breen and Marco away. "What you said to Maura was just the right thing. And you lifted Sinead's heart."

So many more had come in since she'd stopped by that table, Breen saw. So many more voices. And she hadn't no- ticed because the memories had all come so fast and strong. And with them the feelings.

She'd loved them, loved them all, as only a child could love. Absolutely and purely.

She cried for them when she'd gone away.

Now there was Keegan standing with his mother at the head table. Him in black with a dull silver waistcoat, Tarryn in a dress of white flowers over blue.

"You'll sit on Keegan's left," Minga told Breen, "and Marco beside you. Don't sit until he does. There'll be a goblet of wine, but don't lift it until after he speaks."

"Okay." Nerves jittered straight up from her toes. "Am I supposed to say something? Please say no!"

"Only if you wish. Tonight is for welcome and joy."

"I haven't seen Brian," Marco began.

"He'll come soon, I'm sure, and as Keegan thought you would wish it, he sits beside you tonight."

She led them around the table to their places, then took hers on Tarryn's other side. A man with dark blond hair and quiet blue eyes stood on Minga's other side, and took Minga's hand to kiss it.

Og, Breen thought, who'd traveled to a world of gold sands and blue seas to find love.

"These are your people," Keegan whispered to Breen. "You've no reason to fear them."

"I don't." Exactly, she thought.

He waited a moment as the voices turned to mutters, and the mutters died away.

"We have known battle and blood, joy and sorrow, and we will know more as nights pass and days dawn. And we will know peace, as we vowed, as those before us vowed, a thousand years and more to take it, keep it, hold it. What each knows, so all know. We are one. We are Talamh."

They cheered him; he waited.

"This night, we are here, in this place. We are in the hills and the valleys, the forests and the fields. We are in the caves, the cliffs, the shore, and the sea. We are one. We are Talamh. And as one we welcome Breen Siobhan O'Ceallaigh, granddaughter of Mairghread, daughter of Eian, child of the Fey, of men, of gods."

He lifted his tankard, turned to her. "Pick yours up now," he murmured.

He spoke first in Talamhish, then translated. "As you are ours, we are yours, you are home. And so a thousand welcomes, Breen Siobhan O'Ceallaigh, daughter of the Fey."

He tapped his tankard to her goblet. "*Sláinte*. Drink," he added under the calls of "*Sláinte!*" from the rest.

They cheered again when she did. As she stood, her throat closed, but not with nerves. With gratitude.

"I—"

Marco took her free hand. "You can do it."

"Okay." She breathed out. "Thank you." The room quieted on her words, so she repeated them. "Thank you for your welcome, and your kindness, and your patience . . ." She glanced at Keegan. "Well, patience from most."

It surprised her to hear the shouts and laughter. Maybe it shouldn't have, she realized.

"I've come back to Talamh, and though I have family on the other side, I have my brother with me." She lifted her hand joined with Marco's. "I have family among the Fey, and with them, through them, I found myself. I've come back to Talamh. I've come home."

"Well done," Keegan told her under the cheers. "Now sit, or they'll only want more."

Relieved, she sat, laid a hand on Bollocks's head when he rested it on her knee. "What now?"

"We eat," Keegan said simply.

They ate. Platters of meats, boards of breads, tureens of soups, and more. Music and voices rang out again, and Breen used them to keep her words only for Keegan's ear.

"Shana? Have you found her?"

"Not as yet. She has few resources," he said almost to himself. "And as she's rarely gone beyond the village, she doesn't know the land, the people well. She can't hide long."

"When I was teaching, I'd always have a handful of students who'd been overindulged at home, and who thought rules and consequences for breaking them didn't really apply to them. And a few of that handful would always find a way to slide away from consequences or strike out, enraged, when they couldn't."

"You taught children. She's not a child." Then he shook his head. "But you've the right on this. In many ways, a child is just what she is."

"And that's why you're worried."

As she spoke, she saw Kiara slip into the room, a man with ginger hair beside her. He led her to a table where those sitting immediately stood to embrace her.

So many good hearts, Breen thought, so the cold one chilled more deeply.

She started to turn to Marco, so saw Brian come in through a side door before he did. Brian touched a hand— one with Marco's gift on his wrist—to Marco's shoulder, and moved on to Keegan.

He bent over, spoke quietly.

Keegan nodded. "Sit. Eat." Absently, he tossed a bite of beef to Bollocks. "No one's seen her as yet," he said to Breen. "Everything that can be done is being done, so put it aside for now."

He leaned toward his mother when she spoke to him, then took a long drink of wine.

"I'm to start the dancing." When he rose, held out a hand to Breen, she just stared at him. "With you." Rather than wait, he just took her hand.

A heart could sink into the belly and freeze there, Breen discovered, as he pulled her around the table and into the wide, clear space.

"What kind of dance? I don't know how—"

"Left palm to my right, and your right on your hip, then switch when I do, three times. You know how to dance. I've seen you. Eyes on mine."

It helped to look at him, only him, and not think about anything else. She heard the music, heard hands clapping and feet stomping to keep the beat, but if she looked at only him, she didn't think about how many eyes watched her.

He talked her through the steps, even when the tempo quickened. A turn, a touch, and with that quickening tempo a turn became a spin, a touch an embrace. And with her blood beating in time, she wished for more.

The wishing made her breathless when, his hands firm on her waist, he lifted her up, into a half circle, brought her down so their bodies pressed together for just one aching moment.

He stepped back, but brought her hand to his lips as he did so. He kept her hand as he led her back to the table. Others flooded out to dance when the music picked up again.

"I need to dance with my mother, Minga, others. I would rather with you. This is a problem for me."

"A problem for you?"

"Aye." He pulled out her chair. "You should sit, as you won't be given many chances to be off your feet now."

"I don't know all the dances."

"You'll figure it out." He hesitated, then leaned down, spoke quietly. "You'll dance with others, as you should, and you'll enjoy. But I'll ask you don't look at any of them as you looked at me. I want that for mine."

He straightened, turned to his mother, held out a hand.

Marco leaned over to Breen. "Sexy dance!"

"Stop."

"I see what I see, know what I know."

"Go dance with Brian."

She'd barely said the words when Morena's brother Phelin came up to her. "Let's dance, shall we, to spots of rain and leaping frogs."

"You weren't always annoying." She smiled at him as she rose. "I remember you made up games when you lowered yourself to play with—you called us girl babies."

"Well now, I was, I think, all of six at the time, so far superior."

Her big brother. That's how she'd thought of him then, and how, she realized, she felt now. "I don't know the dance."

He winked at her. "I'll talk you through it then. Girl baby."

Shana watched Breen dance. She watched those who'd professed to be her friends fawn over the witch from outside. The despair she'd begun to feel as she'd found Keegan's lackies guarding Loren's house, keeping her from seeking shelter and help against this horrible betrayal, had hardened, had heated into a burning rage.

They searched for her in the forest, from the skies, in the village. As if she'd broken laws instead of defending herself, her place, her rights.

And when she'd come back, so tired from hiding herself in trees and stones and high grasses among the sheep, she'd had to sneak into the castle like a thief in the night only to find the door of her own room barred to her.

The door to her parents' room guarded against her.

And with her own kind searching the castle, the grounds, with empaths searching for even a whisper of her thoughts, her feelings, she would soon find herself unsafe in her own home.

And all because the one from the other side, the one who didn't belong, had somehow turned the taoiseach against her.

Had turned so many so now they feted her like a goddess.

But Shana would break that spell, she would retake her rightful place. When the other from the other lay cold in her own blood, they would thank her for ridding them of that false goddess. Keegan would pay, just as the usurper paid.

Then she wouldn't be wife of the taoiseach.

She would *be* taoiseach. And everyone, anyone who turned from her, like Kiara, would live in misery in the Dark World.

Let her dance. In a blur of speed, Shana plucked a knife from a tray. More than one head turned in her direction, but as she slid along the stone wall, she saw puzzlement, then dismissal.

Let them all dance, she thought as she worked her way slowly to the wall behind the head table.

The night should have been a celebration of Keegan's pledge to her. Instead, the night would end with blood when she slit Breen's throat.

Breen wondered if she could get back to the table and off her feet for two minutes. Clearly, the Fey could dance all night.

When Marco grabbed her hand, she remembered he could, too.

"Come on, girl. Let's show them how they dance in Philly."

The table wouldn't do it, she thought, as she'd still be in plain sight.

"Air. I need five minutes outside in the air. I'm not sneaking off," she promised. "Bollocks and I are going to step out—as I imagine he needs to for different reasons than mine. And we'll be back."

Marco looked down at the dog. "You make sure she comes back."

She slipped out, and Bollocks made a beeline for the gardens, where a few couples wandered.

She just lifted her face to the sky, to the shine of the moons, and breathed in.

Maybe her feet ached some, but the rest of her felt buoyant. Music pumped against the doors and windows behind her, and voices raised in song joined it. Wine flowed, and laughter swam on it.

She felt the beat of that joy in the air, in the countless hearts surrounding her. If she could have chosen a night to lock in so she could return to it whenever she liked, it would be this one.

Then she felt another heart, and the fury pounding in it. Snarling, snapping, Bollocks tore through the gardens back to her.

Breen whirled as Shana blurred from the castle walls, knife raised. On instinct Breen lashed out.

The knife in Shana's hand blazed. She shrieked, utter shock, as it fell from her hand, flaming still, to the stones. Even as Bollocks leaped, she shot away.

"No, no." Breen grabbed the dog before he could give chase. "You won't catch her, and God knows what she'd do if you did."

Trembling, she sank down to her knees and hugged the dog.

Not just spoiled, no, Breen thought as she fought to slow her heartbeat. Not just unstable. Twisted. What she'd seen, what she'd felt had been twisted.

"Breen." Kiara hurried from the garden to the terrace with the man with ginger hair. "Are you all right? We thought we heard you cry out."

"No, no, I'm fine." She rose, shifted to block the knife, blackened by the fire.

"I'm Aiden." He held out a hand to take hers. "I know you helped Kiara today, and she's dear to me. So you are dear to me as well."

"I'm so glad to meet you, and to see you looking happy, Kiara. I wonder if you'd do me a favor."

"You've only to ask," Aiden assured her.

"Would you mind finding Keegan?" Her voice wanted to tremble like her legs, but she fought to keep it steady and light. "There was something I meant to tell him, and it's so loud in there, it's hard to talk. If he wouldn't mind coming out for just a minute."

"Sure we'll get him for you. Though it may be for more than just a minute he wants to stay out here with you." Kiara embraced her, whispered, "I am forever obliged to you. I am forever your friend."

When they went in, Breen cooled the knife, picked it up. "She would've killed me. She meant to."

Because her legs felt weak, she walked to a bench, sat, with Bollocks all but glued to her side. "Best dog in the world. In all the worlds. A part of me felt sorry for her. She didn't kill me, but she killed the part of me that felt sorry for her."

She stayed where she was when Keegan stepped out. "I'd as soon you not wander about by yourself until we've settled things."

Saying nothing, she held out the knife.

"Shana tried to settle them just now. I burned her—I—"

"Are you hurt?" Gripping her shoulders, he lifted her off the bench.

"No. She is. I burned her. Her hand, where she held the knife. The same way—you and the sword. I didn't think. She came at me, so fast, and—"

"Wait for all that. Where did she go?"

"She ran that way. Something's snapped in her, Keegan. I saw, I felt . . . You need to know—"

"We'll get to all that." Cróga circled above, glided down. "Up, the both of you," he said, and all but threw her on the dragon's back before he leaped on.

"Are we going after her?"

He flew up to the topmost tower, and as Cróga hovered, leaped onto the balcony. He plucked Breen off, patted a leg so the dog jumped after her.

Turning to the doors, he held a hand to them so they opened into his room. "You're safe here."

"Keegan—"

"I need you safe. I need to leave you safe and start the search for her. She didn't hurt you," he continued when she would've argued. "Because you stopped her. She may hurt someone else before they can."

"Yes, you're right."

"Stay here. I'll be back when I can."

He went through the door. "Close them behind me. I think it's not something snapped, as you said." He leaped onto Cróga. "I think it's something broke free."

She watched him fly down, leap off again as the dragon hovered. He'd gathered those he needed for the search, she thought. A search for something lost that even if found, wouldn't be saved.

# PART III
# VISIONS

*Deep into that darkness peering, long I stood there, wondering, fearing,*
*Doubting, dreaming dreams no mortal ever dared to dream before.*

—Edgar Allan Poe

# CHAPTER TWENTY-ONE

Shana ran, far and fast. Without any sense of direction, with her hand screaming in an agony she'd never known, she ran through the forest, over fields, beyond the village. With her dress in tatters, her heart tearing through her chest, she ran and ran and ran.

When the blind panic faded into trembling fear, she stumbled onto a stream. Plunging her hand in the cold water, she wept, wept tears so bitter they burned into her soul like acid.

Desperate for relief, she dug at roots with her hands, gnawed them with her teeth to make a poultice. Even when it cooled enough to stop her from gasping, her hand throbbed.

Shaking with shock, she ripped strips from her skirts.

She sobbed, muttered, sobbed as she wrapped her hand. With her good hand, she scooped water from the stream into her mouth to ease her throat.

And she heard them. Elfin ears caught the sound of riders. Hunting her. She damned them, damned them all as she gathered herself.

So she ran, and now as she ran, she plotted vengeance. Deep, endless, bloody vengeance.

While Shana fled, Breen paced.

She lit the fires—in what she realized was Keegan's bedroom, in the sitting room. She lit the candles, the lamps, but couldn't find any real comfort. She paced to window, to doors, to window, and finally, though she knew it would irritate Keegan, opened the doors to the terrace and stepped out.

In the sky she could see dragons and riders, faeries on the wing. There would be others, she knew—and even now spotted a trio of riders on horseback. Combing the roads, the hills, she thought. And there would be elves and Weres on foot surely, searching through the forests and over the fields.

The knock on the door made her jump, but as Bollocks just wagged, she had to assume friend not foe. She went back in, closing the terrace doors behind her.

"It's Tarryn."

Relieved, Breen hurried to unlock and open the main door. Tarryn stepped in, then simply folded Breen into a hug.

"I came to see for myself you're not harmed."

"No, I'm not. Jittery—shaken up a little—that's all."

"Sure and who wouldn't be—jittery. I like the word." She closed the door, drew Breen to a chair.

"Marco?"

"I told him I'd check on you myself, and report back to him. Not all know, but as Brian's been called into the search . . . We'll have some wine. You had little, as we kept you busy dancing."

She poured two cups, then sat. "And to speak truth, I'm bolstering myself, as when I leave you I have to go to Shana's parents. They need to know of this before the rest. And this will break their hearts so they'll never again, never again be mended."

"It's so hard for you."

"Duty often is. And I'll tell you now, as I'm sick in my heart, I'm asking myself if I could have done or said something at the right time, in the right way, to stop all of this."

"She made her choice. Isn't choice the core of Talamh?"

"It is, aye, it is. I'm so fond of her parents, but I never had fondness for their child. She used her beauty, she used their love, used the loyalty of a dear heart like Kiara's, the love of Loren, and so many others. In small ways, in small, selfish ways. And when she caught Keegan's eye as well—she has beauty and charm and wit—I worried. Not that his heart was in danger."

She sat back, sipped wine. "I worried because I could see what she wanted—not him, I could have softened toward her if she'd loved him. But it was what he is, not who, she wanted. And I worried what she would do when she understood, at last, he would never give her what she wanted."

Tarryn squeezed her eyes shut. "But even then I never thought this. I thought of tantrums and hard words, some scheming to gain some power on the council. I thought of that, but never this. And I think I never thought of it because I disliked her, and saw myself with that bias."

"I don't know her, but I don't think . . . The love potion, I can see her holding that as a kind of last resort. But the rest—what she did to Kiara, what she tried to do tonight? That came from rage, impulse, fury, not planning."

"She would have taken your life tonight. And so there's no coming back for her, as the judgment's clear. There was hope before. Loren, and she deceived him, stole from him, used him to try to bind Keegan to her—he asked Keegan to allow him to take Shana away. To ban her from the Capital, and let him take her away."

"Yes, Minga told me."

"Keegan agreed to that, and would have persuaded the council. She could have had a life with a man who loved her. A different life, aye, than she wanted, but a life where in time she might have been content. And now, when she's found, she'll be cast from Talamh to the Dark World. And my son will carry that weight."

Now Tarryn leaned forward, reached out to take one of Breen's hands. "You're the key in the lock, Breen Siobhan. The bridge, the shield. She would have cut you down. Taking a life, any life, would have damned her. But taking yours, if she'd succeeded, could have damned us all. There is no one in Talamh who would give her shelter."

"Where would she go? I was trying to think where I'd go in her place. The Welcoming Tree?"

Tarryn nodded. "It'll be guarded and well. And the falls."

"The falls? That leads to . . ."

"Aye, to Odran. We take no chances. I can only hope they find her quickly, and before she harms another." She set the cup aside. "Should I send someone to keep you company?"

"Thanks, no. We're fine."

Tarryn smiled down at Bollocks, stroked the head he'd propped on her knee to comfort her. "You are well guarded, no doubt, by such a brave heart, and you're safer here than anywhere in Talamh. That helps keep Keegan's mind clear while he deals with this."

She rose. "Try to rest. I'll see you in the morning."

Alone, Breen sat by the fire and began to search the flames. Maybe she'd see, though as yet she'd been unable to call a vision, only see what came when it came.

But she sat, as Bollocks curled loyally at her feet, and tried to look through the smoke and flames to the heart. Nothing cleared for her, and she wished she had her globe, that she'd thought to send for it.

And remembered how once Keegan had shown her how to transport something as simple as a glass of water.

So she visualized the globe sitting now beside her bed. The size of it, the shape, the weight, the colors. How smooth it was in her hand, how worlds shifted inside it.

She imagined its path to her, through stone and wood and air.

And cupping her hands, she called it to her, let the power inside her rise, spread, reach.

"I am Breen Siobhan O'Ceallaigh," she heard herself say. "I am child of Fey and man and god. I am my gift, and my gift is I. Now I use it for the light."

She felt it burst, so strong, so hot, so bright.

A violence in it, as something turned in her, as for a moment, just a moment, she no longer sat in the chair, in the tower, in the castle.

A fury and a purpose, a striking out.

For an instant she stood somewhere else, with water drumming onto water, with chants and screams pounding in her ears.

For an instant her eyes met Odran's.

Then she stood in front of the fire, in the tower, in the castle with the aftershocks of power coursing through her.

And in the firelight, with the candles flickering, she held the globe in her cupped hands.

"Was that the same as before? Was it then or now or not yet? God, my blood's on fire. And it feels . . . right."

She looked down at the globe, saw her hands held steady. "What does it mean that I can do this, and feel I've crossed some bridge or boundary, scaled some wall?"

It left her breathless and thrilled and triumphant.

She lifted the globe, watched the firelight play over it, watched the glow from the candles, from the lamps swirl into it.

"Show me what I need to see."

And she saw, in those depths, a figure running through shadows, through forest shadows that shifted and swirled like water.

Shana.

But that shifted, changed, and the figure she saw running

was a child. A faerie, for she saw wings, just the blur of them fluttering.

Very deliberately, Breen focused, looked deeper.

A child, a girl. Of the Sidhe. Naked.

The child from the waterfall. The sacrifice. Odran's side—where, somehow, she herself had just been.

She wanted to push herself into the globe, push herself into that world again, to the child. The child, she saw now, shivering with cold and shock as she ran, as her wings lifted her up a few inches off the path.

Dilly. Her name was Dilly. She was only six.

"This is happening now. It's all happening now." She was as certain of it as anything she'd ever known. "And I was there, even though I was standing right here, I was there to stop the knife, to break the chains holding the girl. How did I do it, and why can't I get back and help her?"

As she tried to clear her mind again, bring back what had flooded into her, she saw the cat.

The silver cat streaked across the child's path, so she stumbled to a halt, breath heaving, eyes glassy with fear. Then he became a man, and Sedric brought a finger to his lips. He laid the other on his heart as he crouched down.

When he opened his arms, the girl fell into them, and holding her close, laying a kiss on her tangled hair, he slid into the shadows.

Only seconds later, only seconds it seemed, a pack of demon dogs charged down the path. One paused to throw up its head, scent the air. But they ran on.

In the shadows, Breen saw a glimmer of light flash—here, then gone.

"She's safe now. It's now, and she's safe. She's in Talamh again. Sedric and Nan have her."

Exhausted, Breen let her head fall back, let it all drain. She dropped down into the chair again, with the globe in her lap, the dog at her feet. And slept.

Keegan found her there an hour before dawn. Bollocks gave a couple of taps of his skinny tail, then went back to sleep.

"And why would she sleep in a chair when there's a perfectly good bed in the next room?"

Baffled by her, annoyed with her for no reason he cared to name, he rubbed at the stiffness in his neck.

He should wake her, send her to her own bed. If she wanted to take out the dog or go for one of her walks, he'd have someone go with her.

Or he could just carry her into his bed, take the chair for himself, as he didn't expect sleep to come to him for a while yet.

In any case, he wanted a drink and time to sit, just sit and think.

He started to lift her up, and the moment he touched her, she shot awake.

"Keegan." She laid a hand on his chest. "You're back. What time is it? Did you find her?"

He straightened, decided on whiskey. "Plain to see I'm back," he said as he poured three fingers into a cup. "What difference is the time? And we didn't find her."

"I'm sorry."

"No more than I. I never thought her clever enough to hide more than a few hours at best. Not in the dark and the cold when she's used to soft beds and warm fires."

Because it grated, he sat with his whiskey and said what had circled in his mind throughout the search. "It's a lowering thing to understand I never knew her, not as I thought. I knew the flaws and faults, but they seemed shallow things and nothing I couldn't overlook for my own pleasures."

"Stop. She doesn't deserve to have you blaming yourself."

He shrugged at that, drank. "I see the shallow things she had no qualms in letting me, or anyone, see hid deeper flaws. Darker ones. And for all her love of soft beds and good wine and shiny things, she's evaded more than two dozen who search for her through the night."

"She's desperate, and desperation gives her an edge."

"When the light comes, the word will go out, and more will search. Who might she hurt in her desperation before we find her? And when we do, the law allows only one end."

He turned the cup in his hands, stared into the whiskey. "She'll never know a soft bed again. You'll have to speak at the Judgment, and I'm sorry for that. And so will Kiara, and I'm sorrier yet for that."

It tore at him, she thought. All of it tore at him.

"She never understood you, or that the power you have carries such weight. Shiny things like these gorgeous rooms don't balance that scale."

He sat back, watching her as he drank. "Are they gorgeous then?" He glanced around. "I'd rather be home, in the valley. In the quiet."

"So would I."

He looked back at her, smiled. "Would you now?"

"The Capital's beautiful and exciting, the views are stunning. The people are lovely. But there are so many of them."

"Aye, by the gods." He closed his eyes, just for a moment, then half toasted her with his whiskey. "Well then, you could've kept your mouth shut all those years ago, and not floated around in the lake with your hair all swirling like fire in the water, and telling me the sword was meant for me."

"You'd have taken it anyway. It's who you are. Wait. What did I look like, when you saw me on the day you became taoiseach?"

"As you do."

"No, I mean, as I am—not a kid? You were, what, like fourteen, so I'd have been around twelve. Did I look twelve?"

"You weren't a child. I saw a woman."

"Right. Right." She rose to pace, running the globe through

her hands. "So I was closer to now than then. I might not have done it yet."

"If you hadn't done it, I wouldn't have seen you, so you're babbling."

"I'm not. Whether it's lucid dreams or time travel or astral projection, I was years older than I would've been. So I went back—one way or the other. Maybe this."

She held up the globe. "Or it's a tool, a vehicle, a boost. How the hell do I know? But I did it again last night."

"You went back to the day at the lake?"

"No." She sat again, leaned toward him. "Not there, not then. God, I'd give a year of my life for a Coke. No, I tried to see in the fire, to see if I could help find Shana, but I haven't mastered that yet. I get close, but not quite. And I remembered the globe, and how you'd shown me—well, not shown, but challenged me—to get a glass of water from the kitchen while I was still in my bedroom."

"You didn't quite manage that either."

"No, but I wanted the globe. I wanted to see, to help, to do something. So I focused on it—where I'd put it, what it looked like, felt like. I started to call for it, but I felt something else, said something else. And for a minute—less—I was back at the waterfall, Odran's side. The little girl, the chanting. All of it, and it was now, Keegan. I was there now, and standing here now. It was like a hot wire in my blood, a white-hot fury and a surge of power, like all the switches came on at once."

She took the glass from his hand. She didn't like whiskey, but wanted something. After one sip, she shoved it back at him. "Oh no, bad choice. So, then I was back here, standing right here. And I had the globe."

He kept watching her, eyes intense, body still. "What then?"

"In the globe, I saw the girl—I thought Shana at first— but it was the little girl, her wings fluttering as she ran. Just terrified, and running. Now—well, I mean last night when I saw. I knew I was seeing it while it happened, and I wanted so much to be there again, to help her. I started to try to pull out the same . . . whatever the hell it was, then Sedric was there. His cat form first, then him, and he got her away. I knew—I felt—when he brought her back to Talamh. I saw the light flash in the shadows, and they were back here."

"I don't ask if you're sure, as I see you are."

"You sent him to find her."

"I sent a falcon to him when we arrived at the Capital. He's the only one I know who can create a portal almost at will, and a cat is a clever thing. He'd watch and wait. Word might have come while I was out. I haven't checked. You've given me good news. More than you know," he said.

He set the cup aside. "I'll take you to your room. Until we find Shana, it's best you don't go anywhere alone."

"She's not in the Capital."

"I think not as well, but—"

"I know she's not. I . . . I wanted to see her—where she was—so I brought the globe. And I was focused on that, on her, when I asked it to show me what I needed to see. I think, the first few seconds, I think it was Shana. But what I needed to see was the girl—that was more immediate. So that's what it showed me."

"You may be right, but we'll take no chances."

He rose, so she did the same.

She looked heavy-eyed and pale with weariness, but not, he realized, fragile. Not a bit of that.

"You dressed in stars."

"Sorry?"

"It's what I thought when I saw you in the banquet hall. You'd dressed in stars. I've a yearning for you, and it annoys me I can't shake it away. My life would be easier without this wanting. I've enough to concern me without you being in the middle of my thoughts."

"It's good to be honest," she said coolly. "You've got a case of lust and it's inconvenient."

"Lust is rarely inconvenient, and if only that, I'd have had you in bed every night since you returned to Talamh."

"That assumes I'd want to be there."

"Aye, it does. It's not lust alone, though there's plenty of it to go around. I'm weary of telling myself it's best if I don't touch you. You distract, you crowd my thoughts. If that's the way of it, why shouldn't I have you, as that's not changing, is it?"

Clearly, she thought—nearly amused—he was talking himself into sleeping with her.

"Is this your idea of a seduction?"

"It's not, no. I can do much better than this in that area. It's truth I'm giving you, because we both value it."

He reached out to touch her hair, just the tips of his fingers. "And the bloody, buggering truth is I need sleep, but sleep won't come if I don't have. So you could give yourself to the taoiseach for the good of the world."

And there was just enough humor in his eyes now that she crossed the line fully into amused. "I could." She waited a beat. "Or?"

"You could lie with me, Breen, because I'm a man who wants you, and I see the want mirrored in your eyes."

Now she smiled at him, held out a hand. "Why not both?"

He took her hand, then, as he'd done the first time, in another world, swept her up.

"You dressed in stars," he said again as he carried her to his bed. "And I was lost in them."

"I missed you," she told him. Truth, she decided, deserved truth. "When I was away, and when I came back. I missed you."

He laid her on the bed, put a hand on her cheek as he covered her. "I'm here. Stay with me."

When he lowered his mouth to hers, he let go of all the

worries. She brought him peace, and he no longer questioned why. The feel of her under him, soft and yielding, and still stronger than she knew, brought him hope. And he could hold on to that as he held on to her.

Her arms came around him, her hands sliding up his back, into his hair as her lips heated against his. So the slow, quiet kiss grew more avid, more needy with quick bites, seeking tongues, with bodies shifting to find more.

The line of her neck, the curve of her jaw, the pulse in her throat that beat like hummingbird wings—all those flavors enveloped him, enticed him.

Why it should be her, why it had to be her, he would think on later. But now, it could only be her.

His lips sought the curve of her breasts above the starry fog of her dress, then his hands slid up the filmy layers of it and whisked it away with a wish.

Naked, she shivered once, sighed once, then arched to him. With hands and mouth he took her breasts, feasted, and his hunger only grew.

She'd wanted this, had tried to close those wants away, and had sometimes succeeded. Or nearly. Now the craving to be touched by him, to taste him, to have the weight and shape of him pressed against her were met at last, so the joy, the plea-sure, the passion braided together like a rope of fine silk.

As the light began to shimmer awake with night fading off for the coming sun, she ran her hands down him to spin his clothes away as he had hers.

She felt his laugh against her skin. "You missed a boot."

His hands roamed; his mouth ravaged. She shifted, turn-ing over him so hers could do the same.

"It's hard to focus."

"Aye." He brought his mouth back to hers. "But I've got it." Shifting back, he gripped her hands, then drew her arms up over her head.

In the first strikes of sun she saw his eyes, amber flecks

swimming over green. "Next time we'll take time, but I need you now. Take me in now."

"Yes." She linked her fingers tight with his.

When he drove inside her, deep, strong, and held, just held, her body bowed, her heart leaped, and everything in her burst into wild bloom.

He thrust again, held again, with his eyes locked on hers. "I want to watch what I do to you. Once more."

On the next thrust she cried out in shock and release, quivering, quaking as the orgasm tore through her. In her vision, lights flashed and danced, bright as pixies.

"Breen Siobhan." He covered her mouth with his to taste those hot, helpless cries as he drove her, drove them both hard and fast.

The soft light from the new day spread over them, and birdsong lifted in the air. She let herself fly, just fly, a dragon rider into the whirl of wind. And when the wind swept over her, when she fell into it, through it, she fell with him.

She couldn't catch her breath, and decided it wasn't worth chasing. She'd just lie there gasping until it found her. He still held her arms over her head, but loosely now as he lay, limp as a dead man, on top of her.

Slowly, her heart still banging, her ears still ringing, she focused on the ceiling.

The hills and valleys of Talamh rose and fell, browns and gold and so many shades of green. Seas rolled toward beaches of silver shale or golden sand. From the seas Mers leaped. Others sat on rocks. On the high cliffs stood trolls with their clubs or axes or picks. In the fields farmers plowed, and over the forests and meadows faeries flew. Elves and Weres walked among the trees, horses carried riders or carts along the road. A coven of the Wise cast a circle.

And in the sky blue as the seas, dragons flew.

"It's beautiful. The ceiling."

He made some sound, then rolled to lie on his back beside

her. "It was painted long ago, and reminds the taoiseach that when he sleeps, Talamh should be his last thought, when he wakes, his first."

"Well, that's a lot."

"The first night I spent here, I studied it."

"You were just a boy."

"I was taoiseach. And a boy, so I thought: How am I to do this? There's so much, there are so many. I wanted the farm and the valley, and I'll confess it, I wanted my ma. But I slept, and slept with Talamh over me. In the morning, I went, as is written, to the council. I was terrified."

He turned, narrowed his eyes at her. "I'll deny that for a vicious lie if you should speak that out loud to any."

"I'm a vault."

"And keep it locked. So before all had come in and settled, one of the council came to me. He told me to stand tall, ignore the sickness in my stomach. To remember I chose and was chosen. And if any tried to intimidate me, well, bugger them. It was Shana's father who said that to me, and stiffened my spine that day."

She turned, laid a hand on his heart. "He knew you chose, and though it must hurt him more than anything I can imagine, he knows she chose. And I think, when she was here with you, she didn't look up and see Talamh as you do."

"I never brought her to this bed. Or anyone before you." He sat up, scooping a hand through his hair and wondering if lack of sleep had loosened his tongue. Before he worked out what to say next, Bollocks walked to the side of the bed, sent out an imploring look.

"Oh, right! He hasn't been out in hours. Sorry, sorry, what a good boy." Breen crooned it as she started to roll out of bed. "Where's my dress?"

"Somewhere." Keegan looked around, gestured. "There."

"Looks like I'm taking the walk of shame," she said as she went to get it.

"You're ashamed? Of this?"

"What? No, no. It's an expression. When a woman—and it's always a woman—comes home in the morning in the same thing she was wearing the night before, it's called the walk of shame. Stupid, but since it's my first time, sort of satisfying in a weird way."

"I'll take him. I've things to check on, and he can go with me."

In the act of shaking the dress out, she turned. Keegan already wore trousers, a shirt, and was pulling on his second boot. "How did you get dressed so fast?"

"I've been dressing myself for some time now, so I've got the hang of it. Straight to your room when you've got the hang of your own, and don't go out without Marco at the least. Not yet."

He smiled at her as she stood holding the dress in front of her. "You look all rumpled, and it makes me want to toss you back in bed and rumple you more, but needs must."

He gave Bollocks a pat on the head. "If you don't see us when you come out, call for him."

"All right, and thanks, but—"

He just strode over, gripped her shoulders, kissed her until the thoughts drained out of her head.

"Let's go, lad," he said, and Bollocks happily trotted out with him.

# CHAPTER TWENTY-TWO

She didn't really sneak down to her room, but she made a concerted effort to avoid any who hustled up stairs or down corridors. Still, she couldn't go into her room until she'd let Marco know she was back.

He yanked open his door seconds after she knocked, and an instant later, he yanked her into his arms.

"I'm sorry. I couldn't—"

He just squeezed tighter. "I wasn't so worried because Tarryn came and told me you were safe. You and Bollocks both tucked up in Keegan's place in the tower, but, girl, it sure feels good to see for myself."

He drew her back, then his smile flashed to a grin. "And tucked up's what we can call it. You got that all-the-knots-untied look going."

"They're going to tie up again if I stand out here in last night's dress much longer."

Still holding on to her, he walked her to her door and in. "You can change your loose self in the bathroom or WC or whatever you call it. I'm not leaving. Hey, where's Bollocks?"

"Keegan took him." She grabbed clothes out of the wardrobe. "I want a shower, and I think I can conjure a rain of warm water while I'm in the tub."

"I'm talking through the door," he said as she closed it behind her. "Did that bitch really try to knife you in the back?"

"I stopped her."

She did her best to fill him in while she got out of the dress, took the pins out of her hair, and finally managed to call a shower of water.

It felt like glory.

When she came out, Marco was still talking. "Brian came back a few hours ago, and had to take off again right before you came back. He says they'll find her, that no one in Talamh will help her after this. But—"

"He's worried she'll hurt someone before they do find her."

"It'll be harder since you hurt her, and good. Wish I'd seen it. Let's go dig up some breakfast, and find out what's going on."

It shouldn't have surprised her Marco knew his way to the kitchen, or that those manning it called him by name.

She ate bacon and eggs in the big, warm room while a gray cat slept on a wide stone windowsill and a man and woman argued, as they scrubbed pots, over whether the rain would come by midday or wait until nightfall.

When she and Marco strolled out into the pretty sunlight, she wondered why either thought it would rain at all.

As they walked down to the bridge, she started to call for Bollocks, but saw him—and Keegan—in the training field.

Since she wanted the walk, she kept going. "I'm not sure what we're supposed to do with all this going on. I'd like to explore the woods, but I'm pretty sure they'd want half an army to go with me, and that sort of kills the point. I think I'll try to write for a couple of hours. If I can manage it, it would take my mind off all this."

"I might catch a nap. I didn't sleep real easy last night. It's a pisser, you know, because that was a hell of a party."

As they approached the field, Bollocks spotted them and raced to Breen as if they'd been separated for weeks.

Keegan gestured them over to where he stood with a handful of others.

"Good, I was about to send someone to find you, as I've got to leave. So, Hugh, work with Breen. Archery for her, and I'll warn you, keep everyone back from twenty feet either side of the target, for she's pitiful at it."

"Well now, we'll fix that, won't we?" Hugh spoke cheerfully, gave Breen a quick pat.

"And you, Cyril, you'll have Marco for hand-to-hand. An hour, then switch, and another hour."

"What? Why?" Breen demanded.

"Training," Keegan told her. "You've had enough of a holiday from it. You there, Bran, why aren't you in school?"

"It's not started yet, has it? And I thought to speak to my ma a minute. She's in the next field."

"Did you? This is Bran, Morena's nephew. Seamus and Maura's oldest."

"It's nice to meet you." About ten, Breen judged, with clever eyes. "Your school's nearby?"

"Oh, it's just over that way a bit. I was thinking," he said to Keegan, "I could miss the day there and train instead. With my ma. She'll be fine with it."

"I expect you think to tell her I'm fine with it to try to sway her on it."

With a grin set to charm, Bran lifted his shoulders up to his ears.

"School before training, boy. Warriors need good brains as well as sharp swords. Be off with you, and learn something."

His shoulders slumped, and his feet dragged as he walked away.

"Learn something, and impress me with it," Keegan called out, "and you'll have a ride on Cróga."

Like magic, the boy turned, all grins. "I will, be sure of it, Taoiseach." He raced a few feet before wings fluttered out and he flew.

"Someone else has a good brain as well as a sharp sword," Breen commented.

"Someone else remembers being a boy wishing school away. Train them hard," he added, and glanced at the sky. "With two hours of it, you'll likely be done before the rain that's coming midday."

Cróga glided down out of what looked to Breen like a clear sky. Keegan walked to him, mounted, and without another word, soared up and flew west.

"So." Hugh, as cheerful as ever, gestured to the targets on the far side of the field. "We'll get you a bow and quiver."

Breen mustered up a smile for Marco. "I guess we found out what we're supposed to do today. See you in an hour."

And knowing exactly how Bran felt with his heels dragging, she followed Hugh over the field.

It did rain at midday, but by then Marco was taking his nap, and Breen sat at her writing desk. She knew the minute Bollocks decided to try the bed for his own nap rather than his spot by the fire.

She let that go, and watched the rain fall.

Finally, she picked up the pen and tried to close herself in another world—the world she'd built with words.

After a while, after some fits and starts, she pushed everything away and succeeded.

Shana huddled under a lean-to outside a stable. She'd stolen a dress off a line early that morning. An ugly dress, and one she deemed far too big for her own fine form. But hers had been in ruins after the long night.

She knew, when the sun came up, she'd headed west, and though she tried, she couldn't remember enough of her geography or map lessons to be sure exactly where she was.

She'd slept, what little sleep she'd had, inside rocks, and that burned humiliation into her. She wanted a bath in scented oils, her kidskin boots, and the feel of soft, combed wool against her skin.

Instead, she wore some farmer's hideous homespun dress. She was filthy, her hair in tangles, and she'd had to crouch with a horse under a lean-to while the rain poured down.

Her hand ached and throbbed despite the poultice. Her throat burned from thirst, and her head pounded from hunger.

They would pay for it. And the way to that payment, she saw clearly, lay west.

Vengeance required power, and an ally with it. She knew Odran likely had spies scattered here and there—or so her father said when she persuaded him to speak of council business.

But rooting out spies would take more time than she believed she had.

Far too many looked for her now.

She heard whistling, and though it hurt to move, she clutched a rock with her good hand before merging herself with the stable wall.

She watched the boy come, pail in hand, and the tethered horse turn her head in anticipation.

"It's a downpour for certain, isn't it now, Mags? But you're tucked up dry in here." He poured the grain into her trough, stroked a hand down her as she buried her head in it.

"Hungry, are you? I've got a treat in my pocket, so you'll have a carrot, since I'm in charge today. And wouldn't you know it would rain buckets and more when I'm minding my brothers instead of in school while Ma and Da are off helping to find some loony woman."

Shana's teeth bared at the insult. She leaped forward,

striking with the rock, striking again as the boy fell and the horse shied. Snarling, she reared back for a third blow, but calculation replaced blind fury.

He was near to her size, and he had a cap. It had fallen off so there wasn't too much blood on it. And the jacket looked warm.

Tossing the rock aside, she yanked the fat carrot out of the jacket pocket. The first greedy bites woke more hunger, so she gobbled it all before she dragged off his boots, his trousers.

She'd be a boy, she thought as she discarded the dress, pulled on the trousers—a bit snug, but they'd do. And she'd take the horse. She could run faster, but she tired of running, so she'd ride for now, her hair under a cap.

Just a boy, riding in the rain. Riding west.

Breen blocked out the world and wrote until someone knocked on the door.

"It's Brigid with some tea for a wet day if you'd like."

"I would." She got up to answer as Bollocks trotted over, tail wagging.

"I hope I'm not disturbing you, but I thought you'd welcome some tea and a bite to eat. I brought enough for two, as I thought Marco might be with you."

"He's napping—I think. I've lost track of time."

"We've two hours or so before sunset. Oh, I see you were writing," Brigid added as she set the tray on the little table by the fire. "So I'm disturbing you after all."

"You're not, and I do welcome the tea. Would you like some? Do you have time to sit?"

"It's kind of you to ask, but I don't want to be in the way."

"You're not." To solve the issue, Breen poured two cups, then sat. "Is there any news?"

"Only they're looking for her. There's talk around the castle, in the village, and so on. This one thinks they saw her here, another thinks there, but in truth no one's seen her since yesterday. I was so shocked when we found Kiara. Not shocked that Shana would hurt someone, but that she'd hurt such a friend."

"You didn't like her. Shana."

"Ah, well . . ."

"It's all right. Neither did I."

"I can say she'd never be one to say sit yourself down a bit and have some tea. She was more: I don't want red roses by my bed. Take them out and get pink, or, I need my riding boots cleaned by noon. She treated us who give our work to the castle like servants, and we're not."

"No, you're not. You give your work here because you enjoy it, and you have a gift for it. If she didn't appreciate that, it's her lack."

"My heart hurts for her parents, for Kiara, and for Loren, as it's clear he loved her. Loves her still, I'm thinking. So, well, Hugh says you did well with the bow today."

"He did?"

"He did, aye. He's in the way of family, as I have cousins in the north and he's good friends with one of them. He says you'll improve with more practice."

"I can't get much worse. He gave me a leather guard for my arm, and it saved me from a world of bruises."

Marco gave a *tap-tap* before poking his head in. "Hey, Brigid. Hey, cookies!"

He made a beeline for them as Brigid rose.

"I should get back to doing. Thanks for sharing the tea. Rain's letting up a bit," she commented with a nod to the windows. "We'll have a clear evening after all."

"Did I run her off?" Marco asked when Brigid went out.

"She strikes me as someone who doesn't sit still for long. Good nap?"

"Solid, baby. I was hoping Brian would be back when I woke up, and the elf from hell would be in, like, the dungeon or wherever. Guess not." He sat, grabbed another cookie. "Did you write?"

"Solid, baby. I'm going to get out of this chair in a minute—or two—and take my very good dog for a walk in the rain."

"I'm in on that." He switched to bread and cheese. "They'll find her, and that'll be that. Then we can concentrate on taking out the Big Bad."

They walked through what was more a fine mist than rain while spots of blue cracked through the gray. The sun dipped west.

Dragons flew through the mist, through the gray and the blue. She spotted Cróga, but Bran, the boy Keegan promised, rode him.

So he was back, she thought, or had gone out again on a horse. But since they still searched, Shana continued to elude them.

They walked to the village and back as the mists faded, as dusk lowered. As they started back in, Brigid ran out.

"Girl, you're everywhere," Marco commented, and she laughed.

"Do you think? Well, I'm here to tell you the taoiseach sends for you. He's in his tower workshop. I'll take you."

She led them to the tower, up the winding steps to the floor below Keegan's bedchamber.

Brigid knocked, opened the heavy door at Keegan's "Come."

Breen saw a room as large as his bedroom and sitting rooms combined. Fires snapping on either side, worktables, shelves holding cauldrons and bowls, candles and jars.

And she saw Marg.

"Nan!"

She all but flew across the room, but Bollocks still beat her to wag and rub his body against Marg's legs.

"Ah, there you are." Marg returned the hard embrace. "*Mo stór*, what a time you've had."

"I'm so glad you're here. How are you here? Why are you here?"

"We'll get to that. Marco. Let's have a kiss."

When he'd obliged, she gave the dog the attention he begged for, and topped it off by pulling a biscuit from her pocket.

"There now, take that and sit by the fire awhile. Keegan came to fetch me, and so we traveled back on dragons. And I'm here, I hope, to help find this lost and wicked girl."

Keegan, the sleeves of his black sweater shoved to his elbows, stopped his work with mortar and pestle. His face, Breen realized, looked both weary and grim.

"We have others coming, and we'll see if we can make it work."

"Make what work?" Breen asked.

"A finding spell," Marg told her. "Not near as simple as it may sound. We are, the Fey, born to block and resist such spells. They take away choice, and no spells for finding, but for lost objects, are written."

"You'll have wine. I've not given you a moment to catch your breath since we arrived. Sit and catch it now."

"Well then, I will, and give you time to explain what we know now, and why you came for me."

"She's done something." Breen's stomach clenched. "She's hurt someone."

"A boy, barely twelve. Sit, sit. I want some of this myself," he added as he poured wine. "A little farm in the midlands near the banks of the River Shein. He stayed home from school to mind his two young brothers—not yet school-age—as his parents joined the search."

Saying nothing, Marco took two glasses to Breen and Marg.

"Smashed his head with a rock she did, and took his clothes. Left him bleeding and naked in the cold. Took the horse he'd gone out to feed."

"Is he— How bad?" Breen asked, and Keegan shook his head.

"Healers are doing what they can. He was an hour, they think, before the littles—only four years, twin boys—went to look for him. They had the wit to cover him with blankets, and were running to the nearest cottage when one of the Sidhe scouting the area saw them and flew down.

"They have him in spell sleep, as the damage is great, and will take hours if not days to heal. If it can be healed. She's going west, that's clear."

"The valley, your home, your family." Breen looked at Marg. "Mine."

"They're forewarned," Marg assured her, "and more than able to deal with her. This is not a turn, not a twist. This is who she is. She masked it, and well, and it may be she didn't know, not fully, what she had in her. But it was there. Three times now she's tried to take life."

"She had an hour or more on horseback, and in the advantage of rain. She rides well, and she'd ride hard." Keegan sat with his wine but didn't drink. "And as she's proved more canny—or bloody lucky—than I'd imagined, I'm thinking she'll go on foot once the horse is played out."

"But cold and wet, right?" Marco put in. "Hungry, tired. Gotta be some scared in there, too."

"It won't matter," Breen added. "It won't, because Nan's right. This is who she is. The control might have snapped, but this is who she is. What would we need for a finding spell? Something of hers."

"We have hair from her brushes and combs," Keegan began. "Clothes and jewelry she wore, and she left a few drops of blood on the dressing table from her own spell-casting. We'll use it."

"We write the spell, wind the spell," Marg said. "And find her."

Breen looked around, the twin fires blazing, the tools of

magicks, and with her, three of the Wise ready to work under a ceiling painted with stars and the two moons of Talamh.

This she could do. Here, she could help.

"Where do we start?"

Breen sat with Tarryn when she joined them to work on crafting the words and intent. Marg and Keegan worked on ingredients, mixing fresh potions, distilling oils.

Engrossed, frustrated, fascinated, Breen didn't realize Marco had gone out until he came back in.

"Dinner break," he announced as he came in carrying a pot, and the man and woman who'd argued about the rain followed him with bread on a board, bowls.

Brigid came in behind with food and water for Bollocks.

"I know you gotta work," Marco said, "but witches gotta eat like the rest of us."

"He's right," Tarryn said before Keegan could object. "We'll do better work with food in us. What have we here, Marco?"

"What we've got is what I call kitchen sink stew. I went down to the kitchen and Maggie and Teag let me have at it."

"He's a brilliant cook," Maggie put in as she and Teag set up a table. "We sampled the results, and you're in for a good hearty meal. Gods' blessings on you all for the work you're doing, and our candles are lit for the young boy in the midlands."

"Thank you, Maggie, thank you, Teag, and you as well, Brigid. Come now, let's sit." Tarryn gestured to the table. "And see what the kitchen sink has to offer."

"It smells like it offers well." Pushing back impatience, Keegan turned. "And I'm hoping he left you all more than a sample."

"That he did, Taoiseach." Teag grinned. "And we'll go make quick work of it. The kitchen's yours, Marco, whenever you please."

Tarryn ladled up the stew. "We thank you for the meal, Marco."

"Just want to do my part. Bollocks and I, we'll take a walk after we eat so you can get back to it. Did I hear right? You have to do this outside? Teag said it's going to be pretty raw out."

"Outside's best." Keegan took a spoonful. "All right then, it is brilliant. A coven of seven," he continued. "And seven from each tribe."

"Like on Samhain."

"Aye. I would ask you to be part of it."

Marco blinked. "Me?"

"We would have seven that are not Fey, seven who come from outside. I would have you as one of them if you choose."

"Yeah, sure. Wow. What do I do?"

"Be with us," Tarryn said simply.

"That's simple. I already am."

Deep in the woods stood a dolmen that served as an altar for high rituals and spells of great import. Around this, in the last hour, the seven who stood for the Wise cast the circle.

Though the air held raw, and the wind snapped at her cloak, Breen felt a heat inside as she and six others performed the rite.

It surprised her to find Loren as part of the coven, then she realized that was Keegan's way. An acknowledgment of innocence and faith.

So they called to the Quarters as other circles formed around them. The Sidhe, the Were, the Troll, the Elfin, the Mer in the sea, and the seven from other worlds.

Candles and torches sprang to life, spreading light into shadows.

"For justice, for peace, we seek to find she who hides from judgment." As he spoke, Keegan poured water gathered from the day's rain into the cauldron. "In breaking First Laws, she must face punishment."

"So potions for clear eyes, clear hearts swim into water

mixed by son and daughter." Marg drained two bottles into the cauldron.

Tarryn moved forward. "Now herbs and crystals for power, for light, into this brew bring knowledge, bring sight."

Eyes grieving, voice thick, Loren held his hand over the cauldron. "This pin I gave her. I would I could save her."

The next added a glove, and the next a jeweled brush and comb.

"It is Shana O'Loinsigh we seek to find with this spell we seven wind. Now as the altar goes to flame, seven by seven, we speak the name."

Beneath the cauldron, flames rose up to encase the dolmen. And from the dolmen, smoke spiraled up, white as the moons.

"Hear her crimes one by one, and grant us sight so justice is done. With this blood she sought to bind me, from my own will she sought to blind me." Keegan added the blood.

Tarryn poured in pieces of crystal from her cupped hands. "With this vase now broken, she struck a friend to keep truth unspoken."

Breen heard the dolmen hum under the flames as she lifted the blackened knife over the cauldron. "With this knife she tried to end my life. In her attack, this blade aimed at my back."

Marg brought the bloodstained rock. "She struck a child with this stone, and left him lying all alone. By her malice, his life hangs in the balance."

Keegan's voice rose like the smoke. "At this hour, with joined power, for Talamh and its laws we stand as one. Show us now in flame and smoke so justice can be done."

And in the smoke, and in the flame, Breen saw.

In the woods of the west where the moss grew thick and the river ran fast and green, Shana slipped through shadows, into trees, out again.

Miles back, she'd let the horse go. It had served its purpose, and even with vicious kicks had no longer managed even a trot. But she'd found her way, a way she'd remembered from a ride with Keegan on her single trip to the valley.

There would be a waterfall up ahead, and in it, the portal to Odran. It would be guarded, no question, and she'd yet to work out how to deal with that, or how to open the bloody portal.

But she'd come this far.

She'd avoided the search—riders, dragons, other elves (traitors!)—so wouldn't be stopped here. She'd wanted, so badly, to find a torch and set fire to the farm Keegan so loved. But she'd resisted, slipped by even when she spotted his ridiculous brother keeping watch, and the winged whore Morena doing the same by the Welcoming Tree.

She'd outfoxed them, all of them.

Still, she needed to rest again, to settle and think clear. And gods, she wanted something hot and flavorful to eat rather than the raw vegetables she'd pulled from gardens.

Once again she unwrapped her wounded hand, wept a little at the raw blisters, the red shooting up her fingers, fingers she couldn't completely uncurl without agony.

Stretching out, she lowered her hand into the river, bit back a moan that was both relief and pain.

"Ah, poor thing! Such a mean burn on such soft skin."

Shana rolled over, prepared to run, but the woman who stood over her simply held out her hands. "Be still."

And she couldn't move.

"I haven't watched and waited for you to have you run off so I have to watch and wait again. You're a clever one, Shana, more, I confess, than I believed."

She had bloodred hair in long, perfect waves beyond the shoulders of a gorgeous dress the color of ripe plums with a cloak of gold over it. She smiled from eyes so dark and deep they looked nearly black. Jewels glittered from her ears, around her throat, on her wrists, her fingers.

Even in her fear, Shana envied them.

"Who are you?"

"I'm someone who's about to become a very dear friend to you. Now then, would you like me to heal that hand for you? Stand and be still, and I will. Run, and I'll see the ones hunting you find you—as I've helped keep them from doing so thus far."

The woman's smile went fierce. "You don't think you managed this journey without some help, do you now?"

"Why would you help me?"

"I'm of a mind we'll be of help to each other. Stand, girl, and hold out your hand."

She found her legs worked again, so obeyed.

"Ah, that's nasty, isn't it now?" The woman began sliding her own hand just above Shana's. Layer by layer, Shana felt the pain ease, the throbbing lessen.

The bliss of it had her closing her eyes.

When she opened them again, the blisters were gone, as was the horrible red, the crackles of black. But scars, welts of them, ran over the palm in the shape of a knife hilt.

"There's scars."

"I can see that for myself." The woman snapped it out as she stared at the palm with her eyes glinting with temper. "It's been too long since it happened, so you'll live with the scars. Wear a glove if it worries you.

"Now you'll come with me."

"Where? Who are you?"

"Where you want to go. I'm Yseult, and I've had my eye on you for quite a long time. I'd hoped you'd snare the taoise-ach, but since you haven't, well, you can still be useful."

"I know the name of Yseult. Odran's witch. How are you here when the portals are sealed and guarded?"

"I have my ways, and those ways narrow while we stand here. Do you wish to join Odran, do you wish to punish those who betrayed you? You must wish it for me to get you through, and know until the seal is fully broken, I can't get you back."

She stood in a boy's rough clothes, scars marring her hand, her belly aching with hunger.

"I want them to pay. I want to make them pay."

"Then come with me and hurry. We have only moments left."

Lifting her skirts, Yseult ran toward the waterfall. Racing with her, Shana saw four guards.

"They sleep," Yseult told her. "And only for a moment more."

"Why didn't you strike them down? Why didn't you kill them?"

"Death leaves a trail. As long as they don't know I can go in, go out, even if Odran and the rest can't as yet, they'll do nothing more than they've done.

"Now."

She whirled the cloak around Shana, and wrapping her in it, leaped into the river.

Light shimmered on its surface, bright, then dark.

# CHAPTER TWENTY-THREE

B reen heard wailing behind her. More than weeping, the sound was grief ripped from a beating heart.

She didn't need to turn to know it came from Shana's mother because she felt it in her own.

Beside her, Tarryn gripped Loren's arm. "We have to close the circle, Loren. You can't break it. And you can't help Shana now."

"Wait. I can see. Can you see? Not a door," Breen continued. "Not a window. A . . . breach. So narrow, jagged. Under the falls. Not through, under. Can you see?"

"No." Marg took her hand. "What can you see?"

"The water's swirling, the breach closing. It nearly catches the end of the cloak—so close. And the other side, they have to fight for the surface. The spell's fading. Two faeries, no, four, four go into the water to drag them up. Into the air, gasping. There's blood in the water. Not theirs. She needs blood to open the breach. Under the falls, deep under. Not through. Not yet. Not yet enough.

"It's gone. It's gone."

"We'll close the circle."

When they had, Keegan went to Shana's parents. "Your sorrow is my sorrow." Then turned to Loren. "Your grief is my grief. There's no comfort I can give. She made her choice." He looked to his mother, who nodded.

"Come with me," she soothed, and put an arm around the weeping woman. "Come with me now, Gwen darling, and you, Uwin. And you as well, Loren. Come away from here, out of the cold."

"They'll never heal from this," Keegan said quietly. He gestured Brian over. "Send falcons. Call off the search. Let my brother know I come west, now, and need him to help seal this breach. And you, Marg, I'd ask you to go back with me only hours after you traveled here."

"I will, of course. Keegan, she was lost before she went with Yseult. She went because she was lost."

"I know it, and too well."

"I'm coming with you," Breen insisted. "I can help. I saw where they went through."

"Aye, you're coming. Pack quickly, and tonight take only what you need. Marco, I'll ask you to bring the rest when you ride back tomorrow."

"Tomorrow? Ah . . . Sure, no problem."

"I have much to do, and little time. Be ready," he told Breen. "Half an hour."

He strode off, signaling others, snapping out orders.

"That taoiseach stuff," Marco commented, then huffed out a breath. "Man, she went totally to the dark side."

"He has her now. Odran has her. I don't know if she really understands what that means. If she really knows what she's done."

"She chose," Marg said flatly. "Come, I'll help you pack your things, as I brought little of my own."

She took the pages she'd written and her notes, her globe and other tools, and packed the rest for Marco.

"I got this for you." She offered Marg the amethyst candleholder.

"Ah, why, it's lovely, and clever with it. And full of calm and peace. What a sweet gift. Where did you come by it?"

"A shop in the village here. The woman—she wouldn't take anything for it, so it's as much from her. She said to give you her best, and you might remember her. Ninia Colconnan."

Marg's smile beamed out. "And sure I remember her very well indeed. How did you find her? Is she well?"

"Yes, and her shop's wonderful. She was knitting a blanket for a great-grandchild coming soon. Her twelfth, she said."

"What a fine, full life that is. I'm glad to hear it, and hope to come back and visit her. But now . . ."

"We have to go."

When they went outside, where the wind whipped at them and Keegan, Bollocks, and the dragons waited, Breen held on tight to Marco.

"You'll be all right?"

"I've got this. You be careful. I mean it, Breen. You take care of my best girl."

"I will. Promise. Let's go, Bollocks. Tomorrow," she called as she hurried to Keegan. "I'll see you tomorrow."

At Marg's call, Bollocks scrambled up to ride with her. Marco watched Keegan lift Breen onto Cróga. And with a thunder of wings, they shot up to fly into the night.

Brian put an arm around his shoulders. "Don't worry too much now."

"A year ago she was too nervous to call an Uber, and now she's riding a dragon."

"Uber?"

Marco let out a short laugh. "It's a car thing. I used to push her some to step out of her box, now there's no box that can hold her."

"Then be proud."

"I am. Scared for her, too. Same goes for you."

Brian turned Marco's face to his, kissed him. "No worries now. I wear your protection. Come out of the wind and be with me. In a few hours, we ride west."

They flew through the night, in and out of clouds, along snapping winds. Below, the world slept even while its rivers wound, its grasses fluttered. She saw the dark silhouettes of mountains rising, the wide, rolling sea, and once an owl, ghost white, its wings spread as it soared into the thick dark of a forest.

Beside her and Keegan, Marg rode, her hooded cloak swirling while Bollocks sat in front of her, his eyes closed in bliss as the wind flapped his ears.

An adventure for him, Breen thought. For her? A mission, and one too vital for her to waste time on nerves.

Instead, she scanned the land, tried to gauge where they were. But it was so different riding on a dragon at night than making the journey on horseback in the sunlight.

"How much damage can she do?" Breen pitched her voice above the roar of wind and wings. "Shana, how much damage can she do against you, against Talamh, now that she's with Odran?"

"She knows the Capital, the castle, its grounds. She knows the business of the council, as her father discussed such things with her he surely shouldn't have. If she paid attention, and I trust now she did, she'd know the names of scouts and spies, know their routes and routines. She would know a great deal. And she's shown herself to be wilier and more ruthless than ever I knew."

"You'll fix that. You'll change routes and routines and strategies."

"Aye, and that's begun, but she spent her life in the politics and plannings that brew in the Capital. I can see how she'd be valuable to Odran. And I'm sorry to say I can see clear why she chose him over her family, her friends, her world as, for betraying them, he'll give her what she wants more."

"Power. Standing. And the freedom to do what she wants no matter who it hurts."

"All of that, and the hopes of your blood and mine. My family's, and I think now all of Talamh, as they refused her."

"She's too narcissistic to understand if she doesn't give him all he wants, or he thinks she's no longer of use, he'll kill her without a second thought. I don't know if . . ."

She felt a pull, in her heart, her belly, her mind. Heartbeats, so many, deep and slow. Sleeping as the world slept. But one waking now, waking to beat as hers did.

In hers. Of hers.

Waking. Waiting.

In the dark, she saw the mountain silhouette, rising high so it pierced the clouds that floated around it.

She yearned, and that heartbeat merged with hers yearned.

"What is that?" She pointed toward the mountain. "What is that place?"

"Nead na Dragain. It's the highest peak in Talamh. Dragon's Nest."

"Hugh—yes, it was Hugh—pointed it out to me on the ride to the Capital. But it didn't seem so . . . It seems different now."

"It's night," Keegan said simply. "It's written the first of them became there, and waited for her mate. And when he came, there they flourished before even the first Fey walked the lands or swam the seas."

As one, Cróga and Dilis sent out a roar.

"They speak to their brothers and sisters who bide there," Keegan told her. "Some to rest, some to mate, some to wait. You would have seen Nead na Dragain from the valley on a clear day, looking to the northeast. And as you said, on the ride to the Capital."

"I can't remember seeing it before Hugh pointed it out. It looks different from up here." As they flew on, the pull lessened, and the beat within her beat quieted. "But then everything does. I can't make out where we are."

"Near to the valley now, and there Harken will join us, as will Sedric and Mahon. Aisling as well, as someone will tend the children for her."

Even as he spoke, Breen saw the dragon gliding toward them, great wings spread. Moonslight struck its scales, a glimmer of silver over the blue.

With a swish of tail, it turned to ride in tandem with Keegan and Marg, with Harken and Aisling on its back.

"You made good time," Harken called out.

"The winds were with us."

"Mahon's gone ahead, and Morena with him, as she was with me and wouldn't be denied. They've already been to the portal and back, and all's quiet there. They were to take Sedric on this second trip."

"Well then, let's not keep them waiting."

He veered slightly south, and before long, Breen recognized—or thought she did—the hills, the fields, the forests. And when pixies sparkled light over Finola and Seamus's lush and expansive gardens, she knew exactly where she was.

Nerves fluttered now, but she accepted them. Some nerves, even some self-doubt was probably better than overconfidence.

Especially since she had no idea what she'd be expected to do.

She heard the waterfall before she saw it, and the dragons, nimble as hawks, threaded their way down, through the forest.

Keegan leaped off, said: "Jump." Added, "Now!" when she hesitated.

Holding her breath, Breen swung off and into the air. He caught her, and with no fanfare set her on her feet.

"Aisling's too pregnant to— Oh," she managed when Mahon flew up, lifted Aisling into his arms.

Riderless now, the dragons flew up to circle in the dark sky above the trees.

A deer walked out of the woods, became a man. "All's clear, Taoiseach."

"Keep watch, Dak. We'll want no interference."

Thrilled, Bollocks raced in circles.

"How do we do this?" Breen lengthened her stride to keep up as Keegan walked ahead. "What do I do?"

"Power, light, intent, twined and merged. You know where to find the breach?"

"Yes. Under the falls, close to the far edge. I can't see from up here, but—"

"You won't be up here," he began, and Morena landed lightly in front of them, folded her wings.

"All's clear. An interesting trip you've had," she said to Breen.

"I'll say." She saw Sedric take Marg's hands, kiss her lightly.

"Sure I want to hear all about it, but for now, where do you want me, Keegan?"

"The other bank. You and Mahon flanking Aisling and Marg. Sedric at the falls. I'll speak to you when there's time, Sedric, about the child—thank you for your good work."

"She's a bright one, little Dilly, and the work's not done."

"We'll seal this breach, and the next time Yseult tries to use it to take one of ours, may she drown in her own disappointment." Keegan gripped Sedric's hand. "Our light, one light."

"One light."

"Our gift, one gift," he said as Mahon set Aisling, and Morena set Marg, on the opposite bank.

"One gift."

The one he'd called Dak and others came out of the woods to stand near the falls.

"Our purpose, one purpose."

"One purpose."

Mahon flew over the river, put an arm around Sedric. He flew him straight into the falls. As Mahon flew back to the bank, Sedric stood in the thundering water like a statue.

"He holds the portal," Harken explained as he yanked off his boots. "And holding it there, would know if any try to come through."

It had to be freezing, Breen thought, and pounding on him. Yet he stood as a man might in a pleasant meadow, his palms cupped up to catch sunlight.

"What should I do first?"

Keegan glanced at her. "Strip."

"I'm sorry. What?"

"Boots and clothes will weigh you down in the river." As Harken had, he pulled off his boots, tossed his duster aside, then unhooked his trousers. "Take them off. You'll go in between Harken and me, show us the breach. With one light, one gift, one purpose, we close it, seal it."

He tossed aside his tunic, stood naked and impatient. "Hurry up with it."

"It's a matter of practicality." Harken, obviously perfectly comfortable standing naked in front of more than a dozen others, spoke more gently. "And safety as well."

"Ah, balls." With a flick of his hand, Keegan had her clothes scattered around her.

"Jesus!" Mortified, Breen used hands and arms. "You can't just—"

"The water'll cover you modestly enough, even though it be cold as winter's bitch."

Keegan dealt with it by scooping her up and leaping in.

She'd have screamed if the icy shock of the water had left her any breath.

Harken closed a hand around her arm. "Catch your breath now, and catch it well, as you'll need it. As we need you to show us what we don't see."

"Don't think, don't question," Keegan told her. "Feel and take. One light, one gift, one purpose. Now hold your breath. We go together."

Since he pulled her under, she had little choice. But she could see clearly through the eerie green. He had her hand, and Harken the other, so with them, she kicked down, and forward toward the thunder of the falls.

As her heartbeat steadied, she lost the panicked urge to kick up toward the air.

What she felt inside was stronger. Sedric's quiet courage, her grandmother's unbreakable faith, the light from all who stood on the banks.

The united purpose of the men who held her hands.

She saw the rocks and silt below, the wild churning of the water ahead. In her mind she saw Yseult dragging Shana to the chink—black against the churn of green and white. Black with the red of blood threaded through it.

She tugged her hands free to swim forward to the crack, ink black, thread thin in the water. As she held her hands out to it, the light, the gift, the purpose joined.

The force of the water wanted to shove her back. She fought it as Keegan and Harken pushed with her.

The light, the one light, bathed the water in warmth, glowed like the sun as, white and pure, it covered the crack.

She felt it closing, inch by laborious inch, felt the dark that had breached it struggle to open like a maw. She thought of the child who'd been dragged through the maw to face death, and let the fury come.

For an instant, the heat sizzled and snapped, then with a bare whisper of sound, the breach sealed.

She kicked and clawed her way to the surface to gulp in air. Keegan would have put an arm around her to support her, but she had enough fury left in her that her fist swung out before she thought about it.

And landed handily on his jaw.

"Don't ever do that again."

Harken scrambled up the bank, and grabbing her cloak, helped her out of the water, draped the cloak over her shoulders. "There you are now, Breen darling."

She mustered the tattered shreds of her dignity. "Thank you."

"It's done." Keegan leaped onto the bank. "Thanks to you all. We'll keep watch as we have, here and across Talamh."

He dragged on his trousers as Breen struggled to keep the cloak around her and pull on her own. While he issued orders, she managed to dress. She reached Sedric first when Mahon brought him back.

And she wrapped her arms around him to greet him, and to warm and dry him. "I saw you, with the girl, on Odran's side. How you found her, saved her. They were so close behind, so close. I couldn't see them, but I felt them. So did you."

"She was a brave young thing, and asked about you. The goddess with the red hair who broke her chains."

"I don't know how I did it."

"And yet you did. How proud your da would be."

"I saw you fight in the south. How proud your son would be."

Emotion swirled into his eyes before he leaned down to kiss her cheek. "That is the world to me. The world to me you'd say it. Rest now, and there'll be lemon biscuits for you tomorrow. And something for you," he added, and rubbed Bollocks. "He jumped right in after you," Sedric told her. "Not to play, but to guard."

He smiled over her head. "Come now, Marg, call your fierce dragon and let's put these old bones to bed."

"That I will." She hugged Breen first. "Don't be too hard

on him," she said. "He carries such weight. A little hard, of course." She smiled as she drew back. "For he earned it."

"We'll talk tomorrow," Morena told her. "And Aisling as well, as she had as fierce a dislike for Shana as I—and we're proven right, which is no small satisfaction. Mahon needs to get her home, but we'll hear all there is to hear tomorrow. It was a fine punch," she added, then strolled to Harken as he called his dragon.

When Keegan walked back to her, the faint bruise on his jaw more than made up for her throbbing hand. For a moment, he just looked at her—straight and deep and silent.

"I'll take you to the farm or to Marg's or—"

"My cottage. I want my own bed, and I want the quiet."

"As you like."

When Cróga glided down, she climbed on before he could help her. A delighted Bollocks scrambled up behind her.

After he mounted, they flew over the trees, over the fields. She saw her grandmother's dragon and Harken's, both riderless now, soaring north.

They shot through the portal at the Welcoming Tree, into Ireland, and a gentle rain.

At the cottage, Bollocks leaped down, then surprised her by sitting, waiting, rather than streaking straight for the bay. She slid off, then felt surprise again as Keegan dismounted rather than flying away.

"I'd speak to you a moment. Out of the rain," he added when she said nothing. "If it's the same to you."

She wanted a warm drink, a blazing fire, and time alone to brood, but she turned and walked into the cottage.

Keegan brought in the bag she'd forgotten, set it on the table.

"I'll not apologize to you, as I've apologized to you more in these past months than to all and any in the whole of my life."

Breen hung up her cloak, then walked into the kitchen to make herself tea.

"There wasn't time to waste with you being delicate about the matter."

"Delicate." She'd worked hard on the cool and aloof, but felt the ice crack. "Is that what you call my reaction to being stripped naked, without my permission, against my will, in front of a dozen?"

"They weren't there to gawk at you, and what needed doing needed doing quickly. Bugger it." He strode away, slapped a hand toward the fire to start it, strode back. "It's a body, for gods' sake. Everyone's got one."

Since Bollocks stood beside her, head ticking back and forth from her to Keegan, she got a biscuit out of the jar for him.

Rather than gobble it down, he just stood with it clamped in his mouth.

"Really?"

"Aye, for these purposes. You'd have sunk like a stone in all of that, and until we were in the water, at the breach, how could I know how bad it was? How much it would take to seal it? All the time it took to get there, Yseult had that time to gather herself. She might have tried coming back through, and then we'd need to take her on with Marg and Sedric already weary, with my sister carrying."

She wished it didn't make sense, but still.

"In the time it took to get there, you could have explained things to me, what I'd need to do."

"I didn't think of it. There's a woman I once bedded who tried to murder the one I'm bedding now who's gone to Odran. Her father, a good man, a wise one in the ways needed, has resigned from the council, and I can't find the words to change his mind on it. Her mother will mourn the rest of her days. The man who loves her is no good to me now, and won't be until he can draw himself back, if he ever can."

He paced as he spoke, like a man caged.

"She meant something to me once. Meant enough for me to be with her. And in being with her, I played a part in all of this. I don't take blame for it," he said before she could object. "But that's the fact of it. So I didn't think to tell you that if you went into the water fully dressed you'd sink like a shagging stone, as I thought you had the sense to know it yourself."

"I might have figured that out if you'd told me we had to go into the water in the first place."

"Well, how the buggering hell did you think we'd make the seal if not there at the breach?"

"I don't know."

"Do you want me to apologize for giving you credit for more logic than you seem to have on it?"

She poured her tea, very slowly. "In the world where we stand now, and where I've lived most of my life, we're more private about nudity. Should I apologize for giving you more credit for knowing that than you apparently have?"

"I was in this place once on this side where the women on the stage took off . . ." He saw the hole he was about to fall into. "Well, never mind that. It's war, Breen. I can wish for peace, and for the time and skill to give you the room you need, but I don't have it. What we did tonight we couldn't have done without you. I needed you. We needed you."

She softened enough to get another mug. "You expect me to train and to learn how to fight in this war with my fists, with a sword, with a bow, with my gifts. And I'm trying."

She poured tea into the mug, handed it to him. "I expect you to learn how to explain things to me instead of making decisions for me. I've told you enough about my life here so you should understand what it's like for me when decisions are made for me."

"That's fair. That's fair," he repeated. "I'm likely to be as poor at it as you are with a bow, but I'll work on it."

Satisfied the crisis had passed, Bollocks took his biscuit and went to stretch out by the fire.

After he sampled the tea, Keegan sighed. "I appreciate the tea, but I'm wondering if you've some whiskey to go into it."

She went to a cupboard, took out a bottle. When he held out the mug, she poured some in. And when he made a come-ahead gesture, poured more.

"Thanks for that." He took a drink, then another. "I don't see how there'd be trouble over here tonight—or what's left of the night—but I can't risk it. I can't leave you alone. I'm not asking to share your bed."

He drank again as she watched him over the rim of her mug.

"In truth I'm too bloody tired so I don't think either of us would enjoy that much in any case. I can take Marco's bed, or the divan in there. I'd know you're safe. I need to sleep, and I won't unless I know you're safe."

He looked exhausted, and she realized she hadn't really factored that in. And not just physically, she thought, but in every way exhausted.

"You can share my bed. To sleep," she added.

She set down her mug of tea, opened her bag to take her pages out and lay them on the table. She started to shoulder the bag, but he took it.

"I'll carry it up."

With a nod, she started toward the stairs. "Come on, Bol-locks. Bedtime."

He bolted up ahead of her, was already curled in his bed when she came in. She lit the fire before taking her toiletry case out of the bag Keegan carried in.

She went into the bathroom, shut the door.

When she came out, Keegan, like her dog, was already in bed—and both of them asleep.

She changed into flannel pants, a T-shirt, lowered the fire to a simmer. Thinking what a complicated, often difficult man she'd ended up involved with, she slid into bed beside him.

And dropped into sleep the moment she shut her eyes.

# CHAPTER TWENTY-FOUR

She woke alone, and to the shimmer of sunlight. A glance at the clock showed it was after eight—long past her usual get-up-and-get-going time.

Then again, she honestly didn't know what time she'd dropped into bed.

She got up, grabbed a hoodie, and went down to find her dog.

From the back door she spotted him in the bay, and Keegan on the shore throwing the ball. Time after time Bollocks swam after it or leaped up to snatch it from the air.

She had good reason to know he'd do that for hours.

Leaving them to it, she made coffee and—muttering at herself for being stupid and vain—did a light glamour before she carried the coffee outside.

"Your arm will fall off before he gets tired of that game," she called out.

Keegan heaved the ball again before he turned. "So I've come to know. I fed him, as that's easy enough, but I didn't know for certain how to work the machine for coffee."

"Fortunately, I do." She offered him one of the mugs.

"Thanks. It's good. I've thought of having Seamus try growing the beans, as he's a wizard with such things, but tea's the tradition. I might ease it in after things are settled and done."

"I've never asked you what you plan to do once things are settled and done. I mean what else you plan."

"Ah well, handling the business of peace still needs doing. Seeing the laws are held, the roads kept clean and clear, help's given where it's needed, keeping trades running in our world and with the ones beyond."

He shrugged. "And the bloody politics of it all never goes away. I read your pages."

"What?"

"You shouldn't have left them sitting right there if you didn't want eyes on them. I liked them."

"I barely wrote anything when I was at the Capital."

"What you did, I liked. The words roll. You used the castle and the village, how they feel and look, how they smell. It seems to me people will see it who never go there."

"Thank you. That's the hope."

"You're not so angry this morning." He picked up the ball a soaking Bollocks dropped at his feet, and obliged the dog by throwing it again.

"Maybe not."

"And myself, I'm not so tired. So I can wish I had the time to persuade you back to bed, but I have to go back to the Capital."

"Maybe not so angry doesn't mean I'm ready to have sex with you."

"That's where the persuasion would come into it." He reached out to wind her hair around his finger. "But I have to go and deal with the mess of things there, then come back and shore up what's left of the mess here. If I'm back with enough time for it, I'd like you to go somewhere with me on Cróga."

"Where?"

"We'll talk about it if there's time." Once again he picked up the ball. "You're a demon dog for certain," he said, and threw the ball. "You'll come to Talamh later today. You'll want to write first, have the quiet awhile, but you'll come."

"Yes."

"I'll see you there if I'm able. Marco should be back before dusk. Earlier by far if he flies with Brian."

"I think dusk."

"The last time this is," Keegan told Bollocks as he again picked up the ball. "So make it good."

He feinted a throw so Bollocks dashed toward the water, then back again. Feinted again and sent the dog into leaping, dancing, barking delight.

Watching them made Breen wonder what Keegan had been like as a boy, just a boy, before he'd lifted the sword from the lake. Before he'd shouldered the responsibility for worlds.

"I have to go," he told her. "I need to speak to Harken before I fly east, and see that all's well at the falls. I'm . . . explaining things."

It took effort, but she suppressed the smile and nodded. "I can see that."

"All right then." He put an arm around her waist, tugged her to him. "Kiss me, would you, as it took powerful restraint not to wake you when you lay soft and warm beside me at dawn."

"I might not have minded."

"Now she says it. I'll keep that in mind the next time. Now kiss me, Breen, for the ride east will be cold."

She put an arm around his neck, tangled her fingers in his hair. And took her time about it. Testing her power, she brushed her lips lightly on his, watched his eyes as he watched hers.

Then changed the angle, brushed again.

Smiled.

"You leave me wanting," he told her.

"I could." And that, she thought, was a power she hadn't known she had. "But . . ." She gave his bottom lip a little tug with her teeth. "I won't. Kiss me back, Keegan," she whispered, and took his mouth.

What he felt poured into her, the mad heat of need. It left her staggered, aching, thrilled.

"It wouldn't have taken much persuasion."

"Gods spare me." He dropped his brow to hers a moment, then straightened, stepped back. Handed her the mug. "I have to go."

Cróga landed on the beach behind him.

He turned, mounted, gave her one last look. Then was gone.

She wrote a blog, then tested her skills with magicks, creating images for it from memory. The hillsides, the bridges over the river, and Bollocks leaping into the water, Marco on horseback.

Satisfied, she wrote an email to Sally and Derrick before she treated herself to a Coke and settled in to work.

The words didn't always roll, but it felt good, really good, to be back at her desk, back at her laptop, back in the quiet.

And tomorrow, she promised herself, back into her preferred routine.

She wrote into the afternoon, then pushed herself away. Time for a real shower, she decided, and clothes that weren't pajamas.

Time for Talamh.

As Breen and the dog walked into the woods, Shana stirred awake.

She remembered, vaguely, bathing . . . being bathed?

Warm, scented water.

It seemed like a dream, and what did it matter when everything felt so soft and lovely?

She found herself in a bed that cradled her like clouds, with sheets of white satin against her skin. On the ceiling, painted gods and faeries, elves and strange beasts danced and fornicated while cloven-hoofed demons played pan flutes and sly-eyed creatures feasted on the breasts of laughing Fey.

It was all so gay!

The room with its white silk draperies, its gilt furnishings was easily twice the size of the one she'd left behind. And so much more opulent, with its marble floors and crystal lamps.

She'd dreamed of creating a room just like this when she'd taken her rightful place in the chambers of the taoiseach.

She slipped out of the bed with its towering gold posts and swirled the thin white silk that draped her. The fire, of wood, not peasant peat, simmered in a housing of more white marble with a mantel drenched in fresh flowers.

She drew back the drapes, lifted her face to the stream of the sun, her gaze to the view of a thundering sea.

No tiny balcony here where she could barely stand, but a wide terrace with flowered vines tangled around the railings. She started to step out, but the wind blew fierce so she shut the glass door again.

It pleased her to see her favored scents and creams and paints arranged in pretty bottles on a dressing table with soft gold-backed brushes for her hair, jeweled combs, a gold-framed mirror that reflected her beauty, a chair in the palest of pink velvet where she could sit and admire herself.

Opening the first door of the four-door wardrobe she found gowns, jeweled bodices, flowing skirts, rich fabrics. Squealing with delight, she opened more to find riding clothes, shawls, scarves, furs, an entire section of shoes and boots.

Lush, alluring underpinnings, nightwear, robes of silks and satins.

In velvet-lined drawers she found jewels, the ornate, the elegant, the stunning.

This, so much this, was worth every terrible moment of her flight from Talamh. Damn them all!

To amuse herself, she plucked sapphire stars with a teardrop of diamonds and put them on her ears, slid rings that caught her fancy on her fingers.

As she turned her hands to admire, she saw the scars, the shape of a knife hilt, scored into her right palm. It no longer burned her skin, but it burned, hot and strong, in her heart.

Payment. One day there would be payment.

But today, she wanted only delights, and found more when she wandered into a generous sitting room. She'd barely begun to explore when a knock sounded—almost a scratching—on the door.

Shana lifted her chin, said, "Come."

The girl had straw-colored hair pulled tight into a knot at the base of her neck. She wore a shapeless gray dress, kept her eyes downcast as she carried in a tray.

"To break your fast, mistress."

Shana gestured to the table near the sitting room's terrace doors. The girl scurried over, began to set out the teapot, the cup, pastries, a domed plate.

"Should I pour your tea, mistress?"

"Of course."

"I am Beryl, and will serve you as long as it pleases you."

"Where is Yseult?"

"I cannot say, mistress."

"I wish to meet with Odran."

"I am told Odran, our lord, our master, will send for you."

"When?"

"I cannot say, mistress."

"So far, your service isn't pleasing."

The girl glanced up, just an instant, but Shana saw raw fear. That did please her.

"Go tidy the bed and lay out the blue velvet with the jeweled cuffs and hem, the blue kid boots with gold heels, and the proper undergarments. Then go away. Come back in one hour."

Satisfied, Shana sat at the table, removed the dome to find a pretty omelet and a rasher of bacon.

She thought how painful her hunger had been in Talamh, how she'd lowered herself to eat carrots and turnips yanked out of the dirt.

She ate slowly, savoring each bite, and with each bite imagined her glorious revenge.

When Breen climbed over the wall to the road in Talamh, Morena, Amish on her arm, hailed her from the farm.

"At last!"

"Late start. I'm going down to Nan's."

"We'll meet you there then. I'll get Aisling. My own nan's already there."

With the hawk still on her arm, Morena spread her wings and flew toward the cottage.

Amused, Breen continued on. She'd missed this—only a few days, but she'd missed this walk down the road, past the farm and the sheep. Had missed seeing Harken out in the field with the horses as he was now. She'd missed the quiet low of cattle, the smell of green grass and peat smoke on a brisk fall breeze.

The way Bollocks trotted beside her, she knew he was as happy to be back as she.

"We're not really castle types, are we?"

She veered to the side when a wagon rumbled up, and noted the trio of kids in the back.

"No school today?" she wondered aloud. "What day is it? I've lost track."

She saw the group she thought of as the Gang of Six playing a game with a red ball and flat sticks in a near field, so called out.

"No school today?"

Mina, the de facto leader, waved. "Well, it's Saturday, isn't it? And welcome back to the valley."

"It's good to be back."

One of the boys transformed into a young horse, snatched the ball in his mouth, and raced off with it.

"Foul!" Mina cried, and went elf speed in pursuit. "There's a foul!"

Fantastic as it was, Breen thought as she continued on, it was blissfully simple. Children playing on a Saturday afternoon as children did everywhere.

Or should.

She made the turn toward Marg's cottage, marveled at the flowers still blooming despite the chill. And saw the blue door open. Because she was expected. And she was welcome.

Inside, the fire snapped in the hearth and the air smelled of fresh bread and sweet things.

She heard Finola's quick laugh.

They stood together at the counter, her grandmother and Marg's closest friend. Faerie and witch, laughing together as Marg set a boule of crusty bread on a rack to cool.

"So I said to him, Seamus, if your arse wasn't so warm, it wouldn't invite my cold feet to rest on it. And what does he do but roll right over and . . . Ah, and look here, it's Breen."

Breen walked into the hug. "Don't I get to hear what happened next?"

"What happened next is what you'd expect when a man rolls on top of you in the night." She laughed again, blue eyes sparkling.

"And so it is Fi's feeling chipper today," Marg finished.

"Sure I am. And how are you, darling?" She brushed a hand over Breen's hair. "It's good to have you back in the valley, safe and well. Such a brave one you've been."

"I don't know about brave, but I'm glad to be back. Morena and Aisling are coming."

"I expected they would, so Sedric brought me some fresh buttermilk from the farm for the soda bread. And there's jam he made himself, and lemon biscuits. And," Marg added, going into her jar, "we wouldn't be forgetting such a good dog."

"Where is Sedric?"

"He took himself off, leaving the kitchen to the women as a wise man would."

"What he did last night? It was amazing. I can't imagine what it took out of him."

"He's a lot in him, but I can tell you he slept like the dead, and there was no rolling over."

Finola let out another laugh. "Well now, there's always tonight. We'll have wine, won't we, Marg, for our girl talk?"

"We will indeed. I've a bottle of the sparkling sort I've been saving for such a day."

"I wasn't gone very long."

Marg only smiled. "You traveled farther than you might think. Let's have the fancy plates and such, Finola."

"I'll help with that. I met your son, Finola. Or I met him again, and his wife, their sons, their wives. I remembered them, Flynn and Sinead and Seamus and Phelin. As soon as I saw them again, I remembered."

"Sinead sent a falcon to tell me. It meant that much to her. She loved you so."

"I remember. I remember how Flynn would toss me in the air so it felt like flying, and how Sinead tied ribbons in my hair. I remember the night Odran took me, and you brought me back . . ."

Breen folded the colorful cloths into fans.

"What do you remember?" Marg asked.

"I remember my mother crying and shaking. It scared me. It's not her fault, I don't mean that, but it scared me. And you, Finola, you gathered her up, held her, rocked her, and Sinead took me and Morena into her lap."

She paused as it came back, all so clear. "She must have been frightened. Her husband was fighting a war, but all I felt was her calm. The boys were there, too. They were just kids. And she told us a story about a young dragon and a young girl and a great treasure. I don't remember exactly, but I remember her voice. So soothing. And Keegan—I'd forgotten. Keegan sitting nearby, watching me. Just watching. I fell asleep holding Morena's hand, with Sinead holding me."

"She was born to be a mother," Finola said. "Some are."

"And mine wasn't. I'm not blaming her," Breen said. "It was a terrible night for her. I think it broke what was already starting to crack. She loves me in her way, but her way is limited. I have you, both of you, and Sinead, and Sally in Philadelphia. That's a lot of mothers for one person."

Aisling and Morena came in, and Morena eyed Finola.

"Now, what would bring a tear to your eye today?"

"A sentimental tear. And where are those boys of yours, Aisling?"

"Napping, thank the gods, and I've young Liam O'Malley minding them, as he can keep up with their energies once they wake again. And how pretty it all looks, Marg."

"We've sparkling wine to go with the rest. A few sips for you won't hurt that baby," Marg added.

"The way she kicks—and I'll keep saying *she* until I get

me a girl—she could handle a whole bottle and not slow down."

They sat with bread and jam, biscuits and tarts, and Marg poured the wine.

"*Sláinte*." Morena lifted hers. "One and all. And now I want to hear it. Tell us the story, Breen."

"I've only had bits of it," Aisling added. "And from Mahon, who's a man—as most are—stingy with details even if he remembers them. But tell me first: Is it true Shana tried to put a knife in your back?"

"She did."

"Ah, the devil's whore. We never liked her, did we, Morena?"

"Not a bit. She always looked at me as if I was something unpleasant on the bottom of her shoe."

"She did." Aisling gestured in agreement. "She did indeed. And to me it was a superior sort of smirk, queen to farmwife. And still, I want to know some of what she wore, as she had brilliant clothes."

"There was a green dress, deep green with a sheen and a square neckline, and she didn't quite hide the look that said I was considerably less than expected."

She started the story at her approach to the Capital, her impression of it, and the village, and found as she went on— the scene staged in the courtyard, Shana's visit to her room— their outrage equaled support. She could laugh, enjoy the wine and biscuits, and feel part of something.

A circle of women.

"I like Brian, what I know of him." Morena slathered bread with butter and jam. "I can approve of him for Marco."

"They'll be relieved to hear it, as they really seem to be in love. And Marco looked very handsome for the Welcome, and he'll thank you, Nan, for sending the outfit. As I do for the dress. I've never had anything so beautiful. Keegan said . . ."

Every one of them leaned forward.

"What?" Morena demanded. "Don't leave us hanging on the hook."

"He said I'd dressed in stars, and that's how it felt."

"That's poetic coming from him." Aisling nibbled on a biscuit. "I'll have to see this dress for myself. It must've dazzled."

"I was so nervous. It's so different there. The grandeur of it, even though everyone—except you-know-who—was so warm. The banquet room, all the lights, the ceremony of it all. So lush after the strict protocol of the Judgment, and the heartbreaking beauty of the Leaving."

She put her hand over Marg's. "I missed here, even in that short time, but I got to see why Keegan is taoiseach, why and how the laws work, how the Capital and that community work."

She told them of stepping outside, for the air, for Bollocks, and Shana's attack.

"I know her parents a bit." Finola spoke carefully. "Not well, of course, but I know them from visits to my son, grandsons, their ladies, and their littles. I've watched the girl Shana was, the woman she is. And the darkness in her—I thought, well, it's just from some spoiling. But it's far more than that."

"I can see her using— It's Loren, you say?" Morena shook her head. "I don't know him, as her circle was never mine when I spent time there. I know Kiara, of course, as everyone does. I mean to say I can see her using someone as she used them. I can even see her breaking a First Law by trying the love potion. But I would never have seen her ready to take a life. I think my dislike of her blinded me to the worst of her."

"How bad did you burn her?"

Breen shook her head at Aisling. "I'm not sure—she ran. But the way she screamed . . ."

"Good, and I'm not sorry to say it. I hope it burned to the bone. The boy she struck and left, they brought him out of sleep, but they're still not altogether sure he'll be all right again."

"Only evil can do that to another." Finola poured more wine. "And whatever she believes she'll have with Odran, in the end, more than her hand will burn."

Then she smiled. "But our Breen's back with us, and we've yet to hear her version of sealing the portal."

"Punched Keegan good," Aisling added.

"It was a fine punch, delivered with feeling." Morena bit into another lemon biscuit. "And earned, I agree, though I have to give Keegan a bit of the slack, as it was an urgent matter, and moving quickly could have made the difference."

"Which he explained to me after. If he'd told me all that before, I'd have . . . figured out something."

"Men." Morena cupped her chin in her hand. "So often a pain in the arse. Too often so bloody sure they know the best of things, so we have to take the time and trouble to show them they don't."

She cut her gaze to Marg. "You wouldn't have another bottle of that bubbly wine, would you, darling?"

"I would. Let's open it."


Shana had the girl—she wouldn't bother with the name— help her dress. It felt good, it felt right, to have someone wait on her, do her bidding without any need to placate and pretend.

She didn't trust the girl with her hair, so she did it herself, leaving it long and loose, tucked up just a little over the ears to show off the jewels.

She chose a necklace, circles of diamonds close around her throat with a fat sapphire, another teardrop, she felt went well with the earrings.

She wanted to go out, to see more, but when she'd stepped onto her terrace, she'd seen dogs—demon dogs—stalking the rocky island below, the jagged cliffs across the water.

So she waited, and waiting, grew bored. After boredom came irritation. She started for the door—she'd stay inside, surely the dogs weren't allowed to roam at will inside—when the knock came.

She squared her shoulders. "Come."

Not the girl this time, but two males. Sidhe, she sensed, with hard eyes in hard faces.

"Come with us."

She didn't like the tone. "Where?"

"Odran sends for you. You will not keep him waiting."

She angled her head, inclined it, and walked to them.

In the corridor they flanked her, but she didn't mind. The black glass walls intrigued her, and she admired the way the torch- and candlelight played off them.

So much more impressive than the dull stone of the castle in the Capital.

She followed them down wide stairs that turned from black to gold as she stepped on them. Delighted, she tried to look everywhere.

Jewels sparkled in the black glass; grand windows let in the sun and the roar of the sea.

Statues of satyrs and centaurs and sirens stood on pedestals. She gasped when a gargoyle hissed from its perch, and scrambled away.

They descended to a great entrance hall, where the mosaic floor depicted Odran—she'd seen likenesses in books—in black robes with a globe—no, she realized, a world—held in each hand.

And under his feet, the littered, bloodied bodies of those he'd conquered.

It frightened and thrilled her all at once.

Two others stood in black breastplates by closed doors. Elves, like her, they held spears with keen points.

The doors opened as she approached, and her escort stopped just inside.

A throne room, she thought, and as grand as any could imagine, with those black glass walls glinting with crystals and gems, the floor gleaming gold. Light streamed in to sparkle on the throne, gold like the floors, and the one who sat upon it.

His hair, gold as well, spilled over his shoulders and framed a face so handsome it all but stole her breath. His eyes, smoke gray, watched her approach.

Beneath her skirts her knees trembled.

But his lips curved, and he beckoned.

He wore black, pants fitted to his long legs, a tunic belted with jewels that caught the light.

He sat at his ease and waited.

Yseult stood at his side. She wore deep green flowing skirts, with a snug bodice threaded with gold.

A beauty, Shana thought, but old. And past time to be replaced.

She would not stand at Odran's side when it was done, but sit in a throne beside his.

Shana looked him in the eye, smiled in return. And lowered into a deep curtsy.

"My lord Odran."

"Shana of Talamh," Yseult announced. "Brought to you, my king, my liege, my all, as promised."

No, Shana thought, she would not begin this way. She remained in the curtsy, but lifted her head.

"Come to you, my lord, by my choice. With gratitude to Yseult for her help."

"And why do you come?"

His voice was music, and her heart danced. "To serve you how I can, and by serving you take my vengeance on all who betrayed me."

"So you come for your own purpose?"

"I am your guest or your prisoner, as you will. I have hope that my purpose and yours, my lord, are one."

He gestured, languidly. "And what is my purpose?"

"To take Talamh, or destroy it. And rule the worlds beyond it."

"You are of Talamh, are you not?"

"No longer."

"You have family in Talamh."

"What are they to me now? Nothing." And indeed, she felt nothing for them. Odran's eyes mesmerized. "I am with you."

"And what do you bring to me?" Long fingers tapped, tapped, tapped on the wide arms of the throne. "Have you no tribute for a god?"

"I bring you all I am. All I know. And all the power of my hate for what is behind me."

He gestured, and a woman hurried to him with a goblet. He drank lazily as she bowed and hurried away.

"Hate can cool in time."

"Mine will not cool." She held out her scarred hand. "She did this to me, your granddaughter, the one you seek to have. She marked me, and my hate burns as my flesh burned. I wish what you wish, for you to drain her of power. All that I have I give for that purpose."

He gestured for her to stand.

"We will see. We will see if you bring more than beauty and a dark heart. Those are easily come by. We will see if you prove useful, and if you do, you'll have what you seek. If not?" He smiled and drank again. "You'll find the judgment here is not so soft as in Talamh."

"I will be useful. In any way you wish, in all ways you demand."

"We will see. I'll send for you. Go and wait until I do."

She curtsied again, and with trembling heart left. The guards flanked her once again.

The doors shut.

Odran drank again. "We will see," he repeated, and looked

at Yseult. "She may be useful, or merely an amusement. But her hate, it's real."

"She wishes to rule with you, not under you."

Now he laughed. "She will have whatever I give her. But for now, Yseult, I'm pleased with what you've brought me. See that she's brought to me tonight."

# CHAPTER TWENTY-FIVE

In tune with the world, herself, her friends, Breen walked back toward the farm with Morena and Aisling.

"That was the best time! It's so great, sitting around with girls, drinking wine, eating cookies, trashing a psychopathic elf. And did I tell you? When I walked in, Finola was telling Nan about having sex with your grandda last night."

"You didn't, no," Morena said as she cringed and Aisling laughed. "And I can say with truth I wish you hadn't."

"It was adorable. They're girlfriends! I've got girlfriends. Is it going to be weird if I keep sleeping with your brother?"

"I've no objections in that area."

"Good. Great. Because I'd really like to have sex with him again. And if Odran gets his hands on me and sucks me dry, at least I'd've had really good sex first."

"Don't be saying such things." Aisling gave Breen a quick shake. "We're none of us going to let that happen."

"Because we're girlfriends. And we're going to kick his ass."

"We are," Morena confirmed. "And that slag Shana's for good measure."

"I really want to do that. It's all so violent, and I don't even mind it. We have to save the worlds, right?"

"That we do." Aisling rubbed a hand on the side of her belly.

"Is she kicking? Could I . . ."

"Well, of course." Aisling took Breen's hand, pressed it against the movement.

Life. Light. Energy. Promise.

"Oh wow! Oh, that's amazing."

"Most of the time, not counting the middle of the night when you only want sleep. Have you never felt the kicks and bumps before?"

"No. I mean, I knew women, pregnant women, but I never felt comfortable asking. Hey, it's Marco! Marco's back."

She waved her hands in the air, and got a shout-out from Marco as he and Brian stood in the paddock rubbing down their horses. "Who'd've thought a gay Black guy from Philly would slide right into life in Talamh, and fall for a dragon-riding Sidhe? I so wish Sally could see him."

"Maybe one day Marco will take Brian to meet Sally."

Breen gave Morena and the idea a huge grin. "That would be fantastic."

Bollocks bounded ahead to greet the new arrivals, then dashed over to dance around Mab, a teenage boy, and Aisling's two children. The boys immediately wrestled Bollocks to the ground and fell on him.

"Did those two ruffians behave for you then, Liam?"

"Ah, it was a battle, but I won. Nah, in truth we had a fine time, and I'll confess, we ate the last of the ginger biscuits and left not a crumb behind."

"They're made to be eaten, after all."

"Don't go!" Finian wrapped his arms around Liam's legs. "Stay and play with us some more."

"I'll be back another time, but I've got to be off. And you mind your ma, ya pirates, or you'll be walking the plank."

"Yo ho!" Kavan shouted.

With a laugh, Liam changed from teenage boy to young stag and ran over the field toward the woods.

The boys immediately raced to Aisling to tell her about playing pirates and plundering the seas.

"I have my glove." Finian tugged on it from where it hung in his belt. "Could I practice with Amish?"

Morena glanced back to where the hawk perched on the wall. "He seems agreeable. Where's Harken?"

"He went off with Keegan and Da. They came back but went off again. They said they'd be back before supper. Can I practice now?"

"Put the glove on. I've got them for a while here, Aisling."

"Sure if you do, I'll use the farm kitchen and cook for the lot of them. You and Marco and Brian are welcome, Breen."

"Thanks, but we should get back before much longer."

"You're free to change your mind. Send them in when you've had enough of them, Morena."

"Be sure I will."

With Morena entertaining the children, Breen met Marco halfway as he walked from the paddock. "How was the ride back? You wouldn't believe the night I had! But I had the best day!"

He angled his head, smiling as he gave her a long look. "Been day drinking, girl?"

"Yes, and it was fabulous. I have so much to tell you. Is Brian staying or does he have to go back?"

"He's staying. They're putting more troops in the valley, for the waterfall portal thing. So I want to ask if it's okay if he stays at the cottage at night, you know, with me, when he's not on duty."

"Well, duh!" She gave him a big hug, then snuggled right in. "It's your cottage, too. Roomies!"

"Some serious day drinking."

"I should probably take a nap, but I don't want to. I feel so good. I feel like everything's going to be okay because, damn it, we're the freaking good guys. Or maybe because I've been drinking champagne made by faeries. One of those."

"I'm going to have to get me some of that. Breen's been drinking champagne," he told Brian when he joined them.

"Sidhe or Elfin?"

"Sidhe."

"Best there is. And no matter how much you drink, it won't give you a head to regret it in the morning."

"It's wonderful. I punched Keegan."

"What?" Marco yanked her back. "When? Why?"

"He took my clothes off in front of everybody and threw me in the river. We sealed the breach, but I punched him. It's a long story, but I'm mostly okay with it now since he explained."

"We know you've closed the breach," Brian began, "as we met them briefly on the journey back. Sure I'd like to hear the rest of the story, but I should go see if I'm needed at the portal."

"I'll take your things over," Marco told him.

"It's all right then if I spend time at the cottage?"

"Absolutely, a hundred percent." Breen wrapped him in a hug, sighed out happiness. Then murmured in Brian's ear, "Hurt him, and I'll turn you into a pig and roast you for dinner."

His laugh rumbled against her. "I believe you would." His eyes twinkled at Marco. "You have a fierce and frightening friend in Breen Siobhan."

"Like Sidhe champagne, best there is. Why don't I take you home, girlfriend?"

"I guess. Oh, look. Dragons." She pointed up as Cróga streamed through the sky alongside Harken's dragon, and Mahon beside them.

Mahon swooped down, snatched a son in each arm, and with their squeals soared up to spin them.

Harken swung off, landed lightly beside Morena.

"I was about to come up and have a ride," Breen heard her say.

"I've the milking yet. Give me a hand with it, and we'll have one at sunset."

"Fair trade." She took his hand. "Tomorrow then," she said with a wave to Breen.

When Keegan dropped down, he nodded at Brian. "You made good time."

"We did. Do you want me at the portal?"

"Not tonight, as we're well set, but tomorrow, you'll relieve Dak an hour past dawn. You'll hold there until I send word or come myself. I'll want you patrolling the far west down to the south and back. You've the night free."

"Thanks for that."

"I'll get cooking." Marco rubbed his hands together. "Want in on that, Keegan? I've got a taste for chicken and dumplings."

"It's kind of you to ask, but . . ."

When Keegan looked at Breen, she shrugged. "I'm okay with it. Marco makes the world's best chicken and dumplings."

"Then I'll come and gladly. First I need to take Breen for a bit."

"Then I'll get started, and get Brian settled in. How about we take Bollocks?"

"Yeah, okay." Breen bent down, gave him a rub. "You go home with Marco and Brian. I'll be there soon. He's going to want a swim."

"No problem. See you on the other side!"

"Where am I going?" Breen asked as the men went to get their bags and walk across the road with the dog leading the way. "Why am I going?"

"I told you I needed to take you if there was time today, and there is."

"Brian rode Boy back, and it's a really long trip."

"We're not going by horse," he began, then took a good look at her. "Are you drunk then, Breen?"

"Maybe a little. Slightly."

"Well, the flight should clear your head."

"We're going by dragon?" She perked right up. "This has been an excellent day! Now I get a dragon ride and chicken and dumplings." She cocked her head. "And maybe, if I'm in the mood, I'll let you have sex with me."

He took her hand as he called Cróga. "What were you drinking, so I can see about getting more of it?"

"Sidhe champagne."

"That might have to wait a day or two." He gave her a boost onto Cróga, swung on behind her.

"You didn't say where we're going."

"You'll see for yourself, as you must and should."

Too relaxed to object, she looked down as they rose up. "It's so beautiful. The valley, yes, but the farm. Whenever I see it, I know why my father loved it. I know why you do. It says everything about the peace you work so hard to hold. Where did you live before? I don't think I ever asked."

"The cottage where Aisling and Mahon and the boys make their home."

"Of course. That's why it has the same feel."

As they flew west, she picked out other spots she knew. Nan's cottage, of course, and the one where Mina and her family lived, where clothes snapped on the line and smoke puffed from the chimney. And to the south, the ruins, the dance, her father's grave.

Then they soared up, higher, over towering trees, and on a gasp, she reached back to grip Keegan's hand.

The cliffs, sheer as glass, rose over a tumbling sea. The

water beat at their base, spewed up over rock and shale and sand to fold back into itself. Then rushed in to pound again.

On the clifftops, she saw trees bent and twisted from the wind, and high grasses swept down at each blow.

"It's breathtaking. It was from the mountain, but even more now."

"The Far West."

"Marco and I saw the Cliffs of Moher in Ireland. It's like that, only wilder. There are boats coming in."

"The sea's there to be fished."

Her breath caught again as they flew over the sea, and below a whale white as chalk sounded.

Dolphins leaped, and Mers with them.

On the clifftops she saw another stone circle, larger than the other, a few stone buildings, a handful of cottages.

"We have what you'd call a base here, a training ground. Eyes of the Far West they are. My father and yours trained there."

"Did they? Did you?"

"My father and yours trained us in the valley. The stones there are Fin's Dance, the largest and they say oldest in all of Talamh. At sunrise on the summer solstice, the rising sun strikes the king stone—the tallest—and the light spreads from it, white and bright, stone by stone. And they sing. You hear them sing to every dance in the world, and every dance in the world answers."

He circled once more. "And so their song and the light of the longest day touches every corner of Talamh."

"It must be magnificent."

"It is. And the winter solstice gives the moons; their light is softer and restful for the longest night. But still it spreads, and the stones sing."

She leaned against him as he flew back. "I loved seeing that. Thanks."

THE BECOMING   397

"Ah, that was to clear your head. We've a journey yet to take."

She assumed a short one, as the sun eased toward those peaks in the west. But long or short, she didn't mind. Cróga cleaved through clouds like a boat through the sea, and the wind on her face tasted fresh, crisp. The world below rolled green and gold with rivers and road winding through. They soared over the Troll mines, the dales below them, the forest where the shadows deepened.

And, she saw now, they flew toward that towering peak.

"To see the dragons?" Beyond thrilled, she shoved her hair as it blew in her face when she turned to him. "Oh, what a day! Are there many? Can you feel them? I can feel them. There's such power, such pull."

Even as she spoke, Cróga let out a roar. In response, dragons, every color in the world, rose into the air and answered.

A flood, a flood of bold gems against the sky, and the power, the sheer power of them beat like a thousand drums.

"Oh God! I can hardly breathe. It's so amazing. It's so beautiful." She jumped, then laughed at herself when a dragon, amethyst with eyes of emerald, swung beside them. Cróga turned his head, rubbed it to hers.

"His mate," Keegan said. "They live long, but take only one."

"She's beautiful. Does she have a name?"

"Banrion. It means queen, as she's regal. Her rider is Magda, who lives in the Far West."

"There are so many," she said. "They all have riders?"

"No. Some will have lost their rider, as we don't live as long. And like a mate, they take only one, as a rider takes only one. Others will not have chosen or been chosen, found or have been found. And won't until their rider becomes, and makes the choice. Until, they wait."

She saw caves in the mountain, some huge, and ledges,

steps, a wide plateau. Clouds swirled around them like smoke as Cróga glided down.

"Babies! Or young ones. Smaller."

"A year, a full turn, the mother carries the egg. One to three eggs, though three is rare. And then when laid, she nests a quarter turn—only rising when her mate or another takes her place for a brief time."

The young, big as horses, scrambled, squawked, as Cróga landed on the plateau. And, like children, Breen thought, raced back again to flutter around them. One, shining silver, flew up to stare at her from bright blue eyes, then zipped away.

"They're gorgeous. Am I allowed to touch?"

"They wouldn't come to you otherwise."

And because they did, when she slid down, she held out her hands, touched as they darted toward her, did turns and circles and dips.

"They're showing off," she realized. "Playing. Are any Cróga's?"

Keegan gestured, and she watched a youth, emerald and blue, sliding up Cróga's tail. "His youngest. Watch."

Cróga flicked his tail, sent the youth flying. The sound he made could only be called giddy joy. Cróga soared up after to fly with his mate.

"They have three. Two sons, a daughter. One from each nesting. She carries two now, and please the gods will lay them safe next summer."

"Of all the wonders I've seen here, this is the most—I don't know—compelling. I've always had a thing for dragons. I guess it came from the childhood I couldn't remember. And seeing them like this, free and flying. Full grown, children."

Again she held out her hands. One, the size of a large cat, landed on her arm.

"Heavy!" Laughing, she cradled it.

"No more than a few days old, that one. Fresh from the nesting cave." Keegan gestured to the large opening. "There we don't go unless invited."

"Understood." She stroked the amber scales. "I had a dream, right before we left for Ireland last summer. I was walking by the river, this side of the waterfall, and I saw what I thought were little birds, so colorful and quick and bright. They were baby dragons, like butterflies, circling and darting. One landed in the palm of my hand. But they don't come that small."

"No. But dreams aren't always literal, are they?"

"No, but it felt real. As if we knew each other, the one I held. I even named him."

"What name did you give him?"

"Lonrach. That's strange." The baby in her arms uncurled, soared away. "How would I know that word?"

"Do you know the meaning?"

"Yes. It means—"

Her heart began to pound, and in the beat another beat. Merging to pulse as one. In her mind, another mind, waiting.

Yearning.

The dragon, red tipped in gold, landed on the top of the cave. And watched her while others circled around and around, a ring of jewels.

Love burst into her, a flood, a force, a gift. And her heart wept from the joy of it.

"It means brilliant, because you are." Tears blurred her eyes as she stepped closer, and Keegan stepped back. "And here you are. Lonrach. You're mine. I'm yours."

He flew down to her while the other dragons circled overhead. In his eyes she saw herself, and knew he saw himself in hers.

"I'm sorry you had to wait so long." She touched his cheek,

then just pressed her own against it. "You're mine. I'm yours. We're one. How did you know?" she asked Keegan.

"I've known of Lonrach all my life. The dragon who waits for the child of the Fey to come home. To awaken. To become. On the day of the Judgment, you stood, you spoke, you became."

"I don't understand, not really."

"You didn't see yourself, the light in you, the power of you. When we flew back, and you saw this place, you felt him as you hadn't before. So the wait was over."

Overwhelmed, she pressed her face to the glass-smooth scales. "I feel his heart inside mine. I feel it like my own."

"I know."

"This is what it's like for you and Cróga?"

"It is, aye, and for all who make the bond. Now you'll ride."

"I can ride him? Yes. Yes, I can. I can. I know how. I don't have a saddle."

"We'll get you one, but you'll do fine without."

"He wants to fly." Drenched and drunk with love, she pressed her cheek to Lonrach again. "He wants it. I feel it."

"I'll give you a lift up this first time." When he stepped over, she turned to Keegan.

"I owe you, so much, for this."

"You don't, no, that's foolish."

"It's not, and I do. You knew, you brought me so we could find each other. You knew how and when." She took his face in her hands, kissed him. "Thank you."

"Then you're welcome. Up you go."

She laid her head down on her dragon's neck when Keegan boosted her up. "I have to cry a minute. He gets it."

"All right, if you must. Done?" he asked when she straightened.

"For now." Then she simply thought: Home. Simply put the cottage into her head.

Lonrach rose up. Keegan mounted Cróga to join her.

The dragons roared, a sound of triumph, as she flew over Talamh.

And it was different, she realized, different than being a passenger, as thrilling as that had been. Now the sensation of flying swept through her as if she herself had wings.

Into clouds, around them as the last lights of the sun struck, turned them gold and violet and rose. Over the fields and forests with no sound but the rush of wind.

Then below, she saw Marg and Sedric standing in front of their cottage, faces lifted.

They'd known. Of course they'd known. Laughing, she threw her arms high when Lonrach whipped into a stylish turn because she'd wished it.

Harken streamed up beside her, with Morena riding behind him.

"Welcome, rider!" he called out before they veered away toward the setting sun.

In the valley others came out, to look up, to wave. She saw Aisling with Kavan on her hip, Mahon with Finian on his shoulders.

"How did they all know?"

"Word gets round. It isn't every day rider and dragon bond and take their first flight. Take a moment for them, fly on a bit, and we'll circle."

"I could fly forever."

She lifted an arm, swept it in a wave to Finola and Seamus, flew low enough to smell the glory of their gardens, hear the cheers of children who ran along the road.

They flew over the lake where as a boy Keegan had lifted the sword from its pale green waters, and on, on over hill and forest before turning back.

"Best you follow me through the portal, as you haven't gone through this way before on your own."

As dusk spread and shadows gathered, he banked toward the Welcoming Tree, and Lonrach glided after.

Out of Talamh and into Ireland, over the forest, and toward the bay, and the cottage where lights gleamed from the windows.

When they landed, Breen once again lay herself over her dragon's sinuous neck.

The door opened. Bollocks bulleted out to leap and race in circles. Lonrach lowered, and the dog rose up on hind legs to lap at the great, majestic head.

"They'll be good friends," Breen stated.

"Sure as they're both yours and you theirs." Keegan swung down as Brian walked out.

"So his wait's over. Marco, you'll want to come out."

Wiping his hands on a dishcloth, Marco started for the door. "I just want to— Holy shit! Two of them. What are you doing up there, girl?"

"This is Lonrach, and he's mine."

Keeping his distance, Marco hooked the cloth in his waistband. "You went and bought a dragon?"

"No. He's just mine." She slid down, stroked one hand on the dragon, the other on the dog. "And he'd never hurt you."

"What're you gonna do with him?"

"Ride. Learn. Love."

"Girl, I love you more than my new harp, and that's a lot. But I ain't never getting up on that thing."

With a wink for Breen, Brian put an arm around Marco. "I'm thinking never's not as long as you think."

"It's as long as never. Where's he going to sleep?"

"Dragon's Nest. The mountain. He'll know when I need him. I'll know when he needs me. Tomorrow," she said, then stepped back.

With Cróga, he rose up, the wind of wings blowing through her hair. They circled together as the first stars flickered on.

They skimmed over the trees, and away.

"Huh." Marco just shook his head. "I think we could all use a drink. I got the chicken and dumplings going and put together a charcuterie board. So I think it's time to show off my bartending skills."

"I can smell the chicken, and wouldn't say no to a drink." Keegan started inside. "And what's this charcuterie then?"

# CHAPTER TWENTY-SIX

While Breen and the others dug into Marco's chicken and dumplings, Shana entered Odran's private chambers.

He'd sent her an invitation—a command, but she preferred *invitation*—to dine with him. She'd changed into a more formal gown, one of deep gold with a daringly deep neckline.

She'd draped herself with jewels, and found the servant given her had an acceptable skill with hair. She wore it swept up to showcase her face—and the jewels.

She'd expected grandeur and luxury in the god's private rooms, but they exceeded even her expectations.

The black glass walls shined like mirrors. Hundreds of candles shot light from stands of polished gold. More gold stood as columns flanking the hearth where a fire blazed. Furnishings, a long divan, wide, high-backed chairs wore gold, silk, or velvet—and really, could one have too much gold?

Jewels dripped from lamps on marble tables, and the windows held views of the night-dark sea.

He sat at his ease at a table set for two, luxuriously with gold plates, crystal goblets, platters of meat, serviettes of gold linen.

She dipped into a deep curtsy. "My lord."

"Sit." He waved a hand at a female servant, one who wore only a collar, like a dog, to pour the wine.

"She once sat where you are because she pleased me. Then she did not."

When Odran lifted his wine, Shana did the same. "Then it will be my honor and duty to please you always, and in all ways."

"We will see. You shared a bed with the taoiseach until he tired of you. Tell me what you know of him. The things a woman who's had a man's shaft inside her knows."

Though it burned, she ignored the casual insult. "The Fey see him as strong, the holder of the sword and the staff, the protector of Talamh, and the defender of justice."

Rings glinted and flashed on the hand he flicked. "Such is tradition, and tells me nothing."

"Because they're blinded by tradition, they don't see his weaknesses." She sipped wine. "He leads from duty, not desire. He has no ambition beyond the peace and safety of Talamh. If not for duty, he'd spend his days plowing the fields in the valley with his brother, planting his seed in someone content for only that. He leads, but he doesn't rule."

She shrugged. "This isn't strength. In other worlds, one in his position commands. Rulers don't barter and trade, they take what they want. A ruler, a true one, rules with passion, as you do. Rules with power absolute. Instead, Keegan sits at the council table, where they natter about small things and think nothing of what the powers of the Fey could amass in other worlds."

That had the faintest smile curving his lips. "But you think of it."

"Oh, aye. The world beyond, where the woman with your blood travels back and forth so freely, a world of great size and riches, resources and people with no magicks? It could be conquered like that." She snapped her fingers. "And so could others, could all. And what they have would be ours. Instead, we bind ourselves with foolish laws and weak traditions, we revere choice and freedom as if they were gods."

"But you do not."

"I do not."

He signaled to the woman again. "Serve us." As she stepped over to fill Odran's plate, then Shana's, from the platters, Odran considered his guest.

"And still, this tells me little of the taoiseach."

"It tells you, my dark lord, he's a slave to duty, and would die for it. Like your son, who took him as a son. In other things?" She shrugged delicately as she ate. "He enjoys books and music, has more of an appetite in bed than for wielding the power of his office. He lacks patience, particularly for formalities, and has a quick temper. But a soft heart—too soft for true strength. He bears the weight of leader, but takes none of what could and should be his."

She gestured to indicate Odran's rooms. "You won't find gold or jewels in his chambers at his own castle. I'm told he took the one from outside to the Trolls in the valley and bargained for what she wanted instead of taking. Bargained and drank with them. Trolls."

She sampled the meat on her plate. "He would heed his mother in most if not all things like a child rather than a man grown. His gift is strong. If any tell you it's not, they lie. He is skilled, as skilled as any I've known, and though I haven't witnessed him in battle, I've seen him train others. He's fierce."

"As was the one who came before him, and yet he—the son I created—is with his pale gods."

"Aye, and it's said Eian O'Ceallaigh taught him well. Perhaps knowing the boy he trained would lead one day. And so Keegan knows every hill, every dale, every river, every forest in Talamh, and would know most who live there by name.

Another skill, as it . . . endears him to them. So they are loyal to him."

"But you are not."

She ate delicately. "I have no loyalty to him. If I had taken his mother's place as his hand, I would have used my influence to ease him away from useless traditions. I enjoyed bedding him, but I bedded him with a purpose. If the one from outside hadn't come, I would have achieved that purpose. Then, it would have been my hope to meet with you, and discuss mutual goals."

"And why would you think I would meet with you, or discuss goals with you?"

Smiling, she shook back her hair. "I had hope that you would see, through your great powers or through your spies, that with me there were changes. Some I could believe you would approve of. And you might consider I could help you attain all you want.

"May I have more wine, my lord?"

Watching Shana, he signaled to the woman.

"And now you sit here, defeated in your goals, having made no changes."

"Aye, that's true. And still I would discuss with you how I might help you attain what you wish, and have some small benefits—whatever you deem I earn. My father sits on the council," she continued. "And though my mother has no interest in politics and policy, he found a willing ear with me. I know the defenses and offenses planned against you, my lord Odran. I know the castle as Keegan knows the world, as I made it my world."

As she drank more wine, Shana accepted flirtation wouldn't work here, not with a god who could take any he wanted. But knowledge could.

She would make certain it did.

"And I know what I think your spies and scouts, even any

prisoners you may have taken, do not, as only a handful know. And that is the location of every portal in Talamh, what worlds they open to, and how each is secured. And while I may not know all, I know many of the portals in other worlds."

"You've traveled through them."

"I have not, my lord. And though it is not permitted, my father indulged me by showing me on maps. I would be honored to do this for you if it would please you."

"And in return?"

"In return I would see those who turned against me punished. I would enjoy, after you've drained the one from outside of power, when you have finished with her, putting a collar on her like this one."

"Because she took the taoiseach from you."

"He's but a man, and men are easily come by. But because she took what I worked for, what I earned." Shana held out her palm. "And I have this to remind me. She will have scars, should you grant this wish, to remind her."

"And the taoiseach?"

Her eyebrows rose. "You would execute him if he survives the war. Keegan, his family, a public execution so all of Talamh knows who rules."

For the first time, he smiled. "You like the taste of blood."

"I prefer wine, but what is rule without power, what is power without force? And to hold worlds, there must be fear, and aye, there must be blood."

"And all you want for assisting me is what's left of the girl when I'm done with her."

"Well now." With a laugh, she gestured with her wine. "If you're well pleased with me, I wouldn't mind if you granted me a place—oh, a small one, inconsequential—where I might rule. Under your dominion, of course. Or more, if you're very well pleased, a place to sit beside you. To lie beside you. I could give you sons, and from them, you would take what you will. Power to drink for years and years."

"And if you displease me?"

"I don't believe I will. My lord, all of my life I've wanted what I have at this moment. To sit beside a ruler of great power, of great vision, who will use it to gain more. Who will indulge my frivolous affection for lovely things. For this, I will give all I have to please you."

"Then you'll begin now." He rose. "Dispense with this," he told the silent woman before striding into the next room.

Because she enjoyed the wine, Shana took her goblet with her.

She didn't bother to disguise the gasp at the vast bed, the towering posts of gold, but wandered past another raging fire to circle the vast room.

She could see herself—wanted to see herself—sitting at the long dressing table with its drawer knobs of diamonds as big as a baby's fist, or lounging among the plush pillows on the settee. Standing on the terrace looking out at all she commanded—through Odran, of course. But it would be hers. She would see to it.

Whatever the cost, whatever the price, she would have this.

"Your taste is more exquisite than any. I am humbled to stand in such a room."

"You are not humbled."

She smiled, lowered into a curtsy. "Already you understand me. But I am honored."

"Disrobe."

"Myself or you?"

"Yourself."

"Then I must ask for the assistance of a god, as I cannot unfasten the gown."

She set the goblet down on the dressing table, walked to him, turned her back. "If you would, my lord."

He tore it so the gown ripped in two. Shana merely stepped out of it, kicked it aside. "Such strength. It thrills me. I lack it, but if you'll allow." She turned to him, wearing only the underpinnings she'd selected for this exact purpose, and began to unfasten his doublet.

"I would see you, Odran, god of the dark. And though I know you can take me willing or not, I give myself to you. Now and always, as you wish.

"Ah, such beauty." She ran her hands over his bare chest—slighter than she'd imagined, his skin smoother, but for the small scar at his heart. "Grace in strength," she murmured as her hands traveled down to unfasten his trousers.

She found him already hard, like stone, like the marble columns, and smiled.

When she started to put her arms around him, lift her lips for his, he shoved her against the thick post of the bed, and drove into her.

Cold, cold, like a shaft of ice impaling her. Shocked, she cried out, but he battered her against the post, and for a moment, she thought she felt claws dig into her hips.

She didn't resist, and because he watched her with eyes that had gone to black, she lifted her legs to wrap him, around his hips, and, closing her eyes as if in ecstasy, cried out again and again.

Cold, sharp, vicious—gods, she wanted to scream for him to stop. And feared if she did, he wouldn't until she lay dead at his feet.

She thought of the slave woman in the collar, and held on to him as if enthralled. She would die before she served meat and wore a collar like an animal.

Then something changed, and instead of pain and fear, she felt a terrible pleasure rising through it. Dark and dangerous, it conquered her. Wild with it, breathless from it, she gripped his shoulders, looked into those black eyes, and said, "More."

When he was done with her, he tossed her on the bed. She felt slightly ill, her body throbbing as her burned hand had, and wished only for the oblivion of sleep.

THE BECOMING ✦ 411

Then he climbed on top of her, hiked her hips high as she moaned.

She screamed when he sodomized her. And though she feared he would tear her in two, that dark pleasure broke into her again until she wept with it.

Until she craved it.

He used her over and over, tirelessly, brutally, until she thought the endless pains and pleasures might kill her.

When after the long night he ordered her to leave him, she stumbled naked back to her room, her body bruised, tiny gouges bleeding.

And understood now that she knew those pains, those pleasures, she would rather die than live without them.

When Brian woke, he lay a moment longer in the warm bed with Marco beside him. He had duties, and would never shirk them, but thought how lovely it would be to stay, to wake together.

Another time, he hoped. They would have other times.

Quietly, he rose.

He would use the shower—a much fancier sort than any he'd found on his visits outside of Talamh. Marco had shown him how it worked, and together they had shown each other what interesting things could happen inside a glass box under a hot rain of water.

He'd imagined himself falling in love at some point. In the future. Eventually.

But he hadn't known what it could be, not really. He hadn't known the lightning strike, the floating on a quiet river, the wild flight among stars, the simple rest.

Love was all of that and so much more.

He'd found someone he wanted to join hands and walk with for the rest of his life.

Whatever god, whatever fate had put Marco Olsen in his path, he would be forever grateful.

He dressed in the dark before brushing a light kiss on Marco's cheek.

"I'll come home to you tonight," he whispered, "and every night I can."

Carrying his boots, he walked downstairs.

Though Marco had told him Breen rose early, it surprised him to find her in the kitchen in the first breaths of the new day.

"Good morning to you."

"Morning." She lifted the mug in her hand. "I made coffee."

"Thanks for that, but I don't have a liking for it. I'd make myself tea if you'd show me how this thing works." He tapped the stove.

"Sure." She turned the burner on under the kettle.

"Ah, well then, that's simple enough."

"I'm no Marco, but I could scramble you some eggs."

He smiled at her, this key to so much who offered to make him breakfast. "It's kind of you, but I'm hoping you won't think of me as a guest here."

She smiled back at him. "Okay then, you can scramble your own eggs. Bread, bread knife, toaster." She pointed as she spoke. "Butter and jam in the fridge—along with eggs. The cottage is Marco's as much as mine. You're Marco's so it's yours. That's how things work for us. If you've got this, I need to check on Bollocks. He's already out and in the bay."

"I can manage, thanks."

She went out to drink her coffee in the air while her dog romped in the bay, while the mists rose over it and the waking sun shot tiny rainbows through it.

Keegan had left only moments before Brian came down. He'd taken no time for coffee or tea. He would, he told her, come back to resume her training, but had duties first.

So did she, she thought. A duty to the work she'd chosen, a duty to the dog and dragon who'd chosen her as she had them. A duty to the two worlds she knew, and the people in them.

Keegan left so quickly, and with so much, obviously, on his mind, she hadn't told him about the dreams.

She didn't know what to tell him anyway except they'd been dark, disturbing, scattered, and full of screams of pain, moans of pleasure.

Firelight against black walls, something—someone?—rutting in the shadows.

Then a light, already dim, extinguished.

Probably just a stress dream—a sexual stress dream. Though she hadn't gone to bed stressed. She'd been happy—ridiculously so—then Keegan had made her happier yet—and exhausted, so sleep had come easily.

But she was stressed now, and couldn't say precisely why.

She watched Bollocks bound out of the water, leap through the mists as she heard the door open and close behind her.

"You're wet," she warned Bollocks as Brian strode toward her. "Be polite."

Instead of leaping on Brian, Bollocks sat, held up a paw to shake.

"And a fine morning to you as well." Brian handed Breen one of the slices of toast he held before he shook the offered paw. "I thought you might like some yourself."

"Now that you mention it." Breen bit into the toast he'd loaded with butter and raspberry jam. "Thanks."

"Marco tells me you train—exercise—in the mornings, then write your stories."

"That's the usual routine. I missed a lot of both when I was in the Capital. Marco's not a morning person. But once he's up, he'll work."

"On the machine, the computer."

"He's a whiz on it."

"And with the cooking and the music as well."

"Multitalented, our Marco."

"I love him, and wish for a life with him."

She lowered her coffee, let out a long breath. "That's really fast."

"I know it, but it's as real as anything I've known. This isn't just a moment for me. Not just a day or a week. It's always."

She'd seen it, she admitted, in both of them. Maybe she had a dozen questions about where it would go, where it could go with two people from two worlds. But what mattered, what really mattered, was love.

"You make him happy, so you make me happy. His family—not his sister, but the rest of his family . . ."

"He's told me. I'm sorry for them."

She turned to him now, felt a strong and definite click of connection.

"So am I. That's exactly how I feel. Sorry for them because they can't see how amazing he is. How good and kind and bright and beautiful he is. They only look through one prism, so they can't see him."

"But you're his family, you and Sally and Derrick. He has you, and now he has me. He'll have my family, who'll love him as I do. And when Talamh and all is safe, we'll make a life together."

With that said, they watched the wet dog roll blissfully in grass damp with dew.

"You wonder how we'll make that life," Brian added. "We'll find a way. Love finds it, and you've only to follow. Now I must go, as I have duties. You have duties to your stories, or you'd call for Lonrach. I know what it's like those first days as a rider. You could ride forever."

He handed her his empty mug. "Bright blessings on you, Breen Siobhan."

"And on you, Brian."

She watched him walk into the woods, wings spreading as he did. After he'd flown into the trees, she let out a little sigh.

"Okay, pal, let's go inside. It's time for us to report for duty."

It felt good, she decided, really good to slide back into routine. Get her blood moving with a workout, get her head back into the story with the writing.

By the time she took a break—time for a Coke!—Marco sat at the table working on his laptop.

"You check your email?"

She winced. "Not yet. I was—"

"Good thing your publisher copies me. Anyway, they're thinking of doing a little drawing of Bollocks at the chapter headings. Maybe just one repeated, maybe a variety."

"Well, that would be great."

"What I said. So I'm going to take him out in a bit, get some pictures to send them. They have the ones you've posted on the blog, or I've posted on other social media, but I figured more can't hurt. Did you eat anything?"

"Yes, Daddy. Brian made me toast."

He lit right up. "You saw him? He didn't wake me up before he left."

"I was already up."

"How did I get to be crazy about two people who think it's normal to get up at dawn?"

"Just lucky, I guess."

"You'd be right. He left this on the bed for me."

Marco picked up a small sketch of himself, sleeping with a smile curving his lips.

"Marco, this is you! I mean, it's got you. He's really good."

"He has a little cottage right in the village. More of a studio, really, because besides a bed, it's mostly—well, other than weapons—art stuff. And his paintings and drawings, Breen, they're really, really good. I was hoping they'd be pretty good, so I could say so, but we're talking serious-artist good."

"I can see that by this sketch. You need to frame it." She set it back on the table. "I'm so happy for you."

"I'm pretty damn happy for me, too." And blissful with it, he trailed a finger over the sketch. "Going back to work?"

"Oh yeah. I worked on Bollocks this morning—that's the one they're paying for. But I'm going to shift over to the fantasy for a few hours. I know it's a shot in the dark still, but—"

"Stop." From his seat, he drilled a finger into her belly. "You're a writer, girl. Writers write. You go do that, and I'll finish this. Then Bollocks and I are going to have ourselves a photo shoot."

"He needs to go out." She walked to the door, opened it, and the dog streaked by.

"I'll let him in if I'm not finished before he is."

She left them to it and went back to her desk to dive into the world of danger and magicks.

Here with the words, with the imagery, she had control. Maybe she didn't see the end clearly, not yet, but she saw stages of the journey.

But when she passed through into Talamh, it wasn't just words, just imagery. And a great deal of the journey lay out of her control.

So it soothed and excited her to write, even when she found herself crafting echoes of what she'd seen or heard or experienced.

And when she pushed away from her desk, she hugged herself with the satisfaction of real progress.

She took time to check her email—Marco would ask again—and as always wondered if she'd find one from her mother.

No. Not yet, and, she admitted, maybe never.

She walked away from it, and found Marco in the living room with his keyboard, his headphones, and staff paper.

"You're writing music!" She did a little dance when he jolted, pulled off the headphones. "You haven't been working on your music since we got here. Let me hear it!"

"Not ready yet."

"You don't need to go through the headphones when you're working it. I like to hear you work out a song. It's like back in the apartment. If you're still into it, we can wait to go over."

"No, I'm good. I need to let it simmer—like my pot roast."

"That's the amazing smell!"

"Got it simmering, and it'll do that for about four more hours. So I need you to, like, woo-woo it."

"Do what?"

"Woo-woo it, so it coasts along, and if we can't get back, it turns off. Can you?"

She held up a finger. "This may be the key to my deeply buried cooking skills. I can do that."

"Great. Handy. You do that, and I'll get us some jackets."

She considered it like setting a timer—a magickal one. With a good day's work under her belt, and the prospect of Marco's pot roast for dinner, she set off with him and Bollocks.

"You're going to ride that dragon again, aren't you?"

"Oh, you bet your well-toned ass I am."

"I'm not."

"I'll talk you into it one day."

"You got a lot of words, Breen, but you don't have near enough for that. Me, I'm going to hang out with Colm."

"Who's that?"

"Dude has a cottage right near Finola's. He makes beer and ale. He's going to show me how it's done. Maybe one of these days, I'll start making Olsen Ale."

"It has a ring."

They parted ways on the road in Talamh. To give herself a moment, she sat on the wall across from the farm. She saw Harken leading a horse from the stable to pasture. And recognized the mare as the one who'd mated with Keegan's stallion in the summer.

Curious, she opened herself, and felt the life inside the mare. Would it kick, she wondered, as Aisling's baby did?

She saw the boys just outside Aisling's cottage, Mab on nanny duty. The Capital, she thought, with its crowds and movements, seemed very far away.

Once again, she opened herself, and tried, for the first time, to call her dragon.

The air held a chill, but not an unpleasant one. A man galloped by on a bay and gave her a tip of his cap. The black-faced sheep grazed behind her.

And Lonrach streamed, ruby red, out of the sky.

Her heart just overflowed. "He's coming, Bollocks." She stood with the dog beside her. "Do you want to fly?"

The way his tail whipped, she took it as a hell, yeah.

He landed gracefully, and still the ground shook. Then he turned his head so his eyes looked into hers.

"I want to go see Nan, and Sedric if he's there, but I wanted to fly first. Wanted this." She laid a hand on his head.

Lonrach dipped a wing so Bollocks could run up it and onto his back. Breen did the same.

"Wherever you want," she murmured, and he rose up.

She saw Harken raise a hand to wave up at her.

They soared over the green, over the bay, over cottages and bored sheep. She saw her father's grave below and sent her thoughts to him.

"They're still there, trapped." She studied the ruins below. "We have to find a way."

She'd talk to her grandmother about it.

She thought about asking Lonrach to fly south. She wanted to see the village there, how much of the Prayer House they'd razed, but when he veered off, she realized she'd thought of somewhere else.

The forest, the stream, the waterfall. The portal.

Pulled there, she thought now, without fully knowing it. But pulled so the dragon was pulled.

And little licks of fear slid cold over her skin as they flew closer. "Do you feel it, too?"

Because he trembled, Breen wrapped her arms around Bollocks.

She saw Cróga circling, so Keegan must be there. At the portal.

Checking. The seal needed to be checked, of course. Guarded well, because . . .

She saw Keegan and other Fey below. Some horses. Sedric, silver hair gleaming.

She arrowed down, wind rushing into her face as Keegan looked up. She caught the flicker of irritation, ignored it as both she and Bollocks jumped down.

"I've too much to do to—"

"They're at the portal, on the other side." She snapped it out. "Trying to open it again. Can you feel it?"

She snatched his hand. "Feel it now."

Through her, he did. "It's holding. We knew they'd try, and it's holding."

"Yes, but . . ."

"It holds, Breen."

"There's blood, blood in the water. Demon blood, and next it will be Fey, a sacrifice of their own, as they have no more of ours. For now. And it is now. Happening now."

"What do you see?"

"The blood, so much blood. Yseult wading in it, and the sleep snakes wound around her shoulders like a scarf. She points. An elf, but he's not quick enough, and the others drag him to her. The snakes, they strike and strike, and he screams and screams."

"Enough," Keegan said when she covered her ears with her hands. "Enough now."

"No, no, no. She takes the knife, plunges it into his throat. Blood, more blood. It gushes into the water. Her hands, painted with it. But the seal holds.

"He's not there, but he watches. Odran watches from his tower. And she falls to her knees in the blood and the water when he slaps out with power. Blood on her face now, her own. He turns his back on her, and goes inside. And outside in the storm he brings, she bleeds."

"All right now. Bring her some water."

"It's not right."

"The seal holds," he said again. "And as it does, Talamh holds."

"It's not right, Keegan." She took the offered water, drank deep. "He didn't look at me. He didn't look, but he saw me. I know, I felt. But he didn't look."

"You bested him."

"It's not right," she said again. "It's not, but I don't know why. I wasn't coming here, but I felt pulled. Like it was urgent I come. But the seal's holding, and you were expecting them to try. Why did I need to come?"

Keegan looked back at the falls, brought the portal into his mind.

"To see what he wanted you to see, and feel what he wanted you to feel. There'll be a purpose in that. Call your dragon. You'll bring Marg to the farm. I need to get Mahon. If his purpose is what I think it may be, we have work to do."

# CHAPTER TWENTY-SEVEN

They sat around the big farm table in sturdy chairs. Breen imagined the generations who'd done the same for family meals. How they'd talked and argued, laughed and cried.

Had they reached over the big table for seconds? Had children pushed peas around on their plates hoping they'd somehow disappear?

Her father would have eaten here, as she would have. And her mother, she realized.

They'd been a family once.

Now they sat, another kind of family, not to eat and talk about the day to come or the day that passed, but how to defeat a god hell-bent on destroying them.

Instead of its candlestands and serving dishes, the sideboard held rolls of maps. Rather than sitting at the head of the long table, Keegan stood, the sword still strapped to his side.

"All in Talamh know of the Welcoming Tree, and the portal to the other side through Ireland. By law and tradition, because we were once part of that world, that place, any in Talamh may pass through there.

"All in Talamh," Keegan continued, "since Odran took the child Breen was, know of the portal through the great falls that leads to the world he conquered and claims as his own. By law, this portal was sealed, and is closed and forbidden. And we know through blood sacrifice and black magicks, Yseult breached that portal. With the help of the Pious in the south, Odran was able to create a portal from his world to ours, and that we closed and sealed. These two we guard as they lead only to Odran's world. Breen's seen Yseult's efforts to break through the portal in the falls."

"Yes." She spoke up because he looked at her. "Twice now. The first time I—somehow—went there—as they were about to sacrifice the young girl."

"And so you stopped them, and Sedric went through and brought her back safe. But Yseult used the breach we hadn't found to take Shana through to Odran. And in seeing this, as you saw the other, we knew where to find the breach, so sealed it."

"I won't forget that part anytime soon. But today I saw Yseult on the other side of the falls. They're sacrificing their own now to work the spell, to compromise the seal."

"I don't doubt this is true, and they would kill their own without question, but I don't think he plans to come at us that way."

"From the south again?"

Keegan shook his head at Mahon. "Where we sealed again, and guard, and have, like the falls, concentrated forces."

"He can't use the Welcoming Tree," Harken pointed out. "He still has no way into that world, and even Odran can't break that ancient spell. Nothing passes through—from here or from there—that intends harm."

"He only has those two ways." Morena held up a finger on her right hand. "The south." Then one on her left. "The falls."

"There are other portals."

"Aye, but none that lead to Odran's world, and none all in Talamh know. To use any but the Welcoming Tree, you have to get permission from the taoiseach. If granted," Morena continued, "you're bespelled so the location is hidden from your mind. For the safety of all, for this very reason."

"For this reason," Keegan agreed. "So none taken by Odran, none who choose to join him can give him another way, another world to conquer and destroy. And before Odran, it was tradition. The taoiseach has this knowledge, and holds it."

"Since you wouldn't have told him, he has no way to know . . ." Morena trailed off. "Gods, Keegan, you didn't tell Shana?"

"What do you take me for?" Rather than a sting, his words carried weariness. "But the council, as it advises, as it helps craft the laws, as it is sworn to duty to Talamh and its safety, knows. It's a sacred trust, and such matters are never to go beyond the council room.

"But Uwin is an indulgent father, and Shana a clever daughter. I used the mirror to speak with my mother, and she'll ask him. He won't lie. She'd know if he did, but he won't. If he told her, he did so because he believed I'd pledge with her, and that she would sit at the council table one day."

He turned away a moment to look out the window, the fields flowing toward the hills, the hills rolling toward the mountains, the mountains reaching for the sky.

"I don't excuse him for it, though I understand it. And by law if he hadn't resigned, he would be removed from the council. And I must send him and Shana's mother from the Capital, where they've both served and honorably, for all their lives."

"This is not for you to carry."

He turned back at Marg's cool tone.

"Who else then?"

"He chose, and wrongly. I am a mother who loved her child more than my life. Yet I never spoke of council business with my son, a clever boy indeed, until he himself was taoise-ach. You love your brother, your sister, and this one here who is another brother to you. Yet you have never spoken of these things, never broken your oath to indulge them."

"She ruined them," Breen said quietly. "They let her."

"There you have it." Morena tapped a fist on Breen's shoulder. "That's exactly so."

"A word?"

Keegan nodded at Sedric.

"I know the portals, as this is my gift. And yet never have I spoken of where they are with Marg, nor she with me. Love, the healthy sort, holds respect as well, and doesn't ask another to break a trust. In my time, I've seen you, and those before you"—he laid a hand over Marg's—"lift and carry the burdens of taoiseach, and so I know the staff is heavier than the sword."

Keegan sat. "Would you take his place on the council?"

Sedric smiled. "Not even for you, lad. There's too much cat in me for politics and protocols. But if you intend to use those maps here with those you trust, I'll show you any portal not on them."

"There are more?"

"I have no way of knowing. I know only what I know."

"Wait," Harken said when Keegan started to rise again. "You did take an oath, and can only break it to save Tal-amh, and the worlds beyond it. Must break it for that, but you can't do that on a feeling or a guess, Keegan. You have to be sure Shana's father told her, and even if he did, can you be sure she'd betray her own world? Her people, her family. To do that takes a vicious heart, an empty soul."

"I'm going upstairs now to ask our mother if Uwin gave Shana the knowledge. If he did, as he denied her nothing, the rest follows."

"But does it now?" Harken argued as Keegan strode out. "I know what she's done, and I know if she's ever found again, she must be banished for it. But to help Odran destroy her own people—"

"Men!" Morena tossed up her hands as she shoved back from the table, then used one of them to cuff Harken on the back of the head as she started to pace. "Men, men, men can be the most simple of creatures. And I count you and Keegan as two of the most sensible of the breed. But what does he do but get himself tangled up with a selfish, conniving bitch of an elf, and all for a bit of grinding together in the dark."

"Well now, it was a bit more than that. Not much," Mahon added, "but a bit. She could be charming, and—"

"Another blind spot." Morena aimed a finger at Mahon, and followed it with her derision. "Charm, beauty—the clever mind, sparkling eyes, and quick tongue? Well, they can go either way, can't they? But beauty forever makes a man think with his cock instead of his brain."

"That's not what I'm thinking with at the moment," Harken shot back. "And she wasn't the sort who brings that out in me."

"But you see beauty and charm and it's hard for such as you to see past that and see what it hides. Men! What do you do about them?" she demanded of Marg.

"Patience helps."

"Oh, but I'm tired of patience." She jabbed a finger at Breen.

"I don't know enough about men to know."

"Oh, you'll learn, trust me on it. Aisling, what do you say?"

"I've said nothing to now, as I have two children napping

upstairs here, and a third resting inside me. And every choice I make must have that in mind. I can say what Keegan decides is for him. And I will say I never liked her or trusted her. And while I can't say Mahon thought about the trust, he never liked her. And I'll say to you, Harken, if the question asked me was would she do this terrible thing, my answer would be, well, of course she would."

Morena walked behind Harken again, and this time kissed the top of his head. "I love the quality of you that pulls away from thinking the worst of anyone, even as it frustrates me."

"It's not because she's a beautiful woman."

"Maybe just a bit."

"You're loyal." Breen spoke up because it seemed so perfectly clear. "So it's hard to accept such terrible disloyalty in another, and one your brother had an affection for."

"Affection." Morena snorted.

"Beauty and charm played into that, I suppose, but it was there. You're kind, Harken, and that's as much a part of you as the color of your eyes. She's cruel. I don't know if even she knew how much cruelty she had in her, but it's free now.

"Keegan's right," she added. "If she has the knowledge, she'll use it to destroy. It's what she has left."

"And she has it right enough," Keegan said as he came back in. "My mother is calling the rest of the council, and will tell them what I need to do. I won't wait for them to debate and argue and drag it all out to do what I need to do."

"You're taoiseach," Marg told him. "Your duty's clear."

"Aye, it's clear. I ask you now to be council in the valley, to hold that trust sacred, to swear it. To swear to speak truth to me as you know it, to stand for the law. To stand for Talamh. You've already sworn," he said to Marg, "but I ask you to swear again."

"And so I do."

As he went around the table, Breen felt the doubts want to rise up. But he met her eyes, waited.

"I swear it."

"In the Capital the council has representatives from every tribe." On a hiss, Keegan dragged a hand through his hair. "I can't take time for that at this moment, but will deal with it."

Out of long-ingrained habit, Breen raised a hand. For a moment, Keegan just stared at her.

"This isn't a bloody classroom. Speak if you've something to say."

"I'm going to say you have the blood of all tribes in you. You, Harken, Aisling. So, it could be said you represent all."

Now he frowned, even as Harken gave her a nod of approval.

"I can work with that," Keegan decided. "Politics is bollocks half the time, and that I can work with. But for now we start with the maps of Talamh, and its portals. Then the maps of other worlds, the outside, and theirs."

He took a map from the server, unrolled it on the table.

Breen's first thought was that it was a beautiful piece of art, surely hand drawn and lettered with the dragon banner flying over it. Beautifully detailed as well, as she recognized places she'd been.

The Capital, of course, with its castle and bridges, the sea, the forest, the village, to the Far West and the wild cliffs and stone dance.

Then Keegan laid his hands on the parchment, and it glowed under his palms.

When he lifted them, she saw that markings had appeared. Small circles in dragon's-heart red that shined with light.

"Here are the portals of Talamh, each named for the world or place it leads to and from. There are twelve. There are more worlds than this, of course, and some of these worlds have portals that lead to other worlds as well. A traveler may pass through two, even three to reach the one desired—and approved."

"There's another." Sedric laid a finger in the center of the dance in the Far West. "It's a kind of door, but inside only. Entering here, you can travel to any place in Talamh. It needs precision and care to use, as without that you might come out in front of a galloping horse or, as I did once as a boy, on a crumbling cliff ledge in a high wind."

"It could save considerable time when it's needed," Keegan considered. "I've never heard of this."

"It was rarely used even when I was a boy, and its location closely guarded. As I was told more than one who used it in long times past came to harm, even death by not calculating with accuracy. And as it closes behind you, you have to make your way back by other means."

"One-way trip," Breen mused. "That wouldn't help Odran, as he'd not only have to know about it, he'd have to be inside Talamh to use it."

"Yseult may know." Marg frowned at the map. "And may have found a way to use it to move freely in Talamh."

"If so, she won't find it free to her now. We have the base there, so will keep close watch."

"There was another."

"Was?"

Sedric nodded at Keegan's question and stood to bend over the map. "It lost its light before my time, before the time of the old wizard who trained me in the portals. It may have been lore more than truth, but somewhere in the forest in the Capital. Here, I was told, held the fourteenth portal of Talamh. There may have been more in the long past, but I never found them. And I looked," he added with a small smile. "In my adventurous youth. Though I never found this one, as told to me, I felt some echo of what had been."

"Where did it lead?"

"I don't know, nor does anyone, to my knowledge. I found

nothing written on it, no song, no story, no legend other than what I was once told. What I once felt."

"We have those traveling outside, and even without that, we don't seal the other portals. If Odran's planning to use one to attack, he'd know. While he doesn't, we have an advantage. Mahon, we'll need guards, trusted and seasoned ones, for each portal."

"On both sides."

"Aye. At least one, at all times, who has the gift of sensing a change in them. We have Fey who chose other worlds, but Fey they are, and they'll stand. We'll send travelers through, portal to portal, to see if he means to go through another world to get here."

"The portals won't be a secret and sacred trust," Mahon pointed out. "The council may try to block the strategy that reveals them all."

Keegan just raised his eyebrows. "Have you met my mother?"

With a laugh, Mahon lifted his hands. "You're right, of course. It's this one . . ." He circled his finger above the forest on the map. "It's a worry."

"It is, aye, it is. Why would a portal lose its light? And why is there no story or song about such a thing?"

"A time before time," Harken said. "A time before Talamh made its choice, before magicks were scorned or persecuted? And if its purpose became the dark, would it lose its light?"

"We'll put scholars on such matters, but that's my thinking. Did Odran choose a world to make his own with only one way in and out? Or did he take it, as we've never found another portal leading there, because of this?"

"Two portals at the Capital," Breen said, "and both in the forest? Both to the dark? It's the only place I see on the map where two are—or may be—so close together."

"Could they be connected? That's what you're thinking,"

Morena said. "The locks on the portal to banishment, to the Dark World, have never been breached. But if this is somehow part of it, or connected, could he open both?"

"Fear." Marg looked up from the map. "It may have been fear of what stood behind the portal that stopped those from long ago from recording it, from speaking of it. Perhaps they themselves destroyed it somehow to keep what they fear on the other side. Or what lived on the other side was so dark it swallowed the light."

"It's said Odran fell into the Dark World when cast out," Aisling reminded them. "And wandered there century by century until he found his way out."

"And this may have been his way." Keegan nodded. "Scholars will scour the great library for any mention of this. If I were planning to attack, what better place to destroy than the Capital, what he sees as the power source of Talamh?"

"It's not," Harken said, "only the symbol of its laws and its justice. The power of Talamh is its heart."

"He'll never take its heart. Sedric."

"I'll go, aye, of course. I'll do my best to find it. Not so young as I once was, but wiser."

"We'll go." Marg took his hand. "I can help with this. You'll look after what's mine while I'm gone, Taoiseach."

"I will."

"The boys are up. I hear them," Aisling said as she rose. "I'll take them home, away from plots of wars."

"I'll need Mahon awhile longer."

"I know." She ran her fingers down Mahon's warrior's braid, kept her other on the child growing inside her. "I'm with you on this, *mo dhearthái*. Be sure of it."

As Aisling went out, Breen rose. "If I could have just a few minutes to tell Marco I'll be here for . . . however long. He said he'd take Bollocks down to the bay."

"There's no need. I need Mahon to help choose who might

travel and where, who will guard and where, and Sedric, who may know of portals we don't. I'll call you again, as council, when all's in place."

"They don't need me either. I'll go with you. Safe journey," Morena said to Marg and Sedric. "And good hunting."

"Come home soon." Breen moved over to hug them both. "And safe. Find the tree of snakes." She pulled back abruptly. "I don't know what that means. I just know you should look for it."

"Then we will."

"Snakes," Morena said as she pulled Breen outside. "A tree made of snakes?"

"I don't know, but that's disturbing. And it can't be that. Someone would have noticed a tree made of snakes long before this."

"You've the right of that. He'll send my father, my brothers. My father traveling for certain, as he's done so in so many worlds. And my brothers to guard."

"You're worried for them."

"I can't be." Shaking it off, she held out an arm. Amish soared to it. "It's who they are, and what they are. And if Odran comes, I'll be lifting up a sword. I've grown up knowing that day may come. So."

She raised her arm so Amish took flight. "We live today, and a fine one it is. We'll watch the beauty of my hawk, spend time with your good dog and our friend. As Mahon will likely be off dealing with all this most of the evening if not the night, Harken will go to Aisling's cottage to keep her company and help with the boys."

"I think he's one of the best men I've ever known."

"He is, in all ways. I love him," she said simply. "And I'll go to his bed tonight, as we'll both need it. I'll ask you to invite me to dinner first."

"Sure. You're always welcome."

"I can't tell my grandparents any of this, and it scrapes at me. I find yet another reason I wouldn't want what Keegan has. You can't tell Marco."

"I know, and yeah, it scrapes."

"We'll have leave soon enough to tell them, and that's a more worrying time. And so . . ." The hawk flew back to her. "And there's that good dog playing in the water with the Mers, and another good man sitting and watching. We'll take the rest of this fine day with them, won't we?"

"Yes. I'm glad I've got you, Morena."

"We've all got each other now." Morena gave Breen a little shoulder bump as they walked. "What do you suppose he'll make for dinner?"

Since the Mers provided the fish, Marco tried his hand at fish and chips. The three of them ate with the fire simmering, the music humming, and candles flickering.

An easy meal with easy conversation helped Breen put thoughts of vengeful—possibly psychotic—elves and murderous gods out of her head for a little while.

It meant something, a great deal of something, to see her two closest friends, one from each of her worlds, erase all boundaries to forge a strong friendship of their own.

"I know my fish and chips." As she polished off a second round of the chips portion of the meal, Morena wagged her fork at Marco. "So I can say with considerable authority, this was the best of them I've had in Talamh and on this side as well."

"First time I've made them with fish caught by mer-kids. That might add an extra zip."

"They like you, and a certain water dog."

"Who, maybe for the first time ever, played himself out." Breen smiled over to where Bollocks sprawled sleeping in front of the fire.

"Clancy's cousin in the Far West has a female about to

drop a litter. I'm thinking I'll barter for one of the pups for Harken. They lost their Angel last winter, such a sweet dog she was, and he's not had the heart to get himself another. But he misses having one running about. He'd accept a pup as a gift, then he'd have that love in his life."

"Aww."

She laughed, lifted her beer in a toast to Marco. "I can't be denying I'm soft on the man, but if you preferred women, I'd toss him over without a thought for you, darling."

"For my fish and chips."

"It weighs heavy on your side of the scale."

"You know, the highlight of my life, seriously, was coming to Ireland with Breen last summer. Seeing things I'd only read about or seen in movies. Actually being there. But hitching a ride to Talamh with her tops it. Meeting you, Keegan and his family, Nan and Sedric, going to a freaking castle, learning to ride a horse, finding out my best pal's a witch, all of that. Meeting Brian? The best icing on the best cake in the history of cakes."

"I'm tossing an *aww* right back at you." Morena propped her chin on her fist. "You're mad for him, aren't you?"

"I guess I am. Hell, no *guess* about it. Totally crazy about him. I was hoping he'd make it for dinner."

Breen accepted the quick twist of guilt knowing she couldn't talk about the new council meeting. "I imagine Keegan's got most of the riders doing flyovers, or whatever they'd call it. Since I had a little talk with him—Brian, that is—this morning, I happen to know the totally crazy's mutual."

"You talked with him? About me? What'd he say?"

She ticked a finger in the air. "Sorry, the details are in the vault."

"Hey, hey, hey!"

"But the big picture?" She rose, bent over to kiss Marco.

"He loves you, and in a way that's as gooey sweet as a Hall-mark Christmas movie, and as strong as Iron Man's suit. So I approve, and since you made the best fish and chips in two worlds, I'll deal with the dishes."

"I'll help with that, but what's this Hallmark gooey, and who's Iron Man, and why is his suit so strong?"

"Sit with Marco. He'll explain. I've got the dishes."

"Okay," Marco began. "You're definitely coming over so we can stream Christmas movies, and *Iron Man*—all of them, plus *The Avengers*. Since that's going to take some time, I'll give you the gist."

It was nice, Breen thought, to listen to Marco explain some pop culture to Morena. And entertaining to hear Morena's questions and responses—more enthusiasm by far for super-heroes than holiday romances.

But Marco intended to give her both, apparently, with weekly movie nights.

When Morena left, Breen found it comforting to settle into her room with Bollocks, the fire, her tablet while listening to Marco practice on his harp downstairs.

While he waited for Brian, she thought.

Yes, both gooey and strong. And who wouldn't want both in their lives?

When worries wanted to intrude again, she decided to push them away a little longer. She'd write her blog now, post it with photos in the morning. That would free up more writing time.

She could finish the first draft of the novel in a matter of days—a week at the most. She really thought she could. Then what she should do is set it aside. Just let it sit there while she finished the second Bollocks book.

And wasn't it great to know she could fill her mornings doing what she'd always wanted? Odran couldn't take that from her. Whatever happened, she had this time, she'd done this for herself.

If the novel went nowhere, she'd still have written it. And she'd have done her best.

If Odran broke through, came for her and the Fey, she'd fight, she'd draw on everything she had to stop him. She'd do her best.

Using those thoughts, that determination as a springboard, she started her blog. She'd nearly finished when Bollocks's head popped up. She'd heard it, too—the sweep of dragon wings.

She scrambled up, hurried to the window. She could admit the quick disappointment when she recognized Brian's dragon gliding down. That, she told herself, needed to be pushed aside as well.

Easy to do, she realized as she watched Marco come out to greet him. As she watched them embrace. As she sighed over the welcome-back kiss.

"They look good together, Bollocks." She sighed again, stroking the dog's topknot as her best friend and his love joined hands and walked together toward the bay.

"A moonlight walk. Romantic. Marco's found somebody who understands romance. Some swings and misses before this." She shot Bollocks a look. "I could tell stories there. But it looks like a home run this time, right? And whatever happens, they'll always have this."

She watched another moment, then stepped back. "Let's give them some privacy. I need to finish the blog."

When she started back to the bed, her tablet signaled a FaceTime request.

"Sally!" She dropped down, accepted, repeated, "Sally! Just who I needed. I was— Holy crap, you look gorgeous!"

Sally shook back his shaggy red wig, angled his head. "You like?"

"Love. Gorgeous, sexy, sultry."

"We're doing a tribute to the eighties. Rocking heroines from the decade. Way before your time, baby girl."

"And you're not doing your amazing Cher?"

"I wanted to mix it up, try out a new. So I'm hitting them with my best shot."

"Oh, oh, I know! Of course. Pat Benatar. You'll be great."

"I'm following Dell's Tina Turner, and that's a tough spot. But somebody's got to do it, and I own the joint. Speaking of gorgeous, there's that face. Gorgeous, happy face. I miss you."

"I miss you. I really, really miss you, and I'm so glad you called."

"Thought I'd take a chance you and Marco would be around. Where's my boy?"

Breen glanced toward the window. "On a date. Did he tell you he met somebody?"

"He gave me and Derrick a few crumbs, but not the whole cookie. Somebody he met at a party a week or so ago. Is that the one?"

"That's the one. Brian. Sally, they're in love."

"Hmm." Breen watched Sally pour himself a glass of wine. "That's quick."

"I guess it is, but it's real. I've never seen him so happy, or seen him with someone who just gets him, and loves him because he gets him. I felt guilty about Marco coming with me. So sudden, like I stole him from you."

"Don't be silly. I like knowing he's with you. And I like looking at you right now, knowing whatever you found there makes you happy, and gives you what you need."

"It does. Being able to write here, it's given me just what I needed—and more, it's given it when I didn't really know what I needed until I had it."

"Derrick and I read your blog every day, and it gives me something—as your honorary mom—I need. Hearing the strong and the happy in you. It's opened you, my sweet Breen, being there, the writing, the taking your own."

"It's changed me."

"No, honey, it hasn't changed you. It's revealed you." Sally waved a hand, drank some wine. "I have to stop or I'll get sloppy and ruin my incredible eighties eyeliner."

Love simply filled her. "How did you know you're just what I needed tonight?"

He tapped a finger next to his shaggy bangs. "Mother's instinct. What about Keegan, the hot yet charming Irishman? Still seeing him?"

"Oh, well, yes. I mean, not like Marco and Brian. We're both really busy anyway."

"No one's too busy for love, or lust or just a little romance. What does he do, anyway? I don't think you ever told me."

Tricky, Breen thought. Sally could see through lies like glass. "Oh, he's in a leadership position. The head of a large group."

"No kidding?" Sally paused to repair his lipstick. "He didn't strike me as the executive type. I thought there was a farm."

"Yes, they have a family farm. Keegan, his brother, and his sister, and he bases there when he can. He has another base in the east. He travels back and forth a lot. It's a lot of responsibility. He's a responsible sort. People depend on him, and he takes that seriously."

"That's good to know. I liked him, but I have to look out for our girl, even from a distance. And I'm thinking, if you and Marco stay there into spring or summer, Derrick and I need to take a trip."

"Really?" Twin spikes of joy and trepidation rushed through her. "You'd come to Ireland?"

"Need to see my kids, and if this thing with Brian is the real deal, I want to see for myself. And I want to meet your grandmother."

"She'd love you. You'd love her."

And she'd figure it out, Breen told herself. Somehow, she'd figure it all out.

"We'll talk about it. Meanwhile, one more thing before I have to get my well-toned, leather-clad ass moving. If you do plan to stay that long, I've got a new girl bartending. She's a bright one, and oddly from Ireland herself."

"Really?"

"Not from the Galway area where you are. Dublin—and Meabh knows how to tend bar like she was born for it. You might want to think about subletting her the apartment."

"Oh. I never thought . . . That makes sense."

"I'll send you her information. You can vet her, but I already have. We don't hire just anyone here at Sally's."

"Yes, thanks, but if you trust her, I trust her. I'll talk to Marco, but that sounds like something we should do. I mean it's just sitting there empty."

"You can sublet it furnished, or we can pack up and store what you don't want in it."

"No, it's fine, furnished is fine. We have everything we want. I'll talk to Marco tomorrow. Thanks, Sally. Give Derrick a big kiss from me."

"You can count on that. We love you. Talk soon."

"We love you. Rock their socks off."

Sally winked. "Count on that, too."

When Breen ended the call, she started to go back to her blog. The light rap of knuckles on wood had her looking over. She hadn't shut her door when she'd come, and now Keegan crouched in the doorway, petting Bollocks.

"Your door was open, but I didn't want to interrupt."

"Sally." Breen set the tablet aside as she rose. "I didn't hear you come in. If you need to talk to me more about all this, we can go down. I can make tea, or get you a beer."

He stepped in, eyes on hers. Shut the door behind him. "I've had enough talk for the day."

Not a walk-in-the-moonlight sort of man, she thought. Yet it was strangely romantic the way he stood, watched, waited.

Her choice.

"Funny. So have I."

Making her choice, she went to him.

# CHAPTER TWENTY-EIGHT

It surprised her to find him there when she woke at first light. It surprised her to wish he could stay, and she with him, to take a day without responsibilities and duties.

But that wasn't his way, and she had responsibilities and duties of her own.

She started to get up, to begin dealing with those responsibilities and duties, and in a room full of shadows, he took her hand.

"A moment. Sometimes the day starts too soon."

"It does."

He flicked his free hand toward the fire, so the flames came alive. "The bed's warm, but you won't be when you're out of it. I'd have you stay in it and me with you if the world would just stop for one bleeding day. But it won't."

He sat up, shoved back his hair. "I need to go to the Capital. Likely I should've stayed there last night instead of coming back. I may be back tonight, or I may not."

She sat up beside him and rubbed a hand down his arm, rubbed it down her own. "No strings." On his baffled look, she got up. "It's an expression," she began.

"Aye. I know the meaning, I think."

Since she was naked, she decided to put on workout gear. She'd just throw a jacket over it for her morning ritual with Bollocks.

"I think I see strings on Brian and Marco."

"Yes, very clearly. They'll have a lot to work out at some point."

He watched her pull on leggings, a sports bra. "I like the clothes you wear to do your exercise."

She looked over her shoulder. "Because they're practical for the purpose?"

"No, though I suppose they are that as well. I'd like to use your shower before I go if you don't mind."

She walked back, sat on the edge of the bed. "Let's do something. Let's say when you come here, when I sleep with you, when you're here in the morning, you don't have to ask to use the shower, or eat something, or make tea or have a beer. Whatever."

"I don't want to be careless with you."

"You're impatient, often abrupt, occasionally dictatorial, but you're not careless."

"I was careless with her, I think. With Shana. It's not excusing any of it, but I can look back and see I was careless in assuming we both knew what we had, and what we didn't and never would."

"I'm not Shana."

"You're not, no, and nothing like her. Nothing like anyone else. I shouldn't be with you like this, that's the truth of it. I shouldn't have mixed things this way, but I have. My worry for you should be only as the key to protecting my world and yours and all the others. But it's not now, and can't be again."

She pushed back the urge to stroke and soothe because that wasn't his way either.

"I see, so it's all on you. I didn't have anything to say about it."

"That's clever," he said as he rose. "You have an agile and clever mind. I admire it."

Naked, he wandered to the window. "I've spent more than half my life as taoiseach. I'll hold the sword and staff until I die, to protect Talamh. Odran may see that's sooner than I'd like."

"Don't say that. Don't."

He looked back at her. "I don't fear dying for my world, for my people. I wear the braid and have as a vow to fight, to give my life if needed, as my father did, as yours did. But I fear, as I didn't, as I shouldn't, harm coming to you. Not just for Talamh, but for myself."

"So you'll knock me down, insult my sword work, and mock my archery skills."

"You have no archery skills, and aye, as often as I can, I'll knock you down. That's not being careless with you, as I see it. It's the opposite."

"I don't have many relationship skills either, but I'm pretty sure of this. The fact that we have one, a personal sort of relationship, makes us both stronger."

"And how are you figuring that one?"

"Because it matters more when you care. I'm going down to let the dog out and make coffee."

Odd, she thought, as Bollocks bolted down the steps ahead of her, she'd never had a more romantic conversation in her life. She wasn't sure what it said about either of them, but she was fine with it.

In a cold, steady rain, Keegan flew to the Capital. He found his mother in the council room, as he'd asked her. Only the two of them for now.

She rose as he came in, her look somber.

"A wet journey," she said, and poured him tea.

"Thanks."

"Uwin and Gwen left an hour ago. I found a cottage in

the midlands where they can live. It's simple, it's quiet. They have their horses and possessions, and I had the cottage stocked with food and other necessities.

"You were right to send them away." She laid a hand on his arm. "It was hard for you to do that duty, but you were right. As I'm right to help them make this start in this new life."

He just nodded, sat. "Sedric?"

"He and Marg are already back in the forest. It's much ground to cover, Keegan, but they won't stop. I would have gone to help them, but I knew you were coming and wanted to speak to me. Loren asked to help."

Now Keegan lifted his gaze.

"He wants to find this portal," Tarryn continued. "There's no question of it. And part of him believes he can somehow save Shana. There's no question of that either. But he wants to find it, and he's skilled."

"All right. There's no one's judgment I trust more than yours. You look tired."

"Ah well, that's what a woman likes to hear."

"Ma." He reached for her hand.

"I didn't get much sleep. I'll rest better now that I've seen Uwin and Gwen on their way. And I've three elfin replacements for you to consider for the council."

"None from the Capital."

Tarryn raised her eyebrows. "I thought you'd want someone quickly, and with a sense of the protocols."

"I think we lean too heavy on from here, and those who see too little of the rest. I know someone in the south. She's young, but a little youth may be a good addition. I need to fly south in any case to see the progress, and I'll ask her."

"Nila. The one who took the child the Pious stole back to her family. I know my boy. It's a fine choice, Keegan, and I hope she agrees."

"That saves me the time I thought I might need to convince you."

"I'm your hand, and your ma. You're taoiseach. And I thought you might bring Breen with you this time, as she could be useful in the forest. And with the spell Marg and I've started to plan out."

"I considered it, but we need to take care not to put all the eggs in the basket, right? There may be a portal, and it may be Odran's plan to use it. But there are others. The waterfall they've used before—and with her close, she may sense or have a vision. The Far West, that gateway Sedric spoke of.

"As it is, I'm thinking you might be more useful there as well."

"In the valley?" She just smiled at him. "Save your breath for the convincing. As I said, I know my boy. You think to take me from the thick of it, as all logic says this is where he'll strike. So while you won't ask me to shirk my duty, you'll try to make it seem I can do more away than here. No."

Because he'd known that for a lost cause before he'd begun, he drank more tea. "I have some fine reasoning to wrap around it."

"Well then, save it for another time. Do you want to call the council?"

"No, bloody hell, I don't. I'm for the forest and the wet."

"Then I'm with you."

"You think I should've brought Breen here?"

"I think you'll have to before it's done."

He found Marg first, working with Loren and an elf. He could wish for speed, but Keegan knew being thorough and efficient overruled his impatience.

They'd divided the vast acres of forest into grids, and covering each, he'd learned the previous day, took an hour or more.

"It would take less," Marg told him, "but there's so much here. So much energy, so many heartbeats, so many echoes of power."

They stood in the rain, the air smelling of drenched pine

and earth, and gloom thick as a plank. Like his mother, Marg wore a hooded cloak over sturdy trousers, sweater, boots.

Lifting her hands, she spread them, circled them. The grid map formed in the air.

"You see we've marked over grids we've completed."

"And made some progress."

"Some." Knowing him, Marg smiled a little. "Slow progress. Sedric continues in the north of the forest while we work the south. The others you chose—the empath Glenn with the young Were, ah, Naill, take the east, and Phelin McGill takes the west with another empath. The elves, as our Yoric here, serve as runners."

"We've seen nothing like a tree of snakes," Yoric said.

"Sure you're lucky to see your hand in front of your face in this gloom. My mother and I will take a central grid before I fly south. If we manage no more than one or two, it's still less to be done."

And it all could be for nothing, Keegan thought as he and Tarryn walked through the wet. A story told by an old wizard to a young were-cat, long ago.

But he gave it three hours, then had a meal, as grown man or no, he found it difficult to refuse his mother.

On Cróga he flew north first, where the frigid air turned the wet into icy stones, and then to swirling snow. In the high peaks that speared up along the thrashing sea, he dismounted in snow that reached the tops of his boots.

The portal here opened to a world he'd visited once, and briefly, as he found its reliance on machines, its lack of interaction among its residents, inhospitable.

As no other portals had been found or recorded in that world, he thought it unlikely to impossible Odran could come through this way.

Still, he had six guards on duty.

A fire blazed on a wide, flat rock, and the wave of heat

from it almost thawed his frozen bones. Snow fell in thick, fat flakes, and the wind tossed them where it willed.

If the rain had been a misery, he thought, this was brutality.

And yet Hugh, whom Keegan put in charge of the day duties, greeted him with a rosy-cheeked smile.

"A fine day in the high country."

"Every arse within five miles is frozen solid," Keegan tossed back.

"Ah, sure and a northman's blood runs too thick and hot for that. All's well here. One of us slips in and out every hour as you ordered. They're no more interested in us on the other side than we are in them."

"Stand on then, Hugh."

"So we will. I'm grateful for the service here, as my home is just . . . well, you can't see through the snow, but it's just down in the foothills. So I'll see my lady and our babe when we rotate."

"May your lady keep you warm through the night," Keegan said as he mounted Cróga.

"That she will."

He crisscrossed Talamh on his way south, stopping at every portal. He flew out of the snow and brittle cold—thank the gods—into more rain, an all-too-brief moment of sun, and the smoky fog that followed it.

He stopped in fields, in forests, by the banks of a lake called Lough Beag for its small size.

When he soared over the valley, he took Cróga down at the farm, where the rain had slowed to a drizzle and the sun pulsed weakly against the stacked gray clouds.

He found Harken in the barn sharpening plowshares. Other tools, including three swords, lay already keen on the worktable.

"It's cold as a dead man's arse in the north, wet as a drowned rat in the east. And you couldn't cut the gloom with an axe over the far midlands."

"Warm and dry enough in here."

Keegan took the kettle from the squat stove, poured the hot water through a strainer of strong tea leaves.

"Do you want a meal?" Harken asked him when Keegan sat on the top of a barrel.

"Thanks, no. Our mother nagged me into eating before I left the Capital. I've only got a short time, but wanted to check with you before I go on."

"Quiet. I saw Brian when he came through, and he says Breen and Marco will stay on the other side today until they're needed. They both have work there."

"Just as well for that."

In steady strokes, with sure, patient hands, Harken continued to run the blade over the whetstone. "I can feel you poking at me. I know where I'm needed, Keegan, as I've told you before. That's here. If you need me somewhere else, you'll say."

"And you'll go." Keegan took a long drink, felt the warmth spread that was as much home as a hot drink and a fire. "I had a lot of time to think—you'll have it when you're flying through fucking blizzards and downpours and buckets of bloody hail."

Harken grinned as he worked. "The luxury and glamour of the taoiseach."

"Bloody bollocks on that. I know there are many who would give all, who do give, and they're valued for it, every one. But it's family, Harken, that holds me up. You and Aisling, Mahon, the boys, Ma. Knowing I can go to any of you. This place. I don't work it like you, but I need it like you."

"I know it." Harken lifted his gaze as he worked, met Keegan's. "I don't lead like you, *mo deartháir*, but I need to know you hold the sword and the staff. It holds me up knowing it."

"Yet your sword's sharp and ready."

"So will the plow be when I'm done."

"Gods willing I'll help you use it after the wheel turns to the new year." He rose. "I have to go. I've three more portals to check, and then it's back to the Capital. I'll come back tomorrow if I can."

"*Turas sábháilte.*"

"Safe enough, but likely wet. Harken . . . If we're right about Odran coming through this portal we can't bleeding find in the Capital, and if he gets past us—"

"He won't." After testing the edge, Harken picked up a hooked blade. "But we'll hold the valley, and home."

"I trust you will."

When Keegan left, Harken continued the task, and waited.

A few moments later, the barn door creaked open again, and Morena came in.

"I started to come in before, but saw Keegan, and felt it was a brotherly sort of talk, so went back out again."

"It was that, and thanks for it."

Rain dripped off the brim of the hat she'd pulled on against the rain. Mud caked her boots.

He thought, as he always did, she was the most beautiful creature ever born. And still he waited while she wandered about, so obviously restless, tense, irritated.

"You left quick and early this morning," he said.

"Nan and Grandda needed me. Grandda's making a rocking chair for Bridie Riley to give to her daughter, who's having her first by Yule. And Nan's been making apple cakes for bartering. It's hard not to tell them about this portal that might not even be real."

"It's real enough."

"How can you know?"

"Because it makes the most sense."

She threw her hands up in frustration, and little red sparks of light shot from her fingers.

"Well, none of it makes any bloody sense to me. Why can't

he leave us alone? Do we trouble him? We wouldn't. He has his world, doesn't he, and can lord over it as he pleases. What does he gain by destroying ours? And why are you smiling like that?"

"As I see you're doing all you can to work yourself up into a rage so you don't say what brought you here. Or why you left so sudden this morning, why you've come back, why you're marching around the barn like there's fire in your boots."

"I told you why I left, and I only came back this way thinking I might see Breen."

"She and Marco are staying on the other side today."

"Then I'll go there."

He kept working. "You won't change what is by stomping away."

"I'm not stomping. Change what?"

"What you feel, and what you want." He set the tools aside and stood.

"You don't know what I feel, and have no right to look inside me."

"I don't have to. I see what I see in your eyes. I love your eyes," he said as he stepped toward her. "I love what I see in them, always, but what I see in them now, I've waited for. I love you, Morena. I've loved you a long time, and will for all the rest of time I have."

"This isn't the time to talk about love. What's coming— and if I can feel it, you do—what's coming is terrible."

"It is, aye, so there's no better time to talk of love. Without it, there's no reason, is there? Just survival, and that's not enough. You're ready."

He took her hands, and though she made a half-hearted attempt to tug them back, brought them to his lips.

"Ready for what? Ready to fight? I will, and so will all of us. That's not—"

He simply touched his lips to hers.

"Bloody hell, I thought, I believed, we'd have enough of each other when we started this up. We'd have enough, and go back to being friends."

"I'll always be your friend, but not only. I've waited until you're ready, and now you are. So I'm asking you, Morena Mac an Ghaill, to pledge to me as I pledge here to you. To wed me, and make a life with me."

"I'm stupid in love with you. It pisses me off sometimes."

"I know it, and well, but still, here we are."

"I won't promise to cook for you."

"As you're a terrible cook, I'll say thanks for that."

She had to laugh. "I am a terrible cook. It was . . . sitting at the table, a council. I never expected to be asked such a thing. And sitting there, listening, knowing—even though you hear and you know before—I could only think: Why do I pull away from what I want in my heart when there's so much dark? It's past time for the game of it. So I pledge to you, Harken O'Broin. I want a life with you, and I'll love you through all of it, even when it pisses me off."

He drew her in as she drew him, and kissed her long, slow, deep, in the barn that smelled of hay and oil and burning peat.

"I want to wed in the spring. I don't want to start my life with you in the dark of winter, but in the promise of spring."

"I can wait." He kissed her again.


While his brother attained his heart's desire, Keegan went to the waterfall, the Far West, then flew south.

The air warmed, the skies cleared, and the frigid cold of the north seemed like a hard dream.

It pleased him to see not a single stone from the Prayer House remained on the hill. In its place craftspeople worked on erecting a pillar of white granite. They would polish it and carve the banner of Talamh at its center. At its base would be a pool of fire and water, a flame that would never be extinguished. And above it, in the old language:

IN THE LIGHT LIVE THE BRAVE.

And all who looked on it, he promised himself, would know, would remember, would honor.

As he circled, Mahon flew up to join him. "It's a fine thing, a strong thing. It's the right thing."

"Aye. And the portal?"

"The coven swears the locks and seal hold. No breaches, and no attempts."

"There will be, if they get through in the east. I see repairs are moving quickly."

"Thatchers, carpenters, masons. They're swarming. It's a good potion after the battle to mend and build. In truth, Keegan, I think there's a cloud lifted here with no more shadow of the Prayer House. After the baby comes, I think Aisling and I will bring the children here. I want them to see the memorial, and I want them to build castles in the sand and run in the surf."

"Well, for tonight, you can fly as far as your cottage with me."

"Work here to be done still."

"And you can be back at it tomorrow. Did you send for the elf?"

"I did. I've brought her in from patrol, and she's down there working with the masons. She's a good hand with stone, is Nila."

"Then I'll speak with her. Choose who you want to take charge until morning. She'll say aye or nay, so this won't take long."

He landed Cróga on the beach, much to the delight of a group of children playing in the shallows.

And as he walked toward the shops and cottages, he thought Mahon right. A cloud lifted.

He found the elf rebuilding a wall. Spotting him, she got quickly to her feet.

"Taoiseach."

"That's good work. Mahon said you had a hand for it."

"I like to build things. And watch them built. The memorial is already such a strong symbol."

"Would you walk with me?"

"Of course."

"I want to thank you for your words in the Judgment."

"They were truth, and my duty. And, I don't worry to say, a pleasure as well."

He nodded. Young, he thought, a pretty young elf with a warrior's braid who'd already seen battles and blood.

"I wonder if you would take up another duty."

"I serve Talamh."

He nodded as they walked away from the village toward the trees. "You would have heard of Shana, and her crimes, her flight, her choice to join Odran."

"I have, aye." Nila's face went hard as the stones she'd laid. "Do you wish me to go through and find her?"

Keegan glanced down. "And finding her?"

"To bring her back for judgment. That is the law."

The right answer, he thought, the true answer, and given without hesitation.

"That is the law. But no, I send no one to Odran's world for this, for her. Her time will come when it comes. Her father was on the council, now he isn't. I'd ask you to take his place at the council table."

She stopped short, stared at him. "I don't understand. Taoiseach, I'm not a politician or a scholar."

"You're loyal, brave, you have my trust. You know the law and honor it, Nila. I want that at my council table. Your home's in the south, and you'd have to make a new one in the Capital. It's no small thing I ask."

"I'd make my home where I'm needed, and so my family would want. But I have no experience."

"Neither did I when I took the sword from the lake—and younger than you. It's a choice, Nila, and there's no dishonor in choosing no."

He looked around. Some of the trees bore battle scars, others stood as no more than scorched husks.

And still there was beauty here. And from it, more would bloom.

"How is the child? The little girl."

"Alanis? Resilient."

He turned to her fully. "You would know because you would go and see her, make sure of it. And this is yet another reason I ask you to serve on the council. The law must have heart, it has to beat from it, or it turns to stone."

"I . . . I'm gobsmacked, and that's the truth of it. But I'd be honored to serve Talamh, and you, on the council. But I'd ask for someone to teach me how to, well, do it."

"You'll have my mother for that. I'm on my way back to the Capital now, and I'll see you have rooms and whatever you need. Do you have a horse?"

"I do, aye, though I'm faster on my feet."

"You'll want the horse in any case." He held out a hand. "I'm grateful to you."

"I'll hope you will be."

# CHAPTER TWENTY-NINE

He didn't come to the cottage that night, or the night after. Breen learned of progress at the Capital—slow—from Marg through the scrying mirror. She heard tidbits from Brian, who came late, left early, so she knew Keegan traveled the whole of Talamh every day, and spent hours in the forest on the search for the dark portal.

She immersed herself in her work. It gave her purpose, held off the worry, and stopped her, for hours at a time, from feeling useless.

And she shocked herself when she came to the end.

It wasn't finished, she reminded herself as she stared at her laptop screen. She had to go through it all, edit, fix, polish, obsess.

But somehow it was all there. Five hundred and thirty-six pages of her words, all there.

She had to stand up, walk around the room, so Bollocks's head popped up from his nap on the bed. She had to open the garden door, breathe the cool air. And because he sensed her mood—glazed joy—instead of bulleting out, Bollocks reared up on his hind legs and danced around her.

"Yeah, we'll dance." She held out her hands so he put his forepaws in them. Joy beamed from his eyes into hers.

"I made you a demon dog in the book, I hope you don't mind. You're a good demon dog. An amazing demon dog, the best ever in the history of demon dogs.

"I don't know what to do next. Yes, I do! We have to go tell Marco."

Happy to oblige, Bollocks ran out with her to where Marco sat at the table working. She smelled red sauce and spicy meat. Spaghetti and meatballs, she realized.

Perfect. Everything was perfect.

"Hey, girl." He kept tapping his keyboard. "I'm about done here, and if you can do that woo-woo thing to the stove, I was thinking we could go over and take a ride. Who knew I'd learn how to ride a horse, much less miss doing it? You gotta need a break from writing after two days of pretty much round-the-clock."

"Marco."

"Yeah, two seconds, just finishing up, and I talked with Abby in Publicity about setting up social media accounts for Bollocks—like, his accounts, get it? After the first of the year, get people invested in him, you know?"

"Marco," she repeated.

"And done. Yeah, what?"

He looked up and over, saw her face. "Something's up." He got slowly to his feet. "I think it's good, but I know there's shit going on you're not telling me about. Or can't. And Brian can't. So tell me if it's good right off."

"It's good. It's great. It's ridiculous. I finished the book. The novel. The fantasy. Well, not finished-finished because—"

She ended on a laugh because he swooped her up and spun her around. Not to be outdone, Bollocks reared up again and added a few joyful howls.

"Mimosas! Now!"

"Mimosas?" She laughed again, clung to him. "It's barely two in the afternoon."

"You wrote a damn book—another damn book." He eased back to give her a noisy kiss. "And we're having mimosas."

"I wrote a book. Two books. Well, one and a half, maybe a third, because I still have to edit and expand, or contract, polish it or—"

"Two books," Marco said definitely. "Girl, I'm so proud of you."

"You're a big part of why. If I had to do all that?" She pointed to his laptop, his files. "Well, I wouldn't. I'll take the mimosa. I think I have to sit down. I think I have to cry a little."

"You cry all you want." He drew her in again. "I'm going to cry with you. My Breen."

Bollocks let out a yip, and Morena came in. "What's all this? Why is there crying?"

"Celebratory crying," Marco told her. "Breen finished her book."

"Oh, well now, that's brilliant." She met Breen's anxious eyes. "And all's well."

"I just told Breen I know there's stuff you can't tell me. Bollocks and I can take a walk."

"I'm sorry for that," Morena told him. "But there's no need. All's as it was two days ago, as that's how long it's been since you've come. So I've come to you."

"Good timing, because we're having mimosas."

Now she grinned at Marco. "I know that drink. It's putting champagne in orange juice, and I'll have one and lift it to our storyteller. Can I read it?"

"It's not finished-finished. I have to—basically, I have to go through and make it better."

"Then you will, and we'll drink again when you do." At home, Morena took off her cap and jacket. Then sniffed the air. "And what is that amazing smell?"

"Spaghetti and meatballs." Marco moved to the kitchen to give the pot a stir before he went for the champagne. "You should come to dinner. Hell, I got enough for a small army. Bring Harken, and if Keegan gets back, it's a party."

"I wish I could, believe that, but it's best Harken and I stay in Talamh for now."

"Because of the stuff you can't tell me."

"Let me say this, as Breen would be more careful about it—"

"Morena."

"I know what I'm about." She walked into the kitchen as well to sniff at the sauce. "Oh gods, that's a miracle in a pot. The taoiseach formed a council here in the valley, and Breen and I are on it, and we're sworn not to speak of what's what there unless given leave."

"Okay." With his bartender's hands, Marco opened the champagne with a happy little *pop*. "You'll tell me when I can help."

"No question of it."

"Something's up with you, too." Frowning, Breen studied Morena's face. "I can feel it, but it's not—it's not what we can't talk about."

"Nothing about that, no, and I've been waiting for the pair of you to come over so I can tell you. And bloody talk to you, but you don't."

Marco paused in the act of shaking a bottle of orange juice. "Is it good or bad? I have to know these things."

"Well, it's good. It's passing strange still, but good. I was ready, you see. It was the council meeting that had me realizing it." She wandered back out of the kitchen, in again. "And he knew it, of course. He knows my moods better than I do half the time, which is annoying and, well, comforting, I suppose. So there you have it."

"What?" Marco set down the bottle, threw up his hands as

Breen smiled and started crying again. "Give me a freaking clue here."

"We're pledged, Harken and me. You'd say engaged on this side, though our way of it makes more sense, I'm thinking."

Before Breen could move in to hug, Marco grabbed Morena off her feet. "Girl!" He swung her, as he had Breen— and started the dog up again. "A Christmas wedding? Man, I love Christmas weddings."

"No, not winter," she said as Breen wrapped her arms around both of them. "I want spring, and the light, and the blooms, and the promise. Ah, fuck me, I've lost my mind and I'll be a farmer's wife."

"You're perfect for each other. Just perfect," Breen exclaimed. "And you're right about spring, because that's hope and promise, and it's a sharp stick in Odran's ugly eye."

"I nearly went mad waiting to tell you. When I told Nan and Grandda, Grandda went straight to the farm, claiming he was going to grill Harken like a trout over keeping me happy. Which he didn't, of course, as he loves Harken like his own. Nan cried, then flew into a flurry of talk about dresses and flowers and such, and now is in the mirror with my ma, or they're sending falcons winging back and forth with plans. And I'll leave all that to them, as they've earned it, and will be better at it than I could be."

She took a breath. "Now I'm babbling, but I want to say if either of you, who'd be better as well, want to put your thoughts into it, you're welcome to. And with tradition, when we wed, you have a friend or friends stand with you when you make your promise and join your lives. So you will, won't you?" she said to Breen. "My oldest friend, and you, Marco, as Breen made you mine and me yours. You'll both stand with me?"

"Of course we will."

"I'm going to get these drinks before I start blubbering

like a baby." Marco swiped tears away. "And screw the orange juice."

That evening, Breen took her laptop to her room. She could work while giving Marco and Brian—if and when he came—some privacy. And she could work on her second Bollocks book, something happy to help her hold on to all the good feelings of the day.

Maybe Keegan would come. She'd feel steadier if she saw him, if she heard directly from him. In her talks with Marg she understood they had doubts now the portal existed. Days of searching had given them no sign or sense of it.

Or a tree of snakes.

She didn't know what that meant, only that the phrase had come so clearly, so definitely, it had to mean something.

Unless it didn't.

She'd tried seeing in the fire, tried seeing in the globe, but nothing came.

Unrelenting rain in the east made the search more difficult, and no doubt slowed it. But Marg had told her the rain had moved out to sea that evening, and the next day promised clear.

She wondered if she should go to the Capital, if she could help. And wondered if waiting to be asked—or ordered—was weakness or strength.

Either way, she'd go to Talamh the next day, and practice in her grandmother's workshop. She'd ask Morena or Harken to help her with her training.

And prepare herself for whatever came.

But now she'd write, and she'd wait.

She wrote until late, until the house fell silent and sleeping. Then she threw on a robe, pulled on boots to take Bollocks out for his last round of the night while the pixies fluttered their points of light in the dark.

With Bollocks settled in front of the fire, she settled

herself into bed. She'd work on his book more in the morning, but go to Talamh earlier than usual. She'd take a ride with Marco—stop by Finola's to talk wedding plans—and she'd call Lonrach to give them both the pleasure of a flight. She'd work on her training—both magickal and physical.

She would fill the day, but if nothing changed, she'd ask Harken to let her use Keegan's mirror. He'd just have to find time to talk with her, and accept she needed to go to the Capital and help with the search.

"Tree of snakes," she muttered as she turned off the light. Why would she know it if it meant nothing?

Maybe in the workshop, with her grandmother's magicks all around, she'd find the answers.

Tomorrow, she thought, and drifted into sleep.

When the dream came, it came soft and lovely with a sky of heartbreaking blue. Through the field a stream burbled, and along its banks grew the violet paws of foxglove, the elegant trumpets of columbine, the starry flowers of wild thyme. Butterflies fluttered, birds sang as she walked with Keegan.

"It's all so beautiful."

"Peace." He lifted her hand to his lips. "There's nothing more beautiful. We'll have it, and thousands times thousands of days like this."

"I'm glad you came. I missed seeing you, talking to you. Did you find the portal?"

"We won't talk of such things now. We have this. We have the quiet. We both like the quiet moments."

"We do. I guess that's something we have in common." She smiled when he bent down and picked a buttercup to tuck behind her ear. "You don't get many of them, the quiet moments."

"I could have more if I abjured the staff, if I sent the sword back into the lake."

"You wouldn't. Couldn't."

"Would you have me fight every day of my life, suffer the weight of passing judgment on others?" He turned her toward him. "Or would you have me be with you? Go to your world with you and make it mine?"

"You can't—"

He drew her in. "Can you tell me you don't wish me to choose you over all else? As no one has before? Even your father, in the end, chose Talamh. Chose the sword, its power."

"Duty, not power," she began, but he laid his lips on hers. She felt dizzy from the kiss.

"He could have passed the duties to another and stayed with you." Eyes on hers, he brought her hand to his lips, pressed them to her palm. "You weren't enough for him."

"That's not true. Keegan—"

"I would choose you over Talamh." He pressed his lips to her wrist, had her pulse pounding. To her throat, so the beat doubled. "Ask me."

Weak with want, she nearly did. "I can't."

"If you love me, tell me. Tell me I must choose you." His hands roamed over her; his lips grew hot and urgent. "We'll have peace, and quiet moments. You will be all to me. Tell me! Demand it!"

"If I loved you, I couldn't. If I loved you, it's what and who you are I love. Stop. You're hurting me now."

"I hurt you?" He shoved her back, and the rage on his face had her heart flying to her throat. "What do you do to me with this weak mewling? Would you have me fight against a god for a meadow of flowers? Would you have me die by his hand? Do you wish this for me?"

He swept his hands down his body. Blood poured from his chest, down his arms, dripped from his fingers.

"No. Stop. Let me help." She leaped to him, trying to find the wounds, to heal them.

"My blood is on your hands. Remember this, pathetic child of the Fey. You killed me."

The dark dropped, and he was gone. She stood alone with his blood still warm and wet on her hands.

Alone, but not in the sun-drenched meadow. Now she stood in a forest so thick it felt as though the trees pressed in against her. A thousand heartbeats roared in her head. Terrified, raging, grieving.

Before her stood a tree, black as pitch, its branches gnarled and coiled. Its roots dug into the ground that held no life, as the tree had smothered its breath, its beat.

As she watched, as she understood she stood before the dark mirror image of the Welcoming Tree, those coiled branches began to move, to slither.

To hiss.

"No." She pushed back at it with all she had. "You won't come through."

But she heard the screams, the clash and thunder of battle.

They had come.

So she ran, with no weapon but herself, toward the sounds of war. She tossed light ahead, gasping when she saw blood on the path. And the dead scattered among the trees.

She couldn't save them, so she ran to save others.

But when she came through the forest, the castle burned. Flames ate their way over the bridges, and the river boiled beneath them.

Cróga, his emerald and gold scales smeared with blood and ash, lay dead on the scorched earth.

Screaming in grief, in horror, she dropped down beside him.

Odran walked toward her, the sword in one hand, the staff in the other.

And the power swirling around him, through him, spoke of death.

"Rider and dragon, dead. Hear the screams, *iníon*? Hear how they cry out, how they beg, how they curse the day you were born? Soon, the Fey will be no more, and the world is mine. Talamh has fallen because you did nothing."

He laughed, his black robes billowing as he walked toward her. His gold hair flew around his face, and the gray of his eyes went to red-rimmed black. "Your blood is my blood. Your power is my power. Now come, and let me drink."

She woke with a scream strangling in her throat, and Bollocks on the bed, nosing at her, whining.

She started to wrap her arms around him to comfort them both, but in the dim light, the dawn light, saw the blood on her hands.

"Oh God, my God." Horrified, she shoved out of bed to race to the bathroom, scrub it away. She felt dizzy and ill, had to brace her hands on the bathroom counter to fight off the vicious churn of nausea.

"Not just a dream. A portent? Was it him or was it me?"

She looked up into the mirror at her face—sheet white, clammy with sweat.

Terrified.

"It doesn't matter."

She rushed back into the bedroom and to the globe. "Show me Talamh, as it is now, at this moment. Show me the Capital, and beyond."

What she saw was dawn breaking, and the castle standing quiet and whole, its banner flying against the first hints of light.

She saw dragons in the air, and fields. Sheep and cows and horses, smoke curling from chimneys.

"That wasn't now. If it hasn't happened, there's time to stop it."

She grabbed clothes, dressing quickly—leggings, sweater, boots. She didn't have a sword at the cottage, but reached for her wand, her athame. No weapon but herself, really, so she'd have to be enough.

She sprinted down the hall, rapped hard on Marco's door three times, then just shoved it open.

"Breen, what the fuck!" When he shoved up in bed, alone,

she saw she was too late to borrow Brian's sword or take him with her.

"I have to go. I have to go right now, to the Capital."

"What? Why? What?" He shook his head as if to clear it. "Jesus, coffee."

"I don't have time, I don't know how much time there is. I need you to stay here. Don't go to Talamh today. Don't go until I get back."

If she came back.

"Keep Bollocks. I have to go now."

When she ran for the stairs, Bollocks ran ahead of her. "No, you have to stay with Marco. You stay!"

She grabbed a jacket on the way out, shoved her arms through. As she'd already called Lonrach, he waited for her outside. Even as she yanked the door open, Marco came flying down the stairs in nothing but his Baby Yoda boxers.

"What the actual fuck, Breen."

"I don't have time. I have to go. Stay here, promise me. I have to go or they'll die. He's coming."

"You go, I go. Give me two minutes to get some clothes on."

"Stay here." When he grabbed her arm, she flicked him off with a little buzz of power.

"Don't you pull that crap on me!"

He ran after her, but she mounted the dragon where Bollocks already sat.

"Get down! Stay with Marco."

The dog just stared at her with eyes of stubborn steel.

"Damn it. I'm taking him. Stay here, Marco."

The dragon rose up, soared over the trees.

"The hell with that." Marco slammed the door, stormed upstairs to dress.

She wasn't sure she knew the way, but trusted Lonrach did. Beneath her, Talamh began to wake. Lamps glowed in cottages where mothers stirred the children to dress for breakfast and chores before school. Farmers herded cows for the morning milkings. Night guards settled down to sleep, and those like Brian manned their posts.

It would not end today, she promised herself. Odran would not come through. He wouldn't win.

She wondered if she should have tried the portal in the Far West, but calculated by the time she explained herself, tried to open it, risked using it, she could be halfway to the Capital.

She knew the tree of snakes now, and where to find it in the forest. It seemed impossible they'd searched for days and hadn't found it, but she'd take them to it.

With Keegan, Nan, Sedric, she thought, with all that power, they'd lock it down.

She didn't want to think about the first part of the dream, or the longing she'd felt, the war between it and duty. Did she actually wish Keegan would give everything up and come with her? Did she have that much of her mother in her?

"No. No. No. That's not me. It was just a way to help me see the rest. It was night in the forest. I saw the moons when I came out, so it was night. We have time to stop it."

She flew toward the rising sun.

Since the bloody rain had finally stopped, Keegan decided to stay with the search for the first few hours of the morning before beginning the laborious travel to the other portals. To check on the guards, see they remained alert.

And maybe, with the gloom lifted, they'd find this shagging tree of snakes Breen had told Sedric to look for.

Following his thoughts, Tarryn shrugged. "Portents, as we know, are tricky matters. It may be a symbol of some sort, or literal and on the other side, or we've simply yet to find it."

"We've covered nearly every inch."

"But not every. If we don't find success today, you should go to her tonight. And bring her with you tomorrow. She may be what we're missing."

He looked around. Trees, he thought, full of squirrels

and birds. He could hear the drum of a woodpecker after its breakfast, and the rustle of a fox or rabbit after theirs.

"I'm thinking I'll go now. If she is what we're missing, we shouldn't waste another day. I felt it best to leave her where she is. I'm not sure altogether why, but I felt it best. But now—"

He broke off, looked up. "A dragon and rider, coming fast. Cróga sees them, and wants me to . . . Bloody hell, I told her to stay."

"Breen?"

"Aye, and I told her to stay in the valley, or the cottage."

"You were about to go get her, so this saves you time."

"I told her to stay," he repeated as the shadow of the dragon covered them. With the trees too thick to allow him to land, he glided on.

"I'll get her."

"Don't send her back again because you're pissed off," his mother called after him.

Knowing he'd been tempted to do just that, he kept going. The dog reached him first, but Breen—fleet of foot indeed—came close behind.

"I had to come." Though she knew better, seeing him whole, alive, unharmed had her throwing her arms around him in relief. "You were dead, in the dream. You were dead, and your blood all over my hands."

"For the love of the gods, woman, you don't fly across the world because of a hard dream, and when I told you to stay behind."

"It wasn't just a hard dream." She jerked back. "There was blood on my hands when I woke up, and that wasn't the worst part of it. He got through. I was too late, we were too late, and he got through. And . . . do you remember the vision before, the dream I pulled you into when you tried to pull me out?"

"Aye."

"Like that. The castle burning, death everywhere. And Odran, holding your sword, your staff."

"My sword's at my side." But he brushed a hand over her hair. "My staff's where I left it."

"For now. He'll come through if we don't stop him. If I don't do anything. He said this world was his because I did nothing. There was blood on my hands, Keegan."

"All right." He kissed her absently on the brow as he thought it through. "All right now. I was coming to bring you anyway."

"You found it?"

"No, and there's the problem."

"It's not, because I know where it is. I saw it. I saw the tree in the dream, and I know where it is."

"Show me."

"It's not far."

"We've covered all the not far."

"I can't help it." She grabbed his hand, started down the path she'd seen soaked with blood.

Keegan gave a whistle, and seconds later an elf raced up. "Fetch all the others and find us."

Dread filled her, threatened to block out everything else. "I ran this path after the tree started to move."

"Move?"

"Snakes, forming its branches, its trunk. I ran because I heard the screaming, and the battle. That way." She veered left. "We—you and I—were in the sunlight first. A field, flowers, so beautiful. But you said things you wouldn't have said, wanted me to say things I wouldn't. Then you were covered in blood."

"What things?"

"Later. It's this way."

His mother came first, guided by another elf who whisked off again. Tarryn said nothing as Breen continued on.

When the path narrowed to a gutted track and forked, Breen pointed.

"There."

"I see a tree right enough, and a good-sized one, but nothing resembling snakes. And we've covered this ground."

"There," she said again. "It hides and waits and holds its breath. No bird will nest in it, no creature burrow. Its leaves are false when summer comes, another mask, for nothing grows on it or from it. It eats light and life when it can, in secret, as it guards the door to hell."

She let out a breath. "It didn't look like this in the dream, but it's an illusion. Dark magicks are cloaking it, and blocking the light from seeing or sensing. But I can feel."

She started to hold out a hand, but Tarryn stopped her. "Wait for the others. If it's this strong, we'll want the others."

"He made this, conjured this, created this, so he could come and go as he pleased, take what he wanted. But it took more, powers dimming, and more, powers draining. So he needed a child. He made them, but they weren't enough. Until my father."

She turned to Keegan. "I know it. I don't know how, but I know it. And I know he hasn't been able to open it again. Not since he killed my father. It takes so much, more and more, so he's tried other ways."

An elf raced back, a silver cat on her shoulders. The cat leaped off, and Sedric stood studying the tree. "This?" At Breen's nod, he rubbed her shoulder. "I don't feel it. I'm sorry. Let me move closer."

"Not yet," Tarryn said. "And I think it must be Breen to break the illusion."

Marg came in the arms of a faerie, then Loren, then the others who'd spread out through the forest.

"I think the portal's in it—or it is the portal. Like the Welcoming Tree, but its antithesis."

"Aye," Keegan agreed. "I think you've the right of that.

Illusion or no, we seal it. Destroying it, while satisfying, may rip it open, so we seal it."

"Without seeing or feeling, how will we know?" Marg asked.

"We cast the circle and begin. We close it off from Talamh."

Beside Breen, Bollocks growled low, and she felt herself drift.

"Don't you see it?" She saw it go black, saw the branches coil and begin to slither. "It's swallowing the light."

She threw up a hand and, as she swayed, as Keegan caught her, she stood on the other side with the black castle looming.

"So valiant." Odran laughed. "The key, they say, but not just for them. Your father's blood closed it. And yours opens it. Blood on your hands."

He swiped the blade of a knife over her outstretched palm.

She held it up as Keegan steadied her, showed him the blood.

"He's coming."

# CHAPTER THIRTY

The tree bled. Black streams of blood sizzled down its trunk and carved through to smoke. As the smoke, fetid with sulfur, eked out, Keegan raised his sword.

He turned to the elf beside him. "Go."

She blurred away while, dazed, Breen stared at her bloody hand.

Marg gripped it, and that sudden fresh shock of pain brought Breen back. "Fight. He won't take you, he won't have you, but you have to fight."

Dark drove out behind the smoke. As the cracks lengthened, claws gripped the edges, pulling them wider. A head pushed through, black eyes rolling, long teeth snapping. Keegan severed it, but more cracks opened, breaking the rough bark like a shattered mirror.

The dark pouring out sucked at the light.

With a long sword, Sedric impaled a demon dog as it leaped through, and even as its body writhed on the ground, more came. On a feral snarl Bollocks charged. Breen saw him latch on to the throat of a demon before they rolled away, lost in the smoke.

She threw out power, more from instinct than purpose as the light died to dusk, and they came and came.

So many, too many, crawling, clawing, leaping through the widening portal.

As she stood frozen, Phelin shoved her away from the diamond-point antlers of a black stag. "Defend," he told her as he destroyed it. "Yourself and all."

He took wing, shooting up to send a dark faerie plummeting to the ground. When it landed at her feet, Breen stumbled back. Bleeding, one wing gone, it gained its feet to come at her.

Marg drenched it in flames.

"Fight!" she snapped, then turned to slash her short sword at an oncoming elf.

But she could barely see Keegan, splashed with blood, battling with sword and magicks as more flooded through the portal, and his mother, fighting back-to-back with him.

Then Bollocks ran to her through the smoke, his muzzle bloodied, his eyes fierce and feral.

And he felt, she felt.

*Fight. Defend. Destroy.*

When he leaped at the demon charging her, putting himself between her and the sword, rage replaced fear.

Breen enflamed the sword and the demon with it.

As the smoke thickened, it seemed she fought alone, furious and desperate, enraged and terrified. Surrounded by enemies, by shrieks and screams, all but smothered by the stench of smoke and death, she hurled everything she had.

*Fight. Defend. Destroy.*

She turned a scrabbling gargoyle to dust with her wand, slapped burning power at a demon with wings like a bat so it screamed and burned.

It was nothing like watching a battle in the fire, nothing like fighting wraiths on the training field. She was no observer here, and the consequences would be more than bumps and bruises.

She fought for survival, for the world of her birth and all beyond it. She fought, even knowing they were too vastly outnumbered to win.

Then in a rush, others came to fight with her. Led by the swift elves, followed by faeries and riders, more Wise spinning light through the smoke, they charged into the forest.

Through the terrible noise of war, she heard Keegan's shouted orders.

Arrows whizzed by her, and though two of the enemy drove her back, attacking with power, with fang, her training held. A vicious swipe of called wind shot them both away from her. When she stumbled over a body, she blocked out the horror and took the sword from the dead hand.

Beside her, a tree exploded, a flaming red bomb that sent shrapnel flying. A limb, sharp as a spear, impaled the wizard who'd ignited it, and impaled him, writhing, to the ground.

Bollocks streaked up to her, snagged a gargoyle in his teeth, and shook it like a rag doll. He heaved it aside, took on another as she cleaved the third in two with the sword.

Through the haze, Loren fought his way to her. Soot smeared his hair, his face, and blood—from his own wounds and from others—stained his doublet.

"We're to fall back," he shouted. "I'll get you safely away."

"I have to fight." *Fight, defend, destroy* sounded like a drumbeat in her head.

"And you'll fight. But some have broken through the line to the east and the castle. Keegan wants . . . Shana, don't!"

He shoved Breen back as Shana broke out of a tree and struck out with a knife. Its jeweled hilt glinted in the dim light as she drove it into Loren.

And laughed. "Oops, missed! You got in my way."

He said only, "Shana."

As he fell, as his sword clattered to the ground, he took Breen down with him. The hard fall cost Breen an instant, only an instant. But when she gathered herself to lash out, Shana blurred away.

Breen shoved up to her knees, pressed a hand on the wound and the blood spreading over Loren's chest.

"I can help."

But he gripped her wrist. "Poisoned, dark magicks. Too late." A bloody froth foamed between his lips, and all she read in his eyes was sorrow. "I loved her, but I couldn't save her."

He died on the edge of the forest where the dark and the light clashed.

She wanted to weep, just weep and weep, but she made herself get up and push through to the light.

The castle didn't burn, nor did the bridges, but the battle raged here, too. She lifted the sword, drew her power up. Whatever it took, she'd give.

Then whirled back when she felt the change in the air.

Yseult stood, her two-headed snakes coiled around her waist like a belt. Instinctively, Breen flung out light. Yseult met it with dark, so the opposing powers slapped, shot sparks, then merged into smoke.

Fog, silent, stealthy, crawled over the ground toward Breen. Heart pounding—but not with fear, no, not with fear this time—Breen burned it away.

"You used that trick before. It won't work anymore."

"Learned a few things, have you now?" Tossing her hair, Yseult began to circle. "And you think it's enough? That you're enough? You were created by Odran for Odran. That is your destiny."

"No." Eyes on Yseult, Breen reached deep for power. The sounds of the battle smothered into silence, and they stood alone. That, she knew, was Yseult's illusion. "My destiny is to stop him. But I'll start with you."

"Such confidence! Such spirit." Yseult flicked out. Breen felt the sting, like the bite of an angry wasp, on her cheek, but continued to reach. And wait.

"Why don't you show me what you think you have? You've never been enough, and won't be no matter what they tell you in their pitiful attempts to use you."

Once again, Breen burned away the fog. "Then why do you keep trying to drug me?"

"Only to make it less painful for you, my sweet. I promised Marg I would lessen your pain right before I killed her. It's all she asked of me."

Her world wobbled. "You're lying."

"She fought bravely, but in her worry for you, not well. Nor did the one she took after Odran to share her cold and righteous bed."

"I don't believe you."

"Sure and you do. A cat's a sly thing, and it's said has nine lives. Well, this one used his last today. Gone now, they are, and the dogs feast on what's left of your taoiseach. All dead and dying because of you. Take my hand now, and come with me, and Odran may spare the rest."

It emptied her as the fog crawled closer, as Yseult held out a hand, as the snakes at her waist showed their fangs and hissed.

And it filled her, not with the cold, calculating power she'd sought, but volcanic rage.

"Go back to hell, and tell Odran I'll send him after you."

Not fire, not this time. Her fury burned too hot for mere flames. It shot out in bolts and daggers of hot, searing light. The fog folded in on itself and, scorching the ground, advanced toward Yseult, as did Breen.

Screaming in shock, in pain, Yseult called the wind to deflect the barbs, but they tore through and ripped into her flesh.

"I'll end you," Breen vowed. "I owe you a painful, terrible end."

Eyes wild, bleeding from dozens of tiny wounds, Yseult swirled fog around her.

When Breen shredded it, she was gone.

"I will end you," she said again, and, riding on rage, ran out of the forest to fight.

Two faeries charged her. She took the female first, as she looked stronger, and fisting her hand, Breen crushed her wings like paper. It gave the male just enough time to grab her arm, prepare for flight, before she turned the sword and jabbed backward, and into him.

But more came, and more, and even in her rage and fury she knew she wouldn't be enough.

Roars sounded from above. Dragons and riders streaked across the sky from the west, and faeries flew in like a storm cloud behind them. Wings spread, Morena leaped off from behind Harken and, sword slashing, landed beside Breen.

"Alone?" She snarled it as she impaled an elf.

"There wasn't time. Oh my God, Marco!"

She saw him riding with Brian as the dragon spewed a line of fire over the enemy.

"We have to drive them back!" Morena shouted. "Back through the portal."

The battle raged in the air as it did on the ground. Wings burned, and the wounded and dead dropped like stones from the sky.

"I don't know where it is. You have to lead the way. Harken can deal with this. He'll drive them back," Morena said, "and so will we."

So they fought their way back, through the smoke and the stench, over the bodies and the blood. Breen sensed Bollocks—always close. And alive. She called Lonrach so he'd join the other dragons, and with Morena and fresh warriors, drove the enemy back.

Some ran back through or dived or flew, others crawled,

howling from wounds. From the other side where the dark pulsed, she heard screams, but she ignored them.

Marg stood, alive, whole, with Tarryn, hands clasped as they worked to spread light, to close the portal, to seal the cracks.

Once again she wanted to weep, just weep, but she ran to them, gripped Marg's hand, and joined power.

And that merged power flexed its muscles. Fighting still whirled around them as more and more of the enemy broke ranks to rush back through, but the three women stood focused and unwavering.

Bollocks charged, dragging a wounded dog back and finishing him, and Breen pulled up light, spread it.

It burned, like dragon breath, so some went to flame in the retreat. Where the dark had swallowed the light, now light pulsed, a thousand hearts to close off the dark.

She heard Sedric call out. "We've broken them. You, you, you, guard the three. The rest, go after the stragglers."

Alive, she thought. Alive. Yseult was made of lies.

She wouldn't think of Keegan yet, couldn't.

She still needed the rage—cold now, deliberate now—to find more, to find enough to close the portal and the dark beyond it.

All we are, she thought, all we have. And gave a last hard push.

The portal snapped shut, cutting the demon who tried to climb through in two.

"Closed," Tarryn said. "It must be sealed."

"My father's blood closed it, Odran said, and mine opened it. But . . . he had to pull some part of me to the other side to use it."

She looked down at her palm. She'd healed it so she could use the sword. "Can I seal it from this side?" She looked to Marg.

"Aye. In the light, and given freely."

Breen held out her hands. "You should do it. My blood and my power come down from you."

"*Mo stór.*" Marg took Breen's hands, kissed them. Then, taking the athame from her belt, scored both palms. Then both of her own.

"From mine to his, from his to yours." She pressed her palms to Breen's. "A gift clean and bright."

Breen took it, stepped to the tree, pressed her palms against it. "The light given me outshines the dark. Upon this door I place my mark. What my blood opened it closes tight, it seals with light. Through the power given me, as I will, so mote it be."

She felt it pass through her, and felt with her hands on the portal, with her blood seeping into it, the black rage on the other side.

"Beat your fists," she muttered. "Do your worst. You won't use me again."

Then it drained, it all drained, and she turned to throw her arms around Marg. "She told me she'd killed you. Yseult. You and Sedric and Keegan. I thought you were all dead."

"Oh, no, no, my sweet girl. She lied to hurt you, to weaken you."

"She hurt me, but made me stronger." She held tight. Tighter. "I hurt her, Nan. But I didn't kill her. I swore I'd end her, and I will. I heard Sedric after, so I know he's alive. Keegan?"

She looked over Marg's shoulder to Tarryn.

"He called Cróga only moments before you arrived to join the other dragons and riders. To join his brother. They'll hunt down any who lived and remain in Talamh. So."

She took Breen's hands, gently healed the cuts. "While they do their work, we'll finish ours." Then she drew Breen in, held her. "Your father is proud of you today."

"You loved him," Breen stated. "I feel it."

"I did. Now." She drew back. "We cast the circle, we salt the earth, and this evil thing will never hide what it is again."

It left her shaken. She trembled inside, as she'd learned what she would do, could do. Take lives, and more, with a terrible fury. She trembled inside, knowing she'd do it again when she had to.

So when she came out of the forest with Bollocks at last, started to cross the ground still blood-soaked and scorched, and saw Marco standing beside the dragon with Brian, the weeping she'd held off burst free.

He rushed to her, folded her in, rocked, swayed, and just said her name over and over.

"You were supposed to stay at the cottage." She pressed her face against his shoulder. "I told you to stay at the cottage."

"Hey, you're not the boss of me. Well, you sort of are, but not about everything. Not about taking care of my best girl."

"You rode on a dragon."

"Yeah, and that's not something I want to do again anytime soon."

"Ah now, you'll learn to love it." Brian clapped Marco on the shoulder as he kissed the top of Breen's head. "He wouldn't stay behind, and if I'd left him there, how could he ever forgive me? And how could I ask him to?"

"You came." She turned her head on Marco's shoulder to meet Brian's eyes. "You and all the others from the valley."

"Marco went straight to Harken, and between him and Morena, they gathered enough of us, left enough behind to keep the valley secured if needed. Now we think we've dealt with all the stragglers, but I'm to do another pass."

"Good luck with that," Marco told him, and shifted Breen to draw Brian in for a kiss. "I'm staying down here on solid ground."

"You'll learn to love it," Brian said again, and mounted. Then flew.

"I love you, Marco, and enough I'd put you in a happy trance so we could fly home, but as much as I want to be there, I don't think I can leave yet. I need to talk to Keegan. Need to see him. And I want the longest, hottest shower in the history of long, hot showers. Maybe a gallon of wine just to dull the images in my head right now. I killed, Marco. I know they were evil, and it's war, but I killed."

"So did I." Emotion that mirrored hers swam into his eyes. "Three Sidhe. One was a girl. I mean female. I never thought I could, but I did. I'm not sorry, but I feel a little sick inside."

"Let's go sit down somewhere and just breathe. And let Bollocks swim. He—he killed, too. The sweetest dog in the world—in any world—killed to protect me and others. And—and they hurt him." Tears welled up again. "He had cuts and gouges."

"Oh man." Marco crouched to stroke his hands over Bollocks. "Is he okay? I don't see anything."

"I fixed it, and I took him to a stream so he could wash off the blood. I couldn't stand seeing the blood on him. And you, you weren't hurt?"

"Not a scratch. Were you?"

"Nothing much. Let's just sit down somewhere quiet for a minute."

"Breen." He took her shoulders. "I need to tell you about Morena."

"Oh God, no, is she hurt?"

"It's not her. It's her brother. Phelin. It's Phelin."

"He's hurt? Where is he? I could help."

"No, baby, you can't help."

She stared, then it struck, then it sank in. "No, no, no. I saw him fighting. I saw him right at the beginning."

She'd sent frogs after him once, long ago. She'd danced with him at the Welcome. She'd met his wife. He'd talked about becoming a father.

"Where is she? Where's Morena?"

"She went to tell her parents, her family." Marco brushed tears from her cheeks, and from his own. "She's going to need you, but she's with her family. Harken, he had to tell her. He took out the one who killed Phelin, but he had to tell her."

"All this, so many dead, over me."

"Breen."

"I don't mean it's my fault. I know better, especially now. But Odran used me, Marco. He used me, and Morena lost her brother. There'll be other Leavings. There'll be children whose mother or father doesn't come home again. I'm not going to feel sick inside anymore about what I did today."

She turned to him. "If I begged you to go home, back to Philadelphia, you wouldn't."

"Not a chance."

"I'm afraid for you, Marco."

"That's mutual, me for you, so we stick together." Eyes on hers, he gripped her hand, linked their fingers. "Like always."

She took a breath. "It would've been worse, more would have died, if you'd listened to me this morning. So, okay, I'm going to try to stop. It won't be easy, but I'm going to try. We stick together."

"Except for now. Keegan." He pointed out. "Looks like he's coming down, and you guys need to talk. I'm going to go see if I've still got a room in the castle."

He gave her a hard kiss, then left her.

Cróga glided down. When Keegan dismounted, she wondered if she looked anything like him. Blood on her face, her clothes. Were her eyes that exhausted?

They stood a moment, a dozen feet apart while the sea breeze blew away most of the battle stink. She wasn't sure what to say to him, how to begin, but when he started toward her, she met him halfway.

"Are you hurt?" he asked her.

She shook her head. "Are you?"

"Nothing. No."

But she knew, felt, some of the blood he wore was his own.

"I didn't protect you. They separated us, and I couldn't protect you."

"You trained me to fight. With a sword, with my fists, with my power. And I did. It's not like the training field. You tried to teach me that, too, but I didn't know." Her throat clogged; her eyes welled. "I didn't know. Now I do."

"Don't cry, I beg you. Your tears would break me."

"I came to help—the dream, the portal. But he wanted me to come. He needed me to, to use me to open it. And I didn't see that."

"How could you? None of us did. His tactics, his strategy, all very well planned out for this. To make us believe he'd use the falls for his way in, while he worked here. But we turned that on him, and had troops massed here."

He looked away, back toward the woods. "Not enough, not for the ambush, not without Harken bringing more. We'd seal it, I thought, find it, seal it, and wouldn't that fuck his fucking plans."

"And I opened it."

"The fault's not yours."

"No, it's not, and not yours. It's his. Phelin died." The tears wanted to come again. "Morena—"

"I know it." Closing his eyes a moment, he scrubbed his hands over his face. "He was a friend, a friend since childhood. I don't know all we lost as yet."

But he would, Breen thought. He'd know all the names, speak to all the families, and lead another Leaving.

"Loren." At his nod, she continued. "You don't know how. I was there. It was Shana."

"Ah, gods."

"You need to know. He stepped between her and me. I think, I believe, to try to save both of us. And he took the knife she intended for me. He said it was poisoned, and I couldn't heal him. Keegan, it happened so fast, and I couldn't . . . She laughed, and there was something different about her. In her."

"She's Odran's now. But he couldn't have wanted you dead, so the knife and the poison, that was hers."

"I killed today." She said it flatly, and drew his gaze back to hers. "I'll never be exactly the same because of that."

"I'm sorry for it."

"Don't be. I know who I am now. I fought for Talamh today, and for you, for myself, my father. When Yseult told me—"

"Yseult?" He touched her for the first time, gripping a hand on her arm.

"Didn't your mother tell you?"

"There wasn't time for talk. I know she's well, and she with you and Marg closed and sealed the portal. But I . . . I had to see you for myself, so there wasn't time for talk."

"She found me—or lured me away enough, I don't know. She tried the fog trick again." Breen's eyes hardened. "It didn't work. She told me I'd caused all this. I didn't," she said when Keegan started to speak. "And she told me Nan and Sedric were dead. That you were dead. I said I didn't believe her, but part of me did. I believed her, and I hurt her. I should've killed her quickly, but I didn't want quick. I wanted her pain. She used the fog to get away because I didn't want quick."

"Wait." He cupped her face now to keep her gaze on his. "She had you alone, and she ran from you?"

"Screaming. Shrieking, really. And bleeding. A thousand

barbs, that's what came into my head. Or not my head, I don't know where it came from."

"She's as powerful as any I've known, and surely more since she chose Odran. And she ran from you. I took you to your dragon because you'd become. But it's today, in full, in truth, you've become."

"I'll kill her before it's done."

With a sigh, he lowered his forehead to hers. "I find I don't want this for you. I know it must be, but I find I wish it wasn't."

"I was born for this."

"And so much more, *mo bandia*."

"He'll find another way. Odran. He'll find another way through, sooner or later."

"Aye, until he's destroyed, he'll keep finding a way. But ask yourself this. Why didn't he come through this day? So many of his demons and warriors came through. Even Shana. He sent Yseult through, and with one purpose I see. To bring you back to him. He didn't come through and take you or try. Why?"

"I hadn't thought of it." So much blurred, she thought, with so many moments of clear-cut clarity. But she hadn't thought of that.

"You've a brain in there." He tapped a fist lightly to her head. "And a fine one at that. So think of it. We were taken by surprise, and outnumbered. Even with the warriors waiting for a signal, we were at a disadvantage until Harken brought the valley warriors. Shana found you. Yseult found you. Why didn't he?"

"He can't come through?" Her eyes narrowed as she turned the question into a statement. "He can't come through, not yet. He doesn't have enough power to come through again."

"The gods banished him to that world, and it took centuries for him to build enough power, to drink enough to pass through to Talamh. And what did he do?"

"Made a child—my father. To drain the power from his son because he didn't have enough to take the world, to take Tal-amh. Nan stopped him, and it took him years more to come for me. He sends others through to steal children, young Fey, for sacrifices, for more power. But it's not enough."

"And won't be, I'm thinking. He's a god in that world, but in this? There are weaknesses and risk."

"He's a coward." When it struck her, she gripped Keegan's bloody shirt. "He's a goddamn coward. Stealing and kill-ing children, lording it over a bunch of ugly, asshole demons and—and wingnuts."

"Wingnuts? Faeries?"

"No, I mean extremists. People who choose to belong to some insane, twisted cult because somehow it makes them feel good, feel superior."

She gave him a little shake, paced away, paced back while Bollocks stayed stretched out on the ground and watched her with adoring eyes.

"I've been a coward, so I know beating one isn't just pos-sible. It's probable. If he thinks he won something today, he's wrong. He's just one more step closer to losing."

"I didn't think I'd smile today," Keegan told her. "But here you are."

She stopped in front of him. "I need more training."

"You do, aye. And you'll get it. Sure I think I won't find it so easy to knock you down so often as before."

"I killed today."

"Ah, Breen."

"I killed wicked, evil things today, and I'm fine with that. This?" She held up her arm, turned her wrist to show him her tattoo. "*Misneach*. Courage. That's not just a wish anymore. It hasn't been just a wish for months now. So you'll train me to kill wicked, evil things, and you and Nan will help me learn how to use magicks as a weapon against them."

"I think Yseult would say you've learned that well already."

"I wanted to hurt her as much as kill her, and that was a mistake. I took a sword from a body and used it. You wouldn't have liked my form, but I used it. You'll teach me to use it better."

Giving in to what he'd wanted since he'd seen her standing in the field, he brought her wrist to his lips. "That may be beyond my skills."

"Maybe I'll surprise you."

"You do, every day. If I kiss you here and now, I may never stop."

"I'm all right with that."

He drew her in, brushing a hand over her hair, hair full of hellsmoke but still bright as a flame. He touched his lips to hers gently, once, twice. Then yielded to need, to her, and poured everything, the relief, the longing, the hope, into the kiss.

She locked around him in the light, and answered everything.

"Can we stay here like this?" She pressed her face to his shoulder. "Just for a minute. I want, so much, to go home. The valley, the cottage, so if we could stay like this for a minute. I have to stay for Morena, her family. For the Leaving. I need to be here for Finola and Seamus when they come. I need to help you do all the sad, hard things you have to do."

Murmuring, murmuring in Talamhish, he buried his face in her hair.

"And I need to learn the language so I know what you mutter at me, or shout at me."

"I wish you wouldn't as yet. If you'd come with me to Phelin's family, you'd be a comfort to them. And to all who'd see you at the Leaving, you'd be strength and comfort, and hope."

Nodding, she eased back. "I'm going to need a room."

He kissed her again, lightly. "Share mine."

He took her hand, so they walked toward the castle where dragons circled. They walked back to do all the hard and sad things.

And Bollocks trotted beside them.

# EPILOGUE

On the other side of the portal, where a storm raged because he willed it, Odran stood over Yseult.

She suffered, lying in the soft bed he'd gifted her. He could end that suffering—kill her or cure her—but he found her misery a small pleasure on a day of disappointments.

"You failed me, yet again."

Her eyes, glassy with pain, looked up at him. She wouldn't beg, and he respected her for it. And still, a day of disappointments.

"You bleed, soiling the bed. Why do you not heal yourself?"

"Some of the barbs are too deep. The pain is great, and dulls my powers."

Lightning struck outside. Something screamed.

"I could end your pain, and use your witch's blood to enhance my own."

"If that is your will, my king, my liege, my all."

"Can I have her jewelry?" Shana held up one of Yseult's pendants, posed with it in a mirror. "She won't need it if she's dead." Beaming, she swirled around. "I killed a witch today, one who loved me. A powerful alchemist. It's more than she did."

Odran barely spared Shana a glance. "She opened the portal, you merely went through. Leave us now."

"To your chambers or mine?"

"Mine."

Shana sent Yseult a sparkling look before she glided out.

"I fear, my king, she is more than half mad."

"And fertile. Already she carries a child for me, so she has her uses. I wonder about yours." He walked to the window to watch the storm. "All the time, the blood, the work to open the portal, only to fail to bring her through, to have them close it again."

"There are other ways through."

"And so the mad elf has her uses." He turned back. "But do you? Do you, scarred and bloody, weak and writhing? Defeated by one with only months to learn her magicks."

"She has your blood, Odran, and this is her strength, this is my weakness against her. My life is yours to do with as you wish. If you take it, I pray I may serve you in death. If you spare it, I will use every moment you give me to open the way, to bring her to you."

"I believe you. I know you speak the truth. Still, I dislike failure."

He walked back to her bed, laid a finger on one of the wounds in her arm. The white-hot pain had Yseult's eyes rolling back, her body arching in a rigid bridge of pain.

When he removed it, she fell limply, shuddering.

"You'll suffer." He leaned down until his face loomed just above hers. She saw the red rimming his irises, and wished only death came quickly.

But she didn't beg.

Smiling, he straightened. "But you'll live. For now. Ply your magicks, witch, and serve me well. Or the pain you feel now will be as nothing."

When he left her, the storm snapped off. In the sudden silence, Yseult closed her eyes. The cold, as he'd refused her a fire, had her shivering even as the burn from the wounds scorched her blood.

She would suffer, and accepted it. She'd failed him, and failure paid a price.

But she would heal. She would heal, regain her strength, and amass more power.

And with that power, she would open the next door for her king, her liege, her all. She swore it on all that was unholy.

When she had, she'd drag the bitch-goddess back to Odran and toss her screaming at his feet.

And when he'd drained her, when her god Odran took all he needed and left the mongrel child of the Fey little more than a mindless husk, she would pay for every moment of this pain.

She would pay for eternity.

Turn the page for a sneak peek at
Nora Roberts's new novel

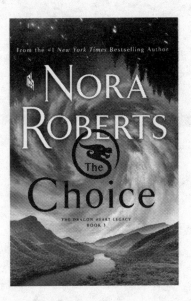

Available now

# PROLOGUE

Throughout the span of time, the worlds of Man often believe themselves singular. Those who believe and accept they aren't alone in the vastness tend to consider themselves superior to those who share the vastness.

They are wrong, of course, as the worlds of Man are neither singular nor superior. They simply are.

In the worlds upon worlds that spin, some proclaim for peace even as they beat the drums of war. That they beat the drums with an insatiable greed for power over others, for land, for resources and riches in the name of their favored deity rarely strikes as wrong, or even ironic.

It simply is.

In some worlds, war is the deity, and the worship of it bloody and fierce.

There are worlds where great cities rise from golden sands, others where palaces glitter under the depths of deep blue seas. And those that struggle to life from hardly more than a spark in the dark.

Whether the denizens of a world climb the high mountains or swim the oceans, whether they live in great cities or huddle over a fire in a forest, whether they beat the drums or rock the cradle, all share one common goal.

To be.

In one such world, in the long ago, Man and Fey and gods existed. In this world grew cities and palaces, lakes and forests. Mountains rose high; oceans ran deep. For a time out of time, magicks shined under sun and under moon.

Wars came as wars will. In some, greed prospered. And in some, the thirst for power could never be slaked, even with the blood of the conquered hot in its throat. One dark god, crazed with power, drank deep of Man and Fey and more, and was cast out of the world.

But this was not an ending.

As the wheel of time turned, as it must, snakes of suspicion and fear slithered into the harmony of Man and gods and Fey. For some, progress at all and any cost replaced the bond between magicks and Man, and the worship of the more took over the reverence once given to the gods.

And so there came a time of choice, to step away from the magicks or to preserve them, to abandon the old gods or respect them. Making this choice, the Fey broke away from the worlds of Man and the suspicions and fears that burned them at stakes, hunted them in forests, condemned them to the axe.

So Talamh, a world from a world, was born.

Those wise enough, with vision enough, created portals for passage between worlds, as by law of Talamh, all and any had the choice to stay or go. There, in a land of green hills, high mountains, deep forests and seas, magicks thrived, and under the leader—chosen and choosing—peace held.

But this was not an ending.

The dark god plotted in his dark world and gathered his army of the demons and the damned. With time, with blood, he harnessed enough power to pass through the portal and into Talamh. There he courted a young witch, one chosen and choosing as taoiseach, and blinded her with love and lies. She gave him a son, and in secret, while the mother lay in enchanted sleep, he drank power from the babe, night after night.

But a mother's love holds great magick, so she woke from this forced sleep. And awakening, led an army against the god to cast him back and seal the portal. When it was done, she deemed herself unworthy to lead as taoiseach, so cast the sword back into Lough na Fírinne and gave the staff to the one who lifted the sword from the water.

So once again, peace held, and in the peace of the green hills and deep forests of Talamh, her son grew. One day, with pride and sorrow, she watched him lift the sword from the lake and take his place as taoiseach.

Under him, peace held; justice was served with wisdom and compassion. The crops grew and magicks thrived.

Fate deemed he would meet and love a woman, a child of Man. Through his choice and hers, he brought her through the portal to his world, and there, out of love and joy, they made a child, a daughter.

The magicks in her beamed bright, and for three years she knew only love.

But the dark god's thirst was not slaked, and his rage only grew. Once again, he amassed his powers through blood sacrifices and dark magicks, aided by a witch who turned from the bright to the dark.

He stole the child, imprisoned her in a glass cage beneath the waters near the portal. While her father, her grandmother, while all the warriors of Talamh rode or flew on wing or dragon to save her, she who had only known love knew fear.

And that fear in one so bright bloomed into a rage as wild as the god's. So her power bloomed with it and struck out at the god who was her own blood, her own kin.

She broke her cage even as the Fey attacked the god and his forces. Once again, the god was cast out and left beneath the ruins of his black castle.

Her mother, human in her fear and with a fear that turned to bias and a bias that tainted love, demanded to take the child to the world of Man, to have the child's memory of magicks and Talamh and all who dwelled there erased.

Out of love for the child, and for the mother, the father granted this and took them through the portal, lived with them in the world of Man, returning to Talamh for love, for duty as often as he could.

But though the love for the child never dimmed for the father, the love between the child of Man and the child of Fey couldn't survive, and his efforts to live in both worlds carved pieces from his heart.

Yet again the god threatened Talamh, and the worlds beyond it. And once again the Fey, led by the taoiseach, defended. The Fey drove him back, but with his dark magicks, with his black sword, the god killed the son he'd made.

So another time for mourning, and another time of choosing.

A young boy, mourning the taoiseach as he had mourned his own father, lifted the sword from the lake, took up the staff.

While the boy grew into a man, one who sat in the Chair of Justice in the Capital or helped his brother and sister with their farm in the valley, while he flew over Talamh on his dragon and trained for the battle all knew would come, the daughter lived in the world of Man.

There, with her mother's fear and resentment, she was taught to step back and never forward, to look down rather than up, to fold her hands instead of reach. She lived a quiet life that brought little joy, and there knew nothing of magicks. Her bright came from a friend who was a brother in all but blood and in a man who stood as a mother of her heart.

She dreamed, sometimes of more and different, but too often her dreams came blurred and dark. And in her heart lived a sorrow for the father she believed had left her.

One day a door opened for her. She made a choice, this woman who'd been taught so rigidly not to risk, not to step forward, not to reach. She traveled across the ocean to Ireland in hopes of finding her father and finding herself. In her travels she found a love for the place, for the green and the mists and the hills.

In a cottage by a bay, she explored those dreams of more, and reached out for those even as she reached in to find herself. One day, she came upon a tree deep in the forest that seemed to grow from a stand of rock. She climbed onto the long, thick branches.

And stepped out of the world she knew and into the world of her birth.

Her magicks stirred awake, as did her memories, aided by the grandmother who loved and had longed for her, by the faerie who'd been her friend in childhood, and by the boy— now a man—who had lifted the sword from the lake.

She learned of her father's death, and mourned him. Of her grandmother's sacrifice, and loved her. She discovered her powers and the joy in them. And though she feared, she learned of her place in Talamh, the threat of the dark god who was her blood, so she trained to fight with magicks, with sword, with fist.

As weeks turned to months, she, like her father, lived in two worlds. In the cottage she pursued her dreams; in Talamh, she honed her powers and trained for battle.

She allowed herself to love the one duty bound to Talamh, found the courage she wore as a symbol on her wrist. She embraced the wonders of the Fey, the winged faeries, the blurring speed of elves, the transformation of Weres, and more.

When evil came to Talamh, threatening it and all, she

wielded fist and sword and magicks against it. She killed what came to destroy the light, faced down the darkest of magicks with that light.

So she became what she had been born to become.

But this was not an ending.